Horns

and

Halos

By: Nia Rose

HORNS AND HALOS

Book design by Poisoned Apple Publishing
Editing by Poisoned Apple Publishing

ISBN: 978-1-955222-15-0

Published by Poisoned Apple Publishing, L.L.C.
www.poisonedapplepublishing.com

Printed in the United States of America

**Coven Chronicles series by
Nia Rose & Octavia J. Riley**
SPELLBOUND & HELLHOUNDS
SECRETS OF THE SANCTUARY
SPIRITS OF THE BLACK FOREST
SAND DUNES AND BLOOD MOONS
SMOKE, LIES, AND GRIMOIRES

**Stand Alone Novels by
Nia Rose**
SONS OF STARS
KING OF CROWS
HORNS AND HALOS

God,
thank You for carrying me through the darkest parts of my
life and for delivering me safely on the other side.

This is for all of the toxic loves that I learned some of the most
valuable lessons in my life from. To the ones who came
behind you and loved me despite all my brokenness. To me,
learning to love myself even though I was not who I used to
be, and I felt fractured in every way a soul can be.
To finding a way to trust in love again.

Sometimes you have to go through Hell before you find your
place in Heaven.

Prologue:

The World We Know

Contrary to popular theorists, it was not difficult to come by simple household items like soap, food, and weapons after Armageddon hit. Too many people had banked off the sea of knowledge Google Search had to offer. Along with people finding way too much time on their hands when quarantine happened fifteen years before the collapse of our world—as we knew it—came to pass, many had new skills and trades learned. They were drowning in baking, do-it-yourself projects, and finally learning how to do a few odd crafts that had almost been lost by time itself. The resurgence of soapmaking, blacksmithing, knitting, and sewing was off the charts. There had been a major rise in the average person having un-average knowledge.

Not such a bad thing, if you ask me.

Also, contrary to popular belief, the world wasn't done in by nukes. It wasn't done in by wars, or poisoning, or sickness. And no, it wasn't zombies either. It was demons. It was rapture. It was scripture on crack and pure nightmare fuel. It was every twisted fear mankind could imagine, and it was spat at us with fury and vengeance.

Personally, I would have preferred the zombies.

Chapter 1:

Close the Gate

They say that the more you struggle, the more you grow. With that theory alone, it stands to reason that we all feel ancient by now. None of us should have gone through this hell. And yet, we have. Saying that we've survived this long is a half-baked truth. We have managed to not die—that much is true—but the price we pay for it is deep, flawed, and only gives more pain to those left living. That is, if we can be considered to be doing that anymore. *Living*. Yeah, I'm not sure that's what we are doing. At least, it doesn't feel like it.

A hundred years ago, people used to talk about how they had seen this coming. Now, no one really talks about the past. Almost like it has been banned from our tongues and minds, or as if it's too painful for us to dream of a time when things weren't like this. When things weren't like Hell on Earth.

I've heard people mention angels in whispers once or twice, a long time ago. I've read it a few times in books that hadn't been lost through the years to raids, fires, and looters. I've never seen an angel before. I doubt that I ever will. But I've seen my fair share of demons, and I've been far too close to devils, so I hope that the winged creatures are out there somewhere. Maybe the angels forgot about us, or maybe we forgot about them. I wouldn't know for sure. My meemaw never explained the reasons for why we were all damned now. That's what everyone said when they trudged through the streets. That we are all damned … forsaken. Most days, I believe them. After all, how can we not be?

When I was growing up, Meemaw told me many things. There were countless times that she would whisper to me stories by the fireside while Momma and Daddy fixed us supper or snacks. Her stories were ones that she said flourished in the faith cities. Grand places that were full of prosperity and peace. I always wanted to go to one. They always sounded so magnificent to me, like they were castles in some faraway and magical kingdom. It sounded like a place that was untouched by the destruction and chaos that surrounded us.

"Sia," she'd say while tightly braiding my long, black curls. "These are the words that they teach in the faith cities. Those places are large enough to withstand the nightly demon attacks. Their prayers and words from these stories build a city stronger than metal," she would whisper fervently to me.

"We have a strong city, too, Meemaw. We have lots of people, even though we live out in the Wastes!" I remember telling her once while my large, blue eyes searched the rich, russet glow of her orbs.

She only shook her head with a deep-set frown. The firelight seemed to make shadows that crept and crawled into every crevice of her aged face, and it made the mahogany tone of her skin darker. Her bright eyes held a sadness that was etched in pain. I wanted to cry while I looked at her then. The hurt mingled with the darkness and blended with the illumination of the flames dancing over her wrinkled skin. That expression scared me.

"No, child. This place is fragile. It's broken in a way that can never be mended. We don't have a strong city. We have a city of glass."

That was the last thing I remember her telling me that night, that our city was nothing more than glass. I didn't understand her when she told me that back then. It was a warning, and I never listened. I wish I had. But there were too many secrets that I wasn't aware of, and you can't guard yourself against a beast you know nothing about.

The front gate that I had once found so much comfort in was now a thing of pure horror. Wind whipped by, sending dust clouds rolling past the massive wall and the two giant doors that stood between the village and the endless stretch of the Wastes. A fine, daunting line was drawn between dry, desolate land and everything I had ever known. And I was on the unfavorable side of it and the comforts the village had provided me with for the past nineteen years.

My mother, father, and meemaw stood on the other side of the entrance with me. My friends and the countless residents had already said their goodbyes to me the night before.

I should have known how wrong this all was, but I had been so blind. Now that I was on the receiving end of this horrid event that I had grown up thinking was normal, it all made sense. It was anything but normal. The lies that I had been told—that all of us children had been told while growing up—had buried the truth that I was still trying to wrap my head around.

Once every year, everyone that was between the ages of nineteen and twenty-three would put their name into the large ceremonial bowl in the center of the village. At the end of the night, they would draw out one of the names. The chosen person would have a grand party.

It was a wonderful event. It was a night full of food and drink and games and merriment. Last night had been one of the best nights of my life. In the morning, the family would say their goodbyes, and the chosen person would leave the city. What I had been *told* was that the chosen one was to be picked up by passing caravans to join another village. As I stood there, I understood why my parents and Meemaw were fighting last night when they thought I was asleep. There were no caravans. There were no travelers that had come to escort me.

The ugly truth was I was a sacrifice.

For the last hour, I had stayed silent as they explained everything to me. I was so lost and confused as I tried to ingest the information that was so closely tied to my fate. A fate I had no choice in. A fate that had been forced upon me.

Once a year, a single, chosen villager was selected to leave the safety of the massive walls in order to fulfill the pact that had been made upon the founding of our village.

"Your family is forever bound to this place, and you can never leave. Once a year, a single person between nineteen and twenty-three is to be cast out of your village in the morning, never to return. They must be chosen at random, and the person may never be swapped. You are never able to receive them if they come back. You are never able to seek them when the gates are closed. You

cannot hide them within the city. If you fail to heed your end of the bargain, my protection over your little village will cease."

That was the deal that the founders of the village had made with the devil that they had encountered so very long ago. The years of protection that we had out in the Wastes weren't because we were favored by luck or because of our trusted walls. The reason the lesser demons and deadly creatures of our world had passed us over was because we were protected by a devil. We were bound by a pact that had sentenced countless to a frightful and lonely death.

… And it was my turn to pay the price.

My mother walked up first and hit her knees as she reached longingly for me. I had just turned nineteen three days before the yearly event. I regretted that fact now as I watched her fall apart. I dipped down to try and bring her back to her feet, but she dragged me down to her. Hurt swam in her blue irises as she held my cheeks in her hands. "Hide during the night, travel by day," she said swiftly, tears rolling down her pale face in droves. "Don't make loud noises. Sleep only during the dusk or dawn." Her hands trembled terribly as she held my face. "But … above all …" She tried to speak, but she couldn't. Her words were snuffed from her existence as pain snatched her up. I could see it. The hurt she silenced as she willed herself to pretend like she wasn't being shattered to pieces. "… You have to live," she finished in a raspy voice. She shook me indignantly. "You hear me? Live! You *must* live!" she growled, but the rivers of tears betrayed her commanding voice.

I held one of her hands in my own. My umber skin looked so dark compared to my mother's. She had a tan from years under the sun, and still, she was milky white next to me. Her blue eyes searched my darker, azure gaze. Maybe I

was in shock, but I wasn't crying. I was scared, I could feel it deep in my gut, but I hadn't screamed or cried or said a single thing about how unfair it all was. My mind was lost traveling down a thousand paths. I felt more hurt for those that I had hugged and wished happy travels to in previous years.

I wondered if they were still alive …

I squeezed my mother's hand and forced a smile. "It's all right, Momma. I'll be fine," I told her, but I doubted the truth of my own statement. I wanted my last words to her to be comforting. I already knew that sleep would not come to her easily in the nights to follow, and there was little I could say to change this. I would try, though.

She practically lunged forward and wailed quietly, making sure that the villagers didn't hear her heart breaking outside the gates. Making sure only I could. It was a sound that would haunt me for the rest of my life.

"Nastasia … oh … my baby. I am so sorry. I love you … I'm so sorry," she whimpered.

Frantically, I hugged her back. "Momma, Momma … it's okay. I don't blame you." I pulled away and forced her to look at me. "I'll never blame you. I love you. This will never change that." I felt the prickling sting of salty water welling up in my eyes. I let the wind dry it as I blinked desperately, hoping that I had hidden the unshed tears.

Daddy came and helped Momma to her feet. "Come now, Marietta, the others might see," he warned, a touch of ice to his words.

I knew my father well. Whenever he sounded like that, he was trying to be strong for everyone. He was masking his own worries and pain so the family could lean on him. He was the quiet rock that never complained as stormy waves relentlessly crashed over him. He helped me to

my feet next and passively looked at the large bag thrown over his shoulder. "It'll be heavy to carry," he stated.

I nodded. "I know," I whispered back.

He shrugged it off. The massive, thick-woven cloth bag *thudded* on the ground, stirring up dust. "It'll get lighter as you travel … because …" he trailed off. I knew he was struggling to speak and look strong. But even boulders can be weathered away over time.

"With each day, it will get lighter because the rations will be lesser, and I'll slowly grow used to the weight," I finished for him.

An unsure smile formed on his lips. "Yes," he managed to croak out.

Rushing forward, I hugged him. He and I never needed many words. We could just look at each other and know what was in our hearts and what was on our minds. "I love you, Daddy," I whispered to him. "I'll be okay."

He pulled away from the hug and undid a thin, leather belt around his waist. His deep mahogany skin was a shade darker than Meemaw's, and I memorized every feature of his darkened face as he handed me the belt and machete that had been attached to it. The look that passed between us said it all. I knew what it was for. Daddy always made me cut wood or help with preparing meat for the village. I knew the force needed to go through bone; I knew what blood looked and smelled like. I swallowed hard. I finally understood why he had made me do that through all of these years.

Meemaw clamped a hand over her mouth and pushed past my parents. "Sia. Oh, my little Sia!" she cried.

"*Shhh*, Mom," my momma begged.

"*Shhh*, yourself," Meemaw snapped back. "I wish it was me that had been drawn from that cursed bowl!"

"It is forbidden," Father warned.

She sobbed and ran her fingers through my braided, ebony strands. "I should have told you sooner … I wanted to, Sia. I wanted to so badly," she cried.

But even without them telling me, I knew why the truth had been hidden. Even if the pact with the devil allowed it, how can the youth grow up and enjoy their moments knowing that every day, every year, they are closer to a nightmare? That isn't a childhood. I was glad that they didn't tell us. I had a lot of happy memories to carry with me. Last night's feast would be cherished by me, too. It would be the things that enabled me to live through the horrors I was about to face. We all knew of the dangers that existed outside the safety of the village. Most had rarely come to see them firsthand. But we had been warned and told stories daily to ever remind us of the fate that would befall us if we ventured too far when scavenging.

"Meemaw, I understand," I told her.

Her wrinkled face scrunched up even further as she frowned and bent her brow angrily. "Nonsense. Stop talkin' like you're an adult, child," she hissed. "None of this is right. It never has been," she protested.

I did the only thing I could to try and calm her down. I hugged her. I wanted to hug them each as many times as I could. I wouldn't be able to do it after today. "I love you," I said as I squeezed her.

I felt her body shudder in my embrace. "Seek the faith cities," she whispered back to me. It was a tone that was hardly audible and meant for only me to hear. "Seek out shelter at night, keep the fires low, and head for the faith city," she urged again.

"I promise I will."

The morning was still early, and the heat would only become more intense as the day went on. I didn't want to leave, but I needed to start my journey soon.

"She needs to head out if she plans to make a decent camp before nightfall," Daddy informed.

We all hugged again. The last to leave my side was Daddy. He helped me tighten the machete to my hip. His deep brown gaze was transfixed on the newly sharpened weapon.

"It'll serve me well, Daddy."

When I spoke, he snapped out of his haze. Slowly, his eyes lifted to me, and I could see the mist forming in them. "Don't stop swinging until you're sure," he stated quietly.

"And then I will swing again to *be* sure," I said.

We hugged one last time, and I watched their sad faces disappear behind the massive, wooden doors as they closed shut and sealed me to my undesired fate.

Chapter 2:

Gnashing Teeth, Scratching Claws

I had left shortly after the reality settled in that the doors would never again open for me. It didn't take long for me to accept it. Besides, there was an arduous journey ahead of me, and sitting at the front gates like a lost soul would do me no favors in the long run.

There weren't a lot of options in which direction to go. My village was about a day's walk from the ocean. There was nothing but miles upon miles of water, sand, and minimal places to hide. To the east was the Wilds. Endless stretches of forgotten cities and towns that were overtaken by fast-growing forests, and they harbored enough shadows to hide countless unpleasant beasts. If there was any chance that I was going to survive a possible one-week trek to one of the faith cities, I'd need to head north and hug the base of the mountain ranges. That way, I would have the potential of hiding away in one of the many caves at the end of each day. If I couldn't, I could hide on a high ledge, giving me the advantage if I were to be attacked. It would also provide me with a landmark to help keep me heading in the right direction.

I was already checking the canteen with quiet calculations. I found it hard to not sip when my mouth felt

dry or when I felt pangs of hunger start to stir. I would need to find a clean water source in the next day or so. It was another reason why the highlands were the better option to traverse through. There was a natural spring in them, and it dumped into the Red River. The river made a sharp turn and split off before cutting to the east, traveling straight to—and through—the Wilds, while the other stream followed the line of the mountains.

As I walked, I noted a rattler and gave it plenty of room to carry on its way. It gave a shake of its tail in warning as it slithered along its course. I picked up a nearby stick and prodded at the ground ahead of me as I continued to walk. I wasn't looking to limp around in the Wastes until I died from a snake bite. However, I much preferred the snakes instead of the darker, crueler things that lay in waiting out in the vast and desolate stretch of dry, barren land.

The mountains ahead were my guide. For however long I'd be journeying, I would follow them and seek shelter along the way within tucked-away caves or nearby towns and villages that dwelled in their shadows. I wasn't sure how many of those communities would openly accept me, so I was already mentally preparing myself with backup plans for when the worst came to pass. It was better to be equipped for any situation when one was cast out into the Wastes.

As I surveyed the area and the placement of the sun in the sky, I stumbled over a large rock and sucked in a sharp breath of air. While rubbing my shin, I sighed and thought about gathering dry wood as I walked. It would be extra weight added to my heavy load that would weigh me down, inevitably slowing my progress. Yet, they were things I was willing to accept because a fire meant warmth, a way to cook, a source of light that could repel creatures, and—if things got really bad—it could become a weapon. They were all pros that far outweighed the cons in my mind.

For the next several hours, I would gather sticks and pieces of wood at the base of the mountains until my arms were practically overflowing. Using the leather belt Daddy had given me, I wrapped it around the bundle and threw it over my shoulder. Every so often, I would repeat this action until the belt couldn't spare an inch. By that time, the sun was starting its slow descent in the sky. As it did, I tried to stifle the growing panic that was rising in me.

With night came shadows and sounds. There came danger, and I didn't want to be left out in the open when dusk would be upon me. I wanted to be holed in a cave that I had thoroughly investigated and snuggled next to a warm fire long before that ever happened. As Momma had said, I wanted to go to bed soon, though I doubted sleep would have much to do with me tonight.

Regardless of whether it would have me or not, I needed to find a safe place, set up camp, and try to get a little bit of rest as soon as possible. It was roughly three in the afternoon. I would need the extra time to do everything and eat before *trying* to get some shuteye. I wouldn't eat meat tonight. I hadn't caught anything, and the scent of fresh blood wouldn't easily wash away if I managed to do so in the next hour. Thankfully, I had enough food in my pack that would last a good while before it would start to spoil.

As I started to climb up the rocky surface, I grasped onto memories and stories to snuff out my ever-intensifying anxiety. It helped to calm me down enough to where my hands weren't shaking as I pulled myself up the face of the mountain. It wasn't a sharp incline, but it was steep, making hiking a slower process than walking, yet not quite as slow as free-hand-climbing.

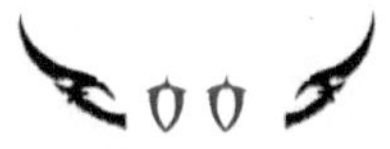

I remembered Meemaw's tales of the grand faith cities. I was heading to the northern one, the city known as Saint Augustine. It was one of the safest places for miles and miles. It was run by what we knew as the clergy fathers, and they were open to taking in wanderers and lost souls. It really was a safe haven for a homeless outcast like me. And anything was better than being huddled in a cramped, critter-infested cave, crying myself to sleep every night until my early end. Finding somewhere I could settle down in and make a new home was definitely a number one goal of mine. It sure beat dodging death daily.

My stomach growled around the time that I had started to think about Momma's homemade stew and freshly baked bread. My eyes misted as the final memory that I had for my family played through my mind. I blinked past the tears as I homed in on a crevice up ahead. It looked like it would be deep enough to house me for a night and keep me safe from both elements and creatures alike. I quickened my pace, pausing only to catch my breath and give my limbs a small rest. I really wanted to get to that opening. And if I could find a way to—in a short amount of time—cover the entrance, I would have a little less to worry about tonight.

Once I reached the ledge that the hole was on, I looked over the side and gauged the distance to the ground below. There was a good bit of space between the rocky shelf and the dry, patchy earth below, making me less likely to be a target when the sun went down. Now, it was time to check out that hollow opening I had my sights set on. Hopefully— as my daddy would say—the stars were aligning for me.

Such a short walk had never felt so worrisome. Around the cave were a couple of thin, sickly shrubs clinging desperately to the little dirt that was collected on the mountain. I checked it with a few good prods from my

walking stick and scouted the foliage to ensure nothing was crawling or slithering away. If a critter saw this as a home, I didn't need to fend it off along with the nightmares that could potentially come knocking on my door later on. So far, everything seemed to be pretty good. Now, how was that space looking?

I peeked in and felt my stomach flip.

The crevice was narrow, with hardly enough space for me to shimmy inside without a lot of finesse and lots of grunting. But it looked like it opened up further in. All good news for me. It would give me somewhere to hide, I could have swinging room if something found me, but it was tucked away enough that I doubted I would have anything come in deep enough to even know I was there. Or, at least, that was what I was hoping for.

I sighed heavily as I dropped my backpack next to the opening. I needed to get in further to make sure it was cleared out and set my things down before I would try to find a way to enclose the small entrance. For now, it felt good just to have the bag off my back. I stretched and felt a few pops along my spine that had me groan with a faint, thankful curve of my lips.

"It's going to be a long trip," I told myself. It was at this moment that I realized I needed to get used to talking to myself. I doubted that I would have any company on my journey.

Deciding that bunking alongside anything that might sting or hiss wasn't accommodations I was willing to live with for the night, I poked my stick into the opening. The end slammed around the stony insides as I tried to rustle up or scare off anything that might call the space home. After hearing no protesting and not seeing anything rush out in a quick escape, I pushed my bag through the crevice and then scooted along behind it.

The opening was small. It took some muscle to scoot the backpack through into the larger opening on the other end. The rocky enclosure squeezed my body, and sharper pieces of its edges threatened to break skin, while the rough walls stung my sides and belly as I pushed through despite the limited space to move in.

With dedication and a few awkward maneuvers, I managed to get myself and everything inside. The entrance to the area had been misleading, and the shadows did me no favors when I had scoped out the spot. It was actually larger inside than expected. And, as an added bonus, there was a small tunnel overhead that opened up to clear skies. Double score for me. I had managed to find a nice hideout that had natural ventilation so I wouldn't be suffocating from the fire's smoke later on that night. Now, all I needed to do was craft a woven door with a few straggling sticks and leaves, and any light from tonight's fire would be hidden. This meant I would live to see another day of trudging through the Wastes.

I propped my firewood against one wall and went ahead with setting up where I would sleep for the night. After the blanket had been rolled out, I gathered up my machete and army-crawled out of the opening to get to work on making a door to lean against the crack.

"If you ever get stuck out in the Wastes, keep noise to a minimum."

"Remember, they feed on negativity. Try to stay positive or neutral at best."

"Stay clean. The scent of blood will call them to you. Never clean what you've killed where you rest."

"Sleep at dusk or dawn. The night is too dangerous to let down your guard."

"Stay hydrated. Stay well-rested. Stay alert."

"Never stop fighting."

The collected voices of those I had grown up around and known all my life sounded through my mind as their words of wisdom reminded me of the dangers that awaited me in the hours to come. I wasn't ready. Even if I had trained all my life, I would never be ready.

I took in another slow breath in hopes that it would calm my thundering heartbeat. It didn't work. I had managed to weave a flimsy door, though. I used a few leafy branches, wove them through the sticks, and nodded approvingly at what I had created. With all my work done, I headed back up to the ledge, fixed the door in place, and shimmied my way back into the space I would call home for the night.

Once inside, I grabbed a ration of food and dug in. My meal tasted bland. My water didn't seem to quench my thirst. The shadows seemed darker, and my mood was steadily tanking. I shook it off and slapped my thigh. "Get over it, Sia. You're not a baby anymore," I told myself angrily. But the harsh words didn't help my sinking spirit.

Momma always was better at this sort of thing. She always knew what to say. Daddy would seal the deal with a big, strong hug as he silently said all the things with his embrace that Momma couldn't with her words. Meemaw would swoop in with a story to steal my attention and make me feel like I was miles away from whatever hell we were all living in. I hugged myself and reenacted the time that my dog, Candy, died.

Daddy had gathered me up in his arms for one of his memorable hugs that stretched on forever. Momma had

managed to sum up everything from how I met her right up until the moment she passed away, bringing a strange peace over me. Meemaw brought snacks and told all the stories of the trouble Candy and I would get into. Before long, my tears had stopped flowing, and I was laughing again. My heart hurt, but I had found things to comfort me.

Slowly, I lay back on my bed and enjoyed the cool press of the stone soaking through my blanket. Now that I was out of the sun, I could feel my body winding down as I cooled off. The sleep I had been worried about not getting was now urging me to give my tired limbs some reprieve. My eyes walked through the small opening, and I could still see the sun through bits of the woven door. If I slept now, I would wake up at nightfall. If the pitch-black didn't wake me, the sounds that sundown brought would.

Pushing those thoughts from my mind, I tried to settle in for a few hours of shuteye. I prepped a fire on the far side of the cave, checked my belongings, took one more sip of water, and curled up in my bed. Though I had to keep my mind from straying to unpleasant thoughts, I managed to fall fast asleep before too long.

It was the undeniable wash of dread that woke me from my sleep. I opened my eyes and—despite my body wrestling with a very natural fight or flight response—I lay still as I scanned the dark, quiet stones surrounding me. It wasn't a strong presence. It was a faint one. Not many things could force me out of sleep with the distinct feeling of anxiety and dread. The creature was probably a leech.

Leeches weren't the worst thing to come across in the Wastes, but they could call others if you weren't careful. They earned their name because they would linger where fear, sadness, and anxiety were, and they consume that same negative energy after they amplify it. This would leave the victim feeling sluggish, depressed, and nervous about every movement and sound, which had a very good chance of gaining the attention of much worse demons. The signs that a leech was in a room was the fear that had washed over me without any reason. That was because leeches emit an aura that causes people around them to feel what they pump out, making it easier to find their prey and consume the victim's negative feelings.

I made sure to keep my emotions in check until I was sure if there was or wasn't a leech in the area. Slow, steady breathing helped while I mentally told myself that I was in control. My eyes pierced through the dusky depths of the cave. To my dismay, I saw it in the far corner.

An oblong-shaped, charcoal-colored ball of writhing worms pulsated in midair as it combed over the rocky walls … searching. It was see-through, but I could still make out the disgusting, wiggling tentacles that slithered and caressed the air in a less-than-appealing way. I focused on mentally blocking myself the way Daddy had always told me to. Fearing that happy memories would turn into me missing my family and friends, I thought of nothing. I focused on my surroundings to list off things that I saw. It made it easier to feel no emotions and be invisible to the leech. Unfortunately for me, there wasn't a lot of scenery to mentally check off. As I fumbled in my tired state, I panicked.

Worst decision …

My heartbeat stumbled, and I sucked in a sharp breath out of reflex. I closed my eyes and thought of nothing

but limitless black and stretches of empty spaces. I thought of the night sky. I mentally imagined the stars and named all of the ones I could remember until I drew blanks. Opening my eyes, I homed back in on the undulating mass and thought of the stone walls while I tried to notice if it had picked up on my blunder. For a moment, I was sure that I had dodged the bullet.

The lesser demon pulsated a few times before it was so faint that it couldn't be seen. A bit of tension left me the moment that the leech blipped out of view. I could feel my heartbeat drumming through my limbs, and that beat quickened to a chaotic tempo when it reappeared in the tiny cave.

Squirming mounds of wormy arms spastically writhed in the air all around the creature. It didn't have any eyes, but it didn't need them to know that I was there. The first, distinct wave of horror crashed into me, and I felt my body buckle to the will of the lesser demon. I could feel my chest tighten, and my mind was flooded with millions of worries that I had ever concocted in my life, and they were all dumped on me in a single moment without warning. I gasped and scrambled to flip over as it manifested into something more tangible and less shadowy.

The fire was nothing more than embers, and I couldn't use it as a weapon. I felt a little more confident when my hand brushed over the handle of the machete. It was sheathed and fastened to the belt that I had put next to my makeshift bed. As I rolled back over, I swiped at the air, and the leech faded from sight a split second before I would have made contact. I silently cursed and quickly realized that I was more exposed than I would have wanted. I had to cut my losses and find higher ground until daybreak. Once the sun came up, I would venture back to the campsite, collect everything, and press on at double the speed of the day before. I needed to put as much distance between me and the area the leech had sensed me in.

There was only one problem with my plan … It wasn't just that it was already several hours into nightfall. It wasn't just that I would be a sitting duck until morning. It wasn't just that I would be trying to free-hand-climb a mountain with zero light on the night before a new moon. All of those things were manageable. Undesirable but manageable.

No. It was none of those things. The real problem with my plan was the two red, glowing eyes that had eerily fixed themselves on me from the entrance of the cave. My heart plummeted, and the urge to scream and vomit hit me at the same time. Neither impulse won me over because, within seconds, my desire to live overrode any other natural reaction to the fear-inducing situation I was in.

I hadn't come this far to be done in on the first night. I wasn't going to be an easy victim. I was going to fight and make them regret picking me because I was going to cut them down piece by piece until I couldn't swing my blade anymore. I may not live through the night, but I made myself a silent promise that as long as I had breath in me, I was going to do whatever I needed to in order to survive.

The demon hissed at me with an unnaturally wide, sharp-toothed grin that was painted in malicious victory. Gray, leathery, translucent skin that looked like it was covered in a thin sheet of slime glistened under the minimal starlight from outside. The thing slowly squeezed through the opening and cautiously crawled toward me, licking its lips with a quiet, wheezy laugh. Goosebumps coated my body as the sound it made was dripping with silent taunts and promises of unfathomable pain. It didn't speak, though, meaning that it was most likely a grunt.

Grunts were not ignorant creatures, but they were far from intelligent. They didn't know how to speak and could only act like wild, starving dogs. IQ aside, it didn't take a genius to realize that it had come across easy prey.

It growled, and a series of guttural, clicking sounds rolled through the small crawl space. The hairs on my arms and the back of my neck rose up—and I swallowed hard. This wasn't good. My eyes darted around, and I saw the leech hovering over me. I felt tired again, and I knew that it had been feeding on my negative emotions. I swung at it, and the ball of worms blipped in and out of sight. Just as I turned around, a maw filled with daggers for teeth was lunging right at my face. Out of sheer reflex, I raised my arm to block the attack and pushed out, and I slammed the creature in the throat. The grunt's claws grazed over the side of my neck, and I felt the blazing trail of heat engulf my skin as its talons scratched me.

My hand clamped down over the inflicted area, and I quickly pulled it away to inspect my palm. My stomach knotted as my eyes took in the few tiny dots of blood. A scratch had never seemed more deadly as it did in that moment.

My eyes fixed on the grunt that I had tossed off of me, and the creature hissed and swiped at the open air while hunched up against the far wall. Dread washed over me, and I felt dizzy. The leech was close enough to feed off of me again.

Swinging wildly, I managed to clip the edge of its oblong body, and a high-pitched sound rang through the cave as it writhed in agony. The grunt scratched at the wall, trying to escape both my swinging blade and the painful

sound of the wounded leech. I stumbled for the entrance, gagged a few times as the fear had soured my stomach, and I crawled desperately for the opening. As soon as I was out in the open, I froze in horror.

The eerie glow of multiple sets of hungry eyes shimmered like dangerous jewels at the bottom of the mountain. I could hear a jackal-like cackle and a series of hisses. I held my neck, but it was too late. From behind me, there was a snarl, and the grunt that had been in the cave darted out and grabbed hold of my ankle. A sharp pain shot through my bone as it clamped its dirty mouth over its prize and tried to rip my foot off. I heard my teeth grinding in my ears as I tried not to yell out in pain. Sure, I was pretty much on death's doorstep at the moment, but I didn't want to go ringing the doorbell to announce my arrival.

I kicked my leg, but the grunt didn't let go. Raising my machete, I pointed the tip down and stabbed it in the head right as it looked up. A second before my blade rushed through its unsuspecting face, it let out an earsplitting cry. No sooner had the noise been made, it was snuffed out with gargles. Wanting to be free of the bloody carcass, I kicked the thing off my leg with all my might, and it slammed into the edge of the cave entrance with a sickening snap.

Turning on heel, I went to address the matter of what little distance was left between me and a hungry horde of demons. The answer was: not a lot. Already, a few were scaling the base of the mountain, and the few that hadn't fallen off were almost near the ledge. Adrenaline coursed through me like a forest fire. Frantically, I rushed over to the crumpled body, grabbed it, and chucked it at the landing where the closest demon was. I didn't hit anything. I wasn't exactly trying to. My goal was to let them feast on the grunt's remains while I made a dash for even higher ground.

The first demon hissed and sniffed at the body before laughing and diving into its meal without restraint. I could hear things ripping and tearing as more joined in to feast. Suppressing the urge to hurl, I ran around a bend in the path and started to climb up. I didn't want my movement to call them to me. However, my bloody scratch would no matter how far I went. I wasn't going to make it easy on them, though. From the looks of it, they were all grunts. Grunts weren't the best climbers. I wasn't either, but I was betting I was better at it than they were.

At least … I hoped that I was.

Without a massive backpack strapped to me, it was a lot easier than the climb I made earlier that afternoon. I hoisted myself up to the first ledge and stole a peek to the ground below. Already, I could see the bony corpse of the grunt peeking back up at me. The few that had had their fill were waddling down the side of the mountain happily, while the others fought over the remaining meal. I clamped a hand over my mouth and stifled the urge to gag with deep, slow breaths.

A screeching cry jolted me, and I lost my footing. I stumbled back to catch myself and grabbed at nothing but air. I could hear the rocks slide under my feet as they gave way, and I fell down. My nails bit into the rocky face of the mountain, and my legs slammed into the hard surface before dangling helplessly. The force of catching all of my free-falling weight at once caused my left elbow to dislocate. I felt it pop, and hanging onto the ledge was bringing me to tears. I still didn't scream, though. But the rocks had made enough noise for me. I looked down and saw a few of the grunts dancing about the ledge as they dodged the falling stones. One of them got mangled by the falling debris, and hungry, nearby grunts wasted no time in putting the limping creature out of its misery.

I turned my head away from the sight, but it didn't save my ears from the sounds. The wounded demon was still howling in pain when the others started to devour it. Fearing a similar fate, I muscled through the blazing pain, managed to get my footing, pulled myself up, and knelt down when I got to safety. My ankle throbbed, and I could feel my sock, thick with blood, adhering to my leg as it dried.

I took a moment to try and gain my breath. It was hard to find a steady rhythm when I felt the pulsing pain steal the air from my lungs. I was going to have to pop my elbow back into place now, whether I wanted to or not. I panted, held my breath, and laid my arm on the ground at a ninety-degree angle. Scooping my other hand under the wrist of the injured arm, I turned the appendage with my free hand until both were palm up. Slowly, I guided my arm up to my shoulder. I growled as I felt searing, white-hot pain rush through the bend of my arm until it went back in place. I wiggled my fingers, double-checked to see that it was fully functional again, and sighed—relieved that the remaining pain was something that wouldn't hinder me and my climbing.

Quickly, I looked over my shoulder to see if I had gained any of the grunt's attention. It was too dark to be a hundred percent sure, but it didn't seem like I had. However, the wails of the (now dead) grunt had gained more dinner guests. I'm sure that the scent of blood in the air was doing no favors to repel the new throng of drooling creatures. I picked up my machete and hobbled around the ledge until I found another way further up the mountain.

Everything on my body felt stiff or sore, and hoisting myself up the steepest incline wasn't my favorite thought at the moment. However, I was willing to muscle through the pain if I could live another day. I found another good spot to climb and tied the machete belt around my waist. Finding grooves within the crag, I started my ascension up the mountain. Blazing discomfort flared through my ankle with each step, and I didn't make it far before my luck ran out. Overhead, I heard the growling and clicking of a grunt, and I gasped as I locked gazes with the creature.

Tiny stones pelted my face as the demon skittered over the rocky side toward me. I tried to sidestep and reach for my weapon, but I was too slow. The grunt threw itself at me and landed on my arm. Immediately after impact, it tore into my shoulder as its claws possessively sank into my flesh. I let go of my hold on the grooves of the wall, and we plummeted a short distance before we slammed against the mountainside and then rolled down to the ledge. My cries mingled with the grunt's as we fell.

Once at the bottom, I could use both my hands to grab hold of the demon's head, and I twisted. I felt resistance. Gritting my teeth, I twisted more. The grunt howled and fought against me until I heard a well-defined snap, and the body went limp. I chucked it off the side without a second thought. I couldn't dwell on what I had done. Survival hinged on my need to keep moving. Checking over myself quickly, I ensured that I had my weapon still attached to my person. I felt a rush of relief hit me when I saw the blade's handle next to my hip, right before the pads of my fingers brushed over the hilt.

Hoots and yips could be heard close by. Some of the approaching demons were already feasting on the new body. But there were more hungry creatures than there was food. I wasn't looking to be their next meal. There wasn't time to climb anymore. The ones that didn't want to fight among themselves for the fresh carcass had fixed their sights on me. I jumped over a small break in the narrow path and hit the ground running with a hiss of pain.

I could hear them behind me, gaining ground. Their talons were scraping over the stone underfoot as they galloped on all fours for me. I couldn't outrun them, not while my ankle was flaring with mind-numbing pain and every thundering footfall I made was soaked in a fresh wave of agony. Eventually, I would have to make a stand. There was no way I could keep this up. There wasn't a lot of time to devise a plan. I had miscalculated the shadows in the distance.

One step.
Two steps.
S
   L
      I
        D
          E

The world became a blur as I rolled down the mountain. Jutting rock slammed into my spine, my hips, my knees. I covered my face with my arms and cradled the back of my head as I tumbled toward the bottom. I tried with all my might not to clench up, but I was sure that I had fractured a rib (at the very least) on the way down.

Drawing in air was painful, and I could feel my whole body shaking as I willed myself to stand up sooner than I would have liked to. My vision swam, and the scene around me swayed like I was aboard a boat atop an angry sea. I hit my knees and dry heaved.

"Get … up, Sia," I growled to myself between gulps for air. "If you're going to … throw up … do it … while running."

I could hear the grunts trying to reach me, but they were heading toward me with the same grace I had exuded on my way down the mountain. Up ahead, I saw my first glimmer of hope on the horizon. The faintest of light could be seen starting to chase away the evening shadows, but it was still about an hour away. Would I last long enough for the glaring rays of sunshine to send the demons back into hiding for another day?

I hoped so. I really, *really* hoped so.

Moving my feet, I tried to run as fast as I could, but—as I did—I could feel every strain on my body. I could feel every sore muscle move against its will as I hobbled further away from the snarling doom behind me. My injured leg was dragged more than it was lifted. My wounded shoulder throbbed with a sharp ache from the bite mark, my chest felt heavy, and I slowly drew out my weapon as I limped along.

It wouldn't be long now. They were right behind me. I needed to save my energy for fighting because it was clear that I wasn't going to make it very far at the rate I was going. Ducking behind a thin collection of gnarled, thorny trees surrounding a few boulders, I tried to calm myself. Emotions can mess you up in a fight. My daddy taught me that, even though my momma was very expressive with how much she didn't like me fighting a man his size. He only told her, "*The world won't care that she's a young girl. I'll teach her how to protect herself so I won't have to weep over a corpse.*" Momma didn't protest anymore after that.

A foolish part of me thought that slipping behind the foliage and rocks would somehow help me, but the realistic side of me knew that I was helplessly trying to survive by running away from certain death. Unfortunately, my wounded body couldn't take me as far as my heart desired. As I stood there wishing that I could manage a miracle and stay alive for another hour, I knew that I couldn't. But I had promised that I would swing my blade until I couldn't anymore. My chest rose and fell rapidly with my labored breathing as I tried to rest as quickly as I could, but every inhale made my upper body feel like I was being stabbed.

It was in that quiet moment that I felt the ghost of an emotion wash over me. Oddly like the residue of dread that the leech had left behind, but this felt different. It felt smarter … crueler. It felt like I had someone whispering to me to run before laughing at my clear misfortune. This thing was watching and enjoying the torment I was going through. There was nothing kind about it, but it made me feel all the more vulnerable. As if, at any minute, some new demon would rise out of the shadows and claim me in ways teeth and claws couldn't. It made my skin crawl and my insides knot up in disgust, but I still couldn't shake the undeniable feeling.

My eyes scanned the surroundings, trying to pinpoint where this new threat might be lurking, but my vision paused when I saw the glimmer of the first set of hungry eyes coming around the boulder. The grunt's victorious, hissing laughter caressed my senses like sandpaper. I licked my dry, cracked lips and quickly lifted my weapon in front of me as I tilted my chin up.

"Forgive me, Momma …" I felt the first tear blaze down my cheek like a falling star, full of heat and destruction. My lip quivered as I whispered, "I tried." Though I knew she would never hear my final moments, I said them to bring me comfort. But I wanted nothing more than for her arms to wrap around me one more time and for us all to be together once more. "I tried so hard," I faintly repeated, and the first grunt lunged at me, slicing a talon across my face. I could feel fresh, warm blood spill from my forehead all the way down to my chin, and a sick, itching feeling soaked my skin. I resisted the urge to hold the wound and grabbed the grunt by the leg and slung it toward the boulder.

Another tried to gain the upper hand while I was distracted. I was quicker. I sliced its arm off as it reached for me, and I kicked it away. As it slid across the desert floor, another dove at me from behind and slashed wildly at my back. Hitting the ground with a piercing cry, I noticed that there were more heading my way. While some of the demons saw the rising sun as the apparent threat that it was, the rest were too hungry to ignore a potential meal. In a panic, I slammed onto my back and repeated the action until the grunt was dazed enough to let me go. I rose to my feet and hacked at the body lying there until I was sure that it wouldn't get back up. And then, like I told Daddy, I stabbed at it again.

Sweat was pouring down my face and brow when I lifted my hardened gaze to the horde of grunts cackling and licking their lips at me. The vision in my left eye was hazy as blood flooded the socket. I closed that eye to keep my gaze fixed on the approaching demons. Rage bubbled inside me. Tears mingled with the crimson liquid on my face. I felt dizzy and tired. But I let all of my anger ball up inside, and I released a bellowing roar to the approaching creatures.

"Come on!"

Chapter 3:

Those Gold, Uncaring Eyes

When the sun rose, I was sure I was going to die. Either from a vengeful straggler, blood loss, or from the elements themselves, but I wasn't going to last on my own. That much was for certain. I reserved myself to that ugly truth as I felt the first rays of light warm the back of my pant legs.

It should have been a moment full of glee and happy tears. Instead, I could feel the hot tears of sorrow rolling down my face as I struggled to take in another ragged breath tinged with a metallic perfume. My mind ticked off a list of things that were in my duffel bag that might help me out in my current situation. However … I didn't have the energy to go get them. No matter how many times I told my limbs to move, they twitched and lay motionless. I opened my eyes after managing to roll over on my back. I wanted to see the sky. I wanted to watch the glittering stars fade from midnight hues and deep purples into a splendid, baby-blue sky kissed with morning sunshine.

From somewhere behind me, I could hear one of the grunts try to crawl toward me. I was pretty sure it was the one with only one arm and two broken legs, as it was taking its sweet time on getting to me. I didn't know if I was upset

or glad about that. I was happy about one thing: I didn't give up. I fought as hard as I could until I couldn't. My body, refusing to react to my commands to get up and flee the area, was proof of that fact. Slowly, I closed my eyes.

After several minutes of quieting the trepidation that had mounted within my being, I had finally stopped crying about my soon-to-be death. A few silent talks to myself had brought me to accept my undeniable fate. I reminded myself that even if I wanted to fight, I didn't have the strength to. I told myself that relentlessly until I didn't think of a way out of my conundrum.

If I just rested my eyes for a moment, maybe I could regain enough energy to fight off that one, lone grunt and hobble back to my stuff to try and rest and mend before racing off to somewhere safer. There was far too much blood around me for this place to be safe. I was bleeding too much.

Drat. I had done it again. I had closed my eyes long enough to fantasize about trying to escape my doom. I had daydreamed about the possibilities of my life existing beyond this moment. The quiet talks that had silenced my natural desire to fight and survive had been forgotten. Lazily, I gave a corner smile and shook my head.

"Silly, Sia ..." I whispered to myself.

Closer now, maybe a few feet away, I heard the hissing of the grunt. I could hear the pebbles as they were dragged over the desert floor under the weight of its body while it scooted closer to me. I could smell its searing flesh as it cooked under the rays of the sun. I let out a slow breath, and my fingers twitched over the handle of the machete.

With my eyes still closed, I suddenly felt the same dread that I had before the sun rose. It was as thick as a humid day in the south and as uncomfortable as a sunburn. It

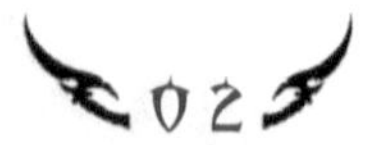

felt like something that you wanted to wash away with a whole bar of soap and a steaming hot shower.

My chest tightened as my heartbeat stumbled over itself involuntarily. It felt hard to breathe. My head felt foggy, and I started to feel dizzy. Fear was choking the very life out of me, and I wanted nothing more than to take in a slow, unrestrained breath of air into my tired lungs. Was something watching me? The longer I felt it, the more that I realized that it wasn't just dread that I was feeling. It was more uncomfortable and more unforgiving than that. My heartbeat threw itself against my sore ribcage, and I winced in pain.

There were only two things that could summon this level of anxiety. I very much doubted that it was the half-dead grunt sliding its way toward me. I froze as a cold, angry tone slithered over my being.

"Pathetic."

My heartbeat fumbled and then quickened in tempo. My eyes darted open. I wasn't sure if I should look in the direction of the voice or not. I didn't want to see what new nightmare was coming my way. But there was a sound that tore my eyes from the sweet, blue sky. A sick *snap* that said—without words—that the crawling grunt's life had been extinguished. It was a sound that came a little too close for comfort. Jerking quickly in the direction of the new threat, I felt the blood drain from my face as I held the new assailant in my gaze.

He was a dark beauty despite his robes of impeccable white and with hair like freshly fallen snow that fell down to his hips. One look at this being told me he was danger incarnate. Trimmings of black and vivid silver framed him in a way that was both refreshing and frightful. His skin was as cold as his voice and sculpted like he had been carved from

alabaster. But those eyes—they were gold and otherworldly, yet they held the breath of winter deep within those brilliant hues.

This wasn't a grunt, this was a … a devil.

My mouth dried up, and my eyes refused to blink, and I watched him glide toward me like a snowstorm in the middle of the desert. I tried to lift my blade, but my strength wasn't there. My arm flopped over, and I struggled and strained to stand. Despite my better judgment, my body reacted on its own and tried to escape the doom that was fast approaching.

Devils weren't like grunts. No. They would torture you first. They would make you wish that you were dead. There were some things that were worse than death, and the devils knew them, used them, and enjoyed every minute of them. I didn't want to be his next mangled toy. Even though my mind knew it was pointless, my body desperately tried to carry out the motions that it simply couldn't perform. I made a small sound of dissatisfaction, and his laugh chilled me to my core and beyond.

"Hahahaha, please … *run*. I do enjoy a good chase."

My legs buckled after two steps, and I fell forward. My weapon flung from my sweaty grip, and I whimpered as I watched the sunshine glint off the blade as it escaped me. It fell with dust clouds and corpses surrounding it. I slammed into the unforgiving ground with a groan of pain. Dirt was now sticking to the tacky, half-dried blood on my face. Frantically, I reached for the weapon as if wordlessly begging it to come to my hand and help me survive just one last fight.

"You did the best you could, darling. Don't beat yourself up. Nothing could prepare you for me," he warned.

My lower lip quivered as I still tried to touch the hilt. Grazing over the edge of it with the pads of my fingers gave

a spark of hope, but it was snuffed out by the shadow of the devil draped in white. His sandaled foot leisurely hovered over me and then ever so slowly stepped onto my aching hand. I wailed in pain and used every ounce of strength that I had to punch at his foot with my free hand. He bellowed with laughter that made my whole body freeze in place.

"Aww, it's so cute that you are trying," he said with a snicker.

His foot lifted off of me, and I was free to move. The devil sneered in disgust at me and swiftly kicked my side. Heat flared over my ribs. Rolling over, I coughed and tasted a metallic essence dance over my tongue. I spit the blood out of my mouth as I gasped for air. My eyes gradually glided over to him just in time to see his nails grow like needles. My mind raced. A thousand ideas and possibilities danced through my head at a speed I could not fathom. Everything moved so slow in that moment. I could see the end that was heading for me and knew that I was powerless to stop it.

Those dagger-like talons raced toward me, poised to kill. They were aimed at my throat and diving down faster than anything I had ever seen. My mouth opened to scream. But, to my surprise, words replaced what I thought was going to be a shrill cry of horror.

My voice sounded like it was made of sandpaper as I yelled, "I want to … make … a deal."

Something so sharp and deadly had never been held that close to my neck for so long. When I swallowed, I felt the tip of his nail graze my throat. Even the drumming of my chaotic heartbeat made the skin jump up just enough to caress the edge of those dangerous claws. The deep scent of spice and smoke swirled around my nostrils as I breathed in his personal perfume. Silence stretched, and I didn't know if he was happy or upset. Not a sign registered over his face to

give me some sort of clue. His eyes, however, held me in a
way a madman would. Ticking off his options while trying to
decipher which one would bring him the most enjoyment.
There wasn't a sliver of concern for me or my well-being in
that gaze. There were only the quiet calculations of a sinister
being.

The smile that graced his lips made my skin crawl.
Something deep inside me knew that the smile he wore was
all for show, and he didn't feel anything. He had somehow
learned how to master the art of a smile and made it look
appealing. But my soul knew. Like Meemaw would always
say, "*Your spirit knows things that your mind doesn't grasp the
understanding of yet. And we call it gut instinct, but it's really the
spirit telling us the truth we fail to accept right away.*"

He knelt in a way that was deadly and alluring. As if
I was watching him float like a ghost of misty white to my
side, but those nails never left my neck. The smile changed
then. It became a grin. A flash of white teeth behind a wild
curl of lips that was almost inhuman. A light flickered like
amber fire within his golden gaze.

"What kind of deal?" he purred darkly.

After an entire day's walk, we had made quite the
progress considering that I was walking on a gimp ankle. A
long way off, a village could be seen, though the details
beyond the rooftops peaking over the spiked tops of the
defensive walls couldn't be made out. It was the first town
that I had seen since I had left my own. The heat carried by

the lonely wind washed over my cheek. I touched the puffy skin on the side of my face and heard him speak behind me.

"I could've healed that too," he stated.

Back where he found me, I had allowed him to heal my internal injuries, but not the exterior. "At a price, I'm sure," I answered in a raspy voice. His dark chuckle that swiftly followed my reply made the hair on the back of my neck rise.

"Everything comes with a price, my dear."

"I'm not willing to pay it."

"I'm not terribly picky. You can let someone else pay for you."

I looked over my shoulder and glowered at the devil. He replied to the look with a slow curl of lips and a wink, but he remained standing tall, fair, and unmoved by my anger.

"No," I said finally.

"I'll be here if you change your mind," he said and then laughed at himself. "I'll be here for a *long* time."

His words cut me deeper than his talons ever could have. The price I would have to pay for my recent deal loomed over my head. I was sure that he wouldn't let me forget that I owed him anytime soon. I scanned the land surrounding the little town ahead as I carefully resituated the backpack on my shoulder.

Curiously, I asked, "So … how does this work?"

He blinked at me and sighed. "How does what work?"

"Can … can they see you, or will they?"

"Do you want them to?"

I thought about it. I really thought about it. The answer was a very loud, "No."

"Then no, *they* won't see me."

"Why did you say it like that?"

"I don't know what you mean?"

Great. I was stuck with a devil that thought I was an idiot. "What can see you if *they* can't?"

His eyes flicked to me, and he sighed again before leading the way to the town. "I figured you didn't want me to be seen with you. I don't exactly look like your standard apocalyptic ruffian. However, I am not hidden from other demonkind. Not unless I desire to be."

"Like you were last night?"

The first trace of curiosity tinted his words. "Oh? You knew that I was there?"

I followed behind him and nodded. "Faintly. I could sense something dark, hidden, and watching me when I was fighting the grunts."

"Hmmm …" he hummed. "Interesting."

I let the conversation die off there. The last thing I wanted to know was why the devil found that interesting, and I was more focused on getting to the next village to hopefully barter for a place to sleep, some food, and maybe some extra supplies. If I was lucky, I could do some mild chores and earn my keep and the extra provisions in less than a week. After that, I'd be on my way again. My goal was still to reach the faith city, Saint Augustine.

We were several yards away from the town when an unnatural wind kicked up. I had to shield my eyes from a miniature dust storm. Tiny rocks pelted my face, and I sucked in a sharp breath of air as the slight, stinging pain struck every visible piece of skin on me. Naturally, the devil did nothing to shield me from this annoying burden.

Before I could register what was happening, a tall woman was looming over me. She looked like she could stomp me into the ground without breaking a sweat. My mouth unhinged as her finer details swarmed me.

Her skin was like pale mud with gray undertones that made her look half-dead and like she would be cold to the touch. Her face was sharp and her eyes too large, which made her human appearance twisted. She wore a black, slim, silk dress with spaghetti straps that scooped down dramatically in the front, showing off her very apparent bone structure beneath her sickly flesh. Her smirk was mesmerizing as her oil-drenched fingers curled to me, calling me closer. My eyes drifted over her limbs that were a touch too long, and I noticed that every portion of her body was elongated in a way that made my skin crawl. With how thin she was, it made her seem taller and came off as unnatural. Instinctively, I slowly fumbled backward to put distance between us.

"Another outcast," she purred. "I've longed to play with something that was still breathing." She took a dangerous step toward me, and my eyes grew so wide that they hurt, and the action made her chuckle darkly.

I parted my lips to speak, but my mind drew blanks. My mouth suddenly dried up, and I felt like I was swallowing sand as I attempted to regain my composure and failed.

"She's with me …" my devil warned.

Turning swiftly, the female snarled, "And why do you think I would care who she is to y-y-y … it's you!" Her words were sapped of all confidence, and she instantly hit the ground on one knee and crossed an arm over her chest as she respectfully bowed her head. "Forgive me, my lord. I didn't know that she was claimed."

It was clear that this devil was weaker than the one I was bound to, or she wouldn't be asking for forgiveness. There were lesser devils out in the Wastes just like there were lesser demons. Looks like I lucked out with a powerful devil.

The devil robed in white looked proud and bored at the same time. He waved at the female, saying, "Rise."

"Yes, Lord—"

"*Don't* say my name ..." he ordered before she could think to continue.

Her mouth was left agape as she floundered on how to finish. "I-I-It is not something to be ashamed of," she replied, confused.

His calm demeanor was replaced with anger that quietly lapped at his irises. "Who said I was ashamed of it?"

She practically flattened herself against the dusty earth below. "I meant no disrespect!"

His eyes narrowed at the folded form before him. "I desire to not hear it for now." He sighed audibly. "Forget it." He looked away as he said, "Rise. I forgive your ignorance."

"Yes," she whispered with a raspy quake to her voice.

"I just call him annoying," I admitted with a cheeky smile.

The female rose faster than I had expected any living thing to move, and she bore her fanged mouth in my face with a hiss. "How *DARE* you!"

"Let it go." He looked her over and came a little closer to me. Something I wasn't exactly happy about.

I took another step back from both of them. Honestly, it was the best option. I felt a little safer with the minor bit of distance between us. The closer I was to them, the more suffocated I felt.

She cut her eyes at me, and a low growl could be heard trapped within her throat.

"Bushyasta, calm yourself," he ordered.

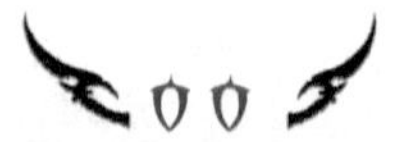

The sound stopped, and her large eyes lost their anger as she turned to him, flabbergasted at his decree. "My lord," she quietly gasped.

He held a hand up at her, and the belled sleeve to his robes danced gently in the breeze. "She and I have not had the delight of trading titles yet."

I forced a smile. "Oh, I guess the blood loss made me forgetful."

He smirked, and an emotion, dark and cruel, swirled in his vision. "My dear, let's not dance on the edge of rudeness … your name?"

There were two very important things that most people learned in the world that I lived in. There is power in a name, and you don't give yours to someone that you don't trust. I looked him over and knew that I didn't want to know his name either. It gave you power over the other person or gave them personal power. Both are dangerous if you don't know how to wield them.

"Sia."

"Sia … you gave me a nickname, eh, clever girl?"

The she-devil snarled. "You disrespectful—"

"Be still. I rather like this game she and I have going."

Good news, the devil wasn't bored with me. Bad news … he wasn't bored with me.

I shivered as he let his icy gaze rest on me. Nervously, I looked away and gained some mental clarity before I returned to him and asked, "And what do you want me to call you?"

"You do not desire to know my real name?"

"Not really," I admitted.

He smirked. "Just call me Draki." He then looked to the she-devil, "I'd like you to refer to me by this name as well. Tell the others."

She bowed again. "Yes, my—I mean, yes, Draki." The look she cut me out of the corner of her eye said that she would have flayed me if I wasn't already branded as his.

"I take it the next village is under your care?" Draki asked.

Turning to face him, she nodded as she said, "Yes, sire. It is my sleepy little village. I'm quite fond of it."

"We will need to venture to it and stay there for a short while."

"What is it that you require? I'll get it for you," Bushyasta stated with an elated expression. "I'd be more than happy to serve you."

"I need nothing," he admitted and lazily pointed back to me. "It is she that requires these supplies and such."

I already knew that she wasn't happy with that explanation. She slowly looked over her shoulder, and I figured that if I was already on her crap list, I might as well have a bit of fun. Waving with an overjoyed grin, I explained, "I just need a place to sleep, some food, and to pick up some supplies for my journey."

"Oh." She swept her ebony hair over one bony shoulder and stood a little more proudly. "I can get you the things you desire."

I didn't like that. I didn't like how she treated me, and I especially didn't like being handed something for nothing. It felt cheap and like I was cheating people. I knew the value of a bed and a safe place to sleep. I knew the cost of a decent meal and life's little comforts. They weren't things that were easily come by. They were earned with hours of relentless work and gathering much-needed items from

around dangerous areas. The price they carried could be etched into the gravestones of those sacrificed for some semblance of peace that we all enjoyed.

"It's fine. I'll do some work for it," I explained.

She rolled her eyes and scoffed. "Suit yourself, *human.*"

Before continuing, I dug through my sack and found my favorite army jacket. It was oversized and would hide most of the blood and wounds from sight. As we walked to the village, I wondered … what price did these people have to pay for their safety? What did they sacrifice for their illusion of freedom and happiness within this demon-infested land? Did I really want to know the answer to that question?

No, I didn't.

And I really hoped to keep it that way.

Chapter 4:

Only Rest for the Wicked

We arrived at the village and were greeted at the entrance. Though I was the only one that they saw, and they were clearly astonished to see me—mangled or not— standing outside their gates asking for lodging and food. I was met with a couple of guards who both wore friendly smiles and urged me to join them despite their confusion.

The first guard was short, had shaggy, russet locks, and green eyes. He looked the happiest to have a stranger approaching the gates. The second guard was bald with a beard, and he had deep brown eyes that sparkled with an untold joke. Both of them pushed the massive doors open and urged me to come closer.

As they approached me, Draki and Bushyasta disappeared, and I honestly felt a little better with them gone.

"What are you doing? Come in. Come in! The hour is getting late. You don't want to be caught dea—" the first guard started, and then rubbed his tattooed arm nervously. The picture was a chain link and came completely down to his elbow. Quickly, he motioned for me to walk through the main gate. "I mean, you don't want to be out there. Hurry up and come inside."

"Thank you. I was hoping to perhaps rest here for a while."

"Yes, yes. Of course!"

"We'll need to take her to the village leader," the second guard informed. He, too, had the same tattoo on his arm, but his was shorter and stopped a few inches before the bend in his arm.

The first guard waved the annoying thought away. "Bah, later." He turned his attention to me then. "So, what's your name? Mine's Gerald." Holding out his hand, he waited for me.

I smiled warmly and shook his hand firmly, just the way Daddy had taught me to. He had always told me that I might look like a village flower, but I could pack a punch, and that I should let my grip do the talking for me. "Sia," I replied.

Gerald winced and sharply drew in a breath of air. "Easy, killer. I'll need that hand for the rest of my guard duty!"

"And for later on tonight, I'm sure," the second guard mumbled.

"Hey!" Gerald whined.

"The name's Alan, Sia. Welcome to our village."

Laughing, I nodded as I thanked him and took a look around.

Erected in the center of the village, there was a massive, carved log with chains swirling around from the bottom to the top. Circling the base, there were eerily carved faces stacked in perfect rows. Each one of the heads looked unique and different, not a single one mirroring another. Looking at it made me feel uncomfortable. It was like I was staring into the frozen, wooden eyes of the dead.

Beyond the homes surrounding the front gates, the village opened up further in, and there were small stalls and barns with a few grazing animals. Next to them were large plots of farmlands and a small field of growing hay. Weeds were choking the life of half the wilted plants that were possibly on the verge of death. A cornfield was far off to one side, and it was drooping from a lack of care.

"What brings ya?" Alan asked.

I blinked and turned to him. "Hmm? Oh, I am venturing to the faith city," I admitted. Instantly, the two men gawked at me.

"Saint Augustine?" Gerald gasped. "Why you headin' there?"

"Did something happen to your village?" Alan asked.

I shook my head. The feelings were still too fresh for me to dive into. I cut off the emotions tied with the event and didn't make eye contact with them. "I'm just trying to find a place to call home."

There was so much more to that sentence, and everyone present felt it. We were all uncomfortable after that. There was no way to deny the fact that we all were very aware of the devils that ruled our world and claimed each village, town, and city that was untouched by the demons surrounding us all.

"Just stopping by on your way there, eh?" Gerald questioned, trying to lift the sorrowful mood that had blanketed us.

I nodded. "Yeah. I'm just needing a place to sleep, some supplies, and a few meals." As I reminded them, I noticed the two men shift uncomfortably and share a look between them. I added, "I don't mind earning my keep. I am not expecting handouts. I'll work for everything. Promise."

To that, the two perked up. Unusually so. "Work?" They said in unison.

"I think it's time you come meet our leader and get that ugly scratch looked at." Gerald pointed to the slash on my face and grimaced. I knew it didn't look pretty. I could feel it. The thing wasn't even fully scabbed over. Churning the air with his hand, he motioned for me to follow him.

Nearby windows were opened, and people inside looked out at us. Others came to their doorways and watched me as I passed by with Alan and Gerald leading the way. I struggled with making my limp less pronounced. Sweat was trailing all over me and seeping into my half-dried gashes and cuts. It stung, and the one on my ankle itched. If I didn't tend to it soon, infection would settle in. Mentally, I started making a list of things I needed to tend to as soon as possible.

As we passed by the various buildings of the village, I noticed that the barns didn't have anyone working around them. The field was bare of workers, the well was free of conversing villagers, the looms felt like they had been abandoned, and the pottery stations were dry as if they hadn't been used in weeks.

"Is it a holiday?" I asked.

Again, the two men shared a look and then faced the path in front of them. I was starting to get the feeling that the reason behind the lack of work wasn't a joyful one. Had someone died? All of a sudden, I felt horrible for asking.

"No. It's not a holiday," Alan answered finally.

"This is just how we are," Gerald added grimly.

Both of them went tight-lipped, and their expressions became twisted with ghosts of their past that they didn't want to talk about. I had a feeling that, eventually, it was going to be explained to me. If I didn't need the food and shelter, I would hit the road again and cut my losses.

However, I didn't trust Draki to keep me as safe as I would want to be. I just couldn't bring myself to trust a devil.

The rest of the walk to the leader's home at the back of the village was quiet, and I felt like I was a criminal marching toward the gallows. I swallowed hard and shifted the weight of the backpack on my good shoulder.

"Rather rude of them not to be the conversing sort on a long walk, don't you think?" Draki whispered in my ear. I jumped and screamed, which halted the two men in front of me.

"What! What is it?" Alan shouted.

"Are-Are you okay?" Gerald asked, concerned. Meanwhile, Alan looked me over like he was trying to pick me apart with his eyes.

I shook my head and bit the side of my lip. "I saw a spider," I said meekly. I even shivered for show. It wasn't a lie. I was really afraid of spiders. I'd been bitten by one in my sleep when I was younger and had a nasty fever and a sore spot on my leg for over a month. I didn't actually see one, but it would defuse any thoughts on their part that there might be something off with me. With light chuckles and a nod of understanding, they continued on.

My vision cut to Draki, and my frown expressed everything I couldn't verbally state at that moment. He drew in a sharp breath and gave me a devious grin. "Oh, did I frighten you?"

I rolled my eyes.

"Hahahaha. Poor thing. I thought you would want the company."

I narrowed my gaze at him, and I could feel his delight in my annoyance with him. I whispered, "I'm fine."

Gerald heard me and laughed. "Right you are. Just a little bug. No need to feel bad about it. Alan here looks like

he could split heads with his bare hands, but he passes out at the sight of blood."

"I do not!" Alan declared.

"Do too. Don't you remember fainting when Bethany gave birth to your son?"

Alan paled a bit. "Don't remind me. That was different. I didn't know a woman's body could go through all that."

I couldn't help it, I laughed. I remembered similar situations happening back in my village. Men and women alike had fainted during childbirth or when they saw too much blood. It was why butcher jobs and medics were only taken on by those that could push past the gruesome images.

While the two guards were distracted, I mouthed to Draki *"Go away"* with an angry countenance.

"Suit yourself. Call out my name if you need me," he stated with a deep sigh that expressed his boredom rather than any form of sadness.

We reached the home, and I stayed outside as the two guards went to inform the leader. While I waited, I looked back behind me to the tall, strange totem in the village's center. How odd that all of the faces were frozen in fear or anguish. Even now—with them being at a distance— they still disturbed me.

"I wouldn't focus on that," Draki warned as he appeared at my side.

Not expecting him to show up again so soon, I shuddered and lay a hand over my overworked heart. After taking a moment, I spoke softly while still looking at it. "Why?"

"It'll become a problem if you do."

I turned to ask him what he meant, but Alan and Gerald had already returned, and Draki had vanished once more.

Alan said, "She'll see you inside."

"I wish you luck," Gerald expressed with a toothy grin before he started back toward the village gate.

"Thanks," I stated in passing while following Alan into the home.

The house was two stories tall with a thatched roof and a second-floor balcony that was woven with sticks and vines. Mud and clay made up the walls, and I could see the bark of logs poking out through the dried mixture. Inside the home was cool, and a few potted plants adorned the exposed windows and were nestled next to the doorways. Further inside, near the back, a woman was eyeing over the many flowers and the half-wilted farmland beyond. Her skin was a touch darker than mine, and she wore an elaborate headdress with brightly dyed feathers that swept the floor as she walked about the enclosed back porch. I could see that her hands up to her forearms were painted in a deep crimson paint, and that same paint was smeared across her eyes. She wore a long, earthy-green dress, and in her dark brown eyes I saw a sadness that danced with wisdom.

"You must be Sia," she said, facing me.

"Yes." I wasn't going to give anyone I didn't trust my full name. Devil or not. It was like handing someone a sharpened blade that you cherished. It could protect you … or cut you down. "What should I call you?" I asked.

"Everyone in the village refers to me as Matulia."

"Nice to meet you, Matulia."

"And very nice to meet you as well, Sia. Come," she said, holding her arms straight out to me, palms up.

I took it as an invitation to take her hands, and I made no hesitation in doing so. Something in her eyes made me trust her without a second thought. Her fingers wrapped around my palms, and she pulled me closer to inspect me silently.

After a long moment, she smiled and gave a small nod. "Whatever brought you here doesn't need to be explained. How can we help?"

A burden was lifted from my shoulders. Feeling relieved, I told her, "I was hoping to do some work in exchange for food and lodging … maybe some supplies if you have them to spare?"

There was something that flashed in her eyes, but it was too quick for me to catch. She was quiet as she contemplated, and when I thought silence was all I would receive, she lightly squeezed my hands. "I think that could be arranged. Perhaps Marcel and Janet could help you make a list and start working."

"Really?" I asked, perking up. I was beginning to think that I was asking too much of them.

She laughed and shook her head, and the sound of the feathers brushing over her body brought peace to my spirit. "Yes," she withdrew one hand to touch my braids, and sadness crashed to the surface of her dark brown eyes. The moment stretched on longer than I was comfortable with, and she noticed. Snapping out of her daze, she smiled at me and let my hair fall away from her grasp. "I'll take you to them. Alan, please see yourself back to your post," Matulia directed.

He bowed slightly to her. "Yes, Matulia."

As he left, she placed my hand on the bend of her arm, saying, "Walk with me."

"Can I ask why everything feels so …" I was at a loss for words. It felt barren and empty, like everyone had stopped working in the middle of their daily chores and just let everything go.

Even from the side, I could see the expression on her face. It was the mask we all wore when we denied the fact that we were kept safe from demons by pacts with devils. It was the same look we all gave when we'd throw open the closet door and expose the skeletons therein.

"It is our curse," she said finally.

And with that, I sort of understood what she meant. The state of their village wasn't necessarily by choice but forced upon them. "You aren't allowed to work?" I whispered, unsure if this was a conversation that should be held at levels that others could hear.

She shook her head with a deep sigh. "We are limited to the amount of work that we can do." She motioned with her chin to the arm that I was holding. I saw a chain tattoo. It mirrored the same one that Gerald and Alan had. Only hers was just a few links long and closer to her shoulder. "If we do more than our share of work that day, the chain grows."

"Yours is so short," I blurted out, and I cringed at my own rudeness.

She noticed the expression and laughed lightly. "It's all right. It's a natural thing to be curious, especially in a new village. I'm the leader," she said. For a brief second, her vision swam with the ghosts of things long since passed. Shaking her head slightly, she began again. "The leader has to lead. They can't be at risk and ever constantly changing. The links must remain short on those that rule over our village."

I dared to ask, "What happens when the chain gets down to your hand?"

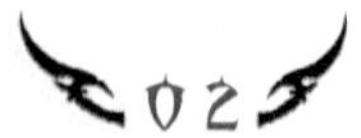

She patted me with a warm smile, but there was a touch of hurt in the curl of her lips. "Don't fuss over such matters. It is our burden to bear. Don't worry. The curse doesn't affect outsiders."

Despite it being the relief that it was, I could feel a weight rest upon me. The type that makes a home in your being when you want to be of some help to someone, but you know there is nothing that you can physically do to aid them. I felt so helpless, and I didn't like that feeling in the slightest. It reminded me of when Momma hugged me when I was thrown out of the village. It reminded me of being trapped between a leech and a grunt in the cave … and it reminded me of being so helpless that I ignorantly made a pact with a devil to stay alive.

We walked behind one of the homes, and I saw three people sitting on a porch with several baskets. There was a man, a woman, and their older son peeling the leaves off of corn with glum expressions. The father had strawberry-red locks and pale blue eyes. His freckles were speckled all over his cheeks and nose, making his pale skin look adorable. But the tired circles under his eyes made his cute, round face seem aged beyond his actual years. His sleeves were rolled up to the elbows, and the visible links peeked out a few inches down his forearm.

The mother had chestnut curls and a brighter set of blue eyes. The skin of her face and hands seemed sun-worn, and her youthful glow was stolen by the hidden appearance of years of endless worries. Her own chain link tattoo was

almost to her wrist, and the image was smeared with sweat and dirt.

The younger man had short, messy, light auburn hair that glinted gold in the summer sun. His eyes were hazel and his smile bright, though the sadness in his hues doused any joy that the curve of his lips implied. He had faint freckles dashing across his cheeks and the bridge of his nose. Stubble lined his chin in a slightly darker shade than his hair. And his tattoo was visible on his shirtless body. Links traveled from the shoulder all the way down to the back of his hand. It was like walking the line of a visible curse with my eyes … because I was. He looked as though he might be a year older than I, and yet I felt like I was looking at a dead man.

"Put the ears of corn by the steps. We'll gather water from the river in a little while so we can wash them," the woman gently explained to the young man.

In a low whisper, Matulia said, "Marcel is the father. That there is Janet, the mother."

"And him?" I breathed, feeling pain take hold of my chest as I asked.

"Elijah," she replied back.

"Elijah," I quietly parroted.

After taking a few steps closer, Matulia called out to the family. "Good day, Roier family!" They all looked up, and I watched as the gloomy expressions on their faces slowly faded away.

Marcel spoke up first as he stood and dusted off his jeans. "Just another day, Matulia. I see you have a new friend."

"And any friend of mine is a friend of yours. She's looking for somewhere to sleep and a few warm meals."

"I'll work for them," I reminded.

Janet gave a weak smile. "We thank you for your help."

I waved my hands from side to side. "I'm just earning my keep. No need to thank me."

"Anyone willing to do extra work around here is a walking miracle to us," Elijah explained.

"Would it be okay if she stayed with your family?" Matulia asked.

The family exchanged looks, turned their eyes to the ground, and fidgeted in silence for a short while. All of a sudden, I felt like I was asking for a favor that caused them all physical harm. But when I looked to them all, it was Elijah's hazel eyes that I was met with.

"We have a spare room you can sleep in," he said.

"Elijah," Marcel whispered angrily and then looked to the mother, worry in his gaze.

Janet shook her head with a painful upturn of her lips. "It's okay, Marcel. It's been three years. Time that room saw more than cobwebs and dust."

"Are you—" Marcel started.

"As sure as the day that I married you," Janet quickly affirmed.

The father nodded and stood a bit taller. "Very well. If you say that it is okay, I'll agree."

Janet smiled, and there was a touch more warmth to the expression. "I'll go prepare an extra place at the table and freshen up the room for you. I'm sorry that I'll have to leave you with these two blockheads," she teased with a wink and dashed through the entrance before her husband could playfully slap her backside.

Matulia patted me before she slipped away, saying, "I know you are in good hands. I've got much to tend to, so I'll leave the three of you to get acquainted and settled."

Turning, the father jutted a thumb out to the field. "I'm going to gather the last of the baskets and meet you all back inside the house. Supper should be soon, and we can finish this up later."

"I can help," Elijah exclaimed.

"No!" The single word was practically barked. He looked to me and the leader before drawing in a slow, calming breath before lowering his voice to say, "You've done enough today. How about you keep our new guest company?"

Not really giving his son an inch to argue, Marcel was hopping off the porch and heading out to gather the lone baskets of corn deep in the field. Shortly after, Matulia headed back toward her hut.

The young man sighed as he was left alone with me. I'm sure he was feeling as awkward as I was. It radiated off the both of us. We avoided eye contact and made weird, throat-clearing sounds for a solid three minutes before he rubbed the back of his neck and reluctantly faced me.

"So, where are you heading? I doubt you are planning on staying here for long if you are picking up supplies."

I took in a deep breath and faced Marcel out in the field, but I wasn't looking with my eyes. I was miles away. What I was seeing in my mind was the glorious faith city that Meemaw had always told me about. "I am heading to Saint Augustine," I admitted.

"The faith city," he breathed. "How I envy you."

Blinking out of my blissful trance, I turned and asked, "Why is that?"

"You have freedom. I know the price we all pay for living out here in the Wastes. We seem like we are well off … but we're not." There was a pause that was more like a

respectful moment of silence, where we both mourned for the dead. "You can go anywhere you want."

I half-laughed. "There is always a price."

"Oh, what price are you paying?"

I stiffened to the question. I felt like he saw through me and could sense my pact. He knew, right? I wiped my hands on my pant legs and smiled awkwardly, trying to mask my inner panic. *There is no possible way he could know. Get a hold of yourself, Sia.*

I settled with answering him with a half-truth. "What price? For starters, there's the nightly battle with grunts."

"Is that where you got that?" he asked, pointing to my face.

I nodded my head, and his eyes widened. Then he looked me over, and it was apparent he was searching for more injuries. I still had on my army jacket, which hid the wound on my neck. My pants—though mangled and coated in blood—didn't visibly show the torn flesh on my ankle. I lifted the fabric and turned enough for him to see the gash. Unfortunately, I could see it too. It was puffy, red, and angry-looking. I grimaced at it and let the material fall back down. I then moved the collar of the jacket from my neck to reveal the scratches. Slowly, I pulled it further off my shoulder and revealed the bite mark.

"You need medical treatment!" he gasped, grabbing me by the wrist. Guiding my arm, he put it around his neck and aided me in walking. "How are you not limping around on that?" he asked as he quickly shuffled across the porch and through the entrance to his house. "Mom! Get the first-aid kit and some hot water!" he yelled.

Janet came to the doorway of a nearby room and looked to her son with a concerned expression. "What's wrong, Elijah … Oh. OH! My word. What happened?" Not

waiting for a reply, she rushed over to grab a pot of water. "I didn't know that it was fresh."

"That isn't the only wound," Elijah informed his mother as he sat me down in a rickety chair at the kitchen table.

"Why didn't you say something, my dear?" she asked.

As she poured the water from the kettle resting next to the fireplace, I replied, "I honestly forgot." Truthfully, I hadn't. "I thought I was fine," I lied.

"You've got wounds that would leave most knocking on death's door, and you are sitting here claiming you forgot and you thought you were fine. How can you ignore yourself like that?" Elijah scolded me softly.

I looked at him and opened my mouth to reply but paused when those eyes collided with mine. That look, I knew it. I craved something like that from my family. I figured a friend would show it to me, but I never expected it from a stranger. *Don't look at me like that … please.* Turning my head from him, I replied in a low, drone tone, "I'm pretty sure death wants to watch me suffer first."

Out of the corner of my eyes, I could see his expression twist into something that was filled with hurt and curiosity. But that view was (thankfully) cut short by his mother squeezing between the two of us as she put the hot water and a pile of folded cloth rags on the floor. "You go grab the first-aid kit, child. I'll clean her up. This is a job for a fellow woman."

He blushed a bit and stood up quickly. "Right," he said, rubbing the back of his neck. "I'll be right back."

The mother responded with a hum and wrung out a freshly dipped cloth. As she dabbed at my face, she asked, "Where else?"

"Oh, um, on my neck, shoulder, and ankle. I think that's all," I admitted.

She sucked at her teeth. "To think a young thing like you stuck outside the safety of a village." Janet shook her head with a heavy sigh. "You're lucky," she whispered as she wrung the water out of the cloth and wiped my chin.

"I think you and I have different takes on luck, Janet."

She looked at me and let one side of her mouth twitch in a nervous half-smile. "What is our world but trading one hell for another? You live out there and fight to live or …" she looked around the house, tracing the walls with her tired eyes, "or you're trapped in here fighting for one more day." She faced me then. "But at least out there, you're free of the chains holding you to your village. Out there, you can try every day to reach a faith city. You can live free of debts you never asked for."

Only, I did ask for it. I almost died for it, but the chains I had been free of for a single day were reattached within hours. I had my own devil. I had my own hell. I couldn't tell her that, though.

"I suppose you're right." I wasn't lying. She was right. I only cheated my way there. If anyone else like me had been outcasted or sacrificed to the Wastes and made it to the faith city, they fought longer and harder than I. I only fought through a night.

Elijah came back with the medkit and put it on the table with a long face. "There's no more alcohol."

"What about the bandages?"

"Maybe enough for her ankle, but nothing more."

She tossed the bloody rag onto the floor. "Drat. When did those get used up?"

"After I had to wrap my blistered hands from working the fields that morning you and Dad slept in."

A look of shame came over the mother. Standing, she wiped off her hands on the side of her skirt and grabbed her son, jerking him over toward me. "You finish cleaning her up, and I'll go ask Matulia for some bandages and alcohol."

"And an extra bar of soap, her ankle is messed up pretty bad."

Janet waved at her son as she rushed for the door. I could hear her call for Marcel as she darted across the porch. She was probably going to tell her husband what had happened and where she was going. Again, I was left alone with Elijah.

Slowly, he knelt down, grabbed a fresh washcloth, and dunked it into the water. "You know, if I didn't see these wounds, I would have thought you made a deal with a devil to stay alive out there."

For a brief moment, my heart stopped. I masked the expression well enough. At least, I hoped that I did. I smiled and said, "You don't say?"

"Not many come passing through. I'm sure you know this, too."

I nodded. I knew it. I knew it all too well.

He motioned to my ankle. "Let's get this one taken care of next."

I didn't disagree. Rolling up my pant leg, I revealed the angry wound. He and I both made a face at it. Mine was filled with pain, and his expression was full of disgust.

"That's one nasty bite there. Someone ate well last night."

I laughed. "His belly wasn't full for long. I gutted him soon after."

It was his turn to chuckle at my joke as he cleaned the torn skin. "I find it oddly comforting to know that when you leave here, you'll know how to keep yourself safe. It kind of gives me hope."

"My being able to slit a grunt in two gives you hope?"

He nodded then. "That there is a chance someone can make it to the faith city."

"Why is that so important to you?"

His eyes naturally drifted down to his arm and traced over the many interlocking links that made up the chain tattoo. "I suppose it gives me hope of escaping a debt I never agreed to pay."

I understood him. I never agreed to this life. At the same time, I didn't feel like I had to struggle to survive like I did before. A devil sort of made things a little easier on you once you make a deal. However, I did feel the desire to secure a safe place so that I could come back to save my family and friends. None of us desired to live like this. Many of us just wanted to live a peaceful, happy life. That was so scarce in our world now. But—if I could find the answers on how to break these debts and curses—I might be able to save more lives than just my own. I was willing to put my life on the line for that, for a glimmer of hope.

He pressed on the side of my ankle, and I drew in a sharp breath. Involuntarily, I jerked my foot, and he latched onto the back of my calf with his hand. His fingers were stronger than expected, and they dug into my skin to the point of almost bruising. "Don't," he whispered.

"That hurts," I yelped angrily.

"I hope so. You've got a tooth sticking out of your bones!"

"Holy—you can see my bone?" I shrieked.

"Yeah. This is bad … uh …" He looked at me with pure perplexity. "Sorry to be wrist-deep in your blood and asking this now, but what is your name?"

I blinked as I stared at him. *Did I never introduce myself? Where were my post-apocalyptic manners?* "Sia," I said.

"What would you say your pain tolerance is?"

"I, uh, can get my shoulder mangled by a grunt and not scream like I'm dying?"

He nodded. "You might want to brace yourself. This isn't going to feel great. I think you'll be all right, though."

"The words of my dreams," I teased.

He smiled at me, and my own smile quickly faded. I frowned and looked away. My whole demeanor changed in the blink of an eye. One moment, I was warming up to him and cracking tasteless jokes. The next, I was colder than an ice storm as I said, "Just get it over with."

He waited a few seconds as I focused on my breathing. I remembered to do what Momma always said. I remembered to not hold my breath. It was like child labor. You kept breathing deep and steady. By the time I closed my eyes, he tugged on the lodged tooth. I grunted in pain, and he chuckled.

I must have looked angry because he held up his hands to show he meant no harm. "You're tougher than me," he said with a wide grin. "I would have cried." With that, he revealed the large, sharp tooth held between his fingers.

Reaching forward, I took the fang and inspected it. I smirked and stuffed it into my army jacket. "That'll be turned into some nice jewelry later."

"By the way, do you have an extra set of clothes?" he asked.

I nodded and then looked down at my bloodstained attire. "Suppose I should burn this outfit."

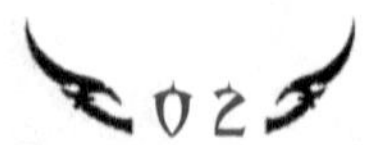

His eyes glossed over like he was hiding something as he said, "We have some old clothes that might fit you."

"I don't want to be a bother."

He shook his head. "They're just collecting dust."

Even though I wanted to ask why they had extra clothes that might fit me, part of me already knew the answer. I was sure that they didn't belong to his mom. Drawing my lower lip into my mouth, I softly chewed at it. From then until Janet showed back up, we remained quiet while he cleaned my injuries. I didn't really feel uncomfortable until he was working on my shoulder. I didn't look at him, but I could feel his eyes on me. It was that special way a guy looks at a girl when he wants to bring her flowers and talk to her, so he could find out what she liked. It wasn't me being snobby about my looks or anything, I could just tell. I could feel his eyes on me like little prickles of energy. During that time, I did everything in my power to look at anything but him. Thankfully, I was saved by his parents walking through the door.

His mother shuffled over and shooed Elijah away. "Let me handle the rest."

"I had it, Mom," he griped.

"Come on, son. Let's go get something fixed for dinner for everyone while your mother tends to the young lady."

Chapter 5:

The Chains that Bind

Not long after Janet was finished patching me up, the men announced that dinner was ready. I was happy to hear the news because I was hungry. Now that my wounds were taken care of, I had almost forgotten about how little I had eaten in the past twenty-four hours. However, I felt comfort knowing that the inflicted areas were cleaned, bandaged, and had a lesser chance of becoming infected.

The moment I sat down, Janet asked me, "So, how long have you been out of your village?"

The question caught me off guard, and I awkwardly stared at each person seated at the table around me. "Two days and one night," I admitted softly.

"That's a long time to be out in the Wastes by yourself," Marcel commented. "Surprised you don't look worse than you do."

"I would if it wasn't for the machete my daddy gave me before I left," I explained. "I might need to sharpen it before I leave. Cleaving through that much bone last night might have dulled the blade." I looked up just in time to see each person with a spoon poised over their bowl and their eyes fixed on me in amazement that was coated in disgust. It was at this moment that I realized that this probably wasn't

the best topic for discussion while at the dinner table. Swirling my spoon around in my bowl of beans, I laughed awkwardly and swept my braids over my shoulder. I hoped that they didn't see my very apparent grimace at my social blunder as I dove into my meal.

The silence was deafening and did nothing for my nerves. Elijah pushed a plate of cornbread toward me, and I eyed him over suspiciously before reaching for a square. "Thanks."

"I might be able to help you out with sharpening it," Elijah said, his eyes full of warmth.

"You have other things to tend to," Marcel stated coldly. "You know the rules."

"I'm just trying to help."

"Gentlemen, let's not discuss work at the table." Janet's words were more like a command rather than the plea she had disguised it as. Both men stared at their own meals in silence after that.

Later on that night, I lay in bed while looking over the list of work Janet had written out for me. Suddenly, I felt the mattress shift as Draki manifested next to me. I parted my lips to scream, but his hand quickly clamped over my mouth.

His face was too close for any sort of comfort to be present as he said, "You really should get used to me appearing out of nowhere. It would be bothersome if you were to scream every time I come around." He leaned in closer to me. Our noses were practically touching, and those gold orbs danced with mirth as his gaze bore into me. "There

will come a time that I will want you to scream, but now isn't that time."

My brow bent angrily, and I slapped his hand away from my mouth and scrambled out of the bed. But the taste of his perfume lingered on my lips. It was the bitter taste of smoke mingled with the pungent scent of spice. "What are you doing here?" I growled the question.

"Checking in, of course. I thought that would be clear."

"I doubt that you are checking in on me. What do you want?"

Draki stretched out on the bed, propped his head up on his hand, and bent one leg. As his robes slightly came undone in the front, he looked like he was modeling for a calendar rather than getting comfortable. I turned away from him. The sight of it was more appealing than I wanted to admit, and it made my stomach feel sick at the thought. I shouldn't be this drawn to a devil. I shouldn't want to be held by him. His deep chuckle mocked me from the other side of the room.

"You're just bored," I whispered.

"You're not wrong," he stated. "However, I wanted to warn you. This place has rules about work, and you aren't exactly fully healed. If you don't pace yourself, they'll use what little vitality you have left."

"So?"

"So … Sia, I thought I would make this easier on the both of us and heal you."

"No."

He narrowed his eyes at me. I wasn't getting the feeling that he was denied often. It took everything in me not to gulp audibly as I faced his unwavering glower.

"No?" he repeated in a fashion that came across as if he was giving me the chance to change my answer.

I nodded.

"Do not forget who belongs to whom here, little girl."

I felt my confidence waver for a moment. "I haven't forgotten."

"I realize now why you didn't want me to heal you out in the Wastes. You did it so you could convince them to let you into the city and to give you an audience with the leader. It worked, and I commend you for it. Most would have been too concerned with their well-being and required healing from me. You, on the other hand, used your injuries to prove your innocence and gain the trust of these villagers." He grinned then. "Who's the devil here, again?"

I didn't like what he was saying. "I did what I had to."

"Most of us do."

"Anything else?"

"Let me heal you." It was stated as a demand rather than him asking me.

I shook my head. "Give me a day before you try to heal me."

He rose from the bed and spoke as he glided over to me. "Don't overdo it tomorrow. It is one thing to be entertained and another to be burdened. I hope you understand what I'm saying, my dear. You've proven to be quite sharp thus far."

"I understand," I replied coolly. "Now — if you don't mind — I want to try and get some rest.

He motioned to the bed, and I brushed past him to lie down. When my head hit the pillow, all I saw was his dusky form and two golden eyes glowing from the corner of the room. The vision unnerved me, and I rolled over. Even

though he was the farthest thing from safe, I knew I was protected. Sleep claimed me without resistance.

The next morning, before anyone else was awake, I was out in the field before the sun had risen too far over the horizon. The last thing I wanted to be doing was straining myself under its unrelenting rays and putting my injuries at risk. I wanted to get work done but without breaking myself in the process. Unfortunately, Draki thought that it was a good idea to join me for those few hours of work.

Brushing a cornstalk out of his way with a sneer, the devil grumbled audibly, "Aren't I lucky that you're such a diligent worker?"

"You are. Otherwise, we'd be here longer than necessary."

He rolled his eyes. "We wouldn't need to be here in the first place if you would let me handle everything."

It was my turn to roll my eyes. I snapped a few ears of corn off the stalk and tossed them into the waiting basket at my feet. "Your help comes with a price," I reminded him heatedly.

He grinned wildly. "I'm sure that we can come up with a reasonable payment arrangement."

I wiped the sweat off of my brow and said, "No." My reply was short and clipped and heavy with my distaste for his suggestion.

The cornstalk in front of him was snapped in half. When I turned in his direction, I was met with an angry stare that sapped me of any defiance. "Remember what I said …"

he warned with a slight growl. "Your life is no longer just yours. We have an agreement. I have every intention of upholding my end of the bargain. Be warned, Sia, I won't give you rest even in death. Do you understand me?"

I turned away from him to continue with my work. "I do," I mumbled before tossing two more ears of corn into the basket.

Red mist formed around me and quickly dissipated as Draki manifested in front of me. His hand snapped out and grabbed me by the jaw. He tilted my head up to look at him as his baritone voice rolled over me like thunder. "Do you?"

I went still in that grip. Instinct wanted me to reach for a weapon. Logic told me slapping a devil with a vegetable wasn't going to be very effective. I didn't want to, but I locked eyes with him. "Are you afraid that I will work myself to death to escape our pact?"

His grip said it all as it tightened around my lower jaw. I winced in pain but managed to not whimper. "I'm letting you know that if you're dumb enough to have such a thought, I won't give your soul a moment's rest in the afterlife."

"The last thing I want is that. I assure you … I'm only trying to earn my keep. These people suffer enough. They don't need me leeching off of them," I stated firmly.

For a long moment, we stared at each other in a quiet, heated battle. He was weighing my words, and I was letting him know (silently) that when I made a promise, I kept it. Even if I didn't like it. After several seconds that felt like hours, he released me aggressively and swiped his hand through the air. At first, I thought that he was aiming to slap me. I closed my eyes and turned my head, waiting for the stinging blow, but it never came to pass.

When I opened my eyes, I saw the remaining baskets full and the stalks bare of ripe corn. I turned to face him, but his form was already fading, but his voice was clear as a bell. "Consider this a favor, human." There was a pause. "Tend to your new wounds … before you go off to do more work."

There were blisters on my palms and a few minor scratches on the backs of my knuckles. He had noticed something so trivial. Did that mean that he cared? Or was it just that he cared about whether or not I could carry out my end of the deal? I balled my hands into fists and sucked in air sharply as the pain swiftly followed after.

"Are you crazy?" Elijah's voice called out from behind me.

Turning to face him, I tried to hide the fact that I was making sure that Draki wasn't around me. Recently, I was finding that you never knew when and where that devil was going to pop up. After realizing that I was in the clear, I groaned and rubbed my lower back. "I couldn't sleep well last night," I stated honestly. I wasn't sure if he was listening to me or not because his eyes were walking the rows of corn and noting the full baskets at the end of each one.

"This … this is too much, Sia."

"What?"

"How many hours did this take you?"

I scratched the back of my neck and thought about how only half of the baskets were from my work. The rest were from Draki. I really needed to come up with a reliable answer for how I got all that work done in the time frame I had actually been outside. Even if Draki had tried to ease my burden, I couldn't help but feel like he was joyfully watching me flounder for a reply. I wasn't left with an honest answer, that was for sure. "You'll be surprised how much work you can get done before sunup if you just opt to get as little sleep as possible."

Elijah frowned at that. "You're injured. You should have been resting."

I went to wave the thought away, and he caught a glimpse of my blisters. Instantly, that hand was hidden from sight as quickly as I could manage to. But the damage was done. I still tried to pretend like I hadn't noticed him realizing that I was only adding to my list of wounds. "I'm sure I'll rest better tonight."

"Have you ever picked corn before?"

"A few times, when I was younger."

He looked at me and motioned to my hands. "I should wrap those for you."

"Don't worry about it."

He wasn't taking no for an answer because before I could change the subject, he had managed to storm up to me, grab my hand, and inspect the blisters. "Sia, you don't need to push yourself like this. What you've done today alone is enough to pay for your medical supplies and room."

"It's just a couple of blisters. I'll be fine," I said, pulling my hand away from his grasp.

He looked at me with worry, and I felt my stomach knot. "Your injuries keep stacking up, and you're not focusing on trying to heal at all. You need to be more careful."

I knew that look in his eyes. I knew those words. He was concerned for me, that much was clear. And anyone caring for me on any level was dangerous. I jerked out of his grip and pointed over to the barns. "I still have work to do," I muttered and took a few steps back. "If you carry the baskets back to your home, it doesn't …"

He sighed and shook his head. "It won't count toward my work."

I nodded, feeling relieved, and started to walk away. "Good."

"You're not going to let me look at those?"

"I'm fine," I reiterated.

"Sia!"

I didn't want to stop. I didn't want to turn around. I didn't want him to convince me to take a break. I just wanted to speed-walk away and drown in work, earn my keep, and leave as soon as possible. I didn't need to get tangled up in anything else … I couldn't afford to.

I could hear him call out to me again, and I didn't give any indication that I heard him. "At least take a break before you do more work!"

Even though I didn't want to say anything back to him, I mentally agreed. So—when I got over to the barns—I rushed for the hay bales in the back and threw myself onto them, panting lightly. White hair spilled over a hay bale stacked next to where I was resting. Rolling my eyes, I groaned.

"What, Draki?"

"Such a nice young lad."

"Don't start. I'm not interested."

There was a dark chuckle and the sound of movement as he peered over the edge at me. "Oh? You really haven't given him enough time to see if you would be."

My heated glare pierced through him. Devil or not, I wasn't going to be manipulated into feeling anything for someone else. "I have to leave here. There isn't a point in getting close to people that are tied to their village." He knew that. I knew that. Even if I wanted to try and get romantically

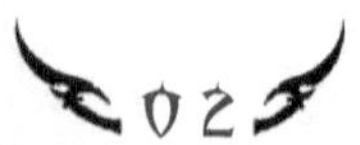

involved with someone, why would I put effort into someone that was bound to their village, to their own devil?

"You could take him with you." Most would think he was being kind. I, on the other hand, knew better.

"There isn't a devil out there that will let go of something or someone that they've claimed."

"Not without a price."

"That is exactly my point."

"But it is still doable," he sighed.

"You're brave to assume everyone is willing to pay for someone else's freedom."

"I'm wise, my dear. I know people are willing to pay steep prices for things that are hard to come by. An unimaginable amount of lived years has taught me that."

I turned over and plucked a few pieces of straw out of the bale. "I'm tired," I admitted meekly.

There was no sound implying that he had moved, but I suddenly felt him at my feet. Moving enough to view where he sat, I looked at his back as he watched the horses and goats graze lazily. I watched his white hair sparkle like diamonds under the early morning rays of light and his clean, white robes sway in the gentle breeze. He looked regal, even if he was sitting on square bundles of straw.

He didn't face me when he said, "Rest. I'll keep watch." He must have read my mind because he stomped out my worries by saying, "Even when you can see me, they cannot. Sleep, Sia. Nothing would dare harm you while I'm here."

There was nothing in me that believed he was doing it because he cared for me. But when you were being watched by something as powerful as Draki was, it was hard not to find unwavering comfort in his words, close your eyes, and drift off to sleep.

About an hour later, I heard Draki whisper to me, "Someone's coming."

I yawned and stretched. Slothfully, I rubbed the sleep from my eyes before sliding off of the hay bale and sluggishly walking into the barn. Along the way, I didn't happen to come across anyone. Not until I reached the entrance of the building. It was Elijah that was marching toward me. Internally groaning, I dipped into the barn and located the barrels of dried, milled corn, cornhusks, cornstalks, corn leaves, and … well, it was just a lot of the corn plant that would normally be thrown away. We don't exactly live in a world where we can let anything go to waste. I was told that I would need to mix it with a bit of water and feed it to the cattle.

As soon as I cracked open the barrel, Elijah came strolling through, saying, "Are you going to avoid me every chance you get, or can you slow down for a tick?"

"I'm not avoiding you. I'm just trying to get my work done."

"Sure feels like you are."

"Well, I'm not," I lied.

"Could have fooled me. I can't get a clear read on you for the life of me. You're hot one minute, cold the next."

I threw the lid back down onto the barrel. "Maybe I have my reasons."

He stuck his hands in the air and bowed his head in surrender. "Fine. You have your reasons. But could you just

take a pause for a minute? I brought you something to help you with your work."

"What?" I asked grumpily while slightly feeling bad for snapping at him.

He walked forward and placed a set of gloves on the lid.

Looking from the gloves to him, I pinched my brow in confusion and looked them over. They looked like they were just my size, and … new. "Where did you find these?" I asked, reaching for them.

"In a trunk back at the house," he said with a smile.

But I saw it. There was another link on his tattoo, and my heart sank. "What did you do?" I breathed the question. He didn't answer me. He just looked away. "What did you do?" I barked.

Squinting as my loud voice bellowed through the barn, he looked off to the side and shrugged. "I don't know what you are talking ab—"

"Don't treat me like I'm stupid. What did you do for those gloves?" I yelled as I stormed over and shoved him.

It was his turn to bend his brow in confusion, and he turned red as he snapped back to me, "I didn't *do* anything for them!"

"Oh, and you thought I wouldn't notice the extra link?" I growled, pointing to the tattoo.

His whole attitude changed so swiftly that if I hadn't seen it happen, I wouldn't have known that it had transpired. Elijah straightened himself up and washed his face clean of emotion as his gaze fixed on me with an unwavering stare. "I made them."

"Why?" I asked, at a loss for words.

It was his turn to be mad. "Oh, I'm sorry … you can be concerned for my well-being, but I can't be concerned for yours?"

"I—" I didn't know what to say. For a moment, I floundered for a response. "I would have been fine without them," I grumbled, but the anger was sapped from my words.

He rolled his eyes. "Yeah, because your hands were looking so great already. Why would you need something to protect your hands with? Hmmm? I'm so cruel to have thought about trying to keep you from being injured further."

"My hands aren't going to fall off, Elijah. But I highly doubt that tattoo of yours has a good outcome once it reaches a certain point."

"Let's not talk about that, okay?"

"Why not?"

"Because it doesn't concern you."

"Oh, but it does. The moment you made those and it gained you an extra link on that attractive arm, it concerned me!"

"It's not something that … wait …" He stopped, shook his head, and started to smile faintly. "You think it's attractive?" He raised his eyebrows in interest.

My face flared with heat, and I turned around to swipe the gloves off the lid and slipped them on. Turning around, I wiggled my gloved fingers at him and said, "They fit. You can leave, now."

He chuckled then, and it only made me blush harder. "Back to avoiding me, are you?"

"I have to work now," I practically yelled in a sing-song voice as I started scooping out the feed.

"Right," he replied with laughter woven into the single word. "Want me to bring you some water later?"

"Busy!" I shouted and walked away.

"I'll take that as a *yes*, and see you in a little while."

With that, Elijah left, and I felt my heart slam against my chest like a caged animal. I took off one of the gloves and fanned myself with it while pressing the back of my bare hand against the side of my face. I felt heat kissing my skin, and I knew I was in trouble.

People will let you down. You can't trust anyone. He is just interested in what you can do for him, nothing more, I thought.

It's easier to push people away when you demonize them. It's easier to not get attached if you make them out to be the bad guy. I couldn't afford to care for anyone. My mind couldn't handle the consequences otherwise.

"Such a nice lad," Draki stated from somewhere behind me.

I didn't care to look at him as I said, "Don't start with me. I'm not in the mood."

"You *are* in a mood, though," he stated.

To that, I hastily turned to look at him. He was grinning wildly as he leaned against the barn wall next to the ladder that went up to the loft. He looked so out of place standing there. This regal creature was draped in varying shades of white while surrounded by dirty stalls, urine-drenched hay, and weathered walls with peeling paint. I narrowed my eyes at him and asked, "Are you going to help me do this?"

"I'm content with watching you struggle."

"Ugh. Then do it quietly, at least?" I growled. At that point, I didn't care what he did. As long as he didn't try to bring Elijah up in a conversation, I would be golden.

"Are you mad at me?"

I didn't reply. I focused on my work to drown out his question. But without warning, he was behind me and snatched my wrist in his grasp, and he spun me around to face him. The flaming touch of his fingers graced the skin of my jaw as he tilted my face up. Eyes of molten gold tore through my soul. A breadth of a moment passed before his voice asked in a growling whisper, "Or are you mad with yourself?"

His words shattered me. I didn't want to self-reflect. There were too many thoughts that I was running from. Letting down my guard to contemplate over one of them would open a floodgate of ideas that I wasn't prepared to endure. "Is there really a difference?"

"So, you're mad at both of us."

I wasn't going to cry! "Maybe," I whispered, fearing that my voice would betray my false confidence.

"Perhaps you need to remember that honesty is worth its weight in gold."

"Funny for a devil to say that."

His grip tightened as his eyes narrowed at me, and his voice dropped to a frightful pitch. "There are many things that I will accept in our … *relationship*, Sia. Know that disrespect is not among them."

I raised my chin higher, proudly displaying that I chose to be held in place without fighting him. "Know that I have the same warning for you. Don't manipulate my emotions or thoughts."

His lips twitched into a one-sided smirk before it quickly disappeared. "As you wish, Sia." Letting his hold of my chin slip from his hand, he gave a quiet laugh. "It's quite delightful having someone boldly stand toe-to-toe with me."

"I'll gladly fulfill that role for you."

"I'm sure you will," he said with a grin. "I'm sure you will."

Chapter 6:

All That We Stand To Lose

After feeding the livestock, brushing the horses, cleaning the stalls, and laying down a layer of fresh hay, I went back to my previous resting spot and watched the animals graze in the early afternoon sun. I was physically there, but in my mind, I was a million miles away, lost in a sea of memories and fighting off the tide of emotions that it brought in.

I could remember it all so clearly. Momma would be rubbing Daddy's shoulders as he washed the dinner dishes, while Meemaw and I would sit by the fireside. The flames would eat away at the crackling logs as she braided my hair, and I would read a passage from one of my favorite books. How I missed the feeling of her fingers running through my hair. How I miss hearing their voices as we went through the mundane moments of our day.

Thinking back on it made me fear the deal I had made. I feared the outcome. I didn't want to be the maker of chaos and destroy someone's life, feelings, memories …

Groaning, I stood up and dusted myself off to carry on to my next task. Much to my disappointment, Draki was standing in my path. In a moment of weakness that was

coated in curiosity, I asked, "What would happen if I didn't uphold my end of the bar—"

"I would destroy anything you hold dear, starting with your parents, and I would eat my way through the land, dragging you along with me to see the destruction that a broken promise would bring." He didn't move or blink in a way that insinuated that he felt bad for what he said. In fact, his voice alone made it very clear that he meant every word of it. Part of me was sure that he'd even enjoy watching me suffer through it all.

I stared at him in horror, and my jaw went slack. "Oh," I whispered, unsure of why I ever asked him what I was thinking in the first place. Any hope of backing out of the deal was quickly snuffed out. Searching the area around me, I tried to wash my mind of his words. I drowned myself in the scenery of the quiet village while hugging myself. Suddenly I felt cold, but it wasn't the kind of chill that came from the air.

As if the event never took place, he asked me, "Where are you off to now?"

I sighed. Was I really expecting a devil to care? Cracking my back, I replied, "To the pottery wheel. The village is lacking in bowls and cups. I was going to try and make them."

"You don't know how to slow down," he muttered to himself. "Have you ever worked with one before?" His eyes trailed over me and rested upon my lower back as I rubbed at it. He seemed deep in thought as he faintly hummed to himself.

"A few times, though, I was never good at it," I admitted awkwardly.

"We'll be here the rest of the day," he griped.

"You could just wave a hand like you did earlier. Neither one of us would have to suffer, then."

He eyed me over with a deadpan expression. Looking away, he said, "Give a man a fish, and you feed him for a day; teach a man to fish, and you feed him for a lifetime."

"What?"

"It was before your time. Come along. It seems we both have some work to do."

We walked through the village to a rundown hut that had a thatched awning. Under it, there was a table littered with various types of clay-created objects. Inside, the whole building looked like a gang of toddlers tried—and failed—to make pottery. Dried bits of red clay were everywhere, from the counters to the windows, to the floors, and entirely covered the man-powered pottery wheel in the far back of the building. Upon reaching it, I gave it a spin. Though it whined in protest, it eventually twirled without further restraint. It was a little rustic, but functional.

Draki sighed at it. "What a pitiful artifact. They could at least have something a little less primitive." He shook his head. I didn't really understand what he meant, and he further confused me by saying, "I feel like I'm about to reenact a scene from a movie." He proceeded to laugh.

All the while, I stared completely clueless to his jokes. I knew what movies were … or what they were supposed to be. Plenty of books I had read described them. I hadn't seen one myself, though. Those lucky enough to live in the faith cities might have seen a handful. They had the luxury of electricity. How I longed to see a light that wasn't a flame. How I wished to see a moving picture. I smiled at the thought.

That moment of dreamy happiness was broken by Draki's voice ordering me around. "Stand over here."

"You're going to turn the wheel for me?"

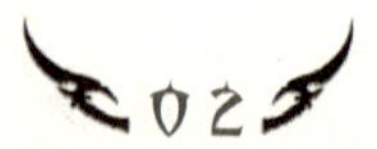

"But of course. How else would I have a front-row seat to your sad attempt at sculpting a cup?"

I frowned. "I don't know why I bother with you," I mumbled.

"Honestly, I don't know why you do, either."

Now that the banter had ended between us, he motioned to a wooden door on the floor. After lifting it up, I saw several clay pots full of murky-looking river water. In the center was a large clump of clay and a small shovel. I didn't need prompting to know that I needed to scoop out a helping and get to work. My nap earlier had set me back on where I wanted to be with my list of chores.

Slapping the lump onto the wheel, I took off my jacket, threw it on a nearby table, wet my hands, and waited for Draki to spin the wheel. As I tried to form the clay, I heard him sigh … a lot. Pushing past the annoying sound, I focused on attempting to build up the clay to look more like a cup. The clay folded in and plopped in on itself. I growled loudly at my failure.

"That's it. I cannot endure hours of this. Watching you fail isn't as fun as I thought it would have been," he announced, standing to his full height. Tossing a layer of his attire onto the same table as my jacket, he fussed with his sleeves and came to stand behind me.

Uncomfortable with the action, I started to sidestep out of his way. A strong hand caught me and moved me back to in front of the wheel. "I didn't tell you to move."

"I don't need your permission."

He sucked in air, and it sounded like a hiss. I boldly turned around, standing face-to-face with him. The moment I did, I regretted it. My bravery wavered when our eyes collided. His white hair slowly fell over his shoulder and framed his pale face. Golden hues blazing with a fire stared

back at me. Per usual, when his grin was washed from his features, his face was sculpted in perfection and free of any emotion aside from hidden, prideful anger. My vision traced every dip and curve and rested on his smooth lips. *Why did I think of kissing them?* I shook my head slightly to free my mind of the vision I had been assaulted with.

"I wasn't asking what you wanted, Sia …" His words trailed off. I watched as he took in a deep breath, closed his eyes, and saw the tension in his shoulders leave him. Opening his eyes, he finished with, "Do not thwart my efforts to help you when you are clearly struggling. Per our arrangement, your best interests are in mind whenever I act."

As much as I wanted to snap back something angrily, I knew our heated arguments weren't going to help us have a more peaceful relationship. And although pushing the limits of his patience daily was fun, it wouldn't help me get my work done any faster. So, I chose to let go of my hostility and whispered, "Okay."

"Good girl," he said while turning me around.

Some of the irritation rose back up in me. It swiftly died when his hands slid over my own and placed them on the cool surface of the clay. I looked over my shoulder, and his face was so close that my nose ever so slightly grazed over his cheek. I tried to pull back, but he held me steadfast in place. The tantalizing smell of spice and smoke calmed me as it had now become a scent that I had associated with him and protection. I loosened up slightly.

"You are putting too much pressure on the clay when trying to form it," he informed huskily.

His hold on me lightened, and one hand went to spin the wheel. Quickly, it returned to guide me, pushing slowly in as the clay slipped underneath. "Your hands are guiding the clay. You are using every bend and curve of your hands

to morph it the way you want it to go." Again, he spun the wheel, and I watched the clay rise as I pushed in gently and then pulled the clay up. His thumbs dipped down over the rim, and the jagged edge became smooth. No matter how mad I wanted to be, I saw the clay transform before my eyes, and I felt accomplished. His hands fell away, and I smoothed out the outside of the cup on my own.

The wheel stopped spinning, and the cup that was left on top of the platform was as good as anything I saw Mr. Freeman make back in my old village. I couldn't help it. I gaped and then smiled wildly. For such a long time, I thought I was only *okay* at many things. Never good … that is, unless it was chopping up animals and wood. I marveled at the work that I had done and felt tears well in my eyes.

"I … made that?" I asked.

"With my help, but, yes. You made that."

Too scared to touch it, I withdrew my hands even more. "I …" I didn't know what to say.

"You're welcome," he expressed as he went to sit in a chair over by the wall.

"I want to make another one."

"Humans are such strange creatures. You show them how to do something well, and they don't want to stop." He motioned at me with a wave of his hand. "Go on. This is your chore, not mine."

I turned to face him and smiled. "Thank you!" I exclaimed.

His eyes widened, and he went stiff before shaking his head and turning away from me. "It would have been a bother to wait all afternoon for you to figure it out."

I didn't care what he had to say. Using a flat, wooden spatula, I removed the finished cup and placed it on another table to be baked later. I still needed to make a lot more cups

before I would need to move on to the bowls. They weren't going to be cooked in the kiln until tomorrow. Just making them was going to take me the rest of the afternoon, and maybe a chunk of my evening too. But they had told me that they didn't need to be perfect.

It wasn't too much longer after I had started the third piece that I saw someone's shadow pass by the windows. The one who cast it was quickly approaching the main entrance. For a brief moment, I worried that they might see Draki. Peering over my shoulder at the devil, I noticed that he was sitting in a chair by the table with our jackets. He was free of any signs that he had previously helped me, as there wasn't a single spot of clay on his attire or skin. He shooed me before disappearing. I looked back to the unexpected guest.

Elijah stood in front of me with a tray of food. "Before you attack me, my mom told me to bring this to you."

The look on my face softened as I heard him say that. "Oh," I mumbled.

He looked around for a clear space to place down the meal, but it was all eaten up with various items and pottery. Rinsing my hands in a container of water and wiping them hastily off on a bit of cloth nearby, I rushed over, moved my jacket, and motioned to the table.

"Thanks," he stated, putting it down.

The awkward silence stretched.

"Look …" we both started at the same time.

He gave a breathy laugh and said, "Ladies first."

Spotlight on me. Great. I suddenly didn't want to say anything anymore. Feeling heat lick at my cheeks, I said, "I just wanted to apologize for yelling and pushing you earlier."

"What about what you said?"

"What about it?"

"Oh, so …"

I smirked. "Oh, I meant every word of it. I'm just sorry for the *way* that I said it."

He laughed again. "And the pushing."

"Yeah, that too."

We both gave a short chuckle.

"Good to know," he said. Slowly, he rubbed the back of his neck and sighed. "I'm sorry too. I understand why you were so upset with me."

I nodded. "It's okay," I muttered and picked up the spoon to stir the soup. Corn and potatoes swirled in the poorly shaped bowl. "It smells great," I expressed, my stomach growling as the spices hit my senses, awakening the hunger I had suppressed for the past couple of hours.

"Yeah, mom's always been outstanding in the kitchen. I've learned a lot from her and …" he motioned to the soup, "I'm able to mimic her cooking pretty well. Dad can't tell who cooked most days."

He stated the last while I had a spoonful shoved in my mouth, and I practically choked on the bite. Through partial wheezing, I screeched, "You made this?" Even as I said it, I found myself licking my lips and savoring the taste.

He nodded. "Sure did."

I did a double-take from the soup to him and tried to blink away my astonishment. "Wow. You did amazing, Elijah!"

"I've got attractive arms, *and* I'm able to cook. Am I on my way to becoming husband material yet?"

This time, I coughed as I attempted to swallow my second bite. Again, I flared with heat. Putting the spoon down, I dropped my hands to my side and flapped them slightly. Through the patting sound of me repeatedly hitting my thighs, I struggled for a way to get out of the conversation. "Seems like it's going to be a short meal break. I've only managed to get two pieces done, and I was hoping to finish them today so I can bake them tomorrow before I have to go to the river to wash clothes."

Drawing his lips into his mouth, he bobbed his head and said, "I get it." He came over and looked at the lump of clay on the wheel. "Do you want me to he—"

"No," I replied quickly.

"Am I bothering you?"

"No," I answered honestly and then winced at my own answer. It was honest, but I didn't want to … I was playing with fire.

He smiled. "Good. I'll keep finding excuses to see you then." Before I could protest, he winked and headed for the exit. "Eat before it gets cold. No one should work on an empty stomach," he yelled back to me.

With Elijah gone, I practically melted into the chair and went stiffer than the dead when my rump didn't hit the wooden surface. Instead, I landed in a lap. My heart stopped beating for a moment, and my stomach did a flip. An arm possessively wrapped around my waist to keep me in place as long digits ran through my messy braids.

"Take a minute. You've been working so hard," Draki purred darkly.

My skin reacted to his voice in ways that scared me. It came rolling over my body like faint thunder rumbling over the thirsty ground below. He was a storm: unpredictable, full of controlled fury, and brimming with

destructive lightning. His rain could quench your thirst right before he drowned you in it.

Doing my best to control my quivering, I focused on regaining my composure and saying, "I'm fine." As I went to stand and free myself of his blazing embrace, I was pulled back, and I felt a ping of energy zip through every limb.

"Stay," he growled in a low whisper.

What that one word did to me, I would take to the grave. I closed my eyes and swallowed past everything from chaotic anxiety to the dangerous emotions that were running amok inside of me. My chest was wild with a drumming heartbeat that raced with primal fear and confusion as I listened despite my better judgment. My suddenly dry mouth made it hard to voice my thoughts as I whispered back, "I need to eat and work, Draki." Saying his name made me feel like I was slapping on chains to me and him and forever tying our fates together. No matter what I would be forced to face in this life or the afterlife, it would be done with him.

He drew in a deep breath, and it was so close to my ear that I shivered. Closing my eyes, I fought everything I had just thought of and hoped that he would let me go.

"Very well," he stated calmly. "The rain is coming," he said, looking out the window.

"What?" I asked, and then I heard it. Actual thunder sounded off in the distance as the sunshine was shadowed by the churning, black clouds heading toward the village. "I see."

The hold on me was released, and he guided me to my feet. Conflicted, I meekly said, "Thank you."

"Stop that," he snapped, standing to his full height.

I looked back, and he had already turned away from me, looking to the opposing windows that held the view of

the sky free of clouds and encroaching darkness. "Stop what?"

"Thanking me."

He kept his back to me, and I looked around the pottery room. I wanted to ask why, but there was this feeling that told me to stay away from asking the simple question. It was as if anger and an answer I couldn't handle would reside in his reply. I knew what it felt like to try to escape questions that I wasn't ready to answer, so I opted to change the subject. I remembered many days and nights that Mom, Dad, Meemaw, and I would sit on the porch and watch the storm roll through the desert. It came so rarely. In the summer, it brought a reprieve from the unrelenting heat of the sun. We would all eat snacks and talk with neighbors as the lightning would web through the sky.

Looking out the window to the storm and then back to Draki, I asked, "Why are you looking out that window? Don't you enjoy watching storms roll in?"

"You never realize how much you miss the sun until you live a life full of endless storms."

"Storms have their own beauty."

"You say that. Living through it is far different than enjoying the moment of one as it passes."

"So, you like sunny days?"

He went silent. When I thought that he had no desire to give me a reply, he said, "I like what they remind me of."

"Which is?"

"What I've lost."

"Can't you just try to find it again?"

He chuckled softly and shook his head. His golden eyes peered over his shoulder to me and inspected me quietly for a moment. "Do you think everything in life is so easy?"

"Just because it was lost doesn't mean it's gone. You can get it again."

He shook his head. "Sia, some things in life are lost because you forgot where you put them. Others are lost because they are taken away."

My brow bent in confusion. "You're saying that there is no way to get it back because you had it taken away?"

"I did something unforgivable," he half-growled the reply.

"All my life I was taught that if you apologize—and if you are sincere—you can earn another chance."

"And therein lies my problem, my dear. I can't apologize sincerely because …" he faced me fully, and his pose was proud and unwavering as he finished his thought, "I'm not sorry for what I did."

I didn't know if that scared me or made me feel sorry for him. "You miss what you've lost but not enough to apologize for what you did?"

His expression shifted. I didn't know that gold could be so bright and yet be so dark at the same time. His eyes washed over me like a hungry beast calculating where it would make its first bite. His tone was low as the one word carried out like an angry song. "*Yes,*" he hissed.

We didn't talk anymore after that. I went to eat my meal while he watched the sun running away from the dark, angry clouds. As time dragged on, and with the melody of the storm to keep us company, I worked on making the necessary pottery.

Chapter 7:

Sweet Nothings

A few hours later, Draki stood on the opposite end of the building in front of the entrance. As he eyed over the doorway, he grumbled something to himself. "Time to leave, Sia," he announced to me and headed my way.

"Hmmm? Okay, just let me finish this piece," I said, refreshing the spin on the wheel.

Before I knew it, his foot had stretched out and stopped the device from turning. The clay folded in on itself as I stumbled over my handwork, and the almost finished bowl became a fresh clump of clay once more.

"Draki!" I whined. Instantly, I turned to look around me but doubted anyone would hear me with all of the thunder and the downpour that went on all around us. Switching from worried to angry again, I pointed a clay-covered finger at him. "I was almost done with that one. It was the last piece!" I yelled.

"I said it's time to go," he repeated, unbothered by my outburst.

Quickly storming around the wheel, I went to give the arrogant devil a piece of my mind. I slammed my boot down and heard a splash as it connected with the ground. The next footfall slipped on the freshly wet clay, and I started to fall. Just as I was sure I would land on the ground, I was suddenly face-to-face with Draki.

White hair fell around my form like a curtain to hide me away when he leaned forward to catch me. His bright, ethereal, golden hues made me go dreadfully still as they were inches from me. One of his hands rested on my back, keeping me from hitting the ground. The other gripped my arm. It felt painfully strange to have him hold me like that and not want to leave. After a long moment, I squirmed in his hold and looked around the room before resting my gaze on him once more.

"I can stand up, now."

"Yes, but can you listen to me?" he asked, his eyes narrowed at me in suspicion.

I looked away and pursed my lips in thought. "Yes," I mumbled.

Satisfied with my response, he brought me to my feet, and I took a few careful steps away from him. My first instinct when I was righted again was to thank him. Momma always said that you thank someone for an act of kindness, regardless of whether or not you like them. But as soon as I opened my mouth, he cut me a look, and I remembered his request from earlier. "Do you really want me to stop saying thank you?"

"You and I have an agreement, Sia. Do you want me to thank you once it's my turn to collect?"

I shivered at the thought and whispered, "No."

"Then I think you understand why I desire you to stop showing gratitude toward me. It's fake."

"It's habit," I mumbled defensively.

"It's annoying."

"Would it kill you to just let me say it?"

He looked at me and drew in a slow breath. "Very well. If it makes you happy, continue to do so."

I nodded once, satisfied with his answer, and headed for the door.

"Aren't you going to thank me?" he questioned, and I could hear mirth in his voice.

"No, you made a big stink out of it. Now I don't want to."

His chuckle made me feel better about being sassy. The last thing I needed was him angry. As I made my way for the exit, I noted the flow of water that was streaming over toward the potter's wheel. By the time I was on the porch, I realized that everything was flooded despite the building being on a slightly elevated foundation. While I was working, the rain had been heavier than I expected it to be. The river that was now rushing through the streets was easily knee-deep. From across the way, coming from Elijah's house, I saw the young man struggle as he pushed through the water, making his way over to me with a poncho held over his head. Water splashed as he dashed through the street that had transformed into a tiny, raging river.

"Sia!" he called to me as a gust of air rushed by. The plastic bellowed in the gale, and I could see the concern in his gaze. "It's a monsoon!" he yelled and held out his hand to me while he continued to come for me.

There was no second thought. There was no contemplation or doubt in my mind. As soon as I saw him coming for me and I heard those words, I jumped off the porch and leaped right into the water with him. Our hands instantly grasped onto each other. A torrential downpour assaulted my skin, and I drew in a sharp breath to quiet my urge to cry out in pain. Elijah covered me with the poncho, and I didn't mind huddling close to him under the protective covering.

"Steady yourself on me and walk slowly!" He had to yell over the rush of the water, the pelting rain colliding with the plastic of the poncho, and the rumbling of ground-trembling thunder as they were all collectively deafening.

I nodded to him. "Okay!"

Together, we turned slowly. Each step was like we had weights tied to our feet. Fighting against the current was a struggle, especially on a wounded ankle. I didn't know that such shallow water could be so powerful. Watching a box and a barrel drift by us, I swallowed hard and held onto Elijah a little tighter. I could feel the definition of muscle under the wet fabric of his shirt. I had to steady my breathing and focus on walking because my mind involuntarily drifted for a moment. When my fingers dug into his skin, he grunted.

"I'm sor—"

"Don't be. I much rather you hold onto me with everything you have than let you get carried away by the current."

I couldn't help it. I stared at him in awe while I tried to match his steps. Snapping out of my daze, I marched carefully through the water toward his house, which had become the life raft amidst the storm.

Marcel ran to the edge of the porch and jumped down into the water before he trudged to us. Two strong hands reached out and grabbed Elijah and me. I could feel his muscles strain as he dragged us toward him and helped us up to safety. Janet was at our side in seconds and throwing towels over our shoulders before gently shoving us into the house.

"Hurry up, it's not safe out here," she said with urgency and then went to help her husband up out of the water.

Marcel gave her a half-hug before visually sweeping the street for any threats or other people who might be in need. After a short pause, he nodded to his wife and ushered her inside.

Shortly after, my bandages were fresh and dry, and I was in a new set of clothes as I nursed a cup of tea Janet had made for me. Elijah had explained that his mom and dad were concerned about the weather. When I hadn't shown up, and the flash flood had started, he had grabbed the poncho and rushed out the front door. I listened to him explain everything as we warmed up by the fire.

"Thank you," I said.

"It was nothing. I'm just glad you're safe."

I remembered how his body felt under my grasp. I remembered how strong his embrace felt as he held me. Worst of all, I felt my gaze lingering on him in the long stretch of silence. Again, my cheeks became heated with embarrassment.

"I need to rest my ankle," I shot out, and I made a mad dash for my bedroom.

Within seconds, I was in my room with the door shut and locked. In the safety of my personal space within the home, I let out a loud sigh and shut my eyes. A braid of mine was played with, bringing me out of my daze. My lids

opened, and I locked gazes with Draki. The single, woven lock slipped from the devil's grasp as he loomed over me.

"So tough, isn't it? Trying to control everything inside of you, hmmm?"

I slapped his hand away. "It's not that deep."

"Oh," he whispered and practically pressed me against the door. His face inched closer and closer to my own. "But it could be."

Tripping over my breathing, I felt my stomach flip, and I pushed the devil away from me. "Not unless I say so."

Draki pushed me hard in return, and my back slammed into the door loudly. "And what *do* you say, Sia?" he growled at me, lips dangerously close to my own.

Once more, I floundered for a reply. The look in his eyes reminded me of melted gold, but in the depths of that beautiful color were spirits of anger and darker things. Things that fed your nightmares and stole all of your hope. It was a look that promised you every pleasure right before you would have every pain unleashed upon you. It was the sort of look that could make you contemplate making the wrong choice. It called to you … and I almost answered.

Freeing my mind from the thoughts swirling around, I opened my mouth and closed it a few times. Nothing came out. I didn't know if I should reach for a lie or an exaggerated truth.

The knock on the door made me jump out of my skin. Draki didn't move. Neither did I.

Elijah's voice came from the other side. "Sia?" He knocked again. "Everything okay?"

Like a snake, Draki slithered closer and moved the braids behind my ear so that his words could caress my skin without any barrier between us. "Saved by the hero, again." I

could *feel* his smirk as he withdrew from me and disappeared from sight.

Steadying myself had never been so hard. "I-I'm fine," I stuttered and pressed a hand against my chest. "*I'm messed up in the head, but I'm fine,*" I whispered to myself.

"What was that?" Elijah asked.

"I'm okay," I explained.

"I heard a loud bang from your room …"

I smiled and shook my head, even though he couldn't see it. "I tripped and caught myself on the door," I lied.

"Oh."

"I'm tired. It's been a long day."

"Right, right. Get some rest, Sia. I'll help you bring the clothes to the river tomorrow."

"You don't have to," I yelled. But only silence greeted me in return. Elijah had once again made a choice, and nothing was going to sway him from it. Deep down, I was thankful for it. The less time I spent alone, the better. Alone meant I was more likely to be around Draki. No matter what choice I made, I was going to be burned. A very ugly truth was starting to show itself to me, and I was starting to accept that the choice I was going to make was going to be the best option. But it was going to hurt like hell.

Chapter 8:

Carried Away

The next morning, I woke up and stretched. I could smell cornbread and fried eggs, and my stomach let me know that it wouldn't stand for me skipping breakfast. I had made the choice to eat before I would work today. Yesterday, not eating and having poor sleep made handling my tasks a lot more difficult and did absolutely nothing for my attitude.

Stepping out into the kitchen, I saw only Elijah. "Morning," I mumbled as I went to sit at the table.

"Morning."

"Where's Marcel and Janet?"

"Mom went to bring a few things to the river. Dad went to tend to the animals."

"Oh, others are going to wash clothes today?"

He shook his head. "No, we have to spread out with as few people possible so that the job gets done, but we don't get branded with an extra link. She's just taking some stuff there so we make fewer trips."

Now that made sense. "Right."

"You won't need to bake the pottery from yesterday. The whole place will most likely be flooded for a few days. Don't worry about chores right now, though," he ordered with a smile. He then brought a plate of scrambled eggs to

the table. Pointing to the cast-iron pan in the center of the table, he said, "Help yourself to the cornbread and butter."

"Thanks." As I fixed my meal, I spoke to Elijah. "And thank you for yesterday. I should have known better, and I should've been keeping an eye on the storm."

"We all should have. I'm just glad that you're safe."

There was a pause in the conversation as I dove into the plate. After a few bites, Elijah cleared his throat and sat at the table across from me. "Sia," he started, and I gave him a quick look to silently tell him he could talk away while I ate. "I was wondering … how difficult is it out there, in the Wastes, by yourself?"

Choking on my bite, I gasped and smacked my chest while I reached for my glass of water. He didn't say anything. He just waited for me to catch my breath and answer him. I didn't meet his gaze and pushed my eggs around on my plate. "It's not easy," I replied in a scratchy voice. A short coughing fit followed soon after, and I drank more water to fill the silence.

"I was just curious," he half-whispered and looked out the kitchen window.

I thought about all the things that he had told me over the short time that we had known each other. The signs all pointed to him wanting the opposite of what I had wanted. He wanted to leave the village. Maybe I was reading too much into it, but that's what it came across like. "Are you thinking of running away?" I whispered.

He shot me a look and then searched the empty home. "Shhh … don't say something like that."

"I've protected this conversation. Only because I have interests of my own that I'm protecting. I suggest keeping the chatter far away from the topic of him leaving this place," Draki's voice invaded my head, and I made sure not to give any

indication that I heard anyone other than Elijah speaking.

I sighed loudly, sat back from the table, and pushed my almost finished meal away from me. "What is it like?" I repeated quietly. He nodded to the question with a hopeful gaze. I took a moment to recall. Big mistake. The world around me faded, and the memories flashed through my head like a choppy reenactment of that night. Pieces in time were shifted and in different placements, but they all happened, and I was mentally reliving them. I must have drifted off. Because as I saw each snippet, remembered every scratch and bite, and saw the battle ensue in my mind, I went still. Only my breath gave away that I was still living.

Snapping his fingers in front of my face, Elijah broke my trance. "Sia! Are you okay?"

Drawing in a breath, I searched the home and reminded the chaotic melody of my heart that I was safe and no longer trapped and alone out in the Wastes. "I'm sorry. I got lost in thought."

He looked worried as he asked, "Is it that bad?"

"Worse," I admitted and took another sip of water.

"And … you're going back out to it?"

I twisted the cup on the table and watched the contents slosh about. "Yeah." Then, looking up to him, I continued with, "This isn't my home. I'm not even sure if the faith city will be. But I know that once I go there, I'm going to be pointed in the right direction."

When our eyes met, I could see an ocean of questions swirling in his vision. He opened his mouth but slowly shut it. He trapped behind his closed lips every free thought that he denied himself to announce. He looked to the back door and sighed. "Ready to go to the river?" he asked.

We rose to our feet and cleaned up from breakfast before gathering all the laundry and heading for the river.

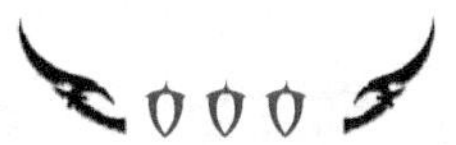

But I didn't feel good. There was a growing danger in the air. I denied sensing it when I first came to this place, but—as each moment passed—there was no denying the subtle hints that had been fed to me. Elijah had a daring spirit tucked away in his eyes. It was the kind of look that a wild animal gives you after being freshly caged. They are looking for the first chance to escape. No thought. No plan. There was only the desire for freedom … even if it meant that they'd be harmed in the process.

The river had grown twice its usual size. The slow, steady churning of water was now frothing and rapid. We stood at the edge with the buckets and basins and stared in awe of the treacherous waters in front of us. Wild waters washed over the smooth rocks lining the banks as I mentally weighed our options.

"I'm not sure that I feel comfortable doing this," Janet whispered to herself.

"We can just gather water and bring it over here to wash them in one basin and rinse them in different buckets. It might take a little longer, but we are already here," I said.

Elijah made a sound that expressed he wasn't completely sold on the idea. "Mmmm … I'm not sure."

"Come on. We just need to be careful. The river was dangerous before, too." They both still seemed to contemplate the idea. "Come on. We knock this out and it's one less thing to do," I expressed with a smile and a thumbs-up.

Janet sighed and then gave a nasally laugh. "Such a charming child. How can I deny you?" Still shaking her head, she started to set everything down.

I tossed my jacket on the ground behind me, and Elijah stared at it with a questioning look. "You sure you don't want to wash that with everything else?" he asked, walking over to it and plucking it up between pinched fingers like it was contaminated. He pretended to sniff it and waved his nose with a Cheshire grin. "Phew!"

"Ha, ha!" I said, swiping it from his grasp. But it did have a bit of a foul odor coming from it, and the dark splashes of blood all over the army design were making it look rather gross. I pursed my lips to the side just as Janet snatched the jacket from me.

"Let's give it another thorough washing, shall we?" Janet smiled at me and placed it into her pile of dirty clothes.

"I'll go grab the last of the laundry," Elijah said and ran off on the fifteen-minute hike back to the village.

Draki was sitting in a gnarled tree rooted near the water's edge. He plucked a thin branch from the limb and brought it to his face. Within seconds, the wood smoked and then burst into flames. I turned away from the view and focused on Janet. She was already gathering water from the river, so I focused on putting soap in the larger basin.

As the moments passed, Janet filled various buckets full of water for us to rinse the clothes in and filled a larger one to use for washing. I started to grind the laundry over the washboard and scrub them free of dirt and grime. It wasn't until we had started to ring out the garments that Janet looked around us with her brow creased in confusion.

"Did you see a string in one of the buckets or baskets?" she asked.

I looked around and tried to see if I could locate it while remembering everything I had taken out. Shaking my head, I said, "No. I haven't."

She sucked at her teeth and draped the recently wrung clothing over the edge of a basket. "Well, this won't do." She propped her hands up on her hips and then snapped her fingers. "Drat. I left it on the kitchen table."

"Do you think Elijah saw it when he went to grab the clothes?"

She thought for a moment and then huffed, defeated. "Best be sure. I'll go and meet him halfway. Worse case, I will send him and those youthful legs back to get it," she giggled with a wink.

I laughed, knowing my mother would have done and said something similar to me. "I can go," I offered.

She shook her head. "No, dear. You've done far more than you should have. I could use the exercise. Stay here and just rinse the clothes."

"Okay."

With that, Janet headed off, and I stayed focused on rinsing. I was over in record time and thought I would start on another round. The water in the washing basin was still relatively clean, so I threw in a few new pieces and started scrubbing away. By the time I started rinsing the clothes, I noticed that the once clean rinsing water was more soapy than clear, and I sneered at it. "Should be a little fresher," I said to myself and picked up the first bucket, chucked out the dirty water, and started for the river.

Draki's eyes were shut, and he appeared to be resting in the boughs of the thick tree. His robes swayed in the breeze like a forgotten favor from a maid in a fairy tale as they hung down from the twisted branches. The thick canopy was hiding his pale face from the blazing sun overhead. I had

to wonder how comfortable one could be resting on such an old desert ironwood tree.

When I was under him, I heard his voice call out to me, "Careful."

I looked up at him, but he wasn't looking at me. He remained lounging lazily in the arms of the ancient branches with his eyes closed. Nodding as if he could see me, I silently slipped by him and went to the water's edge.

I lifted and dipped the large bucket into the flowing water. I never regretted something as quickly as I did at that moment. The rush of the water being caught in the container had far more force than I had anticipated. The bucket was almost ripped out of my hands, but my stubborn mind fought against the river, thinking that I could bring the bucket back to the banks. Not only was it ripped out of my hands, but my stunt had thrown me off balance, and I fell toward the water below. I had managed to turn and catch a glimpse of the setup that we had for the laundry, but any hope of seeing someone there to save me was snatched away as the river swallowed me beneath the current.

Instantly, water engulfed me and filled my nostrils, and I felt my injured shoulder hit the bottom of the river. Fighting the current, I pushed off the floor and tried to swim to the surface. My lungs were blazing, and my nose burned. As soon as I faintly broke through the surface, I gasped for air, and my voice cried out, "Help!" right before my back slammed into a boulder. Hands reached out to grab it, and my nails scraped over the rock. I screamed as I couldn't keep hold. The water was too strong, and I slipped back under the surface. My hands and feet sloppily tried to find a rhythm as I attempted to swim back to the surface. As I breached the waters, I drew in a hasty breath. Sweet air mingled with river water, and I coughed and gagged while I desperately

screamed again, "Help!" I didn't want to die. This wasn't the way I wanted to die. I never knew how much I took the simple act of breathing for granted as I went back beneath the strong current.

I could see bright rays of sunshine glittering on the surface of the churning waters overhead. If I could just reach it again and take in another breath, I could last a little longer. Trying to reach the top, I pushed and kicked my legs relentlessly. Rolling water forced me back down when I was almost there. My heart sank as I hit the rocky bottom. Everything in me wanted to scream in frustration over my failure, over my stupidity. I reached up, trying to swim again. But I saw a shadow blot out the happy beams of sunshine, and then there was a splash. It all happened too fast. My mouth opened, my brain knew I would only get a mouthful of water, but even as it rushed into my mouth, my body reacted on its own and inhaled. I coughed underwater and tried to fix the mistake. But my vision blurred and darkened. I went limp just as I felt hands on me.

The heat from the sun washed over me, and every moment from the river to the shore was a blur. I was on my back, the clear sky greeted me overhead, and I saw Draki look me over and dip down. My tired vision went in and out, and each time the details of the world came back, he was a little closer. I felt like I was still floating, still swimming. It was as if my limbs wanted to move, but I didn't know how to perform the action. Lips were on mine. Heat blazed over my mouth, and I felt a jolt hit me as his hand laid over my chest. Pain blossomed through my lungs, and my eyes shot open. I felt awake again.

"Breathe, SIA!" Elijah screamed as he came crashing down on his knees next to me. "Mom! Mom! What do I do? She's over here! Mom!"

"I'm … coming," Janet panted as she ran over to us.

Turning to the side, I opened my mouth, and water gushed out. Coughing racked my body. Janet turned me fully on my side and patted my back while Elijah moved my braids from my face. His worried expression was burned into my memory as his misty eyes looked me over.

"Are you okay? Sia?" he asked.

I nodded through my hacking and spitting up water. There was another form there, crouched at my feet and watching me quietly as water dripped from his hair and robes. Those golden orbs of his held the same heat as a summer wildfire. He glared at me, and I didn't know if I wanted to be gifted with fresh air in my lungs anymore.

"I told you to be careful," he growled.

I couldn't reply. I could only stare back at him. If it wasn't evident, I wasn't going to make a dumb mistake like that again. I had learned my lesson. Part of me knew that he didn't save me because he cared. It was only because of our deal. It didn't make me any less grateful. I mouthed the words *"Thank you"* before turning to Elijah and Janet.

"Silly child! What were you thinking?" Janet cried as a shaky hand ran over my hair.

My eyes fluttered, and I tried to smile, but when I tried to sit up, I winced and grabbed my shoulder. Blood mixed with the water, and it was running down my arm. Elijah saw it and instantly gasped. "Why were you so close to the water when there was no one else here, you—"

"Fool. Yes … I know," I rasped.

"As long as you're aware," he muttered.

I couldn't help it. I laughed, and it made my chest flare with pain. I coughed again, and he was there, picking me up and bringing me to my feet. "Come on. I'll take you back to the village to patch you up."

"I'm fine. I can still—"

"Go. With. Him. Sia!" Draki barked at me. I froze in mid-sentence and held my shoulder, pretending that pain had halted my speech. "Or I will unveil myself and carry you there over my shoulder."

It took everything in me not to turn my astonished gaze toward him. I remained still and in shock as I stared at the wet imprint I had made on the ground. His powerful voice thundered over me. "Don't forget that I veiled myself because of a request. I'm not *obligated* to stay hidden to perform my end of the bargain."

"Sia?" Elijah called softly.

I shook my head. "It was just really painful for a moment," I lied. "You're right, I need to get patched up." It was directed at him *and* Draki. "Let's go."

"Mom," Elijah started.

She rubbed his back with a soft expression. "Don't worry. I'll finish what I can with the water that we have and dry them. I'm not going close to the river anymore today. It's too dangerous. We can come back in a day or two when the river will be calmer."

Chapter 9:

The Sacrifices We Make

Walking back proved to be quite the chore. What the cold water had numbed away in the field of pain was slowly resurfacing as I hobbled my way back to the village at a snail's pace with Elijah as my new, human crutch. It wasn't my proudest moment—that was for certain. However, I did rather well to hide the pain in my ankle and the soreness in my torso. I think I had damaged a lot more when I was tossed around like a river-ragdoll than I wanted to admit. Despite wanting to heal on my own, I knew I was going to have to ask Draki to heal me. And I had a feeling he was going to do it whether or not I wanted him to.

As soon as the devil slithered into my mind, I remembered him looming over me, and then his mouth on mine. My body reacted to the memory, and I bit my lower lip. *It wasn't a kiss. It was the devil's version of CPR, stupid.* No matter what sort of spin I tried to put on it, my mind didn't want to believe it. Apparently, it was a kiss. A lifesaving, toe-curling kiss. Did all kisses burn? Or just his?

I felt heat lapping at my cheeks, and I tried to talk to Elijah to escape the thoughts in my head. "You got back at the same time as your mom. I figured she would have sent you to the house for the clothesline."

He looked lost for a moment and then gave a nod. "Right. That. My dad had finished his chore early and saw the rope on the table and put it on top of the basket of clothes."

"Oh, so when your mom came to see if you had grabbed it or not …"

"Yeah, we walked back together, but I heard you cry for help. Mom took the basket from me and told me to run. I didn't think twice."

I watched our feet as we walked. "Di-Did you pull me out of the water?"

He quickly looked at me, and I knew the answer the minute we had our eyes meet. "No. I thought that you had climbed out …" His words trailed off, and he looked at me, perplexed. "Didn't you climb out on your own?"

My eyes wandered around our surroundings in a panic, and I tripped over my footwork. Holding me closer to him, Elijah stopped walking to make sure I righted myself first. Once we started moving again, I answered with, "I'm not sure of what happened." It was a partial truth. "I remember crying for help. I remember going under." I paused and screwed my eyes shut. I remembered the loss of hope and seeing the surface of the water out of reach. I remembered inhaling water and feeling it blaze through my lungs. And when I thought death would have me, I remembered Draki over me … his lips over mine. Whimpering, I drew my lips into my mouth and shook my head.

"Don't worry about it. You must have been close to the shore, and the water luckily threw you up to safety."

"Right," I whispered and nodded. "That must be what happened." But I knew the truth. The devil that saved me knew it, too.

Back at the house, Marcel came and took me and helped me inside, asking what happened. While Elijah and I explained everything, I mentally prepared for the pain. It was easy to get lost in my own thoughts. Anything to get away from the agony of a few new stitches and the sting of a thorough cleaning of all the wounds before fresh bandages were applied. As I was mended, I had my memories playing a cruel game with me. I must have looked like I was being tortured because Marcel kept apologizing to me. If he only knew that I welcomed the prick of the needle instead of the tortures that my imagination had me going through. In my mind, all I could see was Draki dripping wet, looming over me, his mouth blazing over my own.

After Marcel was done, I excused myself, saying that I wanted to rest for a little while and did my best to hide the limp in my gait as I headed for my bedroom. I was still pretty shaken up after everything that had happened, and I just wanted to be alone and change into a dry set of clothes.

Behind the safety of the closed door, I pressed my forehead to the wood and sighed. Flashes of me desperately trying to swim to the surface and helplessly being repeatedly dunked deeper into the waters barraged my mind. I held my head, groaned, and stepped away from the door. Spinning on heel, I faced the bed and felt sleep tug at me. My emotions and body had been through so much. I just needed to lie down for a moment. While I could still keep my eyes open, I quickly changed clothes.

By the time I reached the edge of the bed, I felt *him* behind me. Draki was standing there in total silence and close enough that I could lean back and I'd be resting on his chest. I almost wanted to do just that. When he spoke, it was different than when he usually said something to me. It was scarier, but he didn't raise his voice in the slightest. It washed over me like a warning. He didn't need to yell for me to know that I was in deep trouble.

"I told you to be careful."

Those words reminded me again of what he looked like back by the river, dripping wet and full of anger. I turned around and half expected to see him still soaked. His gaze caught me at the same time his hand reached out with lightning speed and squeezed my neck. Out of reflex, I tried to loosen his grasp, only it was useless. In a panic, I kicked and threw punches wildly at him. He acted unaffected by them all. He tilted his head as he watched me. A look of dissatisfaction overtook his usual calm features.

"You defy me at every turn and treat me as though I am your servant." He threw me to the bed, and I was thankful for the air my lungs were gifted with. "Do not forget that everything I've done for you has been me fulfilling requests of yours out of my own generosity … not because it's owed to you, Sia."

Gasping for sweet air, I looked at him while rubbing my neck. "It was … a mistake," I wheezed between choppy inhales.

He moved faster than anything I had ever seen. I almost didn't register the movements. His body loomed over mine, and his golden hues pinned me in place. "It was a mistake that almost took your life from me. We have a deal. You almost turned me into a being unfit of keeping a simple pact," he snarled.

My mouth unhinged, and I felt my heart throw itself against my chest like it was trying to claw its way out of me with every beat. "I'm sorry," I expressed softly.

His lips twitched into a half-smile that swiftly faded. "I'm healing you."

"No—"

"I wasn't asking your permission."

I shut my mouth with a hard frown. We stared at each other in heated silence. He was mad at me for not listening to his request. I was mad at him for not listening to mine. "Aren't we even, now?"

There was another stretch of silence before he smirked and looked away. I was thankful for it. When he wasn't looking at me, I felt like I could breathe a little more easily. When he looked back to me, there was still a sting to his gaze that penetrated my being. "I'm healing you," he said again.

Instantly, I put a hand to his shoulder as if to ward him off. "Wait. Don't. If you do, they'll know that something isn't right. They'll cast me out for sure."

"Why should that bother me? Why should I care? Am I not fit enough to tend to you? Am I not capable of upholding my end of the bargain? I promised that I would protect you, Sia. Why are you hindering me from that objective?"

"I want to feel normal, Draki. I don't want you to make me feel like an outcast wherever I go! I want to make memories along the way. I don't want to feel alone. So, if I have to suffer as I go through the motions, then let me. I can handle the pain. Pain heals."

His face dipped down dangerously close to mine. "I have a world full of nothing but pain that I can share with you since you're so willing."

Fear soaked every fiber of my being, but I glowered at him with newfound courage despite my urge to push him away and run. "No," I whispered harshly.

He drew in air slowly and gave another quick half-smile before pushing one of my undone braids off to the side. His eyes trailed over me, but I didn't feel like he was looking at me. It was like he was looking at things that hovered around me like a second skin. I shifted uncomfortably under the look. He reached up and quickly pulled my shirt down over my shoulder. Instantly, I gasped and squirmed, and his free hand pushed my other shoulder into the bed to keep me still. A claw raced over the edge of the bandage and lifted it from my flesh. A hard expression settled in as he took in the damage that was underneath.

With a sneer, he said, "I'm healing you. Not healing you is putting you at risk, and that goes against our agreement." His eyes flicked back up to mine. "I don't *care* if you want me to or not."

As his words sank in, I realized that he was right … but I didn't like it. I didn't like him being right, and I didn't like him taking away options from me. Slowly, I licked my lips as I tried to blink past my welling tears. "I hate you," I whispered the lie, feeling defeated. My options, the last thing that gave me some semblance of freedom, were going to be ripped away.

He gave a dark chuckle and said, "Love and hate are two sides of the same coin, Sia."

When he healed me, it didn't feel like it. In fact, it felt like the opposite was happening. It felt like fire was kissing my skin and claws were scratching me from the inside out as if they were trying to slowly rip me apart. Though the pain was short-lived, I found new things to torment myself with. For starters, I knew that I couldn't stay past tomorrow. The longer I lingered, the more at risk I would be. And if they turned on me and tried to hurt me because I had a pact with a devil, then Draki would wind up hurting them. No matter what, staying was no longer an option. It was for the best because I felt like I had already overstayed my welcome. If I remained, I didn't know how much longer I could deny what was slowly developing between me and Elijah.

The discomfort from reopening wounds, the excitement of almost drowning, and the sadness that came from leaving a place that could have been home, all made me so tired. Taking a short nap would give me the recharge I was in desperate need of. It would provide me with an escape from Draki, as well. So, I fell asleep sooner than I thought I would have after having my wounds tended to.

A few hours later, I woke up, and the house was eerily quiet. I noticed that the room was darker than it had been when I fell asleep. Throwing my legs over the edge of the bed, I held my head while I yawned.

"It's late," Draki said.

I turned toward where I heard his voice coming from. At first—in the murky depths of the corner—all that was there were two glowing, gold orbs. Their piercing intensity sent a shockwave of ice coursing through every nerve in my body. Instinct told me to scream. Sense told me it was a devil tucked into the shadowed corner. But the fear

was an emotion that traveled with the being. It was part of him. And now, because of our agreement, it was part of me too. He manifested from the darkened void and walked in as he burst through clouds of twisting smoke.

Digging up my courage, I faced him and sighed. "I can see that it's night."

"Then continue to rest. I think we both know that you no longer can remain here in this village."

That hurt. Hearing someone repeat aloud what I had been thinking hurt more than I thought it would. "I know," I whispered.

He motioned to the bed. "Lay down, then. I'm keeping watch over you."

I shook my head and held my stomach. "I'm hungry."

"Very well."

Thankfully, he let me go. I tried not to make too much noise as I crept through the house toward the kitchen. Darkness stretched and claimed any space not cast in the dim glow of the fire from the living room. That included Elijah's form sitting on the couch. He was half doused in firelight and half in shadow. I almost didn't notice him. I shuddered when he spoke to me.

"Hungry?" His voice matched the somber look that was claiming his face.

If I thought of denying it, my stomach wouldn't let me. As soon as he asked, my stomach grumbled. I gave a nervous laugh. "Just a little bit."

He laughed lightly and rose from the couch. "Come on. We'll get you something, and I will help you braid your hair."

I reached up to touch my hair and noticed several braids either undone partially or almost completely. I

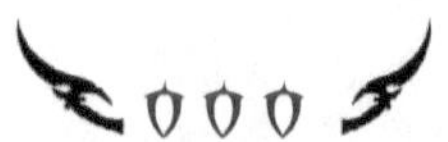

frowned. Meemaw always had to help me because I could never get a straight braid. It always came out crooked, or I would mess them up somehow. Momma always blamed Daddy, saying that it was because he raised me more like a boy than a girl.

"You can braid hair?" I asked.

He nodded. "Yup." Stopping in the kitchen, he stirred the pot, fished out a helping of soup into a bowl, and handed it to me as he asked, "Cornbread?"

Considering how hungry I was for a moment, I paused in thought. "Yeah," I admitted. A square was dug out for me, and he took the bowl from my hands. Instantly, I pouted. "Hey!"

He chuckled and pointed with his chin to my room. "Go grab a brush and meet me in the living room. The firelight will be more suitable than candlelight after I throw a few more logs on."

With fresh understanding, I looked enlightened as I smiled. "Ah. Okay."

I rushed to my room, rummaged through my bag, grabbed my comb, a few hair ties, and then ran back to Elijah. Excitement was quickly building in me as I was thrilled to experience that old feeling of someone playing with my hair by firelight while I ate. It was something that I missed more than anything. If I closed my eyes and let my mind drift, maybe in the small, silent moments, I could pretend it was Meemaw. Maybe I could convince myself that this had all been a horrible nightmare.

I quickly handed him the items needed. Plopping down on the floor in front of the couch, I grabbed the bowl from the side table nearby and cozied up to him without a second thought.

He stifled a chuckle. "Excited?"

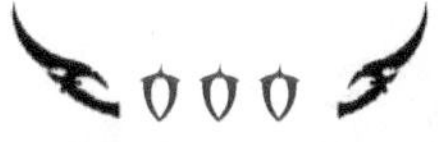

I nodded, dipping the spoon into the soup. "Some of my fondest memories of my old village are of my meemaw braiding my hair by the fire while I ate snacks Momma made for me."

"Ah, I see," he said while putting the ties on his wrist and picking up the comb.

For a long while, we sat in silence. By the time he had finished a couple of braids, I was done with my meal. I sat with my knees tightly drawn up to my chest while watching the flames dance over the logs and listening to the gentle pops of the fire as it ate away at the wood.

"How did you learn to braid hair?" I asked.

I could feel him pause as he grabbed another section of my hair. Silence claimed the room, and he remained still as a statue behind me. Finally, he moved and sighed to himself. "My sister taught me with rope making. It was the only chore I could do in bed."

"In bed?"

"I was sick a lot when I was younger. She would take on my chores because there wasn't a whole lot that I could do to help." There was another moment of silence. He drew in a shaky breath and continued. "I could make rope, though. And she would teach me how to braid with the fibers. She also had really long hair that quite often got in the way, so every night—before bed—I would braid her hair for her." He made a sound that mirrored a sorrowful laugh. "I miss it," he whispered.

I felt that. We both had something dear to us that we missed, something that was taken from us against our will and left a mark upon our memories. The world we lived in was full of pain. It was full of loss, and—oddly enough—we managed to find comfort in connecting through it.

"I'm sorry," I expressed while resting my chin on my knees.

He finished up the final braid and patted me on the head. "Don't be. You gave me the chance to relive something that I missed more than I realized."

"I wish things could be different."

"I do too."

He didn't know how deep my words went. He didn't know that it stood for every painful memory and even the decision that I had made that would lead to more horrible choices in my regrettable future. He didn't know that it meant that I was sorry for him. In a different life, I would have remained here in this damned village and shared the horrible fate that he had been dealt, but I couldn't.

"Hey, that reminds me. While you're here, you should let me take a look at that wound of yours to make sure it didn't rip open in your sleep."

The moment his hand touched the fabric of my shirt, I turned to face him with a smile. "That's okay. We can do it in the morning," I claimed, trying to sound like panic wasn't soaking every word.

He rolled his eyes. "Sia, normally I would listen to someone about this, but people have died over things like this. I'm going to look at it." Fingers traced over my skin, searching for the bandage.

My heart thumped crazily, and I looked around the room. I thought about slapping his hand away. I thought about yelling and waking up everyone in the house. But all of that would only mean I'd have to explain my stupid decision to three people instead of one. Besides, anger would only raise suspicion. I put my hand over his to stop him from lifting the tape holding down the gauze. His eyes flicked to mine, and his determined expression faded into something

else. He wasn't looking at me like I was someone that needed to be mended. That's when the idea hit me.

Rising to my knees, I lunged forward and let our lips collide. I meant for it to be just a peck, but the moment our mouths touched, I didn't want to pull away. The slow, innocent kiss grew into something more passionate, and our hands drifted and grabbed onto each other. He lifted me up and twisted, and we both fell into the cushions of the couch. My tongue plunged into his mouth, and we panted between hungry kisses. I rolled and was on top. I pulled away and fixed my vision on him as he slowly opened his eyes. I just enjoyed the view of him beneath me, but something gold glimmered in the shadows of the room. It was only there for a second, though I knew what it was.

Quickly, I fixed my shirt and scrambled off of Elijah, mumbling, "I'm sorry," before sprinting for the safety of my room.

I could hear him call to me as he jumped over the back of the couch, spurring me to speed up. I managed to close the door and lock it seconds before he could reach me. Meanwhile, my heartbeat thundered in my chest, and I could still taste him on my lips. I held my head and leaned against the door.

"Sia?"

"Please, just let me rest," I whined.

"Okay, but … can we talk tomorrow?"

I could avoid him until I left the city, right? "Sure," I lied.

There was a long pause. Thankfully, I heard the sound of his shuffling footwork as they took him further into the home. A little while later, I heard a door shut across the hall. I let out a burst of air and slid down to the floor.

A slow clap resounded through the bedroom, and Draki was standing in front of me. "Brava!" he thundered with a flash of pearly white teeth.

Anger crawled through my veins. "Don't," I warned.

He threw his hands up in the air. "I wouldn't dream of mocking you, my dear. I'm just amazed at your determination to get that young man addicted to you." Draki's smile was grand and held hints of evil behind the curl of his lips. I remembered them touching mine and how it burned. It was different than the kiss Elijah and I shared, but I liked it just the same.

As the days slipped by, I found less and less things to like about myself. I closed my eyes and drew my knees into my chest. Slowly, I hid my face away in the fold of my arms. "Please stop," I whispered with tears smearing my vision.

He said nothing. One moment, I was curled into a ball on the floor, and the next I was cradled in his arms and surrounded by the smell of smoke and strange spices. Gasping, I unfurled, and he gently laid me on the bed. I must have looked confused because he covered me up, turned away from me, and said, "Rest. I was not trying to upset you."

Chapter 10:

Freedom Has a Price

In the morning, I woke up earlier than usual and finished a few chores before Elijah ever opened his bedroom door. Stepping into the house, I was greeted by Janet and Marcel, who were setting the table. I held my stomach. I had skipped breakfast that morning and had been regretting it ever since I left the house.

"Didn't expect to see you up so early," Marcel said.

"Come, come. Let's eat together," Janet urged.

I smiled. "Thank you. I am really hungry," I admitted, walking over to the table. "I woke up earlier because of all the sleep I got yesterday and thought I would finish up a few things left on the list. I …" I trailed off and gripped the back of the chair. "I need to leave today," I stated a little quieter.

"Oh?" Marcel looked to the table and looked lost in thought. "I'll get the things you asked for by this afternoon. Is that going to be too late?"

I shook my head. "No. That should be perfect." Even as the words left my mouth, I felt my heart sink. A lump grew in my throat, and I hoped that eating would help me swallow it and any feelings that might be growing along with it.

Janet went to wake up Elijah and returned with him shortly after. I tried to hide my flustered expression and focused on eating as he sat down across from me. *Talk about awkward.*

"Morning," he said, and I could feel the smile he wore in the warmth of his voice.

"Mornin'," I mumbled back.

"I'll need you to come with me to the leader's house today, son," Marcel informed.

"Hmmm? Okay," he said chipperly.

The father swallowed a bite and reached for his cup as he explained. "We need to gather up the supplies Sia needs before she leaves today."

Elijah's fork plummeted from his hand and clanged as it hit the table. "What?" he breathed.

I couldn't help it. I winced like I had been struck. I didn't want to be here when this happened. I wanted to avoid all of this. I stood from my half-eaten meal and announced, "I'm full." Another lie tacked onto my growing list.

Elijah stood from his chair so fast that it hit the ground behind him. He slammed his palms down on the table and asked, "When were you going to tell me?" And there wasn't a single thing in this world that could mask the hurt in his voice.

"Elijah!" his mother whispered heatedly.

I looked to the door to the bedroom I had been staying in and saw Draki on the other side of it, watching me with a smile. Peeling my vision from his form, I fully turned to Elijah and saw everything I was trying to avoid written all over his face.

"I came to the decision last night," I answered confidently.

"Is there something we should know?" Marcel asked, plucking up an eyebrow over one eye.

"No," I replied swiftly.

"I guess not," Elijah muttered.

Janet looked around the table and rested her eyes on her husband. There was a silent exchange, and Marcel cleared his throat while standing up. "How about you and I go ahead to Matulia's house?"

"Fine," Elijah growled and stormed out of the house.

Janet stood wringing her hands and mumbled, "Oh dear."

Marcel kissed her cheek and said, "Don't worry about it. I'll talk to him."

She nodded in reply and called to me as I stared at Elijah standing out on the porch. "Mind helping clean up?"

"Huh? Oh, yeah. Sure."

Just then, there was the sound of drums pounding. It was a deep, relentless sound that made me feel uneasy. It rumbled through my body and awoke a sense of fear inside me. As soon as we heard it, Janet dropped the bowls in her hand and cried out loudly as they smashed to pieces on the floor.

"Marcel! No! No, Marcel, it's happening!" she screamed as tears streamed down her weathered face. She rushed to the door, and Marcel grabbed her by her arms. "No! NO! Let me go, Marcel!" she yelled, thrashing about in her husband's grasp.

Shaking the fear-stricken woman, Marcel bellowed out, "Get a hold of yourself!"

As if her legs couldn't hold her up anymore, Janet crumpled and wept. Between sobs, she cried, "She's going to take him. You know that she will."

"We have to face this, Janet. You know that there isn't anything that we can do."

"She's going to take our boy, Marcel!"

"You don't know that!"

"*Look at his chain!*" she screamed.

Reluctantly, Marcel turned and looked at their son. His eyes drifted to the links that stretched all the way down the young man's arm to the back of his hand. Slowly, he turned to face his wife. "We have to answer the call," he whispered, defeated. His shoulders slumped, and he wore a deep frown.

"We have to help him escape," she wailed.

He brought her to her feet and shook her again. "We can't!" Marcel's voice was a symphony of brokenness. A father and husband had been rendered powerless when his family needed him most, and it was made evident in every action he performed and in every word he spoke.

The silence that followed was accompanied by the deafening drumming that poured out of the sky. It felt like it was the morning we were to set out to war, but we had no armor or weapons. It was more like marching off to the gallows. I felt so strange as Marcel looked to me—holding his weeping wife in his arms—and told me, "Stay here. This is a village matter."

As they walked away, I felt a familiar dread wash over me. Part of me wanted to run to them and grab hold of Elijah. I wanted to apologize. I wanted all of this to stop. When they were out of sight, I ran into the bedroom and called out, "Draki!"

"No need to yell, I'm here," he said as he manifested in front of me.

"What's going on?"

He smirked. "Oh, you shouldn't be concerned with it. This is just life as you know it in this sleepy little village. You shouldn't care. You were leaving, remember?"

"Did you do this?"

He balked playfully. "Sia! I have no control over what a devil does over their village."

"*Liar!*"

Any trace of playfulness was erased from his expression, and what slipped into his gaze was darker than the shades of night. Evil spirits swam in his vision, heat wafted off his body, and when he spoke, it sounded like things were crying, wailing, and screaming, and they mingled with his voice until it became a song of torture. A flaming crown slowly appeared over his head, and it slowly spun as two sets of glossy, black horns grew out of his skull. The ethereal glow of his eyes grew to something that was both beautiful and dreadful, and it almost hurt to look at him. Light poured out of him, and his robes rippled in a breeze that I didn't feel. Fangs protruded from his gums and glistened as he snarled to me, "Beg me for forgiveness!"

I took a few fearful steps away from him with my mouth agape and—to my horror—he advanced as I tried to not trip over myself in my retreat. My mouth opened and closed as I forgot how to form words. My throat closed up, and a sharp gasp escaped me.

His unforgiving stride had him upon me in seconds. I tripped in my terror, and his hand snaked out, catching me by the wrist before I could go far. Pulling me with immeasurable force, I slammed into his chest and could only stare up into his molten gaze as he whispered with authority, "Say. It."

"I-I-I'm sorry," I breathed.

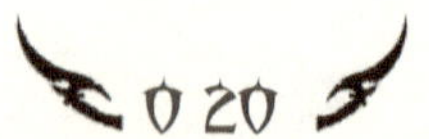

He looked at me for a long moment. As his chin rose proudly, I watched the horns melt away, the flaming crown faded into dissipating smoke, and the light dimmed down until I could look at him without squinting. Slowly, he drew in a deep breath and released it even slower. His free hand ran through his wintery mane, and he cleared his throat before saying, "I forgive you." Dark eyes locked with me. "Don't do it again," he warned.

I nodded, still dumbfounded with fear. When he released my wrist, I stumbled back and rubbed it while lost in thought. *How did that happen? What was I doing?* I remembered then, Elijah! As soon as I looked up to Draki, I floundered on how to ask him for help, so I asked the question I wasn't ready to hear the answer to.

"Is … is Elijah going to die?"

As the devil pondered the idea, his playful expression resumed, and he hummed in thought. "Is Elijah going to die? Hmmm. What a marvelous question, Sia. I do wonder what will happen to him. But I suppose there is a better question that you can ask."

I dared to step closer to him. "What would that be?"

He grinned at me. "Is anyone going to save him?"

I already knew the answer …

"Come," Draki said and swept his hand to the door. "Let us go and watch the show!"

I felt his hand on my lower back as he ushered me toward the exit. Taking an unsure step forward, I drew in a deep, calming breath. One moment, I was in the bedroom, and the next, I was outside next to a building that was near the center of the village. The massive, wooden pillar that haunted me when I first walked through the gates was now surrounded by everyone that lived there. Standing among them was the grinning she-devil, Bushyasta. She flipped her dark strands over her shoulder and rolled her wrist as she pointed lazily to each person present, and shooed those with the shortest visible chains off to another crowd.

Janet and Marcel stood with a group on the opposing side from Elijah. Janet was clinging to Marcel, whimpering as he held her in his embrace. They both looked distraught. A tidal wave of emotions was sure to pour out if the worst came to pass. With the way Draki acted, I didn't doubt a horrible outcome. With how far down Elijah's chain tattoo went, I didn't have a lot of hope to grasp onto.

Bushyasta looked over the few people standing in front of her, gave a side glance to me and Draki by the buildings, and then turned back to everyone. Slowly, she hooked her finger and curled it toward herself a few times. Those standing by her held out their tattooed arms, and she cackled. She slapped one, two, three hands away and grasped the fourth by the wrist, and tugged him out of the lineup.

Turning with his wrist still in her grip, she raised his hand in the air, yelling triumphantly, "We have a winner!"

Janet wailed. Both her and Marcel fell into a heap as tears streaked their tired faces. A unified, "No!" erupted from their mouths.

"Take your place, young man," the she-devil ordered.

Emotionless, he stepped up to the pole, and I watched as the chain on him started to come to life. It undulated and looked like something was swimming under the surface. Suddenly, it pushed out of his skin at the same time that the chain on the pillar burst out of the carvings. Splinters of wood rained down as the chains swayed in the air and headed for Elijah. He bowed his chest, raised his chin, and shut his eyes, ready to meet his fate.

"NO!" It was bellowed louder than any wail from his parents, and it sliced through the still, morning air. "STOP!"

As if by command, the chains paused in their movement, and the she-devil spun on heel. "Oh? Are you offering yourself instead?"

I ran out from where I had been watching. Following slowly behind me was Draki. Only Bushyasta and I saw him. Thankfully, she made no remark on this. I looked at Elijah and then his parents and finally, to the gates to the village.

"Go away, Sia!" Elijah commanded angrily. "This doesn't concern you." He swiped his arm through the air. "Leave!"

"I'm not going anywhere! I can't walk away from you when your life is on the line!" I yelled back.

The she-devil pursed her lips to the side. "Oh, my. Lover's quarrel?"

I glared at her. "Let him go."

She threw her head back and laughed. "This is my domain, little one. You can't come in ordering me around."

I looked to Elijah and then to her. "This isn't fair. They don't deserve this."

"This is what they agreed to!" she barked back.

"Let him go. Please," I begged.

"Are you taking his place?" she asked.

"No!" Elijah roared.

I thought about it, and Bushyasta sighed. "I'll tell you what. Knowing of your own issue that you have, I'll cut you a deal. I'll let him go …" she went still and smiled like she had gone insane, "*if* you can get *two* to take his place." She giggled then and spun around with her arms up in the air. "What say you, sleepy villagers? Who will stand up here and take his place?" Silence was the only reply. "I'll sweeten the deal, I won't take a sacrifice for … mmmm, three years." She held up three fingers and showed them to any who might not believe her. Again, there was no reply. She turned to me and playfully pouted. "Oh, dear … I don't think I have any takers." She stomped her foot and made whining sounds, but they slowly turned into cackles of glee. "Silly girl. Did you honestly think that these people were worth saving?" She laughed even harder. "It's kill or be killed. Eat or be eaten."

I felt like my heart was being squeezed with every word she spoke. I needed to come up with something, a way to save him, but I was drawing blanks. The she-devil turned away from me and waved me away. "If you're done with your interruptions, I need to get back to what I was doing."

"We'll do it," Janet's voice was hardly audible.

"What was that?" Bushyasta asked with a narrowed look in the mother's direction.

Marcel stood up and put a hand on his wife's shoulder as she remained kneeling on the ground. "We'll take his place," Marcel said proudly.

The she-devil gave a short, breathy laugh and shrugged her shoulders. "If that is what you want, go for it. I'll uphold my end of the bargain."

"Let him leave with Sia," Janet said softly.

"Let him what?" Bushyasta questioned.

"Along with your bargain, I want you to allow the boy to leave with Sia," Janet stated with a touch more courage.

"You'll both willingly take the boy's place?" the she-demon asked with a curious look. They both nodded in reply.

"Please, no! Mom, Dad!" Elijah bellowed with hurt splitting his voice in two.

"I'm not watching my son give up. I've already lost a daughter, I'm not burying you, too!" Janet screamed.

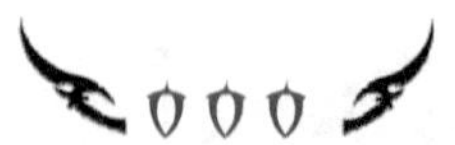

"Very well, it's a deal," Bushyasta announced and then snapped her fingers.

The chain on Elijah was torn out of his flesh, and he hit his knees, screaming in pain. Through his staggering cries, everyone hugged themselves like they could drown out the sounds with the action. Two large, black chains whirled around the pole and then darted for Marcel and Janet. The chains twirled around their bodies and they cried out, and I could see them bite their lips to hold back from screaming any louder. They held onto each other's hands until the chains ripped them apart and slammed them into the pole. There was a burst of flames, a spray of embers, and plumes of smoke. I turned away, but the sound of Elijah wailing would haunt my dreams. When I turned back around, I covered my mouth and felt the first sting of burning tears hit my eyes. Janet and Marcel's faces were now carved into the pole, and they were resting, temple-to-temple, together. Their faces were forever frozen with a bittersweet smile. In that look, I saw a parent's love. They willingly made a sacrifice that few would make, but they left behind Elijah, who never got to say goodbye.

Tears dripped down my face, and I felt Draki's hand on my shoulder. "Looks like we'll have a guest on our trip."

I really didn't like myself at that moment. I forced myself to watch Elijah fall apart and touch the etched faces of his parents while the rest in the village shook their heads as they shuffled their feet back to their homes, leaving the young man to weep alone.

Carefully, I approached Elijah and knelt down next to him. My hand reached out and gently laid upon his back, and he flinched like I burned him.

"I-I'm so sorry." I hated those words as I spoke them. I couldn't find anything more comforting or heartfelt, just *I'm so sorry*.

He sniffled while keeping his eyes on the freshly carved expression of his parents. "I knew they were going to."

"I didn't mean to cause—"

"They were talking about it just before you came. It's not your fault." He drew in a shattered breath and exhaled it like he would break down again. "They were talking about ways to save me. Mom wanted to send me away. Dad said Bushyasta would never let us go." He looked like he was memorizing every dip and curve of the wood under his hand. "They just wanted me to be free," he whimpered.

I put my arms around him, and he let me. I was glad that he didn't push me away or blame me, even if I felt like I was still somehow at fault. That was an emotion I would never be able to rid myself of.

"You're free now," I whispered.

"But at what cost?" he expressed with fresh tears in his eyes, and he wept all over again.

Chapter 11:

The Skin of Our Teeth

I didn't want to be the one to tell Elijah that we had to leave, but we did. When a devil gives you your freedom, you take it before they change their mind or alter the rules. After adamantly whispering to him how we needed to gather our things and head out, he looked around the village like it had become something new and dangerous to him. But I saw—deep down—that there was an excitement there beyond the sorrow.

Back at the house, we separated to pack up and then met back in the kitchen to eat before we'd head out. We had packed everything that we could carry between the two of us and ate while we stuffed the little room left in our bags to the brim with food. We had everything that we'd need for several days: food, water, blankets, and medical supplies. While we finished up, I had a thought hit me.

"Elijah?"

"Yeah?" he said, sounding a touch lifeless.

"Is the reason why you asked me about what it was like out there because you heard your parents talking about … you know?"

He stopped and was suddenly very still for a long time. "Yes," he said, finally. "I knew that they were going to,

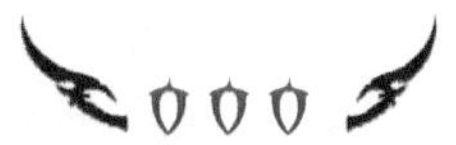

but I … I hoped that they wouldn't. They were my parents, after all. Part of me wanted to protect them, but the part of me that wanted to be saved dared to dream about a life far away from this place."

I nodded. "Oh."

He half-laughed. "I cried for a whole week after I heard them talking about it. Every night their words haunted my thoughts." He looked up at me. "Then you came, and I didn't feel so lost anymore. You were a blissful distraction from everything." He smiled, and it faded as he licked his lips and looked off to the side. "About last night …"

I reached out and touched his hand. My eyes trailed over the dried blood stuck to his skin and followed the jagged scar that replaced what was once a tattoo. I bit my lip and shook my head at him as I met his gaze. "Not here. Not now." I wanted to make sure we got out of here alive *and* to stop him from talking about the kiss. "We need to leave. You were given a rare chance."

"A rare chance indeed," Matulia stated from the door.

My heart stopped beating before picking up in tempo. Were they going to kill him out of jealousy? Joyfully celebrate his freedom? I didn't know. People could be scary things. Sometimes, the worst monsters didn't have horns and broken halos. They had a moral compass that pointed to a different north. Those were the scariest monsters of all because—in their mind—they weren't lost.

"Matulia," Elijah breathed.

"There is no time. Follow me," she said and then turned to wait for us on the porch.

A little weary of trusting someone, we looked to each other with a moment of reluctance. It wasn't like we had a lot of options, though. We threw on our backpacks and headed

out the door to meet up with her. Today, she didn't wear her elaborate headdress and red paint. She was wearing a pair of stonewashed jeans and a tattered T-shirt.

She watched all sides of the house as we approached. After seeing us come out, she looked to the surrounding buildings, and we instinctively followed her gaze. No one was there. She was in front of us when we turned around, and she held a finger up to her lips.

"You have your freedom now. Meaning you two could be offered to that devil for someone else's freedom or used as slaves. There have already been whispers of it." I opened my mouth to speak, but Matulia shook her head. "If you want to get out of here, you need to follow me." She cautiously and quickly scanned the area around us and then darted to the next building over.

We followed the weaving path that Matulia led us through, dodging every person and crowded area possible. Sneaking in through the back of her home, we waited as the village leader gently closed the door. She hurriedly grabbed me by the hand and swiftly led me to the living room. After letting go of me, she shoved a massive chest out of the way and quickly folded the carpet over itself. What was unveiled was a trap door.

Pulling it open, Matulia said, "This was put in here by the founders of the village. They had hoped to use it to escape. Only, there is no outrunning a devil." She shook her head. "Half the village died that night. For the few granted freedom, it has been a way to flee when needed." She looked at us with sadness in her eyes. "I'm sorry that this is all that I can do for you."

Thwack! The front door opened suddenly.

"What are you doing, Matulia?" A male asked after stepping inside the home.

She rose up with a gasp and moved me behind her. "I think we both know what I'm doing."

Elijah poked me with his finger, and when our eyes met, he gave a pointed look to the machete strapped to my hip. I gave the faintest of nods and then went back to watching those at the front door. Three men shadowed the entrance. Two were the guards I had seen when I first came. The other I hadn't seen before today.

"Are you mad? Don't you see what we've been given here? It's a way out of the life we've been living," Gerald said.

Matulia stepped forward, her stance protective. "They're free."

"Which is exactly why we should keep them here. They aren't bound by the rules that we are. They could do the work—"

"They'd be no better than slaves!" she yelled.

"We'd treat them better than slaves, and you know it," Gerald defended.

Alan pointed to me as he spoke to Matulia like I wasn't standing right there. "One of them is a female. We wouldn't have to worry about the she-devil killing off stragglers ever again. We could have a slew of new workers."

"They're kids!" Matulia snapped. "They are free. We should let them go. They never asked for any of this."

"They should stay and help us all from dying! We were born into a life we never asked for! We finally have a way to survive, and you're going to take that from us?" Gerald tilted his head with hurt swimming in the sea of his desperate gaze.

Alan stepped forward, his voice careful and his arm outstretched like he was trying to talk a weapon out of a frantic person's hand. "What would your husband and son

think? If you could save them with labored workers that were treated kindly and respected, would you still send them away knowing that you are sending the rest of us to death, including them?"

The protective arm that Matulia had raised slowly fell, and she quickly looked over her shoulder to Elijah and me. I froze. The panic in my eyes was for all to see. I didn't want to be a laborer. I didn't want to be a glorified slave. I didn't want to be a baby-making machine. I didn't want these people to suffer, but this isn't the life that I wanted. I could see Matulia's heart being swayed. But she shook her head and furrowed her brow.

"They wouldn't have wanted me to keep them here. This is our curse, not theirs. We are letting them go," she commanded with finality.

Gerald's face twisted in anger. "I'm not going to stand back and watch you take this away from all of us."

He lunged forward, and Matulia did the same. They slammed into one another and started to wrestle feet away from us. I heard the trap door open behind us. I wanted to help the village leader, but when the other two came to us, Elijah chucked a chair at the duo and grabbed my wrist to pull me away.

"We need to go," he yelled, tugging at me.

We had only gone down a few steps when I felt the urge to look back. I didn't want to leave Matulia like that. When I turned around, I saw her get hit upside the head with a wooden statue swiped from the surface of the chest. Instantly, she went down, and blood trickled down the side of her face.

"Run," Matulia croaked.

The statue was raised and brought down. Elijah tugged at me and I stumbled down a few of the steps. I heard

the sound of something breaking mingle with wet splatters. I knew. My mind knew, even if I didn't see it happen. I screamed and wailed out wordlessly while Elijah kept dragging me through my breakdown. This wasn't a devil and pacts, this wasn't fighting for survival, this was cold-blooded murder from a fellow human being. This kind of death hit me differently.

"Mat-u-lia-a-a-a!" I cried helplessly.

Any other words were snatched when I saw the first body standing over the trap door. Elijah jerked me, and I didn't need any further convincing.

We ran.

The air in the tunnels was rich with the scent of mildew and must, and the summer heat was intensified by the humid air suffocating the small space. Instantly, I was sweating as we tried to outrun the villagers through the pitch-black while carrying overflowing supply bags. I let go of the duffel bag in my grasp. Who cared about extra belongings? You can't do anything with stuff when you're dead. As soon as it hit the floor, one of the men chasing us tripped over it and fell. I heard Gerald yell and swear as he tumbled.

"Don't look back," Elijah said between panting breaths.

I should have listened. Why do they tell you not to? It only makes you want to … regardless of the circumstance. So, of course, I looked behind us and instantly regretted the action. Alan and the nameless villager were mere feet behind us, and straggling far behind them was Gerald. Not able to control it, I whimpered and turned to face the front.

"Get your blade ready," Elijah warned me. "We can't outrun them."

It was a cruel truth, and the evidence of it was the footfalls that were now closer behind me than they had been a moment before. My tears had mingled with the growing sweat on my face. My lungs burned with every breath. I couldn't even spare a word as we ran. My free hand fumbled over the clasp that kept the blade in place.

Out of nowhere, I had someone dive at me and tackle me to the ground. I screamed and clawed at Elijah's hand as our grip on each other was lost.

"Elijah!" I screamed right before I slammed into the rough ground below. I heard my blade slide across the tunnel and hit a wall nearby. It was too dark to see much of anything. I tried to turn over, but Alan's weight was keeping me pinned to the floor, and I growled as I flailed helplessly, trying to free myself from under him.

"Just give it up. You'll only hurt yourself. We can lose the boy, but we have to keep you," he explained, his mouth right next to my ear. As he forced me to my feet, I thrashed about and looked for my machete. Calling out to the villager that caught up with Elijah, he said, "Don't waste your time if he fights too much. We've got the girl."

"Let me go!" I yelled.

A stinging pain flared over my cheek as Alan struck me with all his might. I saw a burst of starlight invading my vision, and all sound was muffled for a moment.

"I told you to stop struggling!" Alan barked in my face.

"Don't move." This time, the voice was Draki's.

I wobbled for a moment and looked out the corner of my eye. The devil's face was resting on my shoulder as one of his arms rose up to hug my waist. "Don't move," he repeated in a husky voice. I kept my eyes on him as I heard my machete sink into flesh.

Alan grunted in pain, and Draki let go of the blade as he grabbed my hand and made me take a hold of the weapon. I turned to face my assailant, and our eyes locked. His were filled with anguish and mine with fear.

Alan's raspy voice struggled to gurgle out the simple phrase, "You've … got a … devil." Blood dripped from his mouth, and his eyes looked at me with disgust.

With Draki's guidance, I brought the blade down. I heard the sloppy *plop* of something hitting the ground, and I felt my stomach lurch. The devil's bloodied face was all grins, and the ethereal glow of his eyes was like a torch in the thick darkness. His touch on my stomach became warm as he let go of my hand and tilted my face up to meet him. "Hold it together," he ordered. I knew that it was his power—not my own will—that kept me from expelling everything in my stomach at that moment.

He spun me back around as Gerald came toward me, snarling, "You bitch!" as he went to attack.

The blazing touch of Draki washed over my skin as he took each wrist in his grasp and whispered in my ear, "Can I have this dance?" In his words, I could hear the smile he was wearing. He was enjoying all of this carnage. He liked that he was making me do it. He reveled in every motion that I complied with, and his joyful laughter echoed through the tunnels as I followed his movements. I lifted the blade and slashed downward, slicing Gerald's face wide open. His erupting cry of pain was cut short as Draki made me stab the villager through the throat.

Jerking it out, I felt hot droplets hit my face and heard Elijah call my name. "SIA!"

Draki's hold on me fell away, and I felt shock take over, calming my nerves and stopping me from shaking. "Yes," I whispered, feeling like I was a million miles away.

He held my shoulders and strained as he looked through the tunnel for any signs of movement. "Are they—"

"They're dead," I admitted as my voice cracked a little.

He drew me into a hug and then pulled away as if he had forgotten we weren't out of danger yet. "Where's your bag?"

Lifelessly, I pointed behind me in the tunnels. He looked beyond into the blackened void and then pushed me ahead. "You keep heading for the exit. I'll grab the bags and meet up with you. I don't know if there will be others coming."

I nodded, but I felt hollow inside. After I took a few unsure steps forward, Elijah ran off into the pitch to get the bag. I expected to feel alone. I expected to be lost in my own thoughts as I relived the moments that had just passed. Instead, I felt a blazing touch grasp my wrist. Out of reflex, I blindly swung the blade. It went still like I had tried to slice a wall in two. The blade had been stopped by Draki's finger, and his expression was cold and curious as he flicked his eyes from the machete and then to me.

"Not the thanks I was expecting," he said with a grin. He was free of blood, and not a single droplet stained his hair, skin, or clothing. Had it all been a dream? "Come on," he sighed.

With that, the devil slipped his hand down to hold my own and led me toward the exit. When I could see light pouring out from the other end of the tunnel, I heard Elijah running up behind me.

"Let's get the hell out of here," he said, taking my other hand and leading me the rest of the way out of the secret passage.

Meanwhile, Draki let go of me and watched me leave. I looked behind me to observe his form fade from my sight. As I did, his haunting voice echoed through the chamber. "I'll handle the mess back here. Go somewhere safe with him."

Chapter 12:

Nowhere is Safe

Outside of the tunnels, the light was almost blinding, and I had to shield my eyes with my arm as soon as we emerged from the darkened space. After several minutes, I looked to the sky and then searched the surrounding area. The mountain ranges were a dead giveaway to our positioning.

Pointing to them, I lifelessly said, "We need to head that way. North."

Elijah looked at the stretch of protruding rocks rising out of the land and nodded. "Okay."

Some of the fog lifted from me, and I felt more in control when I focused on where we were heading. "We can make camp further up, over there. We headed out later than expected, and we've had a few … setbacks," I said with an expression that swirled with a mix of emotions.

He nodded in reply, and we both silently headed toward the mountains, which would take us a few hours. The good news was that we weren't heavily injured. My face throbbed like I had been hit with a wooden club, but it wouldn't attract any demons later on that night. We were close to the river, too, so we could get water to cook with since Elijah brought a few fresh ingredients from the house.

After tonight, we'd be stuck with rationing cornbread and jerky. We might as well have a feast before we had a stretch of meager meals. We'd also be able to clean up some of the blood and bury the tainted rags.

I was trying to process what had all taken place, and I was sure that Elijah was too. As we walked, I could only hear the dirt crunching under our feet. Draki wasn't around, and if he was, he was even hidden from me and not saying anything. I wondered what it was that he needed to do back in the tunnels.

I must have been sighing a lot because Elijah nudged me with his elbow with a soft chuckle. "You going to talk about what's eating you or just sigh until you don't think about it anymore?" he asked.

I was bewildered. Looking up from watching my footwork, I blinked rapidly at him. "Huh?" It took a second for his words to sink in. "Oh," I stated and then looked back to the ground.

"Should I prepare myself for you to sigh again?"

"No," I said, and before I could stop myself, I sighed again.

We both laughed.

"I'm just lost in my own head, I guess," I explained.

He nodded. "I understand."

I was glad that he did because I didn't have the heart to tell him that I had a deal with a devil. I didn't have it in me to tell him that I felt like everything that happened back at the village was somehow my fault. I didn't want to think about it. I didn't want to admit it. I just wanted to forget for a little while. I just wanted to pretend that it was all a bad dream and that I managed to get by on luck these past few days.

Even if I knew the moment wouldn't last.

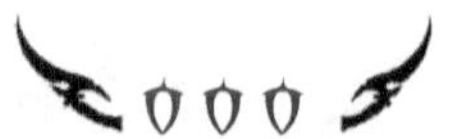

Within a few hours, we made it to a spot with trees and a rocky overhang. It would provide us with shelter. I knew that it wouldn't be enough if I wasn't traveling with a devil. Elijah didn't know that. He also didn't know any better, so his lack of knowledge became my saving grace.

"We need to collect firewood. It's going to get cold," I said.

He tossed the bags down, saying, "Good thing I packed extra blankets from the house." When he turned to look at me, he grimaced and made a face.

"What?"

Elijah pointed to my cheek. "That looks painful," he said, stepping closer. He gingerly took hold of my chin in his grasp and turned my head to the side. He inhaled sharply. "No bleeding, but it's going to be one hell of a bruise."

I gently pulled away and laid my palm over it. There was already a welt, and the skin felt tight over the inflicted area. Sighing, I tossed my things onto the pile. "We're alive. I am going to wash off and bury the rags. With neither of us having fresh wounds, we don't have to worry about the blood attracting demons. I think we should gather firewood, get some water from the river, eat, and sleep before the sun sets."

"Right. I'll go to the river," he stated quickly.

"Are you sure?"

He gave me a look that said it all.

Shifting uncomfortably, I forced a smile and said, "Yeah. I think I've had enough of the river."

Elijah laughed and patted me on the back before going to grab the pot hanging off one of the bags. "You going to be okay by yourself?"

Not like I'm really ever by myself, I thought. "Yeah, I'll be all right."

With one last worried look to me, he nodded to himself and headed off for the river. Meanwhile, I started to collect wood from around the trees. Around the third armload, I turned and stifled a scream. Startled, I dropped the wood and then stared, annoyed, at Draki standing in front of me.

"Could you not do that?" I hissed.

He looked at me as if he were bored. "I honestly don't know how you're not used to it by now."

"Where have you been? It's been hours."

He looked around him and then to the sky. "I suppose I was rather lengthy with my torture session."

"Torture?"

"Mmmm, yes. That little she-devil took her cunning stunt a step too far."

"What do you mean, took it too far? With Elijah's parents?"

He chuckled. "Please, no. I told her if she listened to me, they would willingly give themselves up to her. I just said I wanted you and the boy to go free."

I glared at him. "So, it was you?"

"I merely suggested, dear Sia. As for them wanting to turn you two into slaves … that wasn't part of the plan."

"That was her?"

He nodded. "A very dumb but brave decision that cost her much pain … and an arm."

"You took her arm?"

He waved the thought away. "It'll grow back in a few years."

I balked at him, and he pointed to the twigs on the ground. Muttering a few choice words under my breath, I knelt down to pick up the lumber. "It'll be nightfall in a few hours," I warned with a touch of pepper to my tone. I wasn't

happy with the devil at the moment. He had caused two people to die today, two people that didn't deserve that kind of fate. He also forced Elijah and me into a difficult position that ended with us killing three people.

Draki nodded. "Yes. And I still have something that I need to do."

"Will you be back by nightfall?" I asked.

He smiled at me. "Scared without me?"

"We have a deal," I reminded.

Rolling his eyes, he said, "Yes, yes. I'll be back by nightfall. Even if I wasn't, I've already cloaked you. Nothing would try to harm you if they did come across you. Not without fear of dealing with my wrath."

A sigh of relief quickly escaped me. "Oh, good. I was worried Elijah and I would be sitting ducks."

Draki ticked a finger from side to side and shook his head. "You mistake this little comfort that I've given you. I said *you* were cloaked. Not the boy."

"We have a deal," I whined pathetically.

"He's not part of the deal, yet!" he barked.

To the sound of his booming voice, I fell back with the twigs hugged to my chest. "I can't let him get hurt."

With a wide, toothy grin, Draki bent over and got uncomfortably close to me. "Does that mean you want to—"

"No!" I shot out. "No," I repeated a touch more calmly.

He rose to his full height and fixed his robes. "Then let us hope he gets back from the river before it gets too much later, hmmm?"

"You're a monster," I whispered.

"Correction, I'm a devil and a damn good one."

I gathered myself and came to my feet before storming away to the campsite. "Hurry up and handle your

business. If any of these creatures are as reliable as that she-devil, I don't trust a moment you're not by my side."

He gave a quick smirk. "Such a demanding little thing, but … when you are right, you're right."

With that, red plumes of smoke were left behind, and Draki was gone once more. Within moments, Elijah came back with a pot of water, and he smiled as he set it near where the fire would be.

"You start boiling the water, and I'll fill up our canteens," he said, and then rushed off again.

"Be careful!" I yelled to him as he raced for the river.

The sky was getting dark, and I had been feeling uneasy with each minute ticking by. Elijah still hadn't returned from the river. It shouldn't take this long to get water, should it? I paced around, gazed into the distance, and then paced some more. If I wasn't careful, I was going to make a canyon in the middle of our campsite.

"Where are you?" I whispered and stood on my tiptoes as I watched for his form, hoping he would show up soon. But he didn't. "Ugh," I growled and wrung my wrists white as I walked back and forth again to pass the time. "He should be back by now," I muttered to myself. But all I could think of was what Draki said. I would be safe. Elijah wouldn't.

Worried for his safety, I snatched up my machete and tied it to my waist as I marched off toward the river. It was a slow, sure march that quickly turned into an all-out run when I heard a nearby owl hoot. Nightfall would be soon. Too

soon. And being out in the open like this wouldn't be good. Maybe—if I was lucky—Elijah being near me would cloak him too. That's what Draki said. That I was cloaked, so I was safe to venture out and find Elijah … right?

But why did I feel so uneasy? Why did I feel like something was wrong? Why did I feel like I should have stayed next to the campfire?

The sun was a whisper on the horizon, and my mind was a blizzard of tormenting thoughts. I looked all too happy when I could see the river up ahead. He hadn't fallen into the river, had he? I worried that I was too late. That I was going to find him dead and washed up on the banks downriver. I picked up the pace. Sliding to a stop by the water's edge, I looked around, wondering where to start searching first. That's when I heard it, the distinct sound of water splashing. My heart rose up in my throat, and I raced around a boulder in my path. Instantly, my heart hit the floor of my feet, and I went unbelievably still for longer than I wanted. There was no way that I was seeing what I was.

Its body was gaunt and shaded like the bark of a desert ironwood. Its limbs were long, and the unnerving extra set of arms rested on its hips. Despite the apparent dips and hollow pits that covered its tall body, there was defined muscle under its unnatural skin. A thin stretch of fabric was tied around the creature's waist, and fastened on each side of its hips was a bone medallion with a strange marking carved deep into the surface. All over its form, there were things that looked like a cross between bone and metal, and they protruded from the skin like it had been melted and forcefully made to be armor that was a part of the creature. It was very clear that this was a dreaded soldier.

Soldiers were nothing like a grunt. They typically traveled alone or in small groupings, and enjoyed toying

with humans before killing them. Their whole objective was to break you down and have you lose all hope before they ended your suffering. They were smart, quick, and deadly.

Elijah flopped over as he tried time and time again to stand and fight back. The blood marred his pale skin and hid his freckles. While on his knees, he swung at the demon. But even I could see that it lacked power and was too sluggish to actually hit the beast. How long had he been fighting it? The soldier triumphantly loomed over Elijah. With hissing laughter, it raised its taloned hand. Before the killing blow could be made, a rock bounced off the side of its head.

"Leave him alone!" I yelled after mustering up my courage.

The demon snapped its vision to me and snarled.

"No … Sia!" Elijah croaked.

He was backhanded and hit the ground with a grunt of pain. "Two stragglers," the demon hissed, turning its head from side to side. "I'll have my fill tonight." A roar of laughter left its disgusting mouth. "I was just finishing up playing with this one."

I focused on all the things I shouldn't have. I focused on the orange, glowing eyes, the hooked nose, and the rows of jagged teeth. Shaking off the fear, I made a face at it and took a step back.

"Kind of hard to eat when you're dead," I snapped.

Its eyes narrowed, and the snarky smile was washed clean off of its smug face. "We'll see who will be dying tonight," it growled and then raced toward me, kicking up dust in its wake.

Now that the soldier's attention was on me, I could distract it until … well, I hadn't come up with part two of the plan. A short scream escaped me as I turned and ran,

ducking behind a boulder as I heard talons scraping over the rough surface of the rock in its hot pursuit.

"I'll tear off your pretty face right before I end your pathetic little life!" It yelled and then howled into the bleeding midnight hue that was fast approaching.

Holding my weapon out in front of me, I spun around and took a slash at it. The moment it leaped back to avoid the blade, I turned and ran again. Grunts were small and easily picked off. Heck, I could pick them up and punt them into the side of a mountain. But a soldier? I was no match for a soldier!

Why did I throw that rock?

Frantically, I searched the area, but aside from a few scarce shrubberies, some lone trees, and a couple of cacti, I didn't have a lot to work with. Heat flared through my back as I felt something slice straight through my jacket and T-shirt. I screamed out in agony, and my body lurched forward as I tried to escape the claws that were sinking into my flesh. I hit a knee, and the soldier tumbled as it slammed into my back and careened into the dirt. Scrambling to my feet, I went to get away, but the demon was fast. It grabbed my ankle and yanked. It was the injured one, too. Instantly, I hit the ground. It pulled again, and I was dragged across the desert floor and closer to those haunting eyes. My blade flung out in front of me as I tried to land a blow. With a cackle, the machete was slapped out of my hand like it was a stick. The soldier's maw opened unnaturally wide, and the demon dove at me. I turned my face to the side and flattened myself to the ground with a shriek.

But the attack never came.

I dared to peek out of one eye. At the sight before me, I became a little braver. Opening both eyes, I gawked in

surprise. Draki was standing over me, and the soldier was flailing desperately in his grasp.

"How dare you touch *my* things!" he boomed.

"I-I-I didn't k-know," it cried helplessly.

"Are you that stupid? Could you not smell me on her? Am I that weak that you couldn't tell that I had been in close contact with her?"

It looked around, its eyes bulging. "N-No, sire. Never! I thought that you were done with it. H-Honestly!"

Draki's golden gaze drifted down to me, but not a muscle flinched as he continued holding the soldier by the neck in midair. "Are you okay?"

I nodded and sat up, but the pain in my back flared, reminding me that I had been slashed by the demon's claws. I whimpered and tried to touch the wound. When my hand pulled back, I could see the wet glisten of red painting the tips of my fingers.

"N-No, I didn't mean t—"

Whatever the soldier was going to say was cut off as Draki sneered and squeezed. I looked away. I didn't want to see it. But I heard a *thump* land near my feet while my eyes were closed. I scooted away from whatever it was. Heat kissed my body. The familiar and unbearable warmth that always consumed me when Draki touched me enveloped my body. I felt weightless and knew that (once again) I was in his arms.

In the distance, I heard hoots, hollers, and more hungry cries of encroaching grunts. A new wave of fear gripped me, and I opened my eyes to be locked in place with the devil's gaze. "You're with me. They won't touch you."

"I came to get Elijah. I can't leave him here."

Draki snarled. "You're injured, what good are you to that broken boy? Leave him and find someone else."

I shoved him, and even though it hurt, I twisted about in his arms trying to free myself from him. "I'm not you! I don't abandon things when they become a problem or boring."

"Have you ever tried it? It might be your new favorite thing."

"I'm not leaving him, Draki!"

He forcefully slammed me down onto my own two feet, and I winced in pain. "My job was to protect you. Not him. He's a burden now."

"He's with me on this journey, and you only have yourself to blame. You told the she-devil that you wanted him to go free."

Suddenly, he was toe-to-toe with me. "Maybe I'm realizing I made a mistake, and I'm cutting my losses."

I stood up on my tiptoes and snipped back with, "I'm going to go get him, and you can't stop me." Falling back flat on my feet, I brushed by him.

He grabbed me by the wrist and jerked me back to face him. "You truly will not let him go?"

I shook my head *no*. Draki's molten gaze inspected me, and he took a step closer. Dipping his mouth near my ear, he whispered, "Don't expect me to help you with him ever again. Tonight, I make my first and only exception to our deal. He isn't you. He means nothing to me." I jerked out of his hold and held my wrist like he had burned me as he walked away toward the river. "Pick up your weapon and hurry up, Sia, before I change my mind."

Quickly, I looked away from him to search the ground for my machete. Moonlight spilled over the metal, and I twisted to pick it up, drawing in a hissing breath as my back was attacked with the throbbing ache from the sudden movement. By the time I found it, he was already near the

boulder by the river. I tried to get to him while latching the blade to my hip.

"How are we going to get him back without him noticing you?" I whisper-yelled.

Draki didn't answer me. He just slipped out of my view, and I bolted to catch up with him. As I came around the rock, I stopped in my tracks. The river looked black under the darkened sky that sparkled with the light of the stars. Everything was washed in shadows that gave the world a breath of night, and the melody of the creatures that dwelled within the void swelled around us. The devil's scent was carried in the breeze that was powerful enough to make my jacket flutter in its passing.

Draki looked like a pale ghost mourning some long-lost lover as he lingered by the riverside. His robes rippled in the wind, and his hair flowed like it was gently swaying to a slow song no one heard. He tilted his head to one side, and his vision was fixed on the body of Elijah beneath him.

I shook out of my daze and rushed over. As I picked up the pace, I tried to hide the pain in my voice while saying, "I can carry him."

He scoffed. "You can hardly carry yourself."

I looked around me and mumbled, "I'll let you heal me."

That caught his attention. He glared at me from over his shoulder. "Oh?"

I didn't know what to say, so I nodded in reply.

Turning suddenly, he took a step toward me and let his hand brush over my cheek right before he snatched a handful of braids in his grasp and jerked me closer. I made a small sound but clamped my lips shut before it could fly out of my mouth. Once again, we were too close for comfort. "Even if all I can offer you is pain? Even if I can offer you no

soothing mending, and you'll only feel the sensation of flames kissing your wounds closed? Even if by healing you, I get to see you writhe in agony?"

I remembered how it felt when he healed me before. I knew that if I wanted to carry Elijah, if I wanted to survive and not have my fresh wounds get infected, I was going to have to have him heal me, even if I didn't want him to. Slowly, I licked my lips and felt my mouth dry up as I said, "Yes." But my voice sounded shaky.

He inched closer and drew in a deep breath like he was taking in the perfume of my body. "Hmm, we'll discuss that later. For now, I will carry the boy. If I let you do it, the grunts will get here, and I don't feel like dealing with drooling, hairless dogs." He let me go, and I almost stumbled back.

Rubbing the back of my head, I cut him a look and silently mocked him with an angry pout. When Draki got close to Elijah, he sighed and looked up to the sky.

"I'm doing this because I have something to gain, not because I care," he pronounced. Almost like he was having a conversation with something I couldn't see or hear.

His arms stretched out, and from his form red, curling smoke sparkled and expanded. Levitating in mid-air, the crimson haze swirled. I didn't know that a cloud could look so pretty and yet so menacing, but it did. One moment, Draki looked calm and collected, and the next, his hands tensed and claws extended. Embers fluttered in the air as the suspended smoke darted down and slammed into Elijah. His body spasmed, and then he thrashed about. His back bowed, and a sharp cry of anguish was ripped out of his throat. I watched the devil roll his shoulders forward as if he were putting physical strength behind the magic. Then—without warning—Draki twisted his wrists, his beast-like hands now

palm up, and he lifted his arms. The smoke obeyed his silent beckoning, and it funneled out of Elijah. With a swipe of the devil's hands, the clouds dissipated into nothingness, and the young man went limp in the sand.

"Is he …?"

"I healed him," Draki muttered. Kneeling down, he picked up Elijah and tossed him over his shoulder like he was a sack of potatoes. "He'll sleep long enough for us to get him back to camp."

"What do we tell him when he asks how he got back?" I asked, and raised a curious brow at the confident devil.

He smiled then, but it lacked warmth. "You'll tell him you did. I'll be healing you, remember?" And the dark promise that rested in those words made the walk back to the campsite a dreaded one.

After Elijah was laid down, I felt a sickness rush over me when Draki faced me with his usual, cold expression. There was no attempt to hide that I was afraid of him getting near me. Not when my body responded the way that it did when he was close. Not when he was going to heal me, and the promises of pain were louder than the comforting fact that my wounds were going to be mended. Draki was like fire. Beautiful to look at, but it could consume you within minutes, and there would only be ash left behind. If you were smart enough to pull back before you were engulfed in the fire, you'd forever have scars from the unforgiving burns.

I didn't realize that I never stopped backing away from him and bumped into a nearby tree. Instantly, I felt the bark scrape over my injury, and I closed my eyes and parted my lips to wail out in pain, but a large hand covered my mouth. My eyelids snapped open. White hair, a pale face, and two glowing, golden orbs danced in my vision as his scent of smoky spice encased me. I figured that this was going to be the moment that it would happen. Even though my body wasn't ready for the way that Draki healed, my mind accepted the fate that was going to befall me.

His hand lifted from my lips and drew a line across my skin until he reached my chin. Gently, he pushed against my jawline so that I looked away from him, and I screwed my eyes shut. But I didn't feel pain. I felt the blazing touch of his thumb brushing over my swollen cheek. His voice was gruff and hardly a whisper when he said, "I'm sorry."

My eyes opened, and I turned to look at him, confused. "You are?" Was he sick?

Straightening up, Draki nodded once. "Yes." He touched the welt on my face again with a look I couldn't describe. "You got hurt because I didn't uphold my end of the bargain. I should have stayed closer to you. I didn't think that you would be in trouble," he admitted.

I touched my cheek, and my hand grazed over his. Quickly, I searched the shadowed abyss surrounding us. "I see," I whispered.

"For my lack of upholding my word, I'll grant you one wish."

I cautiously inspected him through slits. "*Anything*?" I questioned.

He sighed and rolled his eyes. "Yes, yes, Sia. Anything," he expressed with a touch of annoyance. Then his expression went dark, and he locked eyes with me as his

voice dropped down to a grim tone. "Within reason, my dear. Don't try to back out of our agreement. My mistake isn't worth the loss of what we've agreed upon."

That idea was dashed before it could ever truly live as a hope in my heart. I had to stop and think a little harder about what I would want from him. The only thing that came to mind wasn't something that would be a good choice for now. The idea itself was great, but the timing wasn't quite right.

Hesitantly, I looked to Draki and searched his eyes as I asked, "Can you set my village free from their contract with their devil without killing them? Not now, but later on, when I'm in a better position to find a way to help them?"

"And here I thought that you were going to ask me to make the healing process gentle," he said with a grin.

"Can you?" I pressed heatedly.

His smile faded. "There is little that I can't do. However, breaking their contract should be simple enough."

I didn't care how it could be done or what process he had to go through. As long as no one was hurt or killed, I was happy. I needed to stress that to the devil in front of me. "And no one will be harmed or killed?"

Shaking his head, he said, "You were very clear on what you wanted. I can do it. Though I don't know how safe they would all be once their devil is gone. When did you wish this to be carried out?"

I thought about it. Even though I knew the answer, I still went through the motions of weighing out my options. "The day before you collect what I owe you," I said finally.

"Very well, then." He let his gaze drift to my cheek, and then his vision flicked back to my eyes. "Shall we proceed with healing you, then?"

Everything in me wanted to say *no,* but I couldn't risk the injury becoming more. I couldn't risk the scent of blood calling various other demons that would put Elijah in harm's way. It was a sacrifice I was willing to make to ensure he would be safe. He didn't need to know what I did for him. I just needed to see him go through as little trouble as possible along our way. He already lost too much. He didn't need to endure anymore. Not because of me or the company that I kept.

"I'm ready," I lied. There was no way I would ever be ready.

He chuckled darkly and took a single step closer. I was pinned by him against the tree, and I gasped as I felt bark dig into the claw marks on my back. His hands clamped down on my shoulders as he said, "You're *mine,* Sia. Don't forget that."

I burned those words into my memory. I engraved them on my soul. I let them echo in me until they became part of the song to my beating heart. I couldn't escape him, so I would embrace him. I didn't close my eyes. I didn't want to hide from this. I had made the choice to let him heal me. *I did this.* He slipped his hands behind me and slid them down my spine. The pain that assaulted me made my legs buckle, but the force of his body pinning me against the tree, along with his embrace, made it so I didn't go very far. My mouth opened up to scream, but I willed every part of my being to remain as quiet as possible. I didn't want to wake up Elijah. I had to suffer through this on my own. Tears streamed down my face, and Draki pressed his lips against the wound on my cheek. It felt like I was being burned alive. All I could feel coursing through my body was white-hot pain. My vision practically went black, my head felt dizzy, and my whole body was racked with my silent cries.

Pulling his fiery lips away from my skin, he then pressed the side of his face against my own and whispered to me. "Every nerve in you is singing with your suffering." He laughed softly. "How delicious."

Abruptly, he let me go, and I fell into a crumpled, weeping heap at the base of the tree. Every part of me was still resonating with the blazing fire that made up how Draki healed. It felt like I was being torn apart and sewn back together. No matter how much I tried to convince myself to stop crying, the tears still kept falling. I sniffled and attempted to rise to my feet.

"I wouldn't do that if I were you," Draki advised.

Determined to defy his words of caution, I found the energy to push myself to stand. I swayed only once and caught myself on the tree. "I'm fine."

"Do you always have to act so tough?"

"Fake it until you make it," I stated with a tired grin and pushed off the tree. I wobbled a bit, and when Draki reached for me to offer help, I slapped his hands away. "You've done enough for one day," I growled in a hushed tone.

He narrowed his eyes at me, but I didn't care. Walking over to the bags, I begged my body to keep up with me as I tried to pull out the blankets to get Elijah and myself situated. I gave up on the idea of separate beds. I was in too much pain, too tired, and too cold to attempt the long-winded process of making two pallets. I had to roll Elijah onto the bed, and he thankfully slept through it. I couldn't bring myself to say much of anything to him about what happened or otherwise. My mind needed a break from everything. But first … I needed to make a fire. The previous one had become nothing more than cooling embers.

◝ 000 ◞

Groaning, I rose up and started for the pile of wood when Draki stood in my path. "I'm trying to get firewood, Draki," I stated, annoyed at his presence.

"I know what you're trying to do. Rest. I'll handle the fire."

"I can do it."

"I said rest, Sia."

I glowered at him. "Are you enjoying this?"

"Do you really want the answer to that? Or do you want to listen to me, lie down, and get some rest before the morning comes and your little man over there starts questioning you?"

Looking over to the male in question, I felt the pride in me dissipate. I didn't want Draki to be right, but he was. I relented on any further objections and sluggishly walked over to Elijah, pulled down the covers, slid in behind him, and cuddled up for the night. He was warm, and his soothing scent brought an unexpected calm over me. Without meaning to, I smiled slightly and snuggled in closer. A soft moan left him when I pressed against him, and his body melted into mine. The warmth of our bodies radiated under the covers and fought off the growing chill of the night. Closing my eyes, I saw one last vision of Draki separated from us by a growing flame as the fire was tended to. It was the last thing I saw before I drifted off to sleep.

Chapter 13:

Unkept Secrets

In the morning, I woke up in bed by myself and saw Elijah poking around by the fire. The pops of fresh firewood filled the early morning air, and the scent of smoke mingled with the cooking food. My stomach grumbled, and I yawned with a healthy stretch.

"You're finally awake?" Elijah asked.

I nodded like he could see me. "Yeah."

His back was still turned to me when he asked, "How did we get back last night?"

I went still and fought with the idea of lying to him. I didn't want to, but I wound up giving up on the idea of telling him the truth. "I made the soldier chase me and killed it when it came around the boulder. I carried you back after that."

"Oh?"

"Yeah."

"Hmm," he said, sounding unbelieving of my tale. "Leaving anything out?"

I felt the first threatening heartbeat choke the air out of me. Holding in my fear, I played it cool and shook my head. "No, I don't think so."

Elijah dropped the spoon into the pot and stood up rapidly, looking down at me as he motioned to his body. "So, you're a healer now, too?"

I opened my mouth, but the words dried up. Sitting straight up, I could only stare back at him in horror. Why hadn't I thought of that? Why hadn't I thought of a good excuse? Why did I let Draki fully heal … wait. Why had he fully healed him? Suddenly, I was scared and mad at the same time. "I-I …" I didn't have a good answer.

Elijah shook his head at me. "You have a deal with a devil, don't you?"

Anything that I was thinking about saying was swept away with that one question. It all came tumbling down around me, and I sighed while curling my legs up to my chest. I was tired of pretending. Trying to keep up with a mountain of lies becomes tiresome after so long. To top it all off, I never liked to lie to begin with.

"Yes," I admitted. The minute the confession left me, I felt a weight lift from me. It felt so freeing, but it didn't wash away any of my fear or guilt.

"Since when?" he asked.

"Since the day after I left my village. Long before I came to you and your village."

"Why didn't you tell me?"

"I didn't want you to find out."

"You weren't hiding it very well."

"I thought that I was," I muttered. "When did you suspect that I had a pact with a devil?"

"The day you fell in the river. You were in the center of the stream one minute and on the bank the next. I suspected then that you had … something keeping you safe."

"I don't understand. Aren't you mad at me? Aren't you scared of me?"

"I think I'd be more scared of you if you hadn't made a deal with one, Sia. You did what you needed to—what we all have needed to do—in order to survive in this twisted world that we live in. Why on Earth would I be mad at you for that?"

"Because you have no idea what kind of deal I've made or whether or not you're even safe around me."

He stared at me, but his eyes looked past everything that rested on the outside. "Tell me a place that I was safe at since you met me."

I opened my mouth and closed it. In our world … was anywhere safe? Sighing, I hugged myself a little harder and shook my head. I didn't know what else to say, so I chose silence.

"I won't ask you about your deal, okay?"

I blinked, looking at him as I asked, "You won't?"

He shook his head and went back to the pot and used the edge of his shirt to grab the hot spoon out of it. "Nah. Just promise me you won't ditch me or feed me to it, okay?"

Slowly, I forced a smile and nodded. "Right, it's a deal," I said, but even I could tell that it lacked conviction.

After we ate, Elijah remembered that he never got water last night from the river because he had been attacked. We didn't want to be caught out in the desert without something to drink, so he ran off to fill up our canteens by himself, even though I offered to help. When he was a good distance away, I stopped breaking down camp and scanned the area. My eyes searched for those detestable, white robes.

"Come out!" I yelled angrily.

There was a loud sigh, like someone being woken from their nap in the most disturbing of ways. It came from the trees where, once again, the devil was lounging in their branches, escaping the rays of the sun.

"There's no need to shout," Draki informed.

I felt rage bubble inside me. "You knew! You knew he would find out!"

"Of course, I knew. I'm not stupid."

"Why? Why did you make things harder for me?" I whined with pepper gracing my tone.

He rose from his slouch, jumped down from the tree, and was on me in a flash. Things like him shouldn't be able to move that fast. I wasn't ready. His fingers wrapped around my throat like a fiery rope, and he pulled me dangerously close. "Because I like watching you suffer, Sia," he snarled in my face. The smell of swirling spice and smoke tinged my nostrils. I felt some of my courage drain from me for a second before I regained my composure.

"What did you think your stunt would do? Turn him away from me? Make him run away before I woke up?"

"Would you miss him?" he asked with a mocking pout.

"You'd miss him more than I would," I growled, my voice dropping in pitch.

He scoffed and let go of my neck. "I think you have it twisted, my dear. I wasn't trying to turn him away at all."

I laughed and crossed my arms over my chest. "Oh, really? Then what were you trying to do?"

"Try?" The grin on his face stole every bit of my arrogance. "I executed my plan perfectly. I just wanted him to bond with you. Now you two have a secret together. Now you have another thing drawing you closer to one another."

He chuckled softly. "Oh, the webs we weave." Each word was uttered slowly and then—in a plume of red smoke—he vanished, leaving only his scornful laughter behind. *"Ahahahaha!"*

I was left alone with my thoughts, and I hated every single one of them.

Our camp was broken down and packed up before Elijah came back from the river. By the time he had returned, I had even doused the flames in heaps of rocky sand and with the remaining soup from the pot. It sucked wasting all of it, but we couldn't take it with us.

We loaded up and headed out. I wasn't sure where the next village was, but if we followed the mountains that hugged the river, we were bound to run into another one sooner or later.

After several hours of walking, we paused for a water break. Our bags were dropped into the dirt, and we stretched our backs with groans as we rubbed our sore spots. We had a little cornbread while we spoke about our options. All the while, my eyes scanned the base of the mountains.

I exhaled forcefully and wiped the sweat that had collected on my brow, although it was a useless act. "Nothing looks good around here that I can see." I could hear the disappointment in my own voice.

Elijah shook his head after scoping out the terrain without any luck. "We can't hit the jackpot every time. Looks like we are going to be sleeping with no shelter tonight."

He was right. I didn't like it. I didn't have to worry much because I had Draki, but the devil had made it abundantly clear that he wasn't going to go out of his way to keep Elijah safe. *Not unless I …* Instantly, I shook the potential thought out of my head. It wasn't an option. I refused to let it be one.

"Vulnerable under the stars," I said softly.

Looking over to me, he gave a faint smile, saying, "It would almost sound perfect if I didn't know that we were closer to death doing so rather than the romantic evening one would think."

I scoffed and held a hand over my heart, like every pump of the muscle was causing me pain. "There isn't anything romantic about it," I grumbled, picking back up my bags.

He followed suit, saying, "Could be." He smirked with a wink as he passed me by.

Why did I like that?

We trudged on a little further and stopped when our bodies couldn't keep going. The bags were heavy, and our backs and arms were aching too much to press on. The sun wasn't helping as the heat bore down on us, making the straps slip and callus our hands or rub our shoulders raw, even with the clothing covering us. Plus, last night's escapades did us no favors in the energy department today. We were suffering quite a bit from it.

"I'll get the firewood," Elijah proclaimed.

"Okay. I'll get the camp ready, then."

We separated to handle our respective jobs.

Chapter 14:

Lose to Me

Returning a few hours later, Elijah and I sat down around the pile of sticks as I tried to light the fire. He blew on the flames while I broke a few twigs. The sunset was beautiful. It was a display of yellows and pinks that painted the sky in a brilliant masterpiece of warm-tinted hues. We watched in silence as the colors faded into deeper shades while the sun slipped from our sight.

"Do you think we'll be attacked again tonight?" Elijah asked.

Shrugging my shoulders, I replied honestly with, "I'm not sure. Nothing is for certain when we're beyond the safety of the villages."

"Nothing is safe in a village either," he muttered, leaning back onto the rocks.

"My village was."

He cut me a look. "If that were true, you wouldn't have been exiled and forced to make a deal with a devil."

"I wasn't exiled," I muttered pitifully.

"Sacrificed, then," he harshly corrected.

He had a point. I sighed, drew my legs up to my chest, and lay my head on my knees. "Yeah. I was. I suppose you're right." I just didn't want to believe that what I had

called home for so long was lumped in with every other danger of our world. I could feel him watching me as I stared at the fire, but we didn't say anything to each other.

After a moment of silence, he asked, "What was your village like?"

"Hmmm?"

"You saw my village. What was yours like? I'm curious."

"Oh." I looked back to the fire and thought about how to describe it. I remembered the front gates. I pushed past the memory of them closing with me standing on the outside of them. I shut my eyes and leaned back on the rocks, listening to them shift under the weight of my body as I mentally walked the streets of the place I had grown up in. I drew in a long, shaky breath and released it slowly as I tried to calm my emotions.

"We weren't in a situation like you were. Our sacrifices were silent and buried under the illusion of a normal life." Opening my eyes, I scanned the brilliant splay of stars that twinkled overhead. "We all helped each other and would hold elaborate feasts at the turn of every season." I smiled, remembering the way we would pass down all the different dishes while talking and laughing and sharing things we had done that day. It was a bittersweet rush of memories, and I let a few tears slide down my cheek before I wiped them away with a short sniff.

"That's not at all what I would expect from a village with a devil pact," Elijah said in amazement.

I laughed. "Well, I mean … we lie to everyone, saying that one lucky person is chosen to leave the village and join another, but there aren't any travelers that come to get you. It's a lie. You are tossed out and left to die. Never able to return."

"Ouch."

"Yeah."

"Do you get to say goodbye?"

There was a pause as I realized that he didn't get to say goodbye to his parents. I was lucky. Just looking at how his life had been, I felt horrible for having a good life up until a week ago. Everything I had been through after that pushed me to make a deal with a devil and lie at every turn. Honestly, I felt like he had a lot more to be sour about in comparison to me. My hardships were nothing to scoff at … but I had been lucky despite all of my pain. It made me realize how cold I must have come across to him as. I didn't need to be *that* guarded, did I?

I nodded as I said, "Yeah. I got to say goodbye." It was whispered sweetly, and I even had a smile to match it.

"That's good." He sat up and tossed a piece of wood on the fire.

I sat up too. "I'm sorry."

He shook his head. "At least I fulfilled their dying wish. I'm free."

Watching him, I felt the question gnaw at me. "What are you going to do?"

"Hmmm?"

I rocked back and forth, holding my knees. "Ya know. Now that you're not bound by your village's devil. What do you plan to do?"

He shook his head. "I honestly haven't really stopped to think about it in depth."

"You haven't?"

"Nah. Being chased down after your parents sacrificed themselves for your freedom, being attacked by a soldier, and worrying about if I'm going to die out here has sort of shoved all those thoughts away."

I understood that. "Yeah. It can put future planning on hold."

"Oh yeah," he said with a chuckle.

I laughed along with him.

He must have sensed it before me because he suddenly dove across the little space between us and put a hand over my mouth. I went wide-eyed with surprise as rocks dug painfully into my back. I looked at him with anger lapping at my irises, but that emotion quickly faded when the dread seeped in.

"Feel nothing," Elijah whispered in my ear, his body pressed against my own in a way that made my mind and heart race.

Easy for him to say.

I tried to look to the stars overhead, but when I did, Elijah was in my view and looking at me in stunned silence. Slowly, I felt his fingers slide away from my mouth, and I heard him dig his free hand into the rocks beside us. My heartbeat was quickly rising as I inspected his face, and my gaze rested on his lips. I knew how they tasted. I knew what it felt like to roll around holding onto that muscular body. I knew, and it scared the hell out of me because I wanted it and avoided it at every turn. Now I was face-to-face with it, and there wasn't an escape. I couldn't move. I couldn't run. I could only focus on the slow rise and fall of our chests as we started to synchronize our breathing. Neither one of us could pull away. It was like we were stuck in a trance, and we didn't try to break free of it.

His face started to dip down, and I didn't try to stop it. I simply closed my eyes and let it happen. I just wanted to feel it one more time. But then, I heard a sound. It was the howl of a grunt somewhere far off in the night. The demon's

cry broke the spell I was under. My eyes shot open, and I whispered, "Don't."

Elijah already looked like he was struggling with himself. He swallowed hard and nodded. "Yeah, not the best time," he whispered back.

"I-Is it gone? The leech?"

He looked over his shoulder, and there was a pause as he scanned the area. A sigh of relief followed soon after, and he groaned as he got up, saying, "Yeah. Seems like it." Holding his hand out to me, he asked, "I didn't hurt you, did I?"

"No," I said, taking his hand. *I should have just let him kiss me*, I thought. "Are you okay?"

He looked himself over. "Yeah, I'm fine."

I pointed to our bags. "We should eat," I said softly.

"Yeah," he agreed.

I started to walk away and mocked myself while making faces at my dumb decisions. A hand on my wrist spun me around, and I slammed into Elijah's chest. My confusion was stamped out when I looked up, and his mouth crashed into mine. I thought about pushing him away. I thought about slapping him. I thought a lot of things, but they all burned away in the passion that consumed us. My hands instantly started to fly over his body, and I gripped his neck and tugged lightly at his hair. He growled against my mouth, and my stomach flipped. We pulled away to gain a breath before we were at it again, and I took a few too many steps back. My mind and body were wrestling with themselves. Our kiss was broken as I stumbled. His hands on me stopped me from falling too far back, but I gave a small yelp as my ankle turned in an uncomfortable way.

"Whoa, are you okay?" Elijah asked breathily.

Panting, I waited a moment before I nodded. "Yeah, I'm just a little tired. We walked a lot today, and I'm pretty hungry."

"Let's get you fed," he said with a smile.

I didn't expect him to change emotions so quickly. He wasn't pressuring me for more affection. I wasn't expecting him to be so happy with our passion coming to a screeching halt. I wasn't expecting him to look at me the way that he did. As he walked by me, he kissed my forehead, and I closed my eyes. It felt like everything that I wanted in a sweet press of lips on the top of my head. It felt like comfort and security and kindness and warmth. When he was a few steps away, I shivered and held myself.

Boy, I was in trouble.

As we ate, we talked about fond memories. Things to chase away the negative emotions that might call to a leech and other creatures that would ensure we wouldn't make it through the night. Though the truth was, I would be fine. Elijah was the one that was more at risk than I.

We laughed at a recent story told, and Elijah tossed more wood on the fire. I sighed, content, and asked, "What are your plans?"

He sighed and hummed to himself. "Ah, yes. The question that I can't really escape from."

"Nope, sorry."

He chuckled again. "Where are you going?" As he asked me, his eyes locked with mine, and they stole my

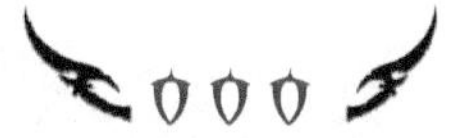

breath from my lungs. I opened my mouth to lie, but my body wouldn't let me.

"I'm still heading for Saint Augustine," I admitted.

Pointing a stick at me, he said, "I'm going to follow you wherever you go."

I didn't expect it. I thought he was going to say that he was going to follow me to the faith city, but not *wherever* I went. Hearing it made my heartbeat stumble, and I couldn't come up with a proper response.

"Why?" I breathed the question as if I could escape the truth a little while longer.

He smiled and said, "Because I like you, Sia. I think that much is obvious."

Thankfully, it was night, and my flustered expression was hidden by the shadowed depths of the twilight hours. Trying to hide the smile, I turned away, rolled my lower lip in between my teeth, and bit down. This man was going to undo every wall that I had built to protect everyone around me. Regaining my composure, I pulled my braids around one shoulder and looked at him. "What if—"

"We'll deal with problems as they come, Sia. Let's not make issues or dream up negative things that might never happen."

"O-Okay."

As I said it, Draki showed up behind Elijah. In a panic, I stood straight up. Wondering what was wrong, he picked up a stick like a weapon and spun around, ready for anything. But when the young man turned, even though he was face-to-face with Draki, he didn't seem to see him. The devil's face peered around Elijah.

"Have I mentioned that he's got beautiful eyes?"

I mouthed "*Shut up. Go away!*" while waving him off toward the endless desert.

Elijah turned around, and I put both hands over my heart.

"Did you see something?" he whispered.

I shook my head. "It must have been the shadows."

He tapped the stick on his shoulder and shook his head. "Should we go to sleep?"

Draki was nodding his head behind Elijah, and I bent my brow in annoyance.

"Did I say something wrong?" Elijah asked.

"Huh? No. I … I was just wondering, do you like spicy food?"

"Do I? I love spicy food."

Not expecting the answer, I lit up. "Really?"

"Yeah. My mom and sister weren't too fond of it, and so we never really made it often."

"I have some recipes that my mom, dad, and meemaw taught me. I'd love to cook them for you."

His smile illuminated the night. "I'd love to eat them."

Draki gave me a look that said he wasn't happy with being ignored. I shot him a quick smile and pressed on with my conversation. "You'll have to make the cornbread, though. I'm not that great at baking."

Elijah laughed. "That's a deal."

I opened my mouth just as Draki said, "I grow tired of these games." And he waved a hand beside Elijah's head. "Sleep," he growled.

Without warning, Elijah closed his eyes and fell down onto the rocky earth below with a *thud!* I covered my mouth to quiet my scream as I watched how hard he hit the ground. Angrily, I shot a dagger-filled glare at Draki and stormed around the fire, yelling, "What in the hell did you do that for?"

Draki followed my pointed finger to the snoring young man and then back to me. "I thought I made it clear that I needed to speak with you."

"No. You didn't. And even if you did, you could have waited," I hissed as I went to Elijah to inspect his head and body. I wasn't seeing any injuries, no thanks to the devil.

"I wait for no one," Draki stated flatly.

"Clearly," I muttered, taking off my jacket and rolling it up to put under Elijah's head.

"Get up. I'm training you on how to fight. It's bothersome to always save you."

"I can fight."

"Sloppily, yes, but not well."

"I fought off grunts," I snapped defensively.

Draki's cool demeanor went up in smoke. Quick steps had him by my side in the blink of an eye, and he snatched me up from the ground. My shirt was gripped firmly in his fists as he stared at me with eyes that burned like the sun. Heat poured over me as his canines elongated like fangs, and he yelled, "Grunts aren't dukes, soldiers, or princes! I might pride myself on time, but teaching you how to fight could be the tipping point between life and death."

"You're supposed to protect me," I reminded meekly, my eyes frantically searching his golden hues.

"I may not reach you in time!"

I was at a loss for words. Was he scared that I would get hurt?

"I may want to see you struggle and be in pain, but I don't want to see you lose to *them*. I don't want to see you lose to someone else. I want you to lose to me. Only to me, Sia."

"And here I thought you cared ..."

He gestured to Elijah snoring on the ground. "Don't make that mistake twice, my dear."

I looked at him and knew that he was right. Walking up the line of Draki's body, I settled in on his gaze as I asked, "So, are you going to teach me to fight?"

He let me go. "Hopefully, you're as competent as I suspect that you are. Grab your weapon. The sooner we can start, the sooner it will be over, and you can rest. You'll need it."

"Why, because of all the walking?" I asked, grabbing my machete.

Looking to the north, he closed his eyes and took in a deep breath. "You should be arriving at the next village tomorrow," he informed blandly.

I fell onto my bedding, heaving like I had forgotten how to breathe. Sweat poured down my face, and I was weakly clutching the machete in my hand. I wasn't sure how long I had been practicing with Draki, but every part of my body was sore. The water canteen was tossed onto my stomach, and I made a sound from the unexpected impact. I didn't have it in me to fuss with the devil for the act. I was more thankful that I had water to drink than I was angry. Shakily, I unscrewed the top and drank while Draki loomed over me.

"You did better than I expected. Good girl. And here I thought it was going to be a total waste of my time."

After drinking, I fell back onto my bed, still panting. "I can't do any more tonight," I admitted weakly.

"You don't need to. Rest. I'm confident that what I've done should be enough to aid you."

"No more lessons, ever?"

"If and when the moment arises, I'll teach you."

I nodded, completely spent.

"Rest, Sia."

Not needing any further prompting, I closed my eyes and curled up where I was. I could feel the canteen taken from me and heard it being put off to the side. Then I felt the machete slide out from under my hand. And—right before I drifted off to sleep—I felt a blanket pulled up over my cold, sore body.

Chapter 15:

A Bitter Tasting Apple

The next morning, we packed up camp and headed out after breakfast. Elijah vaguely remembered talking to me before falling asleep. Thankfully, he didn't question what had led to him passing out.

Later on that afternoon, just as Draki had predicted, we saw the next village in the distance. It was massive! There was a sweet scent in the air, and laughter could be heard the closer we got to it. However, that laughter was unnerving to me because I knew that beneath that laughter and carefree life there dwelled a hidden devil. Happiness like that wasn't free in this world. Not without a hefty price.

By the time we reached the gates, we were greeted by a large gathering of villagers that were full of smiles. They were celebrating our arrival like we were guests that they had been expecting for days.

"We've got travelers!" a female guard with a thick, long, strawberry-blonde braid yelled. Her skin was an ashy-tan and blotched in patches of white outlined in pink. Freckles covered every inch of visible skin, and she had clear, blue eyes like a river. "Well, come in. The things out in the Wastes will try to eat you, but we won't," she said with a hearty laugh.

Her strong hand was on my back, and I was ushered in through the gates before I could say anything or think about changing my mind.

An elderly woman with a crooked nose and drooping wrinkles approached me and took me by the hand. "What's your name, dearie?"

"Sia," I answered, feeling a bit anxious. I looked behind me and saw that Elijah was treated very much the same by a few other villagers.

"I'm Abigail, but folks just call me Abby. You can too. You look like you've been through a lot. Traveling the Wastes will get to the best of us. You need to rest. Let's get you and your husband set up in a private hut, hmmm?"

Everything was happening so fast that I could only focus on one thing she said. "Husband?" I squeaked.

"Oh, I know that blush. Newlyweds, eh?" She leaned in to whisper to me. "Oh, I can spot them a mile away even with these old eyes of mine." She proceeded to cackle as she and the other villagers dragged me toward a private hut at the edge of town with Elijah in tow.

"Really, you don't have to do this …" I tried to reason with Abby, but she was already light-years away as she explained how she and Eustis were in their first year of marriage.

"He couldn't keep his hands off me either," she gushed, slapping my arm lightly as she blushed and giggled.

I forced a smile but felt like there wasn't much that I could do about the situation. At least this way, I had less to be worried about if Draki chose to pop up. So, I let the wave of villagers carry me away to the newlywed hut, which was embarrassing but manageable.

Before we reached the front door, I was able to ask, "Do you all need any help with anything? I don't mind doing

a bit of work to earn the room for a night or two. Maybe we could have a little bit of food for our travels?"

"Oh, of course, dearie," Abby said, patting the top of my hand. She gave a look to a younger man behind us who was slapping Elijah on the back while throwing his head back in laughter. "Daniel, Sia here says they don't mind earning their keep."

"Hmmm? Work, you say?" He rubbed his chin while in thought and gave a toothy grin. "I suppose we could have you work in the orchard for a little bit. This man here can help me make the good stuff!" Daniel laughed again.

A woman with blonde hair and green eyes spoke softly to me as the laughter and stories kept pouring in. Instead of her being hard to hear, she was clear as a bell to my ears. "The only rule that we have here is that you must attend the evening feasts."

I turned to look and ask why, but there was only the fluttering of a pale blue skirt as she disappeared into the throng of people and wandered off in the opposite direction we were all heading in.

"Who was that?" I asked, pointing to the girl.

Abby didn't look. She even lost her smile a bit. Her eyes shifted to others around her, who gave a soft nod like they were trading secrets. Quick as ever, her smile returned. "That's the village leader's daughter, Penelope. Sweet thing, she is." She then changed the subject before I could ask about the village rule. "*Oop*, looks like we're here. Now, you caught us in the middle of our work, so we'll all shoo and let you two get settled. Edna will fetch you something good to eat. You two must have walked a long way to get to our little paradise." She patted the top of my hand again and opened the hut door. "You go ahead and go on, now. Try to get settled and not be too handsy with each other!" She cackled

again, and the door was shut, leaving Elijah and me in the welcomed but sudden silence.

After a brief moment, I turned with an expression that said (without words) exactly how much I didn't enjoy the tidal wave of chatter and touching that came from complete strangers. Normally, I was a bit more relaxed, but after everything I had been through, my nerves felt like they were constantly shot and like I was on the verge of snapping.

Elijah widened his eyes and exhaled loudly. "Well, this is definitely livelier than I expected. Phew, I thought that whole mess would never end," he muttered, tossing his bags by a couch.

The hut wasn't much. Everything was open and in one giant circle. There was a tiny kitchen, a decent-sized living area, and a massive bed. It was obvious what the hut was primarily used for.

"I wouldn't put your guard down in this place," I whispered loud enough for only him to hear.

"Why do you say that?"

I shook my head. "Something about the looks they were giving each other and … I don't know. Something just doesn't feel right."

"You think we could be sacrificed to their devil?"

It was a thought I hadn't really considered, but now it was assaulting my mind relentlessly. "Or that."

He chuckled softly. "Don't worry too much about it, Sia. We won't be here long, and we can keep each other safe."

I looked at him with worry. "You and I can't fight off a whole village."

He sighed and nodded. "You think we should leave after tonight?"

"I'm not sure."

"You could … you know … talk to your …"

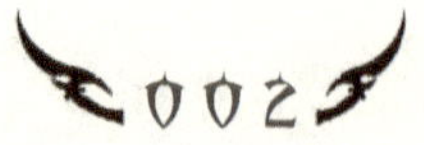

He made motions to me, and it took a moment for the words to sink in. He wanted me to ask Draki? Not expecting the suggestion, I laughed nervously. "I'm not sure I feel comfortable with that."

"He won't answer you?"

"I'm not sure I'd believe what he would tell me," I corrected.

"Words hurt, Sia," Draki said while leaning against the door of the hut.

"Speak of the devil," I sighed and went to toss my bags on the bed.

Looking around the hut, confused, Elijah asked, "He's here?"

"You can't see him," I informed.

"You can change that," Draki suggested.

I held my head. "I can't do this right now."

Thankfully, they both stopped talking and watched me. One, like he was concerned for me. The other, like I was holding him up from tending to some important, pressing matter. After a few deep breaths, I focused on taking things out of the bag that we would need soon as I asked, "Is it safe to stay here for longer than tonight?"

"I fail to see what danger you would be in with me here?" Draki stated, looking like his usual, bored self.

I sat on the edge of the bed and talked to Elijah. "I wouldn't trust it after tonight. I think we should leave in the morning."

"Fair enough," he replied.

Draki chuckled to himself. "Wise choice, my dear." And he disappeared before I could ask him what he meant by that.

After we lightly unpacked, Elijah and I headed back outside. The streets were quiet, save for the occasional sound of a pot or pan clanging in the distance. It was a far cry from the bustling, happy village we had been greeted by. The streets were clean, well-kept, and cold. It reminded me of Elijah's village, but the buildings were not dilapidated and falling apart. Everything was in order and taken care of. However, the silence and lack of bodies roaming about gave an eerie feeling to the town.

"Think they are having a town meeting?" Elijah asked, scanning the area carefully.

"I'm not sure," I replied. My eyes were ever watchful of our surroundings. "Let's see if we can find someone to talk to."

We came around a building, and there was a man with ginger hair and a matching, full, bushy beard. He stood directly in front of us, wearing a bloodstained apron and holding a cleaver with a notched blade. He looked down at us in surprise and raised his blade hand. I jumped back and screamed. Elijah jumped in front of me and took a stance like he was going to start fighting the knife-wielding man.

"Whoa! Whoa!" A tall man that looked to be only a couple of years older than Elijah and me came around the corner. He wore a white, button-up shirt with his sleeves rolled up to his elbows, a black tie was loosely hanging around his neck, and he had on a pair of ebony slacks. He looked really well-dressed for being someone that lived in a village out in the Wastes.

His piercing, hazel eyes darted between the three of us and then flashed a smile to me. "Hey, you must be a new one here, darling." He swept a hand through his deep brown hair and patted the sweaty chest of the meat cleaver man. "Stand down, Patrick. Just the newbies."

Patrick didn't say much. In fact, he didn't speak at all. He nodded slowly while the new male laughed and turned the butcher around. "I'll take care of them. I know you didn't mean to scare them." He faced me and smiled even wider.

"I'm sorry!" I yelled.

Patrick stopped and looked at me. Quickly, he turned his attention to the male in a suit and tie. The well-dressed man waved him down and pointed to me with a smile, put a fist up to his chest, and rubbed it in a circular motion.

Patrick smiled softly and waved at me. He held his pinky and ring finger down and flicked his thumb, pointer, and middle finger out.

"He says that it's okay."

"Oh, thank you …" I pressed, waiting for him to give me a name to go with the face.

"Ah, where are my manners?" He took my hand in his and shook it firmly. "The name's Lucian."

"Real name?" I asked.

He shook his head. "You wouldn't be able to pronounce my real name, love." Pointing to Elijah, he asked, "This your brother?" Extending his hand, he waited for the young man to shake in greeting.

Elijah narrowed his eyes for a split second. "No," he answered deadpan. He then pointed to the hut in the distance. "We're staying in the marital hut."

Lucian wrinkled his nose and shook his head, but he never lost that grin. "Sorry about that, mate. They tend to

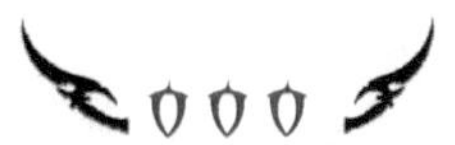

assume a lot here." He looked back in my direction and elbowed me gently. "We can set you up somewhere a bit more comfortable if you'd like?"

I laughed and tried to keep Lucian's attention on me because Elijah looked like he was trying to melt him with his glower. "It's okay. It's only for a night." I cleared my throat awkwardly and looked around the streets. "I was hoping I could find someone to point me in the right direction. I was supposed to work in the orchard, and he was supposed to … uh, 'make the good stuff?'"

Looking confused for a moment, Lucian pondered before he laughed out loud. "Must have been Daniel and Abby." He shook his head. "You'll be working on making wine and ale, buddy. This village goes through a lot of it. Most of the villagers are preparing for tonight's feast. I can take you two where you need to go."

"I don't want to be a bother," I started.

"Oh, stop. I'd be more than delighted to help you out."

Lucian went to put his arm around my shoulder, but Elijah had grabbed my wrist and pulled him to his side. "Lead the way," he said with a smile.

Pursing his lips to the side, Lucian nodded a few times to himself. Those lips curled into a smile once again, though. "Right then, the brewery is this way. We'll drop you off first, and I'll take the lady to the orchard."

Why did I feel like I was being fought over? I didn't like that. I can make my own choices. I was a big girl and didn't need anyone to act on my behalf.

Pulling my hand free from Elijah's grasp, I motioned to Lucian, saying, "Following you."

Silently, we followed him as he weaved his way through the village while we made idle chatter. Once we got

to a brick building, there was a fruity, pungent aroma wafting out from the open windows. Honestly, it smelled absolutely wonderful. After knocking with the back of his hand on the black, steel door, we waited for someone to answer. Within seconds, Daniel stood at the entrance.

"Aye! You made it!" He grabbed Elijah and dragged him inside without another word.

"Sia," Elijah managed to whisper before he was sealed tight behind the door. Daniel could be heard bellowing to the other workers inside that their new helper for the day had arrived.

"Looks like it's just you and me, love."

Turning my head to face him, I saw Lucian closer than expected. He was leaning over me, and his face was inches from mine. I took a few too many quick steps back in my rush to put distance between me and him and almost fell.

"Hold up there now," he called out as he lurched forward and grabbed me around the waist.

"Th-Thank you," I said quietly and quickly righted myself before slipping out of his grasp.

"Didn't mean to scare you."

I nodded. "It was my fault," I muttered and scoped out the area anxiously. "Where is the orchard?" I kept my vision on anything but him.

"Am I making you nervous?" His question was asked in a tone that was curious, but his smile was playful. Almost like he was hoping that he was.

"No. I'm just anxious to get to work. Was hoping to bathe before dinner tonight, and it looks like there isn't much sun left." It was an honest answer, even if it was me stretching the truth.

"Hmmm. Suppose you're right. Let's hurry up then. We definitely don't want you to miss out on tonight's feast."

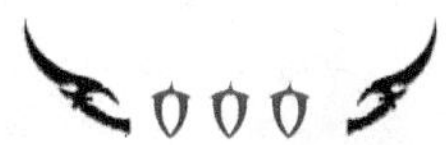

Once again, we set out, and this time I tried to avoid talking with Lucian. The way his attention was set on me had me worried in all kinds of ways. For one, I didn't want to be alone with a stranger. Secondly, I didn't trust the quiet of the streets or even the villagers completely. I would use my machete if I had to, though I didn't think it'd come down to that. Lastly, anyone giving me attention was not good. I was still trying to shake things that Elijah made me feel, and I was failing. I didn't need new individuals to add to my dangerous list of people getting too close for comfort. It would only hurt them in the long run, and that wasn't something I could live with, and it most certainly wasn't something I could die with. If anything, it was something I was desperately trying to forget.

We had passed by countless buildings and barns and were now standing at the edge of what I thought was a field, but it wasn't. It was rows and rows of trees. I had never seen an apple tree. I had never seen an apple. I looked at the stretch of fruit-bearing plants with astonishment. The smell in the air was sublime, and I closed my eyes to drift in the scent.

"How, uh, do you harvest them?" I asked, full of wonderment.

He laughed, hooked his arm around mine, and picked up a basket nearby. "You just find a nice, red apple and twist it free of its branch. After that, it's all yours."

Stopping at the base of one of the trees with a step ladder underneath, he pointed up to the edge of the foliage. "There is a nice bunch. Grab those, would you?"

Making sure I had sturdy footing, I stepped up the ladder and pointed to a cluster of shiny, ruby-red apples. "These?"

"Oh, yeah. They are ripe for the picking. Remember, twist."

Following his instructions, I reached up, grabbed a hold of one, and twisted. A *pop* was heard, and the apple was free from the branch. I grinned at what I held in my hand. "Wow, it looks great." I snapped out of my daze. "How many should I pick?"

"Hmmm … I'd say fill up this basket and then wash up. You don't need to do too much for a bed and a bit of food. We manage just fine on our own."

"Oh. Okay." Stepping down, I put the apple in the basket and then looked up to the branches. "Are you sure?"

"I'm sure, Sia."

My eyes went wide with amazement, and it quickly changed to confusion. "When did I tell you my name?"

His smile broadened. "Word travels fast when there are newcomers in town. You hurry up and don't forget to come to the feast tonight, okay? I'll be looking for you!"

"Okay," I said to avoid a fight or having to explain myself.

Heading back up the ladder, I forced myself to focus on my job rather than him walking away. He was an attractive man. There was no denying that. *There's no harm in looking*, I told myself. When I turned to look, I was suddenly face-to-face with Draki, who was lounging in the branches beside me, blocking my view.

"Don't have enough waiting for you at home?" he asked with a displeased expression.

Swallowing my heart that had leaped up into my throat, I drew in a calming breath and reached for an apple. "I don't know what you're talking about."

After I plucked the apple, Draki took it from me, inspected the crimson-skinned fruit, and hummed to himself. "Such a long time since I've seen one of these." His vision seemed far-off as he turned the fruit in his hand. His golden

eyes flicked over to lock with my gaze, and he presented the apple to me with a smirk. "Care for a bite?"

"No."

He laughed to himself. "That's the first time I had a woman deny me after I asked a question like that." He chuckled again, and it grew until he was laughing hysterically. The darkness in his mirth made my bones cold. Then, like he had a tiny animal in his grasp, he snatched a bite out of the apple as he winked at me.

I licked my lips and steadied my heartbeat. If anyone could make eating look seductive, it was Draki. Peeling my vision from him, I went on to finish my job. However, with each bite Draki took out of the fruit, I felt unnerved. Something as simple as the act of eating an apple had taken on an ominous air, and it set me on edge.

Chapter 16:

A Glass Never Empty

It took Elijah and me roughly two hours to complete our work and another hour to clean up. I had been dodging wasps, bees, and fruit flies, while he had to battle body odor and horrible jokes told boisterously by a crowd of sweaty workers. We agreed that neither of us had it easy after washing up and changing clothes. Not a second after we were ready to head out to the feast, there was a knock at the door.

Not sure what to expect, Elijah rushed to the door and opened it slowly. With every inch that it was opened, I saw the tension in his shoulders melt away until I saw a girl with soft, blonde hair and wearing a pale blue dress, standing on the other side.

"Penelope," I whispered to myself.

"I'm so glad that you've made yourselves at home here." She stepped off to the side and motioned with a sweep of her arm for us to leave the hut. "Tonight's feast is to celebrate the two of you coming to our village," she said with a faint smile and tilt of her head.

"But, don't you guys have a feast every night?" I asked.

Her green eyes settled on me as she replied, "There is always a reason to celebrate." She motioned again for us to come out.

Once we were out, she led us to the center of the village, where there was a massive garden pergola covered in creeping vines and decorated in brightly colored paper lamps. Under the starlit sky, it was positively magical and mesmerizing-looking. There was a dance floor surrounded by countless tables all piled high with food and jugs of drink. My mouth watered as the smell of all the delectable dishes was carried to me by the faint breeze.

"Oh, I'm eating my fill tonight," Elijah mumbled to me.

I giggled and nodded in agreement. "Yeah. Me too."

The crowd noticed us coming their way, and a few familiar faces waved at us as we approached, and they called out for us to sit with them. Any feeling of worry died off as it felt like we had returned home from a long journey. This place felt genuinely happy and carefree. It was so easy to just forget your worries and slip into their way of life. I dared to smile warmly at Daniel and Abby as they waved at us.

Deeper in the crowd, there was Lucian. He was in a clean, white, button-up shirt, leaning on a table and drinking from a glass. He peered over his shoulder and grinned as he noticed Elijah and me. Slapping a hand down on the back of whom he had been conversing with, he waved goodbye as he broke away and sauntered over to us.

"Good evening, Lucian," Penelope said softly.

He took her hand in his and gave a chaste kiss to her knuckles. "How kind of you to bring our guests to us. Such a wonderful lady you are."

"You're too kind," she purred. Then she curtsied to us. "Enjoy the feast." With that, Penelope turned and headed further into the throng of villagers.

Once more, the feeling that I had forgotten crept back up to the forefront of my mind. Something felt off. There was a lie beneath all these smiles. There was always a sacrifice. There was always an exchange. There was always a price for the safety and smiles and luxuries. What was theirs?

"Look at you so tense, love. You should loosen up. Come on and join the party," Lucian coaxed sweetly.

I felt Elijah's hand on my back. "Do you want me to stay close?" he whispered loud enough for me to hear.

Nodding in reply, I smiled at him and locked eyes with his as I pretended like he had asked me something else. "I would love a plate. You always spoil me."

He kissed my head, and a few people whistled and laughed at us. "You deserve it," he announced in a way that was just for me.

Whether he was playing along or being honest, I wasn't sure. He was that convincing. Hopefully, Lucian would think so too. As Elijah slipped away to get us food, I was left in an air of awkward silence.

"You're not married," Lucian stated casually before sipping from his glass. His eyes were glued to me like he was taking in every thread of clothing and strand of hair and dissecting it.

"I'm sorry?"

He leaned in closer and grinned wildly. He invaded my personal space without a care and was almost cheek to cheek with me. He whispered directly in my ear, "You're not married."

I went still. Was he playing with me? I took a step back and forced a smile. "Whether or not I am should be no concern of yours."

He laughed and licked his teeth. "I was hoping that you wouldn't upset me, Sia. You seemed like a girl that could help me have a fun time in this boring village." He sighed and sipped from his glass again.

A woman passing by was tapped on the shoulder by him. When she turned, she was drawn up to his gaze and went strangely still. He held out his glass to her and said, "You should have a drink."

The woman made no protest. She simply took the glass from Lucian and proceeded to drink. As she did, he turned his attention back to me. "Why don't we play a game, Sia?"

"I'm not fond of games."

"Oh, but I am."

The sounds of the lady gulping grew louder. I turned to look, and it was like the cup hadn't lost any contents, but she was drinking like she was draining it. It wasn't right. The cup should have been empty. With how much she was drinking, it should have been bone-dry by now. Lucian snapped his fingers and pointed to himself. "You really should pay attention to me, love. I really don't like being ignored." Those words sounded off warning alarms in my mind. I knew someone that sounded like that.

"I-I'm sorry, but there seems to be—"

"Where were we? Ah, yes. I wanted to play a game."

I felt my stomach knot. "I think I should leave." I wanted to run. I needed to get Elijah's attention, and we had to get the hell out of here. When I tried to find him, two things happened. One, I saw that Daniel and the others were talking to him and surrounding him so he couldn't see me,

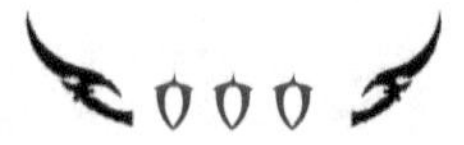

much less get us our dinner. Two, Lucian was in front of me, and he moved fast.

Scary fast.

The gulping from the woman was now a mix of choking and whimpers as she continued to drink from the glass that had no end. It was becoming abundantly clear that Lucian was no ordinary man. In fact, he wasn't a man at all. He was a devil. No sooner had that realization hit me did the woman drinking from the glass fall backward, the cup plucked from her grasp by him as she fell. She hit the floor, and alcohol spewed out of her mouth like a fountain, and she shook about violently before going terribly still. The devil kicked her heeled foot and sucked at his teeth.

"What a party killer," he griped. Slowly, he looked at me, and I froze. "About that game, love." He grinned and wiped off the mouth of the glass and tapped the rim with a single digit. Amber liquid filled the cup, and he took a step toward me. "Are you two really married?"

"Yes," I lied.

He shook his head and ticked his finger from side to side. "Tut-tut-tut. Bad move. I was hoping that this would have panned out differently. I guess you'd rather lie than spend a bit of time with me." He sighed and put the cup between us. Our eyes were still locked, and I couldn't pull away. I felt like I *had* to look at him, like looking anywhere else would take away the air from my lungs. "How about you have a drink?"

My hand wanted to reach for the offered cup. I wanted to drink from it, even though I wasn't one to drink at all. Even though I knew what would happen to me if I did. It was an unnatural desire to consume what was in that glass. The more that I realized I wasn't in control of my own thoughts, the more I panicked. I needed to get away!

"I … I don't like to drink alcohol," I said. But it took *everything* in me to deny him.

He laughed. "Oh, love. You really should have a drink. Just one. It's poor form to be at a party and not partake in its pleasures." He offered the drink again, and I—to my surprise—reached out to take it from him. My eyes remained transfixed on his in a frightful way. I whimpered and felt the cool glass on the pads of my fingers.

Then the world went pitch black.

The sensation of blazing skin prickled over my lids and the bridge of my nose. I smelled the scent of spices and smoke. Any fear that had been growing in me disappeared. As his hand was removed, I blinked at the blinding light assaulting my vision. A forceful hand turned me, and I was chest-to-chest with Draki. His eyes weren't on me, though. They were fixed on the devil across the way.

"I see you've taken a liking to something that is already owned," Draki stated flatly.

Lucian laughed and leaned on the table that was between us. He brought his voice down to a dangerous level as he said, "I don't see your name anywhere on her, mate. Suggest you run along before you get hurt. This is my territory. Next time, don't bring things you cherish to unsafe places."

Draki laughed. The sound was bone-rattling and soul-chilling. It lacked joy and held the promise of darker things to come, and ghosts of anger swam beneath each cackle he made. "Oh, I see you lack manners."

"You're the one lacking manners, walking around in my village like you own it," Lucian growled.

The cup was pulled out of my grasp, and Draki muttered, "Keep your eyes on me, Sia."

"I wouldn't drink from that cup if you want to live. Devil or not, you're playing with fire," Lucian warned.

A chuckle was caught in Draki's throat. "We'll see who gets burned," he stated and brought the glass to his lips.

If he drank from it, he would die. I couldn't have that happen. I didn't want that to happen. I shouldn't have cared as much as I did, but I did. When he drank from it, I started to reach for his arm to stop him. To my surprise, the contents were emptied, and then the cup was gently placed down on the table.

"Mmmmm. That blossoming floral fragrance lingers a touch after the burn. I rather enjoyed it." Draki grinned, and his golden eyes flashed with an otherworldly glow. "I'd love another glass."

Lucian looked from the cup to Draki and very slowly straightened up. "It can't be," he whispered.

"Oh, I assure you, it's me."

"I … Forgive me for my insolence!"

Holding me closer in his grasp, Draki drummed his fingers over the top of the table. The party around us had halted. I wasn't sure at what point everyone had stopped the festivities to watch the power struggle play out between the devils, but it was clear that they had seen it all, from my struggle to my devil swooping in to save the day. Waving his hand through the air like annoying flies were swarming, Draki announced, "Forget it. I shouldn't have let her wander about without introductions."

A flash of baby blue to my side brought my attention to Penelope, who was standing with a gentle hand laid upon Lucian's arm. Her eyes were fixed on the devil holding me. "Sir, if it is all right with you, I'd like to invite the young lady to my hut for a private conversation."

Draki flicked his gaze from Lucian to her and then looked down to me. "It's your call."

Staring at the crowd of faces and then to Elijah, who was giving me an expression that had my insides all twisted, I felt all the unwanted attention from the party turn to me. My chest hurt, and I gripped the clothing over my breast as I answered with, "Yeah. That's fine." *Anything to get away from here.*

I wanted to escape the prying eyes of everyone looking at me. I felt embarrassed. I felt ashamed. And the smile on Draki's face wasn't helping me at all. I stepped out of his fiery embrace and toward Penelope. Without a word, she turned and headed for her hut, expecting that I would follow her.

I did.

Chapter 17:

We Can Make a Kingdom

Her hut was nothing tremendous. In fact, it was moderately sized. Inside, the furnishing was intricately carved, and the attention to detail was immaculate. Everything had a high-gloss finish and was free of dust or grime. Finely woven rugs that looked like they were freshly made decorated the spotless, wooden floors. A few oil lamps were lit, and the light bounced off of various mirrors littering the walls, shelves, and the mantle.

"I'm sorry for the scare you must have endured earlier," Penelope stated softly.

She slowly crossed the living room and closed a door, but I saw something on the other side that would stay with me forever. Shrouded in shadows, a leathery body with stringy hair and a mouth agape, showing off a row of uneven, yellowing teeth, was resting in a rocking chair inside the room. The mummified remains had eye sockets that were sunken and hollow, and its nails curled into the wood of the chair.

"Father doesn't like it when we have company over," she said with a faint smile. The door clicked shut, and she

turned around to face me with her hands clasped in front of her.

My stomach felt sour, and I instinctively held it as I tried to swallow past the rising sickness I felt it growing in my gut. I nodded and forced a smile. "I won't be long," I promised.

"Yes. I suppose we should carry on with what I wished to speak with you about." She motioned to the seating area.

Shaking my head, I said, "I'll stand. Thanks."

"Very well," she said. Seating herself in one of the chairs, she flattened out her dress and flipped her blonde hair behind one shoulder. "I shall cut straight to the chase. I saw your devil. I don't think anyone here in the village didn't see him."

I shifted uncomfortably. Biting the corner of my lower lip, I remembered the way Elijah looked at me and felt a ping of pain in my breast. "Yes, well … I don't plan on staying past tonight."

She laughed into the back of her hand. "Oh, please. I'm not worried about that in the slightest."

"Really?" I was stunned. Normally, having a pact with a devil was grounds to be treated like you were filth. Most of us were born into a pact that we never agreed upon. To be free and broken away from that and willingly make a deal with a new devil was lunacy.

She smiled. It was the kind of smile that lacked the sweetness her features made you assume that she possessed. "Oh, yes, really. You see, Sia, I am well aware of the strength it takes to make a deal with a devil."

My jaw unhinged. "You … this village, you made it?"

Proudly, she straightened up a little more in her chair and nodded. "Of course, I am the founder of this village."

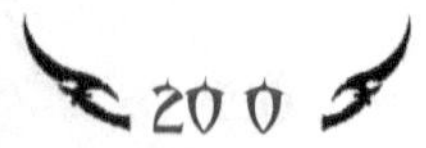

"You guys are doing rather well for it being so new,"
I admitted with an honest smile.

Again, Penelope laughed and shook her head. "Dear,
sweet, child. No, this place is far from new. My father was the
one that broke ground on this village after everything went to
hell, quite literally."

"So … he is the founder, the one that made the pact?"

"No," she said with a glint of something dark in her
eyes. "I did." Her vision crept over to the closed door. "Shhh
… *Father*. Let me tell the story." She flipped her hair again,
settled into the chair, and sighed. "I made the pact a hundred
and forty … mmmm … seven years ago. The price I had to
pay was steep. My debt was the life of my father and," she
motioned to the window, indicating the world outside her
hut, "you saw how Lucian can be. He could go a few years
without touching a soul and then kill a string of them in a
single night. He's quite the fickle devil. But, as long as he is in
high spirits and a party is going on around him, he doesn't
care. He loves watching people indulge in pleasures as much
as he likes taking a life."

I was at a loss for words. If what she was saying was
true, she was … how old? And she looked that young? There
was no way unless she made it part of the deal. As the
thought dawned upon me, I looked at Penelope, confused,
and she giggled. The sound grated against my skin. "You
sacrificed your father for immortality?"

"Of course. He had lived a long life, and I needed to
ensure my investment in our village remained protected and
was run smoothly. How could I pass over this position to
someone that would ruin everything that I worked so hard to
build?"

"That was your flesh and blood!" I yelled.

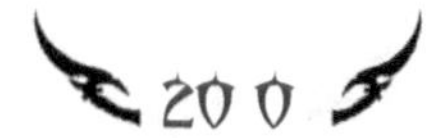

Her tiny fist beat down on the arm of the chair, and she tried to rapidly regain her composure after the anger had flared up in her. "I did what I had to in order to survive and to have this place survive. Look around you, Sia! Is it not thriving and full of life and joy?"

"That joy is a mask," I countered. "Everyone lives not sure that they will see another day, and Lucian loves how on edge everyone is."

"And what about you and your little village? How perfect was it that you were tossed out like yesterday's trash and forced to make your own deal?" She smirked. "Don't preach to me like you are any better. What is your debt?"

Instantly, I straightened my spine like a steel rod had replaced my backbone. "You don't need to worry about that."

She stood from her chair. "Oh, but I want to because I want to offer you a place here. Imagine how much bigger this place could be. Imagine what we could build together. Think about it. You and I could rule this place together with our devils."

"I'd much rather reach a faith city that is free of pacts and devils."

She crinkled her nose, repelled by the idea. "The faith city? Those places are smoke and mirrors. They aren't any better than us out here in the Wastes. Stay and build something that can rival the faith cities with me."

"It comes at a cost."

"It's such a small cost in the grand scheme of things."

"Not to me!"

"Then you are weak!" Her words felt like a slap, and I balked at her. Penelope steamrolled on. "But you could be so much stronger than what you are now. Stay with me. Stay and build an empire."

I was done with this conversation. "I decline your offer." I turned and headed for the door, but her hand was instantly on my wrist, and she jerked me back toward her with a strength I hadn't expected her small frame to possess.

"Don't be a fool, Sia. There is nothing out there that could offer you what I have here!"

Looking at her with disgust, I snatched my arm out of her grasp. "You don't want me. You want the power that my devil could offer you."

Her face twisted into something that looked less human. Her kind and sweet act had fallen apart right in front of me. "What are you going to do with him, hmmm? Run away to a faith city and then pay your debt, live and die with the guilt of whatever your payment is? At least I'm not being pathetic like you."

"I gave you my answer. Back off." I started for the door again.

Screaming, Penelope rushed at me and yanked on my braids, forcing me to stumble backward as my hands tried to hold onto the hair she had a grasp of. Before I could yell at her, I felt the air in the hut change. Heat wafted through the home, and carried with it was the scent of the spice and smoke, and then I felt her grip vanish from me.

Draki tugged me toward him and guided me to stand behind him. The walls rattled, and the wood whined as he looked down to the girl cradling her hand against her chest on the floor.

"Someone is a brave little thing," he muttered through gritted teeth.

"She is worthless. Let me make a pact with you. Together, this village would grow beyond what anyone could imagine. You could *have* me. You would never be bored," Penelope promised with a smile that turned my stomach.

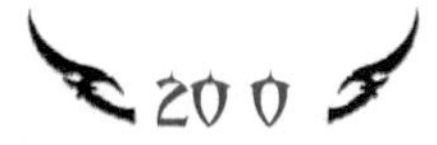

He scoffed. "I'm already bored here. You, my dear, are not in the slightest bit appealing to me." He stepped closer and loomed over her. "But—mark me—if you lay a hand on her again, I will rip your devil limb from limb in front of you, kill every villager, and walk away while everything burns to the ground with you tied in the center of it all."

Her eyes widened, and her face paled. Tears welled up in her eyes as she stuttered and crawled toward him. "You wouldn't. Don't. I don't want to die. *Shut up, Father.* I've got this! We won't touch her. Go. Go. I'm sorry." She reached for him.

Draki backed up before she could touch his robes. "I'm glad that you understand."

"Please, I know you!" Penelope barked out.

It happened so fast. I could hear her inhale to speak, and then she was snatched up by the throat. Draki's grasp squeezed as he snarled in her face. "Say my name and I'll have your tongue!"

She nodded, and tears continued to fall as her face turned colors. Her hands scrambled over his, trying to loosen his grip so she could breathe.

I laid a hand on his shoulder to stop him. "Draki," I whispered.

He looked to me, and some of the anger in him subsided. He tossed Penelope onto the floor and wiped unseen dirt from his attire. "Enough of this. Come, Sia," he commanded, taking my hand and leading me to the exit.

As soon as we burst through the door, Lucian was standing there. The two devils stared each other down for a long moment before Lucian calmly said, "I see you left her alive."

"Only because I was in a good mood," Draki warned.

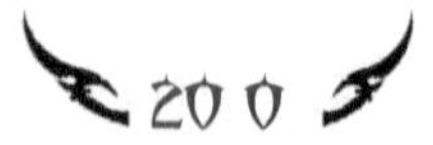

"Hmm. Careful, they might be mortals, but there is something positively alluring about them and their short little lives," Lucian stated while letting his hazel hues slide over to me. He looked me over, starting from my feet and walked his line of vision up my body. After he rested on my eyes, he winked, and I looked away. He chuckled. "I'm off to pick up the pieces. Sleep tight, love. Call me if you need a good time."

"She'll be far too busy with me," Draki snipped and led us away.

When we got back to the hut, there was no fire, and not a single oil lamp or candle was lit. The small home was pitch black and quiet. I wondered where Elijah was, and for a moment, I feared that the unspeakable had happened to him. Turning, I reached for the doorknob.

"Where are you going?" It was Elijah's voice, and he sat up from the couch with empty eyes.

I had to squint to see him in the shadowed depths. "Elijah?"

"Yeah," he grumbled and fell back flat on the couch.

"Are you—?"

He held up a thumb before I could finish the question. "Yup. Everyone wants to be your best friend when they think you're married to a woman who has a more powerful devil than them."

I walked to the couch and leaned over the edge. "Are you okay?"

He raised a flat hand in the air and twisted it from side to side. "Meh."

Sighing, I went to get a blanket to cover him up with, but he quickly jumped over the back of the couch and hugged me from behind. Not expecting the action, I went still and looked around the room like something in it would help me escape his embrace.

"Elijah. It's been a long night. We should sleep."

"Do you care about him?" he breathed the question against my neck, and I shivered. "Do you?"

I could smell the alcohol rolling off of him. "You're drunk and need to lie down."

"Is he the reason you're distant with me?"

I spun around and lay my fingers over his mouth. "Stop. Just stop. We have other things to worry about. We need to leave at daybreak."

"I want to talk with you."

"Tomorrow," I urged him. I knew it was a lie. I was going to avoid it again. I was going to avoid it at every cost. "Right now, I need you to sleep. Okay, handsome?"

He grinned after I complimented him and let me guide him back to the couch. "Handsome, huh?"

"Mhmm." I hummed as I rushed to grab the blanket, ran back, and covered him up.

"Tomorrow?" he slurred sleepily.

"Tomorrow," I replied.

Chapter 18:

Escape Artist

Outside the hut the next morning, there was a burlap sack full of apples and a note that said:

"Think of me each time you take a bite, love."

And I knew who had left them. I wasn't going to complain, though. It gave me something other than cornbread to eat, and I was thankful for that.

Elijah was too focused on his throbbing headache to ask me anything while we walked to the exit. Unlike when we arrived, today the gate was empty save for the two silent guards that let us leave. There was no grand goodbye or celebration. If you came and wanted to stay, you were family and practically treated like royalty, but if you were leaving, you were forgotten and left alone.

I looked back once and saw Lucian leaning against the outside wall, tossing an apple up in the air and catching it like it was a ball. He saluted me with two fingers, and I just nodded to him, not sure if upsetting him would be a great idea. I acknowledged the devil and moved on because there was nothing for me back there.

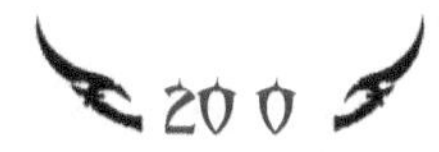

"No more villages," I grumbled as I passed by Elijah.

"Huh?" he moaned, holding his head.

"We can't trust people in other villages. We're safer out in the open and on our own with swarms of demons, so we need to stick close to each other."

He smirked. "I don't have a problem with that. I won't have anyone trying to feed me booze or telling me horrible jokes."

"Oh, the jokes couldn't have been that bad."

Peering out of one eye at me, he winced in pain. "You've no idea."

I laughed and prodded the canteen on his hip. "Might want to drink up. We've got a long walk." I then remembered the apples and grabbed one and tossed it to him.

Fumbling as he tried to catch it, he gave a glower to the sun rising over the horizon and sighed heavily. The two of us traveled for a long while in silence before we spoke again. Elijah had a couple of apples and seemed to be better after a while of having food in his stomach. I struggled to finish mine. The memories of last night kept replaying in my mind like some horrible nightmare that I couldn't shake, and it ruined any appetite that I would have had. It didn't help that I felt dizzy and lightheaded all morning.

After sipping from his canteen, Elijah wiped his mouth and asked, "What happened when you left with Penelope last night?"

That was a can of worms … "I met her dad."

"Oh? Was he nice?"

"He was pretty quiet considering he was a hundred-and-forty-seven-year-old mummified corpse."

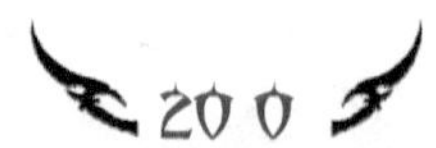

Elijah coughed and sputtered. "A hundred-and-forty-seven-year-old corpse!? Man, it's the quiet ones you got to be careful about, huh?"

"Yeah. Seems so."

There was a silent moment between us before he asked, "What happened?"

The question was so simple, but the memories that I had from last night were anything but that. "She wanted me to stay."

"What?"

I nodded. "Yeah." I sighed and pushed a few braids behind my ear. "She wanted my help turning her little orchard village into an empire."

It took a moment, but when I looked at him, I saw the realization sink in. "Because of your devil."

Again, I nodded. "Mhmm."

He shifted the weight of the bags. "It's a good thing he showed up last night."

I turned to look at him, confusion written all over my face. "Who?"

Staring at me, he finished with, "Your devil."

I let out a short burst of nervous laughter as I remembered the incident and what Elijah had said once I got back to the hut last night. I wondered if he remembered much of what happened before he passed out. "Yeah. I was lucky. There'd be one less person on this journey today if he hadn't been there."

"I'm sorry."

"What? Why are you sorry?"

"I thought I could keep you safe. I didn't think that if I stepped away, it would put you in danger."

I shook my head. "It wasn't your fault, Elijah. Don't beat yourself up."

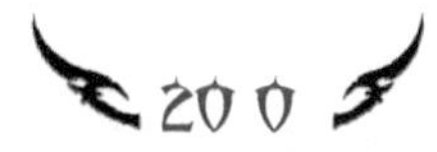

He sighed. "Sia—"

"We won't have to worry about something like that again. No more villages, remember? They aren't safe. We have better chances out in the Wastes with demons and wandering devils than we do in any village." I didn't want to talk about us. I knew without letting him finish that it was the topic he was going to bring up.

He nodded. "Okay."

The disappointment on his face told me that the bravery he had mustered up to talk to me about us had died off a little. It might not last as long as I would hope, but it would buy me some more time. There were more important things to address anyway.

"Keep your eyes peeled for firewood in a few hours. We don't know if the next area will be barren or not."

"Right. I can attach a small bundle with the straps on my backpack."

"Great. I wish I would have had that the first night I was out on my own. I had to carry an armload for a while before using my belt to bundle it all. My hands were sweaty and sore by the time I stopped."

"I can imagine."

"I'll also see if I can spot a rabbit or lizard."

"Tired of cornbread and apples already?"

I made a face, and he laughed at me. I couldn't help but chuckle along with him.

Hours later, we stopped at the first suitable area that we found. The lightheadedness I had been feeling never went

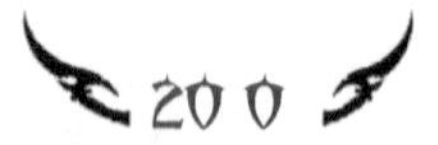

away, and the more we walked, the more groggy and strange I felt. The sweat beading on my brow felt chilled, too. Even when the wind blew, I didn't feel a reprieve from the heat. I must have looked as off as I felt because Elijah pressed his wrist against my forehead while his free hand measured the temperature of his own. The results were less than favorable because he frowned at me.

"You feel like you're starting to have a fever."

Gently, I pushed his hand away. "I'll be fine after we eat and rest," I assured.

His hard expression turned in my direction spoke volumes of the lack of trust he had in my words. "We have more than enough firewood. We have food and clean drinking water. I'll set up camp on my own, and you rest early tonight. We won't make it far if you get worse than you are now."

I wanted to protest, but the moment I inhaled, I felt the world spin. I might be headstrong, but I wasn't stupid. Sighing loud enough to wake the dead, I shrugged off my bags and plopped down to rest against a small boulder. "Fine," I announced glumly.

"And she doesn't argue. Amazing."

"Ha, ha. I would if I felt better," I admitted.

He tossed me the bag of apples. "If you can stomach it, eat one, and I'll set everything up. Okay?"

For the next several minutes, I watched Elijah make our sleeping area, organize our things, and start the fire. It didn't take long before he was helping me to my feet and forcing me to lay down on the blankets.

"I didn't think it was possible, but you look worse now than you did a little while ago."

"What every woman dreams of a handsome man telling her. Be still, my heart." I said it and instantly regretted

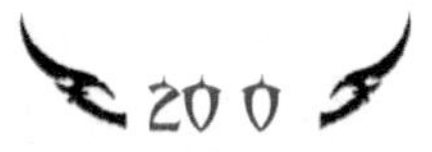

it. The thoughts that he was having were plain for anyone to see. I needed to dodge the bullet and fast. As I lay down, I winced like I was in pain and held my head.

His hands flew out to grab me like I was going to fall over. "Take it slow."

"Water," I rasped.

Elijah grabbed my canteen and handed it to me. I chugged generously and handed it back, saying, "I … I think I'm going to take a nap."

"I wouldn't be too surprised if you're out for the count until morning."

Fear took hold of me then. "Don't stray far from the camp," I sluggishly warned.

"Why?"

"Just promise me you won't go far from me."

"Okay. I promise, Sia."

I didn't want to tell him my devil didn't give a damn if he lived or died. He only saw him as bait and nothing more. If he couldn't serve his purpose, or if he became a problem, Draki would watch him being flayed alive without batting an eyelash. If the devil got angry enough, he just might be the one to perform the action. As long as Elijah stayed near me, he was safe. With me being under the weather, I didn't trust my body to obey my thoughts, which made my ability to save him like last time out of the question.

"Sleep, Sia," Elijah said with a smile. His hand reached out and covered my eyes, blotting out the sunshine.

I couldn't help it. I smiled and closed my eyes. His hand felt so warm. His touch wasn't like Draki's. It didn't burn. It was soothing and inviting. Even though we were out in the Wastes, I didn't feel vulnerable. I felt safe. And despite the hour, I managed to drift off to sleep in no time at all.

Chapter 19:

Keeping the Fires Burning

Elijah sat by the fireside with the machete while watching Sia sleep. Her deep umber skin was glossy with a thin coat of sweat that glistened under the dying rays of the setting sun. He had long ago removed his shirt and used a clean corner of it to pat her forehead dry, but it was to no avail. Though she rested soundly, he worried that her illness would soon worsen. Once the sky turned dark, he covered her with a blanket and tended to the fire.

"She's a rather troublesome thing, isn't she?" Draki's voice asked.

Standing to his feet and pointing the blade into the yawning abyss of the night, he frantically spun in a circle looking for the culprit. He shouted, "Who said that? Who's there?"

A dark chuckle boomed through the camp. "Oh, please. Put the weapon down. You know very well who I am."

Slowly, Elijah complied with the voice. "What do you want?"

"Just to chat, young man."

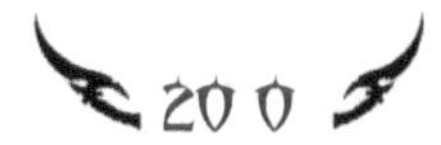

Narrowing his eyes at the pitch black surrounding him, Elijah said, "Show yourself."

"First, promise that you will follow and listen to me."

There was silence as the words were weighed. The fire popped, and Sia turned over with a light moan. Quieter than before, Elijah asked, "If I do, she'll be safe?"

"Please, as if that is even a question. She is mine to protect. As long as she remains in this camp, she'll be fine."

"And me?"

Again, the laughter rose all around. "My, my. Aren't you a smart one? Very well, since you are listening to me, I will ensure you are protected … for now."

With one final look to Sia, Elijah made up his mind. "I promise."

"Stunning."

A small, red cloud of smoke formed in the air, and it grew, stretching and creeping out until it was the size of a man. But the man that came out of the smoke wasn't dark and devious in appearance. He was like a person who had been made from the whitest moonlight and fixed with blazing, golden eyes. His smile was dashing as he stretched an arm out to the side and motioned with the sweep of his vision for Elijah to walk with him. Silently, the two strode away from camp.

In a clearing a few yards away, the devil stopped and turned to face the young man. "I am Draki. Don't introduce yourself. I already know who you are."

Elijah looked angry as he asked, "What do you want?"

"It's nice to see that you don't lack a spine, lad. However, I recommend that you remain polite. You won't find me as kind when I'm upset," Draki warned. The quiet

settled in as the devil situated himself. "I'd be a blind fool if I acted like I didn't know what you felt for Sia."

Any attempt to hide his emotions was forgotten as the young man widened his eyes in surprise. Quickly, he tried to mask it and searched the surrounding barren land. "She's very attractive," he muttered.

Throwing his head back in laughter, Draki let unbridled mirth echo into the night. "My boy, you may find her beautiful, but the emotions that you have for her go further than her pretty face."

Elijah blushed at that. "Is she supposed to be off limits or something?" he asked heatedly.

"Ha, quite the contrary."

"What?"

"Did you think I had some claim on her? I promise you, things that I want are far from the flesh."

"You don't … have any ties to her romantically?"

"I'm a devil, boy. Not a lovesick human. I've no need for emotional ties in this world."

"Why are you telling me this?"

"I didn't want you to give up on her. That's all."

Shaking his head, Elijah said, "I don't believe you."

Sighing, Draki stepped closer as he spoke. "Honestly, she is on a time limit. Though I may not like all the stipulations that she put on our deal, I will adhere to them. One of the conditions is that I had to keep her best interests in mind. That is where you come in."

"How so?'

"Let's just say that you caring for her is a form of protection in itself."

"You want me to be with her?"

"To put it quite simply, yes."

"What does she want?"

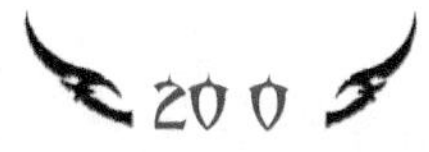

The devil grinned. "I suppose if you give up, you'll never know the answer to that."

"I'm not forcing her—"

"You won't have to. She's struggling with finding excuses on why you two can't be together and failing as it is."

"I still don't understand why you are telling me this."

"Because I'm fulfilling part of my deal with her by doing so. If she keeps this up, it's going to push you away, and that is only going to end horribly for her. I'm merely giving you a pep talk, man-to-man. Don't give up on her. She deserves a guy like you in a world like this."

Chapter 20:

Seeing Double

I woke up to the sound of whispers. My head was pounding, and my face felt swollen. I held my brow, and instantly a cold sweat drenched my palm. Grimacing at the unwelcomed feeling, I peered through one eye to the top of the tall boulder I was lying next to. There were two forms there, watching me while I slowly woke up. I instantly went still. As my vision came to and focused on them, I could make out their finer details despite the surrounding shadows.

The first was thin with hair down to the top of his shoulders that held soft waves to the blond strands. His full lips looked like they were permanently stuck in a pout, and his soft-blue eyes looked like they were full of unspoken sadness. He wore a billowy, white, button-up shirt with frilled sleeves that belled out. His pants were black leather and looked as though they had been painted on him. The outfit suited his lithe-framed body. The firelight danced over his smooth, glass-like skin as he looked down at me with an intense stare.

"She's too pretty," he almost whined.

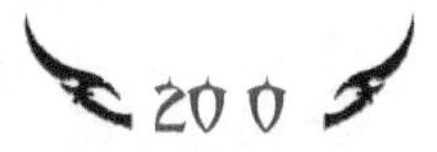

The second figure replied in a voice that felt like sandpaper over my skin. It was rough, slow, and disturbed things deep inside me. "If you like her beauty, take it."

This one had blue eyes like the one next to him, but his azure gaze was colder, and it complemented his short, blond hair. Unlike the thin and dainty being at his side, this one was bulky and large. A scar dragged down over his left eye, making the iris a milkier white than the one in the right socket. The scar itself was ugly and pronounced and disrupted the chiseled features surrounding it. He wore a red T-shirt and a pair of deep blue jeans. His arms alone looked like they could snuff out my life. Everything about him was beefy, and not an inch of skin went without muscle.

I tried to reach around me, looking for my machete, but I came up empty-handed. A quick glance at the campsite told me that Elijah wasn't there. It didn't take me long to presume that he had probably left to get something and took the blade with him for protection. Maybe he went to the bathroom, or … my gaze drifted back to the two perched on the rock next to me.

"Looking for something?" The larger male asked with a narrowed gaze.

"Hopefully, it isn't a weapon," the thinner one muttered. "That would be rude."

I swallowed hard and went very still. "What do you two want?" I knew they were devils. They had to be wandering ones.

"We were passing through, and you looked most peaceful and elegant. I told Midas that I wanted to watch you sleep." His stare burrowed into me in an unpleasant way. "I really do like her eyes, Midas. They remind me of the river."

I didn't like the way he said that.

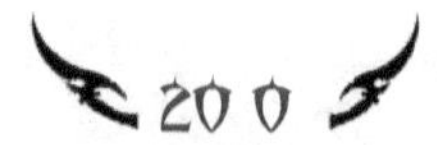

"Her eyes, eh?" Midas watched me as he seemed to weigh something over in his mind. "I suppose I can get them for you." He leaped down from the rock and landed next to me, but I didn't hear him hit the ground. My heart clawed up my throat as he loomed over me with his hands slowly reaching out toward my face.

"No need, Midas," the thin male expressed.

Midas stopped in mid-action. "Are you sure, Cain? I can get them for you if you want them."

Cain sighed. "No. They look better on her …" He gave me a look and smiled, but the curve of his lips came across as sinister rather than kind. "For now."

My eyes widened in fear. I wanted to instinctively hold my hands over my eyes. Should I thank him for letting me keep them? Was there any real etiquette with a devil, or did you just pick what you wanted to say carefully so they wouldn't devour you out of sheer anger? Hopefully, they didn't see me as too weak to defend myself.

"Shouldn't you be thanking me?" Cain asked with aggression lining every word spoken.

"You can't expect much of her. She is only human, after all," Midas grumbled.

I never thought I was going to have to thank someone for letting me keep what was already mine. My foggy brain stumbled for a reply. "Uh …"

Scoffing, Cain pointed his nose in the air as he said, "Of course, you would have horrible manners. I don't know why I expected more of you. It really is such a shame that you have those beautiful eyes. They are quite remarkable."

"Thank you," I whispered.

"Ha. You're welcome," Cain mumbled, flipping his soft curls behind his shoulder.

"Are you sure you want her to keep them?" Midas asked. "You could put them in a jar."

"I changed my mind," Cain said.

"Please leave," I said quietly. Instantly, my hand balled up on the ground and squeezed the sand in my palm like I could make water come out of the grains in my grasp.

"What a nasty little thing you are," Cain said with a snarky laugh. He slipped from the boulder and drifted down like he was a human-sized feather and gently landed on the shoulder of Midas. Perched on the larger male, his eyes followed me as I slowly rose up from my bedding. "You're a brave girl to try and tell me where to go," Cain growled.

"Or stupid," Midas snarled quietly.

Waving the thought away, Cain tilted his head up smugly as he said, "And here I thought she was going to be someone worthy enough to take to our village. We've collected so many pretty things over the years." He sighed as his eyes rolled over my body. "I think she would dull our collection now that I've gotten a closer look."

"Then you should have your eyes inspected," Draki replied as he stirred the fire. The flames rose and lit up the area, making his stark-white appearance more like a haunting image as the orange light swayed over his robes and hair. "She is a treasure to me. Are you saying that I have bad taste?"

Both of the devils gasped. Cain jumped off of the larger devil with wide eyes of surprise. Once on his feet, Midas protectively pushed Cain to stand behind him as he eyed over Draki and tried to gauge his next move. "You want this human?"

The twig was tossed into the pit, and the fire consumed it with ease. "Oh, please, like you didn't smell me on her. I'd love to hear your reasoning for why you thought it

would be wise to pester what belongs to me. Are you that incapable of controlling your desires and urges that you have to steal from other devils now?"

"We were only curious," Midas said confidently.

"Perhaps you were, but … what of Cain? Was he really curious, or was he here to try his hand in attempting to take something that doesn't belong to him?"

From behind the protection of Midas' mammoth body, Cain looked to Draki through narrowed slits. His pout looked angrier, and his expression dripped with vile emotions as he took in every perfect inch of the devil that belonged to me. "I wouldn't dream of taking something you've staked claim to, my lord."

"Good, then. Leave," Draki ordered, and his eyes told the two that they were to leave in the direction he had silently chosen.

Slipping past the two devils on the defense, Elijah tapped me on the leg and mouthed *"Are you okay?"*

I nodded in reply.

In a huff, Cain kicked at the dirt and stormed off into the night, mumbling things under his breath. Midas bowed to Draki as he said, "Forgive our intrusion." Right after, he disappeared from sight as he rushed to catch up with the other angry devil.

"Are they going to come back?" I asked as I watched until the shadows swallowed up their fading silhouettes.

"Not if they know what's good for them," Draki snapped under his breath.

Elijah crawled closer and placed his wrist over my forehead. "Hold still. I want to see if your fever has gone down any." There was a moment of silence as he checked to see if it had eased up. "You still feel pretty hot. You need to get some more rest," he informed.

Honestly, all the excitement had almost made me forget about how crappy I felt. Almost. As I turned to look at him and lie about feeling fine, the world spun, and I felt like I was going to be sick. I swallowed the lie and mumbled, "Yeah. I think you're right." There wasn't a point in denying it. As the words left me, a new wave of sickness overcame me.

Elijah must have seen it because he helped me lie back down after wiping the sweat from my brow. "Come on. You don't need to push yourself so hard, Sia. Lay down already."

I didn't want to fight it anymore. Momma always told me rest was best. Meemaw would always agree with her, and—on the nights that I was really bad—Daddy would always check my fever, wipe my brow, and make sure I was covered up throughout the night. Maybe it was the fever, or maybe it was the sudden sleep spell that hit me, but it felt like I was back home for a moment. Surrounded by people that loved and cared for me. Even though the blankets harbored tiny rocks and bits of sand and the fire crackled loudly, I could close my eyes and feel like I was there again. In no time at all, I was fast asleep.

Chapter 21:

Fever Dreams

Throughout the night, I tossed and turned. I rarely stayed comfortable for long. I was hot. I was cold. I was drenched in so much sweat I could have wrung the water out of the blankets. Every time I turned over, the world felt like it was swaying from side to side. I hadn't felt like that since I was little. I would constantly touch the ground to tell myself that everything wasn't spinning, but it didn't help for long. The fire was both a blessing and a curse as its flames lapped and curled around the wood it ate. The heat was desired one minute and despised the next. The occasional breeze was no different. I smacked my lips and felt them drier than the dirt around me. I tried to flop around and find my water canteen but would fall asleep before I could. It felt like this went on for hours, though I wasn't sure.

Time felt like an illusion. I felt someone lift my head, I felt cool water touch my lips, and I heard his icy voice as he said, "This isn't the kind of suffering I want to watch you go through." And then—feeling a slight reprieve from my torment—I fell asleep again. Only, my dreams were less kind than what my fever was putting me through in the waking world.

The world looked more desolate than I remembered it to be. The entirety of the surrounding stretch of desert and sky were washed in dull hues of sandy yellow, making everything feel dingy and worn. Like a filter of aged filth had been plastered to my eyes. I could taste the heat in the air, and as the wind picked up, dirt struck my cheeks, and I had to cover my face to keep my vision free of the flying sand. Once the strong breeze died down, I lowered my arm and tried to understand where I was. Everything felt familiar and yet very strange.

In the distance, I could hear people talking, and I saw my village, but the surrounding wall was no longer standing. It had been removed. I could see Momma, Daddy, and Meemaw standing outside our house. Frantic to feel their arms around me once more, I ran toward them. However, my legs didn't know how to move right. I kept falling, and no matter how much I struggled, I couldn't run. Opening my mouth, I tried to call out for them as I crawled on the ground. My throat felt tight, and my voice couldn't produce more than a whisper. Tears of frustration welled in my eyes.

"Please, hear me! Momma! Daddy! Meemaw!" But it wasn't loud enough. It was hardly louder than the wind. The sun was setting, and everyone was waving goodnight as they turned to go to their respective homes. My hand stretched out to them as they turned and went inside. I don't know why, but watching the action broke me. I didn't want them to go inside the house. There was a danger that was riding on

the coattails of the setting sun. There was a darkness that was
hidden within the encroaching night.

"Stop. Come back," I begged.

They didn't listen to me, though. The door shut. The
sun's rays were no longer touching our little village.
Suddenly, there was a scream from deep within the collection
of homes. A woman ran between the buildings and then was
tackled to the ground by a group of hungry grunts. I covered
my mouth as the tears spilled down. My eyes darted from the
vision of the woman being devoured alive. Without warning,
the thatched roofs were covered in hungry flames that were
spreading faster than what I thought fire could move. My
heart was in chaos, my mouth was unhinged in horror, and
my ears were hearing a symphony of destruction. Every
noise and vision was drenched with terror. The air was
drowning in drawn-out howls, the wild popping of the
spreading fires and blazing embers, and the tormented
screams of the villagers.

My attention was seized by the shifting shadows that
surrounded the place I had grown up in. Around it were
people that I had met along my journey, and they were
linked—hand in hand—with one another as they joyfully
danced in a circle around my burning house. Inside, I could
hear my family cry and scream in distress. All the while,
those standing outside cackled and skipped about merrily.

"Stop!" I shouted, coming to my feet and trying to
run to them. I could save them if I could get there fast
enough. I know I could.

Penelope turned around. She was broken away from
the circling dancers, and her eyes were full of rage as she
spoke to me with an intense heat lacing each word she spoke.
"This is all your fault! They were safe until you broke them

free. The devil was keeping them safe. You destroyed this village. You'll destroy us all. Stop trying to save us!"

I felt like I had been slapped. "No. You're wrong!" But I could hear the doubt in my own voice.

"You'll take away their only protection. This is your fault. Your fault!" Penelope shrieked.

From within the home, I heard Momma scream, and I saw Daddy's hand slap against the glass of the window. His fist began to pound on the surface, trying to break free. The door bowed as my family slammed their weight against it to try and get out. Gerald and Alan kept it shut while laughing and mocking my family's panic-stricken voices.

"Let them out," I begged.

The smoke and bright, glowing embers from the fire rose and mingled until they blacked out the little remaining light that spilled out from behind the nearby mountains. Starlight was hidden with billowing, ebony clouds, and my heart felt like it was stuck inside the clenched fist of a possessive demon.

Someone tapped my shoulder. Fear gripped me. I noticed that I was holding the machete in my hand. I wasn't sure when it had appeared, and I didn't care. It was a way for me to protect myself. I turned and thrust the blade into whatever was behind me and growled, but my eyes instantly widened. I gasped as I realized who I had sunk the blade into. Elijah looked down to the metal sticking out of the middle of his chest as blood poured out of his mouth.

Torpidly, his eyes drifted back up to lock with my own. "Why, Sia?" he whined in a voice strained with unfathomable agony and then slumped into the sand.

I screamed and didn't know what to do with my hands. I didn't know where to touch him. I was too afraid to touch him. "No. No. No. I'm sorry. Please," I hiccupped and

sniffled. "Please don't die, Elijah. Stay with me. I didn't mean to. I didn't mean any of this. Please!" Nothing that I said was working. He was still bleeding, and I was still to blame. "I'm sorry! Please!" I wailed.

From across the way—not far from the chaos—stood Draki, the perfectly white blizzard amidst the unforgiving desert. His robes billowed and hair gently flowed around him. A faint smile formed on his face as he fixed his gaze upon me. Slowly, he opened his arms, saying, "I can stop all of this. I can take away the pain, and I can stop the torment. Just come to me. Choose me, Sia, and I'll save them."

I didn't care if it was a lie. I believed it and ran to him, weeping. "Save them, Draki. Please. Please. I'll do anything."

His arms fell around me, and then his fingers bit into my skin. I whimpered and looked up to his molten golden gaze as he breathed, "*Anything*?" And his face dipped down to mine. His mouth pressed against my lips, and every fear was burned away.

A blazing kiss consumed my lips, and I didn't fight it. I didn't even try to stop him. Instead, I kissed him back like it would save all of their lives.

I woke up screaming at the top of my lungs, and I could feel every article of clothing clinging to my sweaty body. With one look around me, I noticed that the fire was still burning, and it was just before dawn. Elijah jolted out of his bed and hurriedly crawled over to me.

"Did you have a bad dream?" he asked, his voice thick with sleep.

I took in a breath, and my mouth felt unbearably dry. Nodding to answer him, I looked around me for my canteen.

"Yours is empty," he informed and rushed to gather his and brought it to me. "Here."

Graciously, I took it and chugged. Pulling it away from my mouth, I panted. "I had a nightmare," I whispered.

"Want to talk about it?" Elijah asked.

I looked at him, confused. "My nightmare?" Why would anyone want to talk about the horrors our minds cooked up while we slept? You went through it once. Why relive it?

"Yeah. My mom used to do it with me when I was younger," he said with a smile. "After hearing what scared me, she'd tell me that it was over and that I held all the power. After that, she and I would sit in my room for a few minutes to turn my nightmare into a dream by going through each part of it and changing how it happened."

"You made your nightmare … into a dream."

He nodded. "Yeah. That's what we did."

And it clicked in me then. I felt like I had been locked in a cage and tortured, and Elijah had just handed me the keys to my freedom. It was an enlightening moment, despite the headache that consumed my mind. As I held my hands over my eyes, I could see Elijah look me over with concern from between the slits of my fingers.

I waved him away, saying, "I'm okay. Just a headache."

"Let me check the bags and see if I packed something that will help reduce your fever."

I didn't want to nod. Every movement made my brain hurt, so I sat still and waited for him to go check. A

minute or two passed before he returned and dropped a pill in my hand, saying, "Take this."

Without a second thought, I did. Then I laid back down. "We'll need to leave soon."

He laughed at me. "Not with you in this state. We'll have to wait until tomorrow. Besides, I need to refill our water before we go anywhere. You went through a lot of it last night."

"What? We have to keep moving toward the faith city!" I declared.

"Whoa, there. The faith city isn't going anywhere, Sia. You need to rest and heal up. If we try to drag you along while you aren't in good health, we could just make matters worse. Then we won't be in a better situation and might have to wait longer before we can continue."

I groaned and looked away from him. "I'll be fine," I lied.

"That's you being stubborn."

I sighed. "So?" I expressed with a pout.

"Just let me take care of you. As soon as your fever breaks, we'll be on the move again, okay? But, please, trust me on this."

Slowly, I turned back to him and felt my heart break at the vision of his pleading eyes. That look reminded me too much of my nightmare. It reminded me that I was dangerous to anyone that would ever try to get close to me.

"Why, Sia?"

"You win," I stated in a hushed tone. "We'll wait."

He dipped down and kissed my forehead, and my heart flipped. I was too weak to fight him off, and the feeling of his lips pressed against my skin was welcomed. Everything inside screamed for me to kill the emotions that were surging through me, but—for just this once—I let them

travel through me without hindrance. Soon after, I closed my eyes and drifted back to sleep.

Chapter 22:

On the Road Again

For the next day, Elijah watched over me and made sure that my fever was broken whenever it rose. Our water was replenished, and the last of the cornbread was eaten with a side of sliced apples. Though I was angry that we were not making progress on our journey, I was thankful for a day of resting. No chores, no labor, no responsibilities, and no running for my life. I just lounged about as Elijah cut apples and fed me slices despite my protesting and constant giggles. I couldn't blame him for continuing to do it. It's kind of hard to believe a girl laughing and snatching food from your grasp while trying to bite your fingers playfully was actually upset with you. For all the negatives, a day spent with a fever and lying around by the fireside wasn't so bad.

Shortly after lunch, we agreed that it would be safe to head out the next morning. Draki hadn't made an appearance. I honestly hadn't expected him to and was thankful for it. By the time the sun had set, I knew that the devil had his twisted reasons for letting me suffer through the fever and not traveling for a day.

The night passed by quickly. By the light of the following day, we packed up, doused the fire, and headed out once more. We made sure to keep a steady pace that wouldn't push my weary body too hard.

A few hours before nightfall, we found our next campsite. Quickly, I dropped everything I was carrying and sank down to rest. I might have been ready to be on the move again, but my body wasn't happy about it.

"You didn't push yourself too hard, did you?" Elijah asked as he set down his things.

"Not like I could if I wanted to. Between you dragging your feet and my weak body, we never moved above a snail's pace."

He chuckled at me. "Since you're still not at a hundred percent, I'll gather firewood for tonight."

I listened to him as my eyes scaled a small mountain. "That incline isn't so bad, and even though it's small, it could give me a pretty good survey of the land."

He looked over to it and nodded. "Yeah, you're right. You sure you don't want me to do it?"

I shook my head. "No. I'm hoping that I can sweat out any of the remaining illness in me by climbing it. I'd like to see more than rocks and sand anyway."

"All right, but be careful," he warned. "Last thing we need is you getting a broken leg because you don't know how to take it easy."

I rolled my eyes with a smile. He knew me too well after such a small amount of time. I didn't know if I should be thankful or if I was cursed. "Yeah, yeah. I'm just hoping to spot a lizard to cook up. I think I'm turning into an apple," I muttered.

"I'll keep an eye out too," he stated, waving around a long stick he had sharpened before heading off to gather wood.

He stayed close by while I climbed the mountain. Though it was more of a steep, enormous hill than anything. Once I reached the top, I stood in awe of the beauty stretched out before me.

The river ran up and split far ahead. The mountains were hugging the stream of water as it cut through the land. I could see scarce wooded areas, endless cacti rolling over the rocky terrain, and sandy dunes further beyond our camp. But the real beauty was the silver city that sprung up miles away like a glistening spire sprouting out from the dusty land. It was a beautiful beacon of hope, and there were no words to describe the emotions that swelled within me when I gazed upon that city. I had never seen a faith city. However, I didn't need to. Just one look at it from afar, and I knew—without any doubt—that it was Saint Augustine.

There was no controlling my tears or the excitement as I bellowed out, "I see it!" Gleefully, I turned around with a grin splitting my face in two, and laughed without restraint as I half-slid my way down, shouting, "I see it! I see it!" over and over again.

Elijah rushed to the bottom of the incline after hearing all the commotion. "What's going on?"

I practically jumped into his arms, and he quickly dropped the firewood so he could catch me. I laughed loudly and hugged him around his neck. "Saint Augustine, the faith city, I can see it! We are only a day away … maybe two," I admitted joyfully.

His embrace tightened around me, and he quickly spun us around. Elijah's laughter spilled out from his mouth like the deep ringing of a bell. I could tell that this made him happy, too. A place not ruled by devils. A place free from demons. A place within this vast, empty world that we could call home.

We could call it home.

No more wandering around the Wastes dodging grunts and vicious demons of every rank. No more devils and pacts, just a place where we could settle down and live out the rest of our days. As Elijah whirled around with me in his arms and those thoughts hit me, another (far crueler) thought slithered into my mind. I remembered the nightmare and Elijah being stabbed by me. I remembered the sadness in his eyes as he asked me, *"Why, Sia?"* All my happiness came to a screeching halt. Gently, I patted his shoulder and awkwardly cleared my throat.

"Sorry about that. I got carried away," he said with a nervous cough. Looking down, he realized the pile of wood he had dropped and gasped as he turned to look at the sky. Groaning, he shook his head. "I need to get back to gathering more firewood. You won't be mad if I leave this for you to gather together, will you?"

Laughing lightly, I shoved at his arm and pointed with my chin to an area that was most likely going to have more lumber than what was around us. "Go. I don't mind."

He gave a quick smirk and kissed my cheek before darting off to finish his task. I held my cheek and felt a sickness take over me. One that was caused by knowing that I felt pure happiness when he did little things like that, and all I could offer him was pain.

I spent the next few minutes hating myself as I gathered the sticks, took them to camp, and started setting up our space for the night. No matter how hard I tried to tell myself that everything was going to be all right, I didn't manage to convince myself. In fact, it felt like a nightmare. And that is why I used the little time that I had left before Elijah came back to turn it all around. It could be a dream. I could erase every horrid thought, action, and feeling and turn it all into something new, right?

I had to. If I wanted there to be anything good left in this world, I needed to change how I viewed things. Or I could only blame myself for the outcome in the end.

The dying breath of the sun was extinguished behind the face of the mountains just as we had given life to our fire, which would keep us warm throughout the night. Luckily for us, while Elijah was gathering the last of the wood, he had come across a black-tailed jackrabbit and cornered it. Needless to say, he used his sharpened stick and a rock to finish the job, leaving us with a meal that would give us the energy we'd need for the days ahead.

Oddly enough, pairing the cooked meat with a couple of raw apples brought out the flavors of both and made eating the fruit a little more bearable. We both longed for something more, though.

"I wish we would have come across some wild berries or vegetables. Eating nothing but apples and cornbread for days on end is doing nothing for my energy levels," I admitted. It felt like it was a contributing factor to my recovery time taking so long, too, which only left a sour taste in my mouth.

Elijah was stoking the fire with the stick as he replied, "Yeah. I've noticed that it's been harder for us to wake up lately, too. Our bodies are trying to make up for the lack of a decent diet."

Tired, I massaged my face and agreed. "Yeah."

"How long do you think it will take, again?"

"Hmmm?"

"You know, until we get to the faith city. How long do you think it's going to take to get there?"

I took a moment to think about it. Remembering the distance, I sighed as I came to accept the reality that I had denied when I saw the glistening city. "Probably going to need to split it up into two days," I admitted.

"Oh," he replied with a crestfallen expression.

I sympathized with him. I didn't want to spend any more time out here than he did. Especially because I knew that he was in far more danger than I would ever be. Knowing that little tidbit of information made me want to lift his spirits. "It won't be that bad. Just one more night sleeping under the stars. After that, we'll be at the front gates of Saint Augustine."

"I wonder what it will be like," he stated with a far-off look in his eyes.

Lying down, I stared up at the glittering night sky as I pondered what it would be like. A slow smile crept over my lips. "It'll feel like we are free. No fear of being attacked. No worries on how we'd survive. It will just feel like we are at ease."

He mirrored me as he settled in for the night. "I like the way that sounds."

When I looked over at him, the scar on his arm snatched my smile away and reminded me that the life I lived in my village was happy compared to his. He was raised in a world where every daily task was soaked in worry. In his world, if you did too much, you would perish, and if you did too little, the place you called home would fall apart, the farms would wither, and the people would starve. He lived in constant worry of whether or not his actions were too much or too little, and his body and mind bore the marks either way it went. A fresh wave of guilt hit me just as he turned to look at me with a warm curve of his lips.

"I'm sorry," I whispered to him.

Looking confused, he asked, "For what?"

I looked away as I replied. "For life not being fair … for any of us."

He gave a short, soft burst of laughter. "It hasn't been, but in two more days, we won't have to say *sorry* to each other ever again. Not unless we do something wrong."

The words hurt. They hurt so much because I couldn't promise him that I wouldn't wind up doing just that. "Yeah," I said in a hardly audible tone. I was glad that it sounded like I was tired. I was happy that he didn't say anything else because I was battling myself, and none of it was pretty. As my emotions threatened to rip the ability to speak from me, I said, "Goodnight," before my words would sound too rattled. Closing my eyes, I hoped that we could sleep peacefully through the night.

A sound nearby had jerked me awake. It wasn't morning yet. I lay completely still for a moment, afraid that my movement would bring attention to myself. My eyes walked the space between where I rested and where Elijah had made his own bed. He was staring back at me, and my heart skipped a beat as I hadn't expected his eyes to be open and looking right at me. As the panic ebbed from my limbs, he raised a finger in front of his lips and pointed to behind me.

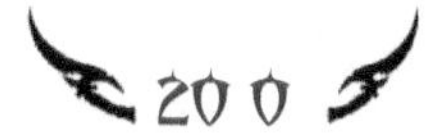

Even though I was riding the fear that was gripping me, I had to wonder where that worthless devil of mine was now. He always seemed to be gone when I needed him. He always saved me, but how many of his actions were for me, and how many were an elaborate scheme that fed his own personal enjoyment?

The thoughts were broken as the sound of a snapping twig snatched my attention away, and I turned swiftly to face the direction the noise had come from. Straining my eyes, I tried to search the murky shadows blanketing the land around us. As my vision adjusted to the lack of light, I could see a huddled form hopping around a few yards away. It took a pause and lifted its face into the air as it sniffed, and I could see its eyes glow in the moonlight.

It was a grunt.

From what I could tell, it was alone and probably attracted to the fire. But when I had that thought, I remembered roasting the rabbit earlier, and my face twisted with disappointment at my own stupidity. The remains of our dinner hadn't been disposed of properly. It wasn't attracted to our fire. It was attracted to the scent of fresh blood and meat!

Quickly and quietly, I turned to face Elijah again. I gave a pointed look to the leftovers from our dinner, and he followed the line of my gaze. As soon as he saw it, his face contorted in frustration. Balling up his fist, he went to slam it on the ground in a fit of rage and stopped inches from the dirt. Silently, he opened his hand and gently placed the palm on the ground to help steady his weight as he attempted to crawl over to it. Once there, he pointed to the carcass and then motioned that he would toss it over behind the grunt. I nodded. We didn't need the creature passing by us, and (hopefully) when its stomach was full, the grunt would

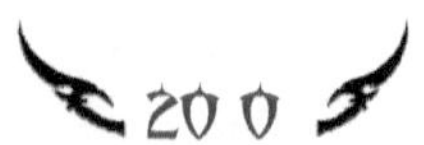

wander away from our camp. Even though the strategy seemed sound, my hand still instinctively wrapped around my machete as I tried to think of a backup plan … just in case.

I had been so lost in thought that I didn't realize Elijah was already about to throw the leftovers. Watching as he picked up the remains, I held my breath and hoped that everything would go according to plan. Realizing that the fire could gain the creature's attention, I grabbed my canteen and slowly snuffed out the flames. A hissing sizzle sprung out from the fire right as I heard a *thud* in the distance. Flashing my vision in Elijah's direction, he nodded in confirmation that it was him throwing the leftovers. Within seconds, the grunt gave a short, clipped hoot of curiosity before it scrambled over to the discarded meat and bones, sniffed it, and dived into its meal.

No matter how much I wanted to feel some form of relief over how everything seemed to be going as expected, my mind wouldn't let me. If I let down my guard, it could spell the end. As I sat there in a torturous limbo, I thought of how Draki had aided me in learning how to do more than senselessly hack at the air in blind fear. I remembered how he told me to hold the weapon. I remembered how he told me to stab. I remembered how he explained that I had to be in control of the blade's actions or I would be at the mercy of whomever I was protecting myself from. And I remembered that demons had no mercy.

"*Sia*," Elijah whispered. The frustration in his voice told me that he had tried to get my attention for a while now.

Blinking, I looked at him, confused, and replied back in a hardly audible tone, "What?"

Without a word, he pointed behind me and then put his hands up to his face. I didn't understand what he meant.

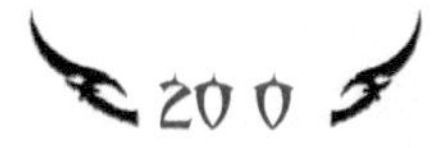

The look on my face told him that clearly. He looked exasperated and pointed to me and then, again, put his hands up to his face, hiding his features from me. Bending my brow, I clumsily attempted to decipher the message he was trying to convey. Just then, I heard sniffing and a twig snapping. It was close. Too close.

My body froze. The sudden realization of what Elijah had been trying to tell me was finally clear. He had been telling me to hide. Now I was worried that it was too late to. Slowly turning, I let my eyes scan the surrounding area where I had heard the grunt. It was hopping around and sniffing at the air. Getting up on my knees, I started to crawl backward and further away from the creature. The surrounding bushes hid most of my movements, and the fire, recently being put out, gave us more shadows to hide in. I wondered how long it would last, though.

A hand brushed over my own, and I flinched as the fear swelled within me. Noticing that it was Elijah's, I relaxed immediately and resumed looking forward. We were shoulder to shoulder and crouching as we kept our vision locked on the curious grunt's form as it hobbled and hopped behind the thin veil of the nearby bushes.

Elijah's mouth was close enough to me that I could feel his lips brush over the edge of my ear. I suppressed the urge to shiver and hyper-focused on the words he spoke. "We need to head away from camp. It seems like it will be lurking for a while."

Frowning, I looked over our simple chosen area. It wasn't much, but wherever we put our blankets down and lit a fire at was a temporary home. I had come to accept that. Feeling like I was being forced out of that made me angry and upset. It made me feel helpless. But all of those emotions were replaced with bitterness when I realized that Draki

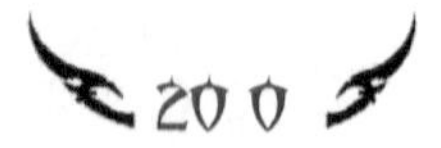

wasn't there to help me. It didn't seem like the barrier that was normally around the camp was present tonight. I hadn't seen him for a while. It almost felt like he had abandoned me. I didn't know how I should feel about that. Happy? Sad? My mind was a mix of emotions, and I didn't have time to really pick it apart because of the current threat. It didn't stop the ache in my chest or the sinking feeling from creeping over my whole being.

"Sia?"

Snapping out of my daze, I dared to look at Elijah and nodded while saying, "You're right. We need to find someplace further away from here." Then I started to head back to my sleeping area to try and grab a few things, or—at least—my bag.

Elijah's hand reached out, grabbed my wrist, and squeezed it in a vice grip. Looking at me, he shook his head. I didn't like that. I didn't want to think about how he was telling me to abandon everything. I never wanted to feel the way that I did that night that I fought for my life.

… I didn't want a reminder of everything that led to me making a monstrous deal with a devil.

He pulled at me and motioned with a pointed look and a jerk of his head in the opposite direction. We needed to get away before things got worse. Grunts might not be smart, but they were annoyingly persistent. If we didn't leave (and soon), we risked more than just one nipping at our heels.

Quickly and quietly, we turned and started to head away from the camp. We could wait it out somewhere safer until morning and come back to grab our things. The last thing I wanted to do was leave everything here. I couldn't let myself stop and think about what we were leaving behind. We needed to focus on surviving.

As we cautiously walked backward, we kept our vision glued to the grunt rustling about the shrubbery. But it was the sound of something snorting behind us that made my blood go cold. There was a laugh, one that was soaked in bloodthirsty snarls of delight.

A second grunt hissed at us.

Elijah spun around and spotted the creature. Not a fraction of a second passed before he drew back his leg and then kicked with all his might. The demon was punted further into the desert. Without skipping a beat, he took hold of my hand and spoke in a hoarse voice. "Run."

I didn't need to be told twice. I wrapped my fingers around his hold, and we both started to run just as the first grunt burst through the bushes with a bloodstained face and a howl of anger. We were already going as fast as our feet would carry us by the time the demon turned its mouth to the sky and shrieked, calling for its brethren. The sound made me spare a look over my shoulder. Letting Elijah guide me, I looked longer than I should have, and there wasn't a single thing I saw that I liked. Within the depths of the night, there were eyes—more than I could count—and they were all set on us. Shadowed bodies hovered around our camp, ripping open our bags and searching the contents therein. The rest of them were racing in our direction.

"Elijah," I whimpered.

"I know," he shot out.

In the darkness, we weaved through the vegetation and hoped we didn't come across a snake or other demons as we rushed through. The moon was a sliver of light in the blackened sky and gave little illumination along our path. As I felt the thundering of endless footfalls thrum over my own pounding soles as they collided with the earth below, I realized how screwed we were. But that thought only

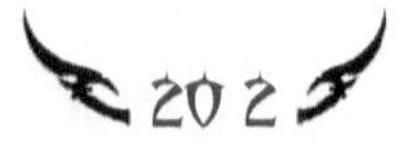

intensified as a high-pitched screech came screaming at us from somewhere off to the side and hidden behind the cacti littering the surrounding area. The blob that emerged and floated about made my stomach drop to my feet. A leech. Any hopeful thoughts were ripped away from me as the cry of the shadowed, wormy mass was answered by something deeper within the desert. It sounded larger, stronger, and like it was just another issue stacked onto our growing list of problems.

"This way!" Elijah yelled before tugging me toward the more rocky terrain.

My feet complied before I could register what he had said. "We're going to need to climb," I yelled to him.

He let go of my hand as he said, "Yeah. I see an opening further up. Maybe we can hide from them in there?"

"Hopefully," I said. However, everything in me doubted that we could hide from everything that was chasing us. I wanted to stop and think, but I couldn't. My body only knew one function, and that was to escape. My mind still felt foggy from my recent sickness, my limbs screamed with pain, my body was tired, and all I could think to do was to run toward the mountain and climb.

Sweat coated my face and dripped from my chin as we practically slammed into the steep incline at the base. My hands swept over the face of the rock as I tried to find something to help lift myself up. As I heard the approaching whoops and hollers, I yelped in frantic panic and searched faster. I only found smooth stone beneath the pads of my fingers. The fear that swelled within me swallowed any sensible thought. I only slapped over the warm surface of the mountain and hoped that I would find a groove … something. *Anything!*

"Over here!"

Elijah's voice made me feel like I had jumped out of my skin. Turning to face him, I saw him higher up, and I smiled. As I ran over, he said, "I'll come down, and you go up first."

"No."

"Sia—"

"Climb!"

Swiftly, I looked behind me and saw the grunts fast approaching. They were tripping over themselves and slamming gracelessly into the bushes and boulders. Flashing my gaze back to him, I shook my head. "No. It will waste time. Climb. CLIMB!"

It didn't take long for me to find the path that he had taken up the mountain, and I followed after him. As soon as the swarm of demons clashed with the base of the mountain, I couldn't help but scream, "Hurry!" up to him. Pebbles rained down on me as Elijah shuffled above me.

"Almost … there," he grunted between labored breaths.

"How close is the cave?"

"Uh …" He paused, and the silence stretched. "Maybe a couple of yards. But the ledge is pretty thin."

I looked down and watched as the grunts below struggled to climb. I eyed the machete at my hip and made a choice. "You hide first. I'll try to draw them away."

He reached the ledge, pulled himself up, and turned to help me. As soon as he had a hold of my arm, he locked gazes with me and said, "I'm not letting you risk yourself for me. Wherever you go, I go. We survive together, or we die together."

As I was pulled up, I let what he said sink in. But the truth wouldn't let those sweet words live long. On the ledge

with him, I replied softly, "Do you really think a devil would let someone die before they collect?"

His expression looked sad. I wanted to wash that look off of his face, but there wasn't time to talk. There wasn't time for much of anything. "I need you to trust that I can do this. You hide, I'll lure them away and come back."

From below, beneath the collected sounds of hungry grunts and cries of surprise as they fell down after failing to climb, there was a deep, unnatural scream. We both rushed to peer over the edge to see what it could have been. Combing through the crowd and flinging grunts out of its path was a larger shadow. Squinting, I noticed exactly what it was.

"A soldier," I gasped.

"We need to go."

I unsheathed my machete and forced Elijah to take it. "Go to the cave. Stay quiet and hidden. I'll come back." I went up on my tiptoes, kissed him, and pulled back whispering, "I promise."

Reluctantly, I pulled away from him and went in the opposite direction from the cave. I was thankful that it was enough of an incline that I didn't have to climb more than I needed to march up in a half-crawl. I took one last look at Elijah, and I watched him fade into the shadows of the cave as his eyes stayed fixed on me until the rocky walls wouldn't permit him to. Then I looked down the side of the mountain and noticed that the soldier was already a few feet from the ledge. I swallowed the urge to scream and quickened my pace.

"You won't get far!" The soldier snarled.

I heard it let out a roar as it leaped up, and its claws scraped over the surface of the ledge as it caught itself, and the demon hoisted itself up over the edge. I tried to move even faster. In my haste, my footing slipped, and I slid down

until I dug my nails deep into the crevices of the stone and halted my descent. Groaning in pain, I twisted and pulled myself up to my knees and started to climb again as I heard the mocking laughter of the demon hot on my heels. Already, a great number of grunts were pouring up over the ledge. Hot tears pricked my eyes, and I felt defeated when I saw some of the grunts head toward the cave.

I had failed.

As that thought crushed me, I felt long, bony fingers wrap around my ankle. I screamed and looked back to see the soldier had caught up to me sooner than I had anticipated. Ensuring my grip was solid, I held on with all my might and used my free foot to kick the creature in the face. It let go and fell only a foot or two away, and it angrily glared up at me as a handful of grunts started to climb up behind it.

I felt overwhelmed. I could hear metal slicing over stone resounding from the confines of the cave. My heart sank as I saw the numbers flooding the mountain. My mind raced. My eyes shifted about to try and find an escape. Finally, I let go of my pride and screamed out his name. I screamed so loud that I was sure something inside me broke.

"DRAKI!"

My pant leg was grabbed and jerked. I felt rocks slicing over my palms and my fingers burning as they tried to keep their hold. I quickly slid on my back, the rough surface tearing the skin as I fell toward the deadly embrace of the soldier.

However, in the twisted storm of demons, vicious laughter, and pointed teeth waiting to consume me down below, there was the flutter of perfectly flawless, pearl robes and long ribbons of snow-white hair overhead. A flash of golden eyes were spared in my direction before they snapped

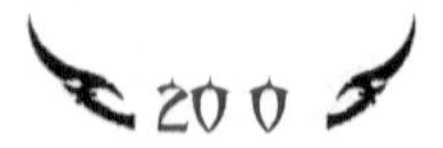

to their new target. A thin, glistening onyx sword was in his hand, and he slammed it into the throat of the soldier and swiftly pulled it away. A spray of crimson erupted into the night air and splattered all around us like red rain. It all happened so fast that I didn't hear him land near me. Draki hovered over me, his eyes burning into mine as I was brought effortlessly to my feet.

"I love to hear you lose all hope and call out my name," Draki admitted with an expression that looked hungry.

The nearby grunts hissed and whimpered as they scattered like cockroaches. Still a bit frazzled, I watched to be sure that it was safe to speak. After only a few seconds, I saw the cave and noticed that the few still brave enough to stick around had chosen the easier prey. I started to go in that direction, but Draki stopped me. Turning to him in confusion, I tried to wiggle my arm out of his grasp.

"Let me go. I need to help Elijah."

"I can't let you do that."

When I looked up at him, I saw that his face was free of emotion, just like when I had first met him. He wasn't teasing me or joking around. I didn't like that. It felt like he was brewing deep, dark ideas. Twisting my arm in his grasp, I tried again to break free.

"Stop it, Draki. Let me go!"

"I said that I can't let you do that. Stop struggling."

But I did just the opposite. I saw the grunts rushing for the opening, and I desperately fought Draki like I thought I could win against him. "Let me go! I have to save him!"

He didn't move. He just tilted his head and stared at me with an expression that felt dead. I screamed and went to hit him with my free hand. I should have known better. I should have known that I was fighting a battle that I couldn't

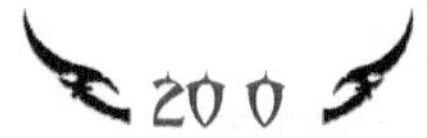

win. Before my hand could ever get close, he caught it in mid-air and glowered at me.

"Is this how you thank me?"

"I'm trying to save him. Please!" I yelled, tears streaming freely down my face.

"Why, Sia?"

"I'll come back. I promise."

"Please?" I begged and felt my chest rack with the urge to crumble at his feet. "Please?!"

Draki yanked me so hard that the feeling of absolute despair was ripped out of me, and I was forced into his blazing embrace. A clawed finger forced me to look up into those molten orbs of gold. "Beg me again," he demanded in a low, cold tone.

My lip quivered. "Please, let me go save him."

He brought his face even closer to mine and searched my gaze. "You realize that you are at *my* mercy, right?"

As he asked me, I heard a cry of pain erupt from down below, and it rolled out of the cave. My heart leaped up into my throat, and fresh tears welled in my eyes. I knew why this was happening. It was my fault. All of it.

"Yes. I'm at your mercy. Please, let me save him. *Please!*"

"Oh? You know that you are at my mercy, yet you have been avoiding your duty to me all this time, and you still have the bravery to beg me for favors?"

"I don't have time for games!" I screamed.

"Neither do I!" He snarled in my face. His hold on me got painfully rough, and I felt like I was being crushed instead of protectively embraced by him. "You've been avoiding the truth. You've been avoiding your end of the bargain. You've been cheating me out of what is mine! I'll hold true to our deal, but remember that you have to do the

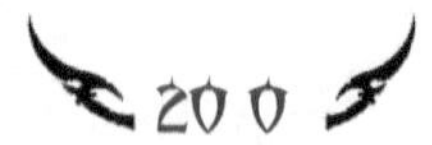

same, Sia." Heat caressed every word that came out of his mouth. Those lips were like fire, his tongue like a hammer, and he hatefully forged each sentence that he had spoken to me.

My face was still tilted up to look at him, but now my chin was forced by the tip of his razor-sharp claw instead of the gentle touch of his fingertip. Another cry came from Elijah as he fought for his life. Would it be better if I just let him die there, thinking that I would come back any moment and that I probably met a similar fate on the outside? Or should I crumble right here, knowing a worse fate awaited him later on down the road?

Licking my lips, I found the strength to speak. "Save him, Draki. I'll stop fighting it. I'm begging you. Save him."

As the grin formed on his face, a fresh tear rolled down my cheek. The devil leaned forward and gently kissed the droplet and whispered in my ear, "As you wish."

His form was there one minute and gone the next. Where the blazing touch had been was now caressed by the chilling cold of the growing night. Where he had once stood was the fading smell of spice and smoke. However, down by the cave, there were unnatural sounds and screams of agony. Fear gripped me, and I scrambled and stumbled down to the ledge and rushed for the opening on the side of the mountain. By the time I reached the entrance, I saw nothing but bodies and blood.

Worried that we were too late, I called out into the night-shaded abyss, "Elijah! Elijah!"

Between coughing and stifled groans of pain, he replied, "Yeah. I'm here."

My eyes slowly adjusted to the dark, and I spotted him deeper inside. The hand gripping the weapon was limp at his side, and his free arm cradled his stomach. I couldn't

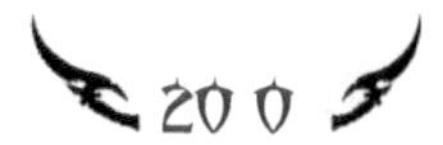

hold it back anymore. Seeing him made me call out his name, "Elijah!"

"I'm here," he rasped.

I never ran to a voice so fast.

As I ran to him, I felt the streams of tears freely falling down my face. This was all my fault. I slammed into him and heard the machete hit the stone underfoot.

"Whoa," Elijah expressed and laughed lightly as he wrapped the free hand around me. I could feel pain flare through my back and didn't care. He was holding me. He was alive. Nothing felt better than his arms around me.

I heard Draki speak to me from the mouth of the cave. Elijah didn't react at all, which meant he didn't see or hear him. I turned just enough to see his snowy attire, skin, and hair surrounded by the pitch of the late evening, and his outline doused in moonglow.

"Don't forget your promises to me, Sia, because if I repay the favor—you won't last a night without me—and Elijah will last even less than that."

Not wanting to see him anymore, I screwed my eyes shut and squeezed Elijah tight. All the while, I repeated over and over in my mind that this was my fault. Every cut and bruise, every fear, every pain, and every drop of blood lost … they were all my fault.

It was all my fault.

Chapter 23:

The Breakdown

I wanted to surrender to everything I had tried to escape from since I started this whole journey. From day one, I wanted to fall apart, but I knew that tears wouldn't save me, fix my problems, or keep me alive. There was no way to stop what had happened. I just needed to go on living and find a way to survive on my own. However, it was surviving that was slowly whittling me down. It was surviving that was a constant reminder that the life I lived was no longer available for me to go back to. Everything that brought me comfort and joy was miles away. I could only settle for shadows of those I loved, of those I left behind. A comb my momma made for me. A blanket my meemaw hand-stitched for me. A machete my daddy strapped to my hip. Reminders that I hadn't made it all up and that I was loved and missed somewhere far away from this dreaded place. It echoed in my broken heart with a sorrowful melody until I shattered into a million pieces. In the darkness of the cave, in a young man's embrace, I fell apart in a way I had never thought that I could. I opened my mouth to speak, but my soul had a song of tears to sing. My voice cracked, my body trembled, and I sobbed like it would mend every problem in my life.

I cried. I cried until my eyes burned, my head ached, my nose ran, and my throat felt raw. I cried until I didn't think there was anything wet left inside me, and then, I cried some more. All the while, Elijah hugged me and didn't say a word. He just let me scream and wail until I couldn't produce anything more than whimpers. He let me open a floodgate and release everything I had been holding back.

Sniffles and soft hiccups filled the cave as I started to regain my senses. My head was throbbing really bad, but I felt lighter than I had in a long time. It felt good to just let everything out instead of pretending I hadn't felt like weights were tied to me since the gates of my village closed in my face. I was tired of waltzing around in the Wastes, ignoring the emotions that I had locked away until I could deal with them. Truthfully, I knew that my life wouldn't slow down long enough for me to do just that, so I went through the motions of my day until I couldn't escape it anymore.

"Feeling better?" Elijah asked in a soft voice.

A shaky exhale left me. Slowly, I nodded and wiped my face off on the sleeve of my army jacket. "Yeah," I expressed with a raspy voice.

"Mind letting me in on why you fell apart?"

"I wasn't falling apart," I tried to lie and smirked even when I heard myself say it.

"Oh, right. This must be someone else's tears and snot," he stated, plucking at his very wet shirt.

"Obviously," I muttered and pulled back just enough to inspect the damage that I had inflicted on his attire. It had become a deeply blotted mess of wetness. Mimicking him, I pulled at the edge of his shirt, and I laughed lightly while motioning to his clothing. "I'll uh … wash that later."

"Yeah, well, let's get somewhere a bit safer first. As charming as a cave covered in grunt corpses is, I would

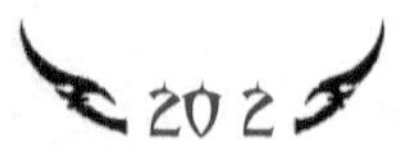

rather my clean shirt not take in their stench."

Wrinkling my nose, I giggled and nodded in agreement. "Yeah. I suppose we should be heading out, shouldn't we?"

"You need to stay put until I return. There is something that I need to handle," Draki explained with very little room for negotiations.

I spun around to face him. "How long will that take?"

"Long enough for me to ensure that the cave will be protected in my absence, so stay put until I get back."

"I take it your devil has given the order that further traveling is prohibited?" Elijah asked with an exasperated exhale.

As Draki disappeared from sight, I looked to the floor and sighed. "Yeah. He says we have to stay here until he gets back."

"And I bet he didn't say anything about an estimated time of arrival?"

"No."

He shook his head and ran a hand through his hair as he looked at each body that lay lifeless around us. "Suppose I should clean up, and we should try to catch some rest."

It was at that moment that I noticed the blood on Elijah's arm. "You're hurt!" Like the words were an incantation, I realized just how badly he had been injured. His arm was the least painful-looking among them. There was a cut on his T-shirt exposing the torn skin beneath it, caked in drying blood. There were puncture marks on his lower pant leg, meaning that there was sure to be a bite or two under the fabric. And, finally, on his forehead was a swelling knot that was accompanied by tiny claw marks.

I had been so absorbed in my own emotions that I hadn't even noticed. And while I fell apart in his arms, hugging him and thankful that he was alive, I hadn't even spared a moment to see if he had been injured. How selfish was I? How long was I going to carry out actions that hurt everyone around me? Why couldn't I be better?

It wasn't surprising that he looked at the wounds and smiled, saying, "I'm fine."

A lie he told me and himself, I'm sure. I pouted, displaying how bad I felt, and shook my head as I walked over to him. Taking his unharmed arm in my grasp, I pulled him over to a spot with the least amount of bodies, saying, "Sit down and let me handle the cleanup. You've done enough."

"Sia, I'm perfectly—"

"Injured. You're perfectly injured. That's what you were going to say, right?"

"Not exactly."

"I don't care what you were going to say, to be honest. I'm going to clean this up. You try to tend to your wounds until I can figure something out while I punt these grunt corpses off the ledge outside, okay?"

He laughed. "Okay, okay. You win, Sia. I'll be a good boy and sit here while you handle the tough stuff. I don't want you to punt me off the ledge, too, if I upset you enough."

"Good, because I just might." I pointed to the spot he was seated in. "Stay here and try to clean yourself up a bit. I'll be right back."

With that, I headed out of the cave with the first couple of limp bodies in my arms. I figured I could mull over ideas and think about a few things while lugging the lifeless demons around. I needed to keep my mind off of the way

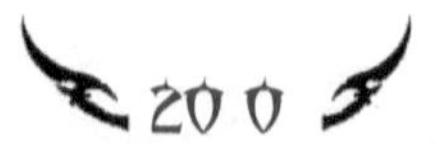

their bodies felt, the way their eyes stared up at me unchanging, like they would come back to life and attack me. The way their gangly limbs flopped about as I toted them along was unnerving. It made my skin crawl, really. Anything that kept my mind off of these disgusting truths was more than welcome.

I thought about trying to head back to get the things from our old camp. If I went now, and there was anything left, it would cut down our traveling time tomorrow. We still needed to get a few hours of decent sleep (at least), and we needed to tend to any wounds that we had. All in all, it was going to aid us in mending, resting, and recouping, but do nothing for our plans of reaching the faith city any time soon. That thought left a sour taste in my mouth. We were so close to where we wanted to be. We could stay here another night, but the pile of dead bodies that were stacking up at the base of the mountain proved that an evening free of roaming demons was less than likely. I tossed another grunt down and sighed. Traveling away from the cave and resting before our final travel was honestly the best idea, even if I didn't like our journey being prolonged. I just hoped that there were medical supplies still intact with our belongings.

After finishing cleaning up the remaining gore, I gathered a few measly twigs and anything that could be burned. My findings were minimal, and I wasn't brave enough to go to the base of the mountain to search for more. The fire would be small tonight.

There were whoops and chitters of excitement growing in the distance. Meaning that there were more grunts on their way. The heap of demons would be feasted on, that much was for sure. I knew that there was only safety inside the cave because of Draki. Still, I didn't want any creatures spotting me.

With my meager findings, I headed inside our newest dwelling and called out to Elijah. "I'm back."

He groaned while he stood up. "Welcome back. What did you find?"

I looked down at the small amount of wood in my arms. "Just some stuff to burn."

"Fantastic. I'm cold and can barely see my wounds."

"I thought you might say something like that, so I started gathering it after taking care of the mess."

"Thanks for all of that, by the way."

"You're welcome."

Slowly, I started to arrange the sticks and searched my pockets. Thankfully, Elijah still had the lighter on him. He produced a flame and held it up against the twigs and a few of the leaves. When the fire started to catch, I knelt down and started to gently blow on it until it grew and caught onto the rest of the piled wood. The glow instantly chased away the darkness that dwelled within. When I looked up, I was stunned by the scene my eyes rested upon.

Strange, white and black markings lined the walls, creating pictures that I couldn't make out from a distance. I stood up and bent my brow in confusion as I inspected them. My feet found themselves walking closer as I studied each line.

"What is i—" Elijah's question was quieted the minute he turned around. "Oh. Oh, I see."

The both of us crept up to the drawings that covered the rocky surface. It looked like the pictures made a story. Around it were words written in letters that looked familiar, yet they didn't form anything that I understood.

The pictures that were there looked both strange and alluring and resembled finger-paintings. Rough lines made images that I'm sure would have haunted me if I had been

alive during the time that the world had fallen apart. The ground was split and jagged, and from the depths of it crawled out black drawings of demons in all shapes and sizes. It bled into towns that were ablaze with fires, and the sky was choked with smoke. From between the billowing clouds were things that looked akin to shooting stars falling down toward homes with people weeping. In the distance, at the far end of the cave where hardly any light could reach, there was a massive pillar of black that bloomed out into a dome. Just seeing it made my stomach knot. I followed the twisted images that told a tale that broke my heart and made me realize just how bad that day must have been. Within the midst of all of these things, there were people kneeling. Around them was a white light, and above their heads was a giant star. They were doing something foreign to me as they bowed their heads to the ground and married their hands. I stared in confusion as I got closer, and tried to make out what was painted there. They seemed sad but … protected somehow.

"They called it Armageddon," Draki said from the mouth of the cave.

I looked over my shoulder to him. "What would you call it?"

His smile was quick and vile. "Deserved."

The look that dwelled in his golden gaze would follow me to the grave. There were a thousand unspoken words drenched in hate and dripping with malicious joy over the fact that people suffered, that they were tormented. It scared me. I drew in a breath quietly, fearing that he would hear it and come closer to me. I needed distance from the devil, but my eyes couldn't pull away from the image of him bathed in the moonlight that made his robes, skin, and hair all have an ethereal glow.

"Is there no one that is worthy of kindness in your eyes?" I didn't mean to sound so pained when I asked him. It just slipped out.

The proud anger he wore melted away and was replaced with an inquisitive look. It slowly shifted into something softer. However, if Draki was going to say something, he never had a chance to before Elijah spoke up.

"Of course not. He's a devil. In his eyes, no one is deserving of kindness without making a steep payment."

The corner of Draki's mouth plucked up, and he shrugged as if he had been caught red-handed, elbow-deep in a cookie jar. I rolled my eyes and went to feed the fire while asking, "So, these are all pictures about what happened that day?"

"More or less," he answered simply. He then gave a pointed look to the fire. "That's pathetic."

Scoffing, I snipped back with, "I couldn't leave to search for firewood. It's better than nothing."

"I'll go look," Elijah whispered after he came to stand next to me.

"You'll die is more like it. There is an army of grunts heading this way. They'll feast on the remains down there and then head out. You'll be an extra set of bones piled at the base of the mountain if you try to go out there now."

"I can go," I muttered.

"Are you crazy?" Elijah gasped.

"Oh, so you can go while caked in blood and littered in wounds, but I can't?" I snapped.

"You've put yourself at risk enough already," he countered.

"I don't mind searching again," I said.

"I mind," Draki warned.

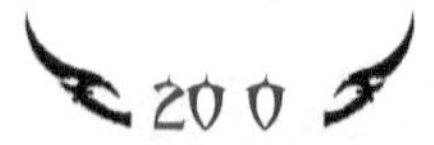

"What do you suggest we—" Elijah's question was cut short with a wave of the devil's hand. Wood magically piled up next to what I had gathered earlier. It would be more than enough to keep us warm through the night.

"I would suggest," Draki began, almost mocking Elijah, "that you stay put for the night like I told you to. Rest up and get comfortable. We all know Sia won't stay still for long once the sun rises."

While Elijah stared in awe at the display of power, I was more focused on Draki as he made his way for the exit. I rushed over to catch up with him. Quickly, I reached out to grab at his robes and gently tugged them to get his attention. He stopped as soon as he felt it.

"Yes?"

"Where are you going?"

He gradually looked over his shoulder to me. "I told you. There is something that I must tend to."

"Will you be gone long?" I couldn't lie to myself, even if I wanted to. When he was gone, I was afraid. The world was full of beasts, creatures, and monsters … but Draki? Draki was the biggest monster in the room. He was what scared the other nightmares away. He was as comforting as the fullest moon on the darkest night. He was what protected me through every evening. Every time he wasn't there, bad things happened. I wanted him to stay with me.

As he looked at me, I saw something flash in his eyes. But that look was snuffed out quicker than I could depict what it was. "I'll be back before morning."

"I …"

"Sia. I did what I needed to in order to remind you that we have a deal. I won't put you in harm's way again. Not as long as you stop avoiding the inevitable."

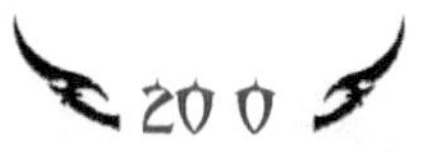

I swallowed hard and nodded. "Right," I whispered, feeling my heart sink.

He brushed my hand away from his robes and gave a pointed look to Elijah sitting by the fire. Drawing my lips into my mouth, I nodded reluctantly and headed over to him. I felt rejected, even though I knew he didn't mean for it to come across that way. Where he was going, I couldn't follow. Besides, I was safe in the cave, and Elijah needed my help with his wounds. We didn't have much, but we could try to do the best we could with what little (very little) we had.

As soon as I turned around and took the first few steps in Elijah's direction, I saw fading, red smoke misting around my feet. Quickly, I turned, and I knew before I looked that Draki was gone. The mouth of the cave held the remains of vanishing, crimson smoke and pools of moonlight. It felt empty. I felt empty.

I clutched the fabric of my shirt around my chest and drew in a sharp breath. I knew what was going on in my head, and I was making no attempt to stop it.

Maybe I was crazy.

Chapter 24:

The Burning Truth

Back by the fire, I had Elijah remove his shirt so I could inspect the deeper wounds more properly. The torn flesh looked angry, and most of the bleeding had stopped, but the edges of the gashes were already red and puffy. Grunts weren't exactly known for being clean creatures. If I didn't want the inflicted areas to fester, I needed to clean and bandage them quickly. Unfortunately, we didn't have the supplies to do it effectively until morning. All I could do for now was ensure that they were as clean as I could get them and covered with … something. Even if I ripped my clothing, it wouldn't be ideal. The fabric was dirty and covered in sweat and blood. It wasn't something I could tear up and slap onto fresh wounds and not expect the worst to come from it.

"These look so bad, Elijah. I'm going to have to go back for our things in the morning," I admitted. Hearing myself say it out loud made the reality of our situation sink in. It made me realize, again, just how close we were to the faith city and how much heading back was going to hinder us from reaching our destination. I didn't want to be out here another night. If Saint Augustine was a symbol of hope, then the Wastes were the absence of it, and I didn't want to linger

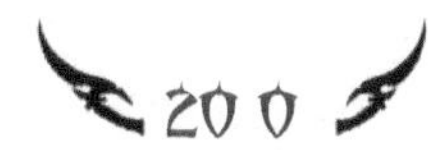

one more hopeless night in the desert filled with nightmares and despair.

"I should be fine until we get to the faith city," he replied softly.

I stared at him in confusion. "We are still unsure if we'll be able to make it there in a day. If infection settles in—"

"Making it there has been just as important to me as it has been for you, Sia. I don't want any more setbacks."

Shaking my head, I said, "No. No, I'm not risking your life so we can stay on an imaginary schedule. We're going to head back and get our things."

"And what if we go and there isn't anything left? What if we waste all the time just to find out that everything is damaged or ruined beyond use? We would have risked it all for nothing."

"It's a risk I'm willing to take."

"We are so close!"

"I don't care," I snapped back.

"I don't get it. We are right there. Surely they will have supplies. We can just push ourselves a little harder."

"And if we can't make it in a day?"

"Then we travel a few hours by night."

"You seem confident that they'll open the gates in the middle of the night."

"I'm more confident in that than I am in the supplies still being intact," he grumbled angrily.

"There isn't any harm in trying. Your injuries aren't just little scratches, Elijah."

"I don't understand why you are so hard-pressed on heading back."

"Because I want to do everything in my power to make sure that you don't get sick. I've seen people die over

less because they didn't get treated properly. Timing and caring for a wound are everything."

He grabbed my wrist. "Are you concerned about me because I'm your friend or because I'm something more?"

I twisted in his grasp awkwardly and lost the heat in my voice. "Let me go," I whispered, though I lacked any conviction.

"Are you asking because you're concerned as a friend or something more, Sia?"

"Elijah, *please*."

He yanked me over to him, and I tripped over the uneven flooring and crashed into his bare chest. He inhaled sharply and then went stiff. For fear of hurting him further, I did everything in my power to minimize movement and felt his muscles shift under the press of my cheek. I could hear his heartbeat thundering in his chest, and I felt his breathing slow down. Sluggishly, I raised my head, and our gazes became tangled.

"What am I to you, Sia?" he asked in a raspy voice threaded with pain.

I opened my mouth, but words failed me. I should lie. My instant thought was to lie to him and tell him that he was nothing and that we were only friends. I wanted to tell him that everything that happened between us was me just feeling lost, confused, and lonely. All I had to do was speak and then spend the rest of my life apologizing to him ... that was assuming he wanted to be in my life after I said everything that was tumbling about in my mind.

"Tell me!" he growled.

I drew in a deep breath, but my words failed me. I slammed into his mouth, and our hands were instantly all over one another. I couldn't tell what I was touching. I just let my fingers trace his skin while I attempted to map out his

body with touch alone. My lips blazed over his, and we panted for breath between hungry kisses. Faded memories of dreams and flames and screams assaulted my mind. I saw blood on my hand, and the machete buried deep in Elijah's gut. Suddenly, I heard Elijah inhale in discomfort.

"Sia, why?"

"Wait. Wait. Wait," I begged between his kisses that trailed from the corner of my mouth, down my chin, and across my neck. Though I was proud of gaining some sort of control over my desire, my body wasn't as happy with me.

His mouth raced back up, and he nibbled on my earlobe. Breathily, he asked, "What? What is it?"

I shivered and licked my lips. "We need to slow down."

His groan was a partial growl. I didn't know how hard it had to be for him to keep stopping himself, and I sympathized with him because it was hard for me too. I had to keep my head straight. I was suddenly envisioning Draki and the way he looked at the mouth of the cave as he was bathed in moonlight and glittering like a winter fantasy in the middle of summer.

"Tell me," Elijah whispered into the cuff of my ear.

I moaned, and I felt him hug me closer to his body. "Elijah, it's complicated," I admitted.

His mouth pressed over my shoulder, and then, right at the base of my neck, he bit down. Shutting my eyes, I rode the wave of pain that mingled with dangerous pleasure. Then his soft kisses fluttered over the teeth marks he had left behind. "Sia, please, tell me."

"More," I whispered.

Elijah went so still that I was afraid that I had said the wrong thing. The fire popped, and my heart leaped at the

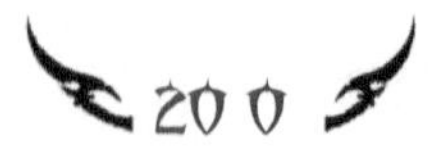

sound. His chest swelled with his inhale, and he asked, "More what?"

Oh, how my body was mad at me! I wanted to just let go and fall into him in a way that made me ache. I felt like I was causing myself physical pain by bridling my passion, but I held my ground and focused on being as honest as I dared to be in that moment. It would be enough to make me feel more at ease. It would be enough to keep him by my side. It would be enough to keep Draki from doing more damage than my slight utterance of truth.

Our lips grazed as we forced ourselves to look into each other's eyes. I saw the suffering in his hazel hues that was both emotional and physical. It all collided with me, and I said the one thing that held so much weight. "You're more than a friend to me, Elijah." He drew in a breath to speak, and I gingerly laid my fingers over his lips to stop him. "But I'm not sure about what that means for *us*. I'm trying to navigate this world, my emotions, and everything else. I need time to figure everything out. You … you understand, right?"

Defeated, he threw his head back and lay there staring at the cave ceiling. After a moment, he responded. "I do." There was another lull before he asked, "Are you going to keep me waiting forever?"

I couldn't answer him honestly on that because I didn't know what the answer was. "No," I said. The lie went down like I was swallowing a sip of bitter tea.

He smiled and said, "Okay."

Just like that, his inner beast seemed to be quelled. His brow knit, and I realized that I was lying half on his wound. The adrenaline was ebbing, and I was sure that the soreness was resurfacing. He grunted in pain, and I scrambled off him as best I could without moving him too much.

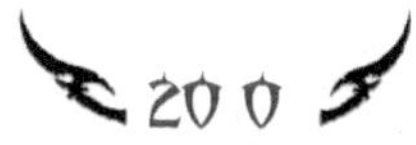

"I'm sorry!"

"You're fine," he mumbled.

"Lay down." I bit my lower lip while looking at him. "I'll try to find a way to clean you up as best I can. Until then, try to not move around a whole lot," I said softly.

He nodded and then groaned. "Yeah. No problem," he stated with his eyes drooping a bit.

I stood to look around for something, knowing I wouldn't find anything. From the corner of my eye, I saw movement at the mouth of the cave. I turned quickly but didn't see a living being standing there. Instead, I saw our belongings from the previous camp piled just inside the opening. I looked around but found no one. Not even a whisper was in my mind. But I knew without asking that it had been Draki. The real question was when he had brought them to us?

Without delay, I went to work on cleaning Elijah's injuries and bandaging him up. After I finished, we both went to sleep. However, the night was full of more tossing and turning than sleep for me, so it came as no surprise that by the time the peeking sun changed the colors of the sky on the horizon, I was up and breaking down the camp. Elijah woke up due to pain when I was nearly finished. Since he was up, I checked the bandages, cleaned the wounds again, and we prepared to set out.

I tried to keep our pace on the slower side, but Elijah wasn't having it. I had tried the whole time to get him to take breaks along the way, but again, the young man ignored my

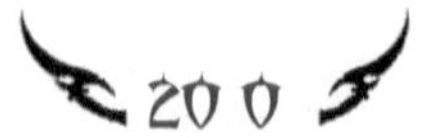

persistent pleas and pressed on like he wasn't hurt at all. Looking to the sun overhead, I scowled at the sky and then to the fast-approaching city.

"Elijah, stop pushing yourself. You'll risk your wounds opening again. We need to slow down."

"We're almost there."

"It won't matter if you pass out before we make it there."

"I won't pass out," he stated in a tone that was muddled with exhaustion.

"You will if you keep pushing yourself like this."

He gave me a look and said, "I'm fine."

"I suppose I should prepare myself to drag you through the front gates if we make it there before nightfall."

"With those scrawny arms? Please … we might as well tack another day onto this trip."

"If you weren't already injured, I'd give you a fat lip for that comment."

He laughed and muttered under his breath, "As long as you do it with your mouth, I won't mind taking the beating even with these injuries."

I felt flush and ignored the heat rushing over my whole body. "My arms are strong enough to slice a limb or two of yours off."

"That reminds me, maybe I should carry that blade for a bit."

I laughed at him and ticked my finger from side to side. "I think it's better attached to my hip, thank you."

We laughed, and I felt some of my anger lift. Again, I looked to the sky and sighed as I noted the position of the sun. Then—slowly—I took into account how close the city looked and pursed my lips to the side.

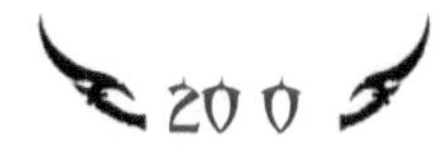

He must have known what I was thinking because Elijah said, "We'll be there before nightfall, Sia."

Looking at him, I tried to erase the worry from my face as I asked, "Are you sure?"

He nodded. "Yes. We can't slow down because of me, though."

"What if your wounds reopen?"

"I'm sure that the faith city will be able to see to my injuries far better than we could imagine. Besides, I'm rushing because one of them *has* reopened," he explained gravely.

The color drained from my face, and my heart slammed down into my feet. Everything in me knew that this was bad. I rushed over to him and forced him to face me. Before he could stop me, I had lifted his shirt and was ready to look under the bandage, but the cloth was soaked in crimson, and a thin stream of blood was traveling down his abs. Fear coursed through my body, and my stomach clenched. Unsure of how to respond to it, I just stared at the wound in disbelief. How long had he traveled like this? Why hadn't I asked him to stop more so I could check on him or change his bandages? I felt sick as I tried to come up with a way to fix it and realized that there was nothing that I could do out in the middle of the Wastes with limited medical supplies. Worst of all, even if we did want to camp out for another night, the fact that the blood was fresh would only call more demons. We *had* to make it to the faith city today.

Elijah gently covered my hands with his and spoke softly to me. "I'm trying to use what strength I have to get there before my body gives out on me. I didn't want to worry you."

"This isn't right, Elijah." I could hear my voice crack as I said it.

He stroked my head and ran his fingers through my braids. "It's not your fault. Don't start blaming yourself."

I didn't know what to say to that, so I met his gaze, and instantly my eyes welled with tears. "I don't want you to keep anything from me like that again."

"I won't keep secrets if you don't," he said in a voice that was so free of worry that it tore right through me.

He never thought that I was keeping more than Draki from him. He didn't think that I had a secret that would make him lose that sparkle in his eyes and warmth in his smile. If he knew the darkness that I harbored, would he still care so much about me? I couldn't bear to look into his achingly beautiful hazel hues anymore. Instead, I looked away, and I was greeted with the pink flesh of his scar on his arm. I remembered how the chain tattoo had been so cruelly ripped out of him, and I screwed my eyes shut. If he had never met me, would he have suffered as greatly as he had? His hand guided my chin up, but I still refused to look at him.

"Open your eyes, Sia."

"I feel like it's *my* fault."

"Open your eyes."

Reluctantly, I did, and I felt the stinging promise of tears burn my vision.

"It's not your fault," he assured sweetly. I pouted, and he laughed. "You didn't send the grunts after me, did you?"

"No," I mumbled.

"Then you have nothing to be sorry about." I watched as he swayed for a moment, and he shook his head lightly. "Come on, we need to get a move on. The city walls are visible. Within hours, we will be there."

I looked over my shoulder to the city that sparkled under the sunlight. Saint Augustine was only hours away, just like Elijah had said. If we were lucky, we'd make it there before dusk, and we wouldn't have to find a place to camp for the night. Even though I wanted him to take it easy, we didn't have that luxury. It wasn't about me wanting to make it to the faith city because of my blind ambitions and a promise made to my meemaw. It was because I wanted him to be safe and taken care of.

"Let's drink some water, and then we can get right back to traveling."

"Fair," he stated, reaching for his canteen.

"And if you feel like you need to take a break—"

"You'll be the first to know," he swore.

Chapter 25:

A Strange Welcome

It was a little before dusk when we arrived just outside of Saint Augustine's walls. I had watched the giant barrier inch closer and closer for several hours now. The polished metal of the wall was almost blinding as its reflective surface sent rays of light extending far beyond its safety and deep into the hopeless stretch of the Wastes. But it wasn't the city's fortifications that I was strangely captivated by, presently. It was the man just outside of them that had my attention.

He was sitting at the base of the city wall. From what I could tell, his garments were tan, tattered, and robe-like, though it was hard to be completely sure as he was covered—from head to his bare feet—in locusts. There were a few flying around him and more crawling about the surrounding ground nearby, but the mass collection of them crept all over the man. He lifted an oddly soft, clean, and olive-complexioned hand into the air, and a lone locust flew over and landed on his extended finger. His head was shrouded in the shadow provided by his hood, and he seemed more fixed on the insect that had just landed on his digit than the new visitors approaching.

"City searchers, aye?" The person cloaked in shabby garbs and locusts asked when we were within earshot.

"Yes. D-Do you know if the city accepts strangers?" I asked.

I heard him give a short, nasally laugh. "Stranger things have entered, and stranger things therein dwell, but if you ask if they will take you, they surely won't turn able bodies away."

"I'm sorry, do you live here?" Elijah asked.

"In the world, in this spot, or within the city?" he countered with a tilt of his head.

A few locusts fluttered by me, and I dodged the small swarm as best I could. I figured I would try a different approach. "We're just wondering if you could give us any advice," I said with a smile. "Mister … uh, what's your name?"

The man tilted his head to the other side and hummed as he stared at us. From beneath the hood, I could see his eyes inspecting me, but it was the familiar way that his look shot through me that set me on edge. Draki could do that with his eyes. Stare at you like he was examining all the parts and pieces that went beyond blood and bone and weighed out every inch of you while you could do nothing but be laid bare before him. I squirmed and hugged myself, which only made the cloaked man laugh.

Slowly, he stood, and the locusts circled him excitedly as he moved about. The cowl was brought down, and I could see that he had heterochromia. One eye was a deep, chocolaty brown while the other was as blue as the summer sky. His short, black locks looked clean despite his appearance, and the stubble lining his face gave him a more rugged look. He smiled, and clean, white teeth flashed back at me.

"Is the lady asking for my name?"

"I … think so?" I stated a bit confused. Was it too late to wish him a good day and walk away?

He laughed again. "Abaddon," he replied with threads of laughter. Then he motioned to me. "And you are?"

I wanted to tell him my *real* name for a moment and had to break eye contact with him. Shaking my head, I looked at him, perplexed. He didn't come across like a devil, but his power was undeniable.

"I'm Sia," I said, finally.

"Do you know anything about the city?" Elijah asked.

"I know a great deal of things, but the sun won't let me list them all if you wish to be safe tonight," Abaddon replied.

"Will we be accepted into the city tonight?" My voice sounded as worried as I felt. Not just because we were running out of time to find a place to camp if we wouldn't be let in, but I took one look at Elijah and knew that his injuries were taking a toll on him. We needed to get him treated and given proper antibiotics tonight, if possible. The only way we could do that is if we got into the city before nightfall.

Abaddon looked up to the walls and then back to me. "Yes."

"Thank you," I quickly blurted out and grabbed Elijah by the hand, tugging him toward the main entrance.

"Sia!" Abaddon called out to me.

"Keep walking," I told Elijah in a whisper. As he walked off, I turned and faced the strange man.

"Be careful of those that dwell beyond the safety of the wall. Not all that glitters is gold. Wolves in sheep's clothing reside within these places. They speak of the power

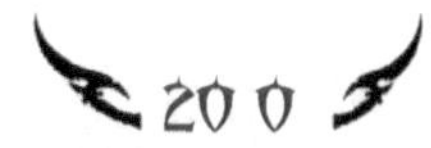

of prayers, yet the one most high never listens to their wicked cries."

"I don't understand."

"You will," he proclaimed as he gradually seated himself back down and pet the locust resting in his hand. "You will."

"O-Okaaay." I drew out the one word and felt that Abaddon was more touched in the head than he was sane. That thought only made me feel like we had a fifty-fifty chance of getting into Saint Augustine without a hitch tonight. I started to turn toward Elijah when I heard the locust-covered stranger speak again.

"Seek the one without eyes but sees all."

"Seek out who?"

"The one without eyes but sees all," he yelled back to me. "I'll be here. I've always been waiting. The walls can't fall until the pure are freed. The innocent must not be harmed," he half-murmured. "We've been waiting for you," he announced a little louder. Again, he smiled at me and then quickly shooed me toward the gate where Elijah was waiting. Something told me that there was more to that man, but I didn't have the time to ask.

Within minutes, we were at the entrance, and a man in a shining suit of armor and wearing a long, red cape stopped us before we could make it completely inside. He had incredibly short, blond hair and deep brown eyes. He was far taller than Elijah and me. He had to be somewhere around six feet four inches in height. I felt like he was

looming over me, and the armor didn't make his presence exactly feel friendly.

"Halt, where are you travelers from?" the knight asked.

I went incredibly still out of intimidation. It took a good moment for me to gather my bravery to speak up. "We're from a couple of villages out in the Wastes," I admitted.

The knight didn't seem moved one way or another by my words. "Did you come across many evils along the way?"

"Plenty," Elijah announced.

A scrutinizing glare flicked over to Elijah and then to me. The knight's eyes narrowed, slowly. "How many days have you traveled?"

"About a week," I answered. A silent moment of quick thinking passed, and I added, "Maybe a few days more than that."

The knight nodded as he looked us over and appeared to be visually counting all of our injuries. "We'll have to seek the Grand Master for final approval."

Another knight standing next to him thumped the first over his chest with the back of his armored hand. "Come now, Harold. You can see that they've been blessed. They've made it across the Wastes for more than a week. They've endured enough." He pointed to our wounds, saying, "Even I can see that."

Harold looked from us to his partner, whispering, "What if they've run into devils?"

The second knight laughed. "Then they'll be safe here. You know that those wicked things cannot dwell beyond the wall."

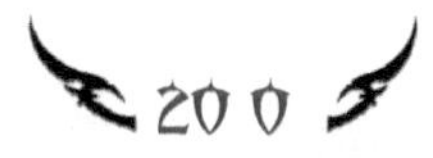

Hope swelled in me. The power of the faith cities was that strong? The devils and other demons couldn't live beyond the monumental metal walls? I dared to smile.

I should have known better.

"What a load of baseless lies, claiming that I cannot pass through these gates," Draki said with a thunderous laugh that only I could hear. He leaned in toward me. "If they think they are free from lesser demons, they are right, but there are bigger nightmares living among them," he cackled. "I've missed rattling the faithful's cages."

"You okay, Sia?" Elijah asked.

"Hmmm?" I snapped out of my private conversation and felt judgmental stares from the two knights. Quickly, I said, "Oh, yeah. I'm fine. I am just tired and pretty hungry. I got lost in thinking about what kind of food they would have."

The second knight tapped the first, announcing, "They're probably smelling Dara's cooking from the inn."

Harold reluctantly nodded. "Yeah. I suppose you're right. It's about that time in the evening, isn't it, Reynolds?" He asked, looking up to the sky and noting the fading light.

"Aye, it is," Reynolds admitted softly. With a heavy sigh, the knight returned his vision in our direction. "Come on then, inside with the two of you. The Hours of Whispered Prayers is about to be upon us."

"Prayers?" I muttered, confused.

"Oi, Francis!" Reynolds called toward another knight slightly further into the entrance.

Quickly, a tall female knight with brunette hair and green eyes approached. Her deep, kind voice sounded rich and instantly made me smile. "You two causing trouble?"

In surprise, I went wide-eyed and lifted up my hands defensively. "N-No!"

She looked at me and laughed, shaking her head. "Not you two," she said. Francis pointed to the other knights that had been questioning us. "I mean these two."

"That's not fair. You're making us out to look like we are always causing problems for newcomers," Harold protested.

Francis rolled her eyes and turned her attention to Reynolds. "Need me to escort them, is it?"

"Aye. Could you, please?" he replied.

She nodded and then smiled at me. "What are your names?"

Elijah informed her by pointing to each of us as he listed our names. "Elijah and Sia."

"Welcome, Elijah and Sia, to the faith city, Saint Augustine," Francis happily announced, motioning for us to walk further beyond the great wall.

I don't know what I had expected the city to be like. Honestly, I had never really thought about it. For so long, it was nothing more than a story, a fairytale. It wasn't until this whole journey was forced upon me that I dared myself to dream and think about what this place would look like. It couldn't hold a candle to the vision that was before me now.

If someone told me a city could be more beautiful than this, I wouldn't believe it. Never before had I seen such buildings. They were tall and sturdy, and the very stones looked like they were embellished in concrete lace. The walls looked like they were made of more windows than they were stone. It was an elegant and beautiful sight to behold. As if it were on cue, the streetlamps came alive and illuminated the roads that were clean and free of dirt. As my eyes drifted on past the shorter rooftops, the buildings became not only taller but more ornate. Windows with magnificently colored glass twinkled with a warm light that was beaming from within.

Spires twisted up from the tops like a thousand stretching fingers reaching for the evening sky, and—in the distance—there was a mammoth-sized building that looked like it was layered in towers and bridges and balconies. It loomed over the rest of the city like a great and wondrous structure of beauty and hope.

"It's beautiful," I whispered.

"The streetlamps are all gas, but the homes are fully powered. A few places here and there still have wiring issues. But, I assure you, all buildings have running water, heat, and at least a single fireplace," Francis informed.

"R-Running water?" I stuttered.

"You have … running water?" Elijah asked in amazement.

"Indeed, we do. We also have heat and air. Most of the city runs off of solar panels and wind power. The rest is run off of gas. We manage to do quite well for ourselves," Francis informed.

I was in awe as I listened to her speaking. It all felt magical and strange, like it was something out of a dream. She listed off the luxuries like they were nothing. To me, they sounded like something out of a fairytale. I wanted to ask when we could wash up. Instead, I walked behind her and heard my stomach grumble as loud as a grunt when I smelled herb-roasted meat drifting in the early night air. I held my stomach and smiled sheepishly when both Francis and Elijah turned to look at me in surprise.

"Well," Francis started. "I suspect that the lady is hungry." Joyful laughter erupted out of the female knight as she resumed escorting us.

"What are the chances of being able to eat before we see the Grand Master?" Elijah asked, looking a bit pale—

which had me worried—but he gave me a look and shook his head.

"Hmmm, I'd say they are pretty good. The Grand Master is usually pretty busy with work and then the evening mass. Not to mention, he has to ensure that the Hours of Whispered Prayers doesn't have any issues. I'd say you have time to get some grub, settle into a lodging somewhere, and get washed up. You don't want to look like something that the cat dragged in when you meet with the Grand Master. Best be looking proper and clean when you stand before him."

Looking around, I became worried that we wouldn't be able to pay for anything. "We don't have any money, but we do have supplies that we could trade."

Francis waved the words away like they were annoying, swarming flies. "Nah, don't worry about it. There's plenty of work to be done, especially with a few of the inns. We'll get you squared away in no time. No able body is overlooked, and no person goes hungry. We each have a role to play in the city." She paused and looked back at me. "We have to take care of each other, or everything falls apart."

Elijah looked toward a few people laughing in the street across the way and calmly asked, "You guys seem to really be kind and caring here. Is there really no one that goes without food or work?"

"Yes, sir. Not an empty belly within these walls, and no job goes undone. Many of us here came from villages outside of the faith city, so it stands to say that most of us here know what it's like to go without. The principles of Saint Augustine were built upon this knowledge. We never want anyone to feel like a burden, like they are unwanted, or like there is no hope for them. We have a weekly food drive in case any families or individuals are struggling with making

ends meet, and there are four employment houses in the city where folks can sign up and be paired with a proper job."

"Sounds … wonderful. It really seems like you all have it all figured out," I said.

"*It does sound wonderful, doesn't it?*" Draki muttered in my mind.

"Is there no crime here?" Elijah asked.

"Only crime right now is your bellies being empty," Francis announced with a chuckle.

We were standing outside a building that had muffled sounds of laughter and chattering sealed away behind a large, wooden door. The glow of the lamps inside cast orange hues over the clean, crystal-clear glass of the inn. A sign swung overhead that read *Arrow's Ale and Inn*. We entered the establishment and were greeted by someone at the front desk. To the left was the bar, to the right was a lounge with a quieter dining space surrounding it, and just behind the service desk was a set of stairs. Standing at the receptionist area was a short, young boy with unruly, blond, curly hair and blue eyes. He had a faint splash of freckles over the bridge of his nose and a smile that was as warm as it was bright.

"Francis, fancy seeing you so early in the nigh—" The young male stopped abruptly and peered around the female knight to the two of us. "Oh, I see you've brought newcomers."

"That I have. They were hungry and needed a place to rest. Dara normally handles these matters well. I don't suppose you would mind me going to the back to fetch her while you mind the front, Micah?"

"Not at all, Francis. You know your way around the place. Leave these two with me," Micah stated, waving with

a nub instead of a hand. Without a second look, the female knight waltzed off.

I couldn't help but stare. Naturally, Micah couldn't help but inform me of my blunder. "Was born with it, if you were wondering."

My jaw unhinged, and I flushed as I floundered for a reply. "I'm so sorry, I didn't mean to …"

He waved the thought away. "Don't be. Not like this is something you see every day, now is it?"

"I insist on apologizing. I shouldn't have stared, and I should have asked. It must have been uncomfortable to have a stranger gawking at you when there isn't anything wrong with you. I was just curious," I said.

Micah smiled at me. "I like you. What's your name?"

"Sia," I softly replied. Then I pointed to the man at my side. "This is my friend, Elijah."

"You two look like something the grunts tossed about in the mud," he expressed with a chuckle.

"Not far off from the truth," Elijah admitted with a muted groan of pain.

"Is there a doctor close by?" I asked.

Micah nodded. "Oh, aye, but I suspect that they'll be coming to you after you get settled in and washed up. It's standard procedure for bringing in stragglers."

"We don't have any way to pay—"

"Bah. I'm sure that Francis told you that you don't need to worry about that when you were being debriefed on what you could expect from the city. You don't need to worry about paying for anything right now. We'll get you settled and then give you a role for the city. Until then, don't worry about it," Micah explained.

Elijah placed his bag on the ground and rubbed his arm, saying, "We're still adjusting."

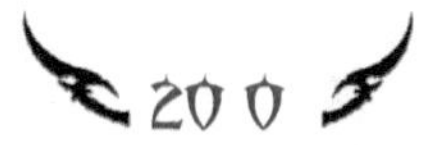

"Understandable. But things get easier when you realize that we all are always adjusting. It never stops," Micah softly explained.

"That sounds more scary than it does reassuring," I admitted.

"It should sound inspirational," Micah said with a short laugh.

"Really?" I asked.

"I can see why it could be seen that way," Elijah started. He waited for us to look at him before he finished with, "Because it means that you're always growing and changing. That means that it's okay if you don't feel like things are working out the way that you need them to because you're still adjusting."

That didn't just make sense, it made me feel like I didn't have to be perfect all the time. If we are always adjusting and trying to be better, then it left room to make mistakes. It meant that we could always give it another shot and fix our strategy. It was a refreshing outlook to have on life, one that I would like to apply to my life right away, so I could stop beating myself up for all my shortcomings and faults. At the end of the day, I was just adjusting to … life.

"This guy gets it," Micah stated with a grand smile.

"And here they are, as promised, Dara. Two young and able bodies," Francis announced from the hall that extended further beyond the staircase.

A sandy, beige-skinned woman walked down the hall next to the female knight. Her silky, straight, black hair reached her lower back and swept from side to side as she made her way toward the front desk. Large, brown eyes were fixed on me as she straightened out the length of her white, lacy top. It was cinched around her tiny waist with a tan belt, and the look was completed with a pair of billowy, coral-colored pants that almost looked like a skirt.

She smiled as she looked the two of us over. "Right you are. Very able, indeed. I think I can find them some work until one of the employment houses can set them up with a proper job." She turned her attention to Elijah and me as she said, "I won't overwork you. I'll just make you honest and ensure that you can fend for yourselves until you get settled into the city fully. Don't want you roaming the streets without coin lining your pockets."

"I see my job here is done. I'll leave you all to it then," Francis stated with a lazy salute to everyone.

"I'll take it from here, hun. You hurry off to return to your post," Dara suggested with a smile and a wave goodbye to the female knight.

"Thanks." Elijah waved to Francis as she walked by.

I added, "Thank you!" as she passed.

With a light laugh and a nod, Francis exited the building, leaving the two of us in the care of Dara and Micah.

Chapter 26:

All that Glitters

I wasn't sure how to change the subject gracefully, so I settled with asking about the name of the inn. "Arrow's Inn is an interesting name. Who came up with it?"

Dara's smile grew as she said, "Arrow was the name of my husband. He bought this place a year before we met."

"Oh, that's lovely. You two run it together?" I asked, perking up.

Her smile never wavered as she replied, "He's been dead for five years now. I run everything by myself."

"Oh," I whispered, feeling horrible for asking.

"Hey, I help!" Micah insisted.

She laughed. "Yes, yes. You do your fair share. I can't deny your helping hand in running the business."

Micah puffed out his chest and beat against it proudly. "I'm a strong, young man that will do everything I can to aid you, Miss Dara."

Rubbing his arm affectionately, she softly said, "I know, dear. I know." Turning toward Elijah and me, she asked, "How about I show you two to your rooms before we head to the back together? You can put your things down, get washed up, and come help me in the kitchen. It's just about dinner rush, and I could use an extra set of helping hands."

"Sure," Elijah answered happily. "As long as we can fix up a plate for ourselves."

I nodded a bit too energetically in agreement, which made Dara erupt in laughter. "Of course! I wouldn't dream of denying y'all a full belly. I'm just a little concerned for your friend here."

Elijah might have lost a good bit of blood, but not enough to stop himself from blushing. He swayed on the spot and corrected himself swiftly. "Is it that noticeable?"

"Not as noticeable as the smell of blood coming off of you."

"You can … smell the blood?" I had to wonder if she was part demon.

She nodded her head. "I worked as a medic for a little while. You can never forget the way that blood smells." She looked Elijah over. "As long as you take it easy until the doctor arrives, you can help out."

He raised a hand and put the other over his heart. "Promise."

"Come on, then."

We followed the innkeeper through the lower hall as she explained a few details to us about the building. "Most of the rooms on the lower floor are for workers, newcomers, or those with disabilities and need to avoid the stairs. You two will have separate rooms, and they are right next to mine. So, if you need anything, just knock on my door, and I'll help you."

"We really appreciate this, Dara," I admitted softly. "I'm sorry if bringing up your husband hurt you."

She shook her head. "Don't worry about it."

Elijah cleared his throat and held his stomach. "I can't wait for that promised meal, Dara."

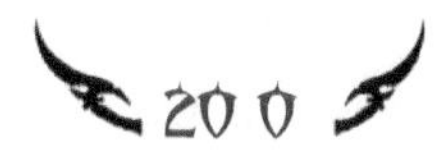

As she played with her keys, she stopped and then looked at us with wide eyes. "Where are my manners? As you two know, my name is Dara. Might I have the pleasure of knowing your names?"

"Sia," I stated, pointing to myself.

Elijah mirrored me, saying, "Elijah."

She smiled again. "Well, Sia and Elijah, for the next few days you'll be staying with us. I hope you'll look at it as home until all of your papers and information is drawn up."

"What papers?" I asked.

She started to walk again as she spoke. "Oh, the usual: your names, jobs, and other information that we write down to keep track of the citizens. Once everything is lined up, they will see what sort of living situation you're seeking and will set you up accordingly. For instance, just a few days ago, a pregnant woman and two men came into town. One of the males was set up with an apartment, and the woman and her fiancé got a small house toward the inner city." She looked back at me and must have noticed how nervous I was. "Don't worry, dear. They talk you through everything and pair you up with the best job and living situation. No one is left feeling like they were forced to do anything."

I felt a lot lighter after hearing her say that. "Thank you," I whispered.

Soon after, we were escorted to our rooms and left alone to clean up and get situated. I wasn't sure about Elijah, but I struggled with figuring out how to get the water working. It took a little finagling, and a few choice words were whispered under my breath, but I managed to get it done. I had never been happier either. Running water sure beat boiling buckets of the stuff over the fire for over an hour to fill up the bath, and it was a thousand times better to flush a toilet rather than walking to and from an outhouse all hours of the day. Yes, sir. This girl could get used to running water.

I didn't want to take up too much time cleaning up. I could always bathe again before bed or in the morning, but I did want to make sure that I wasn't looking like someone that slept with the pigs when I waltzed into the kitchen to help Dara prepare for the dinner rush. I made sure to lather up and rinse off quickly before changing into my last set of clean clothes. I wrinkled my nose at the small heap of dirty laundry. Maybe the coin Elijah and I earned could pay for some extra outfits?

I was still wrapped in a towel when I heard *his* voice coming from behind me on the bed.

"Do you have anything that isn't bloodstained?"

Quickly, I stood and faced Draki with an angry scowl. Waving about my chosen clothing, I snapped back, "Lucky for me, I have one outfit left that isn't."

"We can fix that for you," he growled.

I went still. The kind of still your body underwent when you were faced with a predator that was stronger and was equipped with more teeth and claws than you were. I was frozen in a way where you even hold your breath as you hope the danger passes you by.

His serious glare turned playful as he gracefully stood from the bed and closed the short distance between us. "I won't remind you of our little agreement. However, I will advise you to be on your guard here. This city might appear safe, but it is anything but that."

"You're just saying that."

"No. Not when it comes to keeping you safe."

"It's a faith city!" I whisper-yelled.

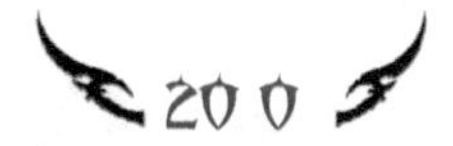

"It's a city of lies!" He matched my tone and was practically nose-to-nose with me. His golden gaze searched my eyes as he let the words sink in.

"You're wrong." But I didn't even believe myself when I heard the words leave my mouth. Doubt was an ugly seed, and the plants it grew took root fast.

"Oh, Sia, not when it comes to this."

"Why? Why are you destroying this for me?"

He grabbed my arms and shook his head. "Sia, I'm not destroying anything. I'm warning you that things are not as they appear. I'm trying to keep you safe."

My eyes stung with the promise of tears. I didn't want to cry. He had to be wrong. I couldn't believe him. I wouldn't. Sniffling, I pushed past the urge to weep and clutched my clean clothes against my damp chest. My free hand made sure that the towel stayed in place. "I need to get dressed," I admitted in a voice that was hardly audible.

He nodded, slowly letting me go, but his final words rattled me nonetheless. "Don't let down your guard."

He disappeared, letting me get ready in peace. Or whatever peace would have me while my mind was plagued with worry. If I had to be careful, did that mean that I needed to warn Elijah, too, or was it all a lie? Did Draki just not want me to be happy? Was he only sowing the seeds of doubt, or were we really in danger? I feared that we would find the answers all too soon.

A short while later, I stepped out in the hall and found Elijah waiting for me. He was resting against the wall

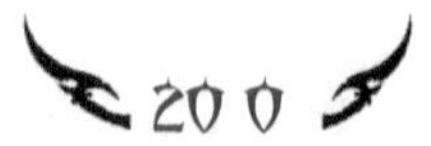

next to my door. He had partially frightened me as I wasn't expecting him to be standing there.

My slight jolt of surprise was noticed by him, and he smirked while saying, "Sorry. Didn't mean to scare you. Thought I'd wait for you and we could walk there together."

"Thanks for that."

"The scare or because I waited for you?"

"The waiting," I snipped and playfully slapped his shoulder.

He hissed in pain, and I covered my mouth before pouting. He shook his head and waved me away like there was nothing wrong with him. "Thought so, just wanted to be sure," he said, but I could hear him straining to sound unaffected by my playful slap.

I sighed. "I'm sorry for hitting you. I wasn't thinking."

"I'm fine, Sia. The doctor showed up. I still feel sore, and I'm waiting for the painkillers to kick in."

"Hey, Elijah?"

"Yeah?"

"I meant it, though. Thank you for waiting for me to come out. Honestly, I get nervous in crowded areas sometimes."

He nodded and whispered, "Me too," before pushing off the wall and motioning down the hall toward the kitchen. "After you."

"This all feels so strange, still, like it isn't happening."

"Yeah, I know what you mean. Everything feels …"

We both said, "Too perfect," at the same time and laughed.

I managed to speak up first after the laughter had ebbed. "I know that I shouldn't, but I keep wondering when

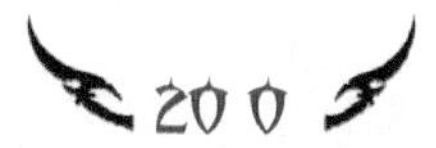

a devil will pop up or when the village is going to turn against us, you know? It's just … I don't even know how to describe it."

"It's just nice to feel like you don't have to always be on your guard," Elijah said with a sigh of contentment.

"Yeah. Yeah, it's exactly like that," I muttered and smiled.

He was right. It *was* nice to feel like I didn't have to worry about demons, devils, or manipulative humans. We could just loosen up and exist. For so long I had been afraid and on guard that when I didn't have tension in my shoulders as I walked a hall, the feeling was alien to me. But I should have known better than anyone that feeling relaxed and at peace wouldn't last long. I had dared to dream for a moment. A silly mistake on my part. My mind was quick to remind me of that.

Don't let down your guard.

I had a feeling that phrase was going to haunt me. There wasn't going to be a single kind gesture that wouldn't go without being thoroughly picked apart because of it. Whether or not I was thankful for that had yet to be decided. It could very well be a trick that Draki was playing on me, or he was telling the truth, and I was in deep denial because I wanted some part of this world to be safe for me and countless others.

There was a series of clangs as we turned the corner. We saw the tail end of a pile of pots and pans hitting the ground while Dara looked distraught at the spill of kitchen cookware.

"Drat!" the innkeeper growled. Noticing Elijah and me in the doorway, she smiled with a look of relief. "Thank the heavens, you're here. I thought it was going to take you two a bit longer to get cleaned up."

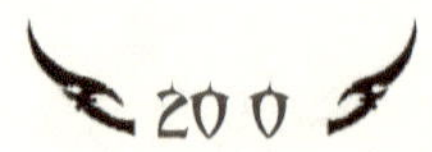

"Didn't want to leave you alone to do it all by yourself," I said.

Elijah raised his hand. "I hurried because we were promised food."

Dara laughed. "Right, heh. I did, didn't I?" She motioned for us to come closer. "Let's get you fed and up to speed so that when the dinner rush comes, you aren't two lost little lambs."

She scurried over to grab a plate and loaded it with meat that was warming high over a pile of hot coals. Next came the roasted vegetables before each dish was finished off with a buttery roll. Elijah and I wasted no time in diving into the meal as Dara gave us the rundown of our duties for the night, which was basically nothing more than plating meals and washing dishes. We didn't even have to cook or leave the kitchen. Two things I wasn't going to complain about. I was too tired and sore to not burn something by accident, and I was too nervous to wait tables. As for Elijah, he didn't need to be moving around a whole lot. I wanted him to rest in his room, but he wouldn't hear any of it.

"Where you go, I go," he whispered to me, and there wasn't any room to discuss the matter further.

Clearing the counter of our empty plates, Dara pointed to one of the sinks in the back. "That there will be your best friend this evening." She then pointed to a couple of metal carousels hanging from a window that could see into the dining area. "That will be the other. All of the orders will be placed there. No need for you to worry about cooking anything. Just plate up the food requested and set it down for one of the staff to take out to the tables."

"Seems easy enough," I said.

"Yeah. Pretty cut and dry," Elijah added.

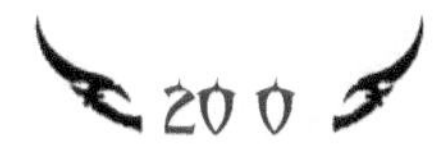

Dara smiled at the two of us. "I have nothing but confidence in the two of you, so let's get ready for the first wave. It should be starting any minute." With that, she stepped out of the kitchen and left us to it.

For the remainder of the evening, Elijah and I worked out a system that made plating food and cleanup a breeze. He handled all of the dishwashing while I fixed up the orders. We were fast and efficient, and there were no complaints. By the time the dining area had died down to murmurs, Dara returned to the kitchen with a grand smile.

"Might just try and keep the two of you for myself," she expressed, wiping her hands off on her apron.

"Won't hear me complaining," I admitted.

Elijah waved, saying, "Or me."

"Just the same, I thank you two. Here," she came close and grabbed each of our hands and placed a few metal coins into them. "Take this, you've earned it."

I turned the shining circles over in my hand, inspecting the strange carvings that were engraved on the surface. "Is this … money?" I asked. I had never seen it before. When I was younger, I had heard a few stories about how some places used it instead of bargaining and trading, so I knew that it could buy things.

She nodded. "It is. It's enough to get you a couple of meals or maybe something in town. It's not much—"

"No. This is fine. We are earning our room and meals to start with. We didn't expect anything else out of the deal," Elijah said.

I looked at him and then the innkeeper and nodded in agreement. "Like he said, we didn't expect more than what was promised. We are thankful for the money. Really, thank you."

Dara sighed with another nod. "Well, you two did better than expected. There isn't a dirty dish in the place, and we managed to make it through the dinner rush and some of the after-hours of the diner. You did more than enough and earned that bit of coin. Save it or spend it, but it's yours."

"Thank you," I said again.

Waving at us with her rag, she shooed us out of the kitchen. "Now, run along, you two. Clean off from tonight and get some good rest. I'll have Micah wake you up in the morning to explore some of the city. Just be back by lunch to help me again."

"What about breakfast?" Elijah asked. "Won't you need help in the morning too?"

She shook her head. "Nah, got a fully staffed kitchen come sunup. It's the afternoons and evenings that I'll be in need of the extra help. Lost my mid-shift and evening help a couple of weeks back, and I have been struggling to keep up with the flow. You two have been a blessing."

"All right then. I guess we'll see you in the morning?"

"I'll have your meals ready. Just come to the bar area when you're ready to eat, and the staff will serve you. I fear I'll be too busy to meet with you before lunch. Running this place isn't easy, but I'm doing the best I can. I know Arrow is watching over me." She laughed and waved the rag at us again. "Look at you two getting me all caught up in the chatter. Shoo. Off with you now."

I laughed and grabbed Elijah by the arm. "See you tomorrow, Dara!" I yelled and tugged my companion to the exit.

"What are you going to do with your money?" Elijah asked once we were out in the halls.

Inspecting the coins again, I let the lamplight in the hall glisten over the face of the money as I tried to envision myself purchasing something. But nothing really came to mind. Shaking my head, I sighed and replied, "I'm not sure. Might just save it until I have a need pop up. We stocked up on a lot of supplies back in that last village. We don't really need soap or medical supplies, and our food and lodging are taken care of by working here."

Flicking one of the coins into the air and snatching it when it came back down, Elijah grinned as he said, "Then we shall save it. I doubt we could buy what we really need with it, anyway."

"What would that be?"

Pocketing the money, he looked at me with a slight frown. "Clothes. We need clothes, Sia. Most of our stuff is stained terribly or shredded by claws. I don't think that Dara would want us wearing those while toiling away in the kitchen around food."

"Do you have anything that isn't bloodstained?"

Cringing, I shook my head with a deep frown. He was right. Elijah and Draki both. We needed new clothing. It appeared that we had to get a proper job as soon as possible because we'd need to save up money to buy it. But the more that I thought about saving money and purchasing things, the more that I felt like I was just preparing to leave again. I didn't like that. I wanted a home. I wanted to belong. I wanted Saint Augustine to be where I put down my roots. For so long, I had struggled to get here to do just that, so,

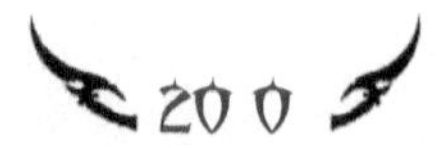

then, why did I feel like I was just getting ready to check off a supply list before heading out again? Why did it seem like there was a knot growing in the pit of my stomach whenever I looked at the shining coins in my grasp? I didn't want to admit it so early on, but something Momma used to always tell me was, *"If it seems too good to be true, then baby … it probably is."* If I acted too impulsively, then I wouldn't feel safe enough to tell Draki to break my village's curse, and I wouldn't be able to bring them here. I found myself holding back and wanting to inspect the faith city more. Did I trust Draki's warning, or had I lost all of my faith in people?

Elijah bumped me with his elbow when we reached my room. "Hey, are you all right?"

"Huh?" I blinked and looked at him, confused.

"You seem like something's bothering you."

I shook my head. "I was just lost in thought. I'm sorry."

"You that tired?"

Smiling, I whispered. "Yeah. Yeah, I'm that tired." It wasn't a complete lie.

"I'd kiss you if we weren't being watched," he whispered back.

To that, my heart flipped, and I felt my eyes bulge in fear. Was Draki watching us from the shadows? I found myself instantly looking to the darkened corners, expecting to see the golden glow of his evil stare from the dusky depths. Instead, I felt Elijah's hand reach up, cup my cheek, and turn it to face him.

"Pretend like we are having a moment," he said in a voice that only I could hear. "It's Micah," he informed softly and flicked his gaze to behind us and then quickly became transfixed on my blue eyes once more. "He's been watching us for a while now."

Resisting the urge to look behind me, I asked softly, "Since when?"

"Since we got here."

"You think this place has something to hide?"

"We live in a world where there are demons and devils roaming about a wasteland, and people aren't safe anywhere but in devil-ran villages—unless they make pacts of their own. This place seems too good to be true."

"Hmmm … my thoughts exactly. Either this place is amazing, and we're jaded, and they are just making sure the newcomers aren't horrible psychos or …"

"Or they are hiding something and hope we are too stupid to figure it out."

"Until we do figure it out, we play the innocent, lovesick couple hiding their passion for one another?"

"I think I can live with that," he said, dipping down to kiss me.

I let it happen even though I knew I shouldn't. As quickly as our lips met, I forced myself to push him away playfully with a giggle. "Elijah, stop. They'll see," I whispered loud enough for Micah to hear.

"Oh, come on. We'll be living together by week's end, I'm sure. Why do we have to hide it?"

"I told you, I want to wait until we're married."

His smile froze, and his eyes lingered on me. "You'd have me?"

Pain shot through my entire being, and I forgot what I was going to say next. "I … We need to rest. We've endured a rough journey and had a long night." I took a few steps back and slowly licked my lips. "Goodnight, Elijah."

"Goodnight, Sia." But there were a thousand things woven into that one statement. I could feel all of the emotions he was trying to hide mingled in the sound of my name. I'd

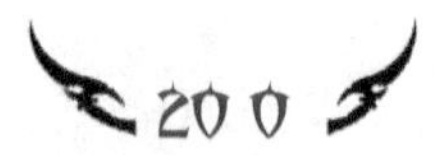

carry it to bed with me and hope that it didn't keep me up all night.

As I slipped into my bedroom, I managed to sneak a peek over to the end of the hall that led to the front desk. It was there that I saw Micah slink behind the corner. I smiled at Elijah, blew a kiss, and felt my heart melt when he whispered, "I'm yours, Sia. Always."

The door shut, and I leaned against it. Everything in me wanted to go to Elijah. Everything in me knew that doing so would mean the end for him. There was too much unknown for me to let down my guard in this place. Until I was sure, I needed to play it safe.

"Pesky little thing ruining such a sweet moment," Draki murmured.

Turning and leaning my back against the door instead, I let out a rush of air and nodded. "You saw it too?" I asked.

Draki held a finger up to his lips and pointed to the door. I looked over my shoulder to the barrier with a furrowed brow, and Draki was suddenly next to me, his breath playing over my neck and the cuff of my ear as he spoke across my skin. "They can't hear me, but be careful how loud you get because they can hear you just fine. And, yes. I saw. You're being watched."

I pulled back enough to see his eyes. "Why?" I whispered.

He grinned as he inched closer to my face. "Because you survived out in the Wastes for so long. One has to wonder … how?"

I opened my mouth and closed it. I couldn't blame them. I wasn't happy about being under suspicion, and I didn't like being followed and watched. But I could understand.

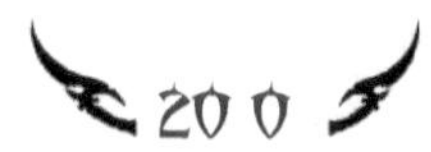

"What do I do?" I asked quietly.

"Do your best to be whatever they want. I don't suspect we'll stay here very long." When he looked back down at me, he laughed. It must have been written all over my face because he answered my question without me ever uttering a word. "I've come to know you quite well, Sia. Once you see this place for what it is …" he looked up and around the room before returning to me, "you'll *beg* me to leave."

"But … there—"

"There isn't anywhere else to go?"

I nodded.

"You could always build your own village." Quickly, he put a hand on either side of me and leaned in until he was practically pinning me against the door. His smile was positively dark as he added, "For a price, I'd be your village's devil."

Chapter 27:

The Trouble with Devils

The next morning, Elijah and I ate breakfast in the dining area before heading out into the city. I was curious to understand how much money was needed to buy standard essentials. I also wanted to see what the rest of the city—and the people in it—were like.

It was slightly irritating as it was distracting to try and consume our meal while knowing that every word spoken, every action made, and every sideways glance was weighed and measured from a distance. Micah was watching us still, and I was willing to bet the little money I had earned last night that Dara was too. I didn't like that because I knew that feeling too well now—the feeling of secrets being kept. Not the kind that were openly gossiped about over tea and cakes. The kind of secrets that meant you had a deep, dark closet hidden away from the rest of the world, and the depths of it was full to the brim with skeletons … and none of them belonged to you. Those were the kind of secrets that were the most hideous because you didn't hide them out of shame. You hid them because you didn't want to get caught.

… Because you weren't done collecting skeletons.

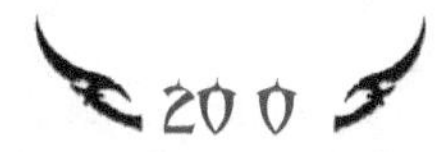

"Come on, let's go," I mumbled, picking up my things and quietly thanking the waiter that came to collect the dirty dishes.

"Ready to go so soon?" Elijah asked.

I was busy pretending to pat down my army jacket and fix my braids while catching glimpses of Micah watching us. I faced Elijah and responded to him. "Yeah, I'm really interested in stretching my legs and checking out the city."

Dara's voice came as a surprise as she exited the kitchen. "You two be sure to start heading back when the bells start sounding off from the cathedral."

"I thought you wouldn't be able to see us in the morning," I said with a smile.

She laughed lightly. "I didn't think I would be able to, either." She pointed to one of the windows. In the distance, upon a large hill, there sat the monumental building that dwarfed any other structure in the city. "The bells start going off around eleven o'clock, so if you start heading back home around that time, you should have plenty of breathing room to get ready and meet up in the kitchen for lunch before the rush hour begins."

Elijah looked the dining area over. "You seem to do rather well for yourself as a diner even though you're an inn."

The smile that we got then was the kind that held traces of sadness. You knew that there was happiness to it, but there was hurt there, too. "That's all thanks to my husband, Arrow," she admitted. "He had a passion for making people feel comfortable and was amazing in the kitchen. He taught me a thing or two over the years." She licked her lips, and her eyes fogged over like she was drifting away to some faraway place that no one could follow her to. "Some days I miss him more than others." She looked to the

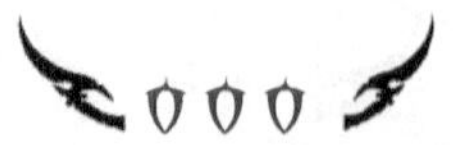

ceiling and sniffed before blinking away unshed tears.
Turning her attention back to us, she motioned to the front
door, saying, "Return when you hear the bells," in a soft
voice that was on the verge of breaking.

I nodded and forced a smile. I hadn't meant to bring
up painful memories again. "We'll see you around lunch,
then." With that said, the two of us headed out and hit the
streets.

For several hours, I had struggled to get used to the
uneven roads. You'd think after falling twice, stumbling
relentlessly, and scuffing my toes over the bubbled
cobblestones more times than I cared to count, I would have
learned how to walk a straight line instead of looking like a
nervous drunk caught in the act during daylight hours.
Unfortunately, my learning curve was far greater than
expected. Aside from mumbling a few choice words under
my breath or laughing to hide my evident embarrassment, I
managed to enjoy my day out. After entering only a few of
the shops, it was clear to us that the money we had earned
was minimal, as promised. It would be enough to buy a
couple of meals, or maybe a small coin purse. Nothing more
than that, though. I had assumed as much, but it was nice to
be sure of that fact now.

There wasn't anything really notable that happened
while we were out. By the time the bells had started sounding
off, we were already halfway to the inn. Every block or so, I
would look back to the massive structure that shadowed
everything. The longer I was in the faith city, the more that I

saw things in a different light. Now—for whatever reason—when I saw the cathedral, the hair on the back of my neck stood on end. The building was both beautiful and haunting to look at. I couldn't stop looking at it as we headed back to the inn.

The lunch rush was similar to the dinner rush from the night before: different meal, same execution plan. Again, we received praise from Dara, who looked at us with a smirk on her lips and a hand on her hips.

"I think I really need to put in a word with the Grand Master about how I would like to keep you two on staff." She looked worried for a moment and quickly added, "Only if you two want to, of course. Don't want you taking on a job that you would wind up regretting later. Don't feel like you're doing me any favors, ya hear? It won't hurt my feelings if you decline so you can get something else that you might feel more passionate about."

"I would love to work with you. I already know the kitchen, I'm familiar with you and the staff, and I know my way around the place fairly well for having just arrived. Besides, cooking reminds me of my parents," I admitted.

Elijah thumbed to me, saying, "I'm with her. Everything she said, I second."

Clapping her hands together joyfully, Dara laughed, delighted with our replies. "Well, that's that, then. I'll write up a letter for you to take up to the cathedral tomorrow. Grand Master Arland will need to look it over, and then it'll need to be stamped by the employment house."

"Do you think we could discuss wages and living arrangements later on tonight?" I pressed. Momma didn't raise a fool.

She wagged a finger at me. "A girl that knows how to bargain. I like that." Stopping to think for a moment, Dara

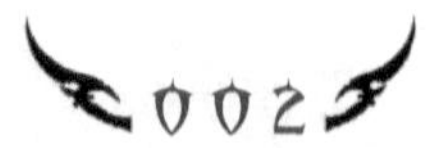

nodded to herself with a slight hum. "Hmm, yes. I believe later on tonight will be perfect. I'll be able to add the details to the letter, and it will make the whole process run a lot smoother for the employment house if we do."

"Perfect!" I gleefully announced. Turning on heel, I called out to Elijah, who had wandered off to scoop out some stew into a bowl. "I'm going to head back out into the city."

"Want some company?"

I shook my head. "No. I just wanted to window shop at a few places that we passed by earlier. I'll be back before it gets dark outside." I looked over to Dara. "I know that the dinner rush starts not too long after sundown."

"Right you are, young lady," Dara said with a proud look in her eyes.

Elijah set his bowl down on the counter and looked at me with concern. "Are you sure that you don't want me to come with you? I don't mind tagging along as you daydream over things."

I nodded. "I'm sure. Besides, you already got yourself an extra helping of food. Sit and enjoy it. I'll be fine on my own. Don't make me remind you that you're still healing from your recent injuries, you'll lose the argument real fast."

He drew in a deep breath and released it slowly. We exchanged a look with our eyes. One that silently told the other that we needed to act normal and that we both needed to be careful, no matter where we were in the city. That included under the roof of the inn.

"All right. I'll see you later on tonight, then." He slid up onto a stool in front of the counter and gave me a weak smile. One that was full of worry.

"I'll see you later on as well. I best be getting back to work. The linen should be dry by now, and there are beds

that need to be made." I barely caught a glimpse of the hem of her skirt as Dara rushed out of the room and into the back courtyard, where the laundry was hung.

"Be back soon." I dropped my voice to a whisper only he could hear as I passed by to say, "Be careful."

"Mhmm," he hummed with a mouthful of stew and gave me a thumbs-up as I left.

Micah wasn't at the front desk when I left. I didn't know if that meant I should be more careful or if he had been listening to our conversation in the kitchen. Either way, it set me on edge knowing that I was being followed around and listened to at every turn. Could I understand why they were being so careful with Elijah and me? Yes. Did I like it? Not in the slightest.

Outside, I took in a deep breath of fresh air and quickly headed in the direction of the shops that I had remembered from our ventures earlier. I wanted to get an idea of which tailoring shop had the better quality clothes. Between Meemaw and Momma, I had an eye for stitching. Tack on the fact that Daddy could tell me the good leather from the bad and which fabrics could hold up through an honest day's work, there wasn't a chance I was going to be swindled by someone trying to earn a bit of money off of my ignorance. Browsing would also give me a good estimate of the wages I should be asking Dara for.

Around the third shop I was about to enter, there was a tall, sophisticated man speaking with another well-dressed male. The taller male had a long face and eyes that looked both sad and tired. His heavily creased brow was bent with anger, and his side-swept, sandy-blond hair made the many folds visible as he argued with the other man.

The second male had deep black hair that held hints of red when the sun hit it just right. It was shaved along the

sides, while the top was short and combed back, but it was long in the back. His hazel eyes also seemed to burn with a crimson undertone, and they came across as if they held a thousand schemes within them. His skin was dark. Darker than Daddy's. It appeared like a black pearl against the pale white of his pantsuit. The ruby feathers that were woven into his hair draped around his neck like a collar, and he had a very thin and finely groomed goatee that made him look a little older than I would have guessed at first glance. A series of black and silver necklaces that were thick and carved in a beautiful design that matched his large earrings were coiled around his neck. I stared a little too long at the deep V of his suit and noted that there was nothing but a bare chest beneath it and not the expected button-up shirt I thought I'd find. When my eyes drifted back up to his face, our eyes met, and he winked at me before he resumed looking at the other male.

The two of them were blocking the path to the entrance and so engrossed in their conversation that they didn't notice me needing to pass by. It didn't help that the one dressed in white made no move to notify his conversation partner that I was coming up behind them. Agitated, I figured I would just walk through the street to get around them. No sooner had my foot hit the street did the chaos begin.

"You, *sir*, are a liar!" the taller man professed.

"Oh? If you believe that to be true, then go see for yourself. I won't stop you," the male in white urged with a suspiciously chipper tone.

"You know nothing," the taller man whispered heatedly. "I *will* go and see. If nothing more than to prove to myself that I was right and you are a sad, cruel man trying to create wedges between two loving people." He stormed off

through the street, bumping into me as he passed. "Watch where you're going!" he yelled at me and then continued on his way like he wasn't the one in the wrong.

I stumbled back and slipped on the curbside as I tried to right myself on the sidewalk. As I failed with my footwork, I found myself caught before I landed square on my backside.

"Whoa there, pretty lady. Careful, the streets are full of angry people."

I shouldn't have been as surprised as I was to see the suit-wearing male holding me in his arms. As I confidently situated myself, I gave a look of disapproval while dusting off unseen dirt from my clothes. "I'm sure you had no hand in causing him to be so angry."

"He simply didn't enjoy me telling him that his wife was enthralled with another man."

"Charming," I said with a sneer and a roll of my eyes.

"Heh, I've angered you?" The way he said it sounded like he was almost proud that he had managed to do it so easily.

I flashed a mock grin in his direction. "It's a stretch if you think my annoyance is anger."

He grinned as he said, "What is annoyance but a single stepping stone along the path to anger?"

I furrowed my brow and narrowed my eyes at him. I didn't like the familiar way his gestures and speech reminded me of a certain devil. I took a step back and shook my head while speaking quietly. "I've no quarrel with you. I just want to look around in the shop up ahead, nothing more."

He plucked a brow over one eye and gave a throaty chuckle. "Oh … oh, you're a sharp one."

"Whether I'm sharp or dull to you makes no difference to me. Either way, you have a good day. I'll just

carry on." I wanted nothing more than to have distance between us. I was willing to pass the shop, even. Maybe head a little deeper into the city before doubling back and rushing toward Arrow's Inn. However, the male had no intention of letting me pass.

Quickly, he blocked my path again and held out his hand. "The name's Kasim."

"Very nice to meet you, Kasim, but I'm pressed for time. I have to get back to work soon."

"Hahaha. Surely giving me a name won't make you late. If a few minutes of your time were going to make you so late to work, I'd dare make the assumption that you wouldn't have had the time to visit this shop you were so keen on looking around in." He grinned then. "Your name?" It sounded like a command, not a polite suggestion.

I drew my lips into my mouth and stared at him, then his hand. I ignored the gesture of handshaking and settled for quickly blurting out, "Sia," before brushing past him hurriedly.

In an instant, he grabbed my arm and spun me back around to face him. "Sia, is it? That's a pretty nickname. But it isn't your *real* name."

"Clever of you to pick up on that. No, it isn't, and I won't provide it for you. So—if you don't mind—I'm going to be on my way now." I tried to pull my hand away from his vice grip, but he wasn't letting go. His smile was like a curved sword, and I saw something flash in his eyes. Out of fear someone would hear me, I whispered to him, "I won't make a deal with you."

That didn't make him let go. In fact, it made him squeeze my arm a little harder right before he jerked me toward him with such force that I almost hit his chest. "Ah, see … there it is. I knew you were different the moment I saw

you. I do love it when the player knows the game. Makes it a bit more fun."

I forced a smile. "I don't know what you're talking about," I lied.

"Oh, my dear, I believe you do." He drew in closer and then inhaled deeply. His eyes fluttered, and he laughed lightly. "You know better than anyone here." He dropped his voice to a dangerous level that was meant for only my ears. "I can smell *him* on you."

I went still. All of my assumptions collided together to form the ugly truth that I was afraid of. He was a devil, and one strong enough that it could reside in a faith city, too. Was this why Draki had told me to be careful? Was it because devils could roam through these streets just like they could out in the Wastes?

His words cut through my thoughts like a knife. "I see I've got your attention now."

"Look, I don't want any trouble ..."

"Nor I. I just want to see if you can resist the urge to lose control." He lifted his free hand and reached for my face.

Looking away, I tried to peel away from his grip, but I found that I didn't have to struggle much. His hold on me was released, and his hand never grazed my skin. Opening my eyes, I saw that he had made sure to put a good amount of distance between us. A devil didn't back off like that because a girl was struggling. No. From my experience, the monsters only backed off when a bigger monster entered the room.

Draki's voice came from behind me as he said, "I see you've not improved on your tactics, Kasim."

"Not everyone can seduce someone into making a deal like you."

Draki laughed and stepped up to my side. "I suppose my charm and beauty are gifts then."

"Not all of us could be His favorite."

The look on Draki's face twisted. "And you see that it didn't get me much further in life than you."

"You've yourself to blame for that."

I heard a growl then and quickly swept the streets to see if anyone else was seeing any of this, or worse, hearing it. But it was like we were in a bubble. No one even gave us a passing glance.

"And I see that you still want what others have," Draki countered angrily.

"What brings you to the faith city?" Kasim inquired in a huff.

"I assure you, it was not my desire to come here. I am merely assisting the young lady," he informed while gesturing to me.

Kasim and Draki both looked at me. Between the fixed attention of two devils was not exactly where I wanted to be. I shrunk a bit on the spot before miraculously gaining more confidence. Draki was to protect me and put my best interest first and foremost. I wasn't in any danger, nothing that I couldn't get out of anyway.

Pointing to the two of them, I warned, "Don't drag me into the middle of this. I have better things to do with my time."

"Why did you come to the faith city?" Kasim asked.

"To find a home," I admitted, ignoring the short, stifled laugh coming from Draki.

Kasim didn't look entertained in the slightest. He shook his head with a look in his eyes that I didn't like. It looked a lot like pity. "You've come to the wrong place for that."

"Why is that?"

"Because home is a place that you humans feel safe at. You'll find out soon enough that you won't find that here. There's a darkness wrapped up in this place."

I stared at him like I was waiting for him to start cackling at me for being naïve. But he only returned the look with an expression I never expected of a devil. It was almost sympathetic.

Slowly, I realized that he wasn't lying to me. The more this reality sank in, the more I felt wronged. I felt like I had finally reached my goal, only to find that it was built on lies. And the more that this thought filled my mind, the more that I found myself thinking that Draki's proposal to build my own city was looking better and better. However, I already had a debt that I needed to pay and struggled with delivering in that department. What was I going to do when there would be more added to that price?

"I'll be the judge of whether or not I call this place home," I muttered and turned to walk back to the inn. I had enough of the city for one day. I wanted to go back and get lost in work, so I didn't have to think about everything that had been dumped on me.

"You'll find that your verdict won't stray far from mine. I see your type more than I'd care to admit. Fun to play with for a little while, but you either turn away from the truth or fall victim to it," Kasim warned.

"I refuse to do either of those." I didn't know if I said it because I simply wanted to defy him, or if it was because I didn't want to believe that those were the only two options I had.

Draki was suddenly in front of me, and I stopped and sighed while looking at everything but him. "What do you want?"

He pointed to the shop behind me. "Didn't you want to look around in there?"

"I did. But I don't find myself wanting to look at clothes right now. I feel drained, and I just want to go back to the inn and put in some extra time or help out around the place."

"You mean you're going back to distract yourself."

"Yes, Draki. I'm going to busy myself so I don't have to think. I'm tired of thinking. I'm tired of searching. I'm tired. Everything I struggled for … I thought that I was going to be able to make a home for myself, and I've been told that I can't achieve that. I don't know what to believe, and I'm just too tired to think about it."

"Then I suppose the only thing to do is to show you."

"Show me what?"

"The secret that this city hides. I'll show you the ugly truth that I know you won't allow yourself to live with. I've come to know you in many ways, Sia. And this will never be your home because you won't be able to wash away the stains this place has."

I felt like crying. Hugging myself, I quietly asked, "And you'd have me leave it all and build my own village where the freedom and well-being of those living there is bought with a sacrifice?"

He gave me a look that said I wasn't wrong. "Everything in this life comes at a price, my dear. The more you fight it, the more the world will try to remind you of it."

"I refuse to believe that is the only way we can live in this world."

"Then you fight the inevitable. Stop being so stubborn and let's leave this place."

"Why are you pushing for me to leave?"

"Because there are things in this life that can't be unseen, there are things that can't be unheard, and there is a haunting anguish that comes with hidden things coming into the light. I'm trying to save you the torment."

I went to walk around him while saying, "You like seeing me suffer."

He grabbed my arm, stopping me in my tracks. "When I'm the one tormenting, yes. This, however, is a different breed of evil. I'm trying to help you."

My eyes searched his. "I just want a place to call home."

Kasim spoke up as he walked closer to us. "Let her see this place for what it is. If it scars her, it's her own fault, not yours."

"You won't walk away from this until you see that it will never be what you want it to be?" Draki asked.

"For now, Draki, I just want to go back to the inn and prepare my mind for work."

He let go of my arm with a sigh and looked me over. "And what of clothes? Were you not out here to try to find some suitable attire for yourself and that *boy*?"

"I was looking at clothes for *Elijah* and myself, yes. But I don't have enough money to buy anything, and it will be some time before I will. It's pointless to get my heart set on something that may not be there by the time my purse is full enough to shop. I was only looking over a few places to see who had the best quality clothes for the best price."

"I see," he said. "Very well, then. Head back."

"Are you not going to follow?"

Kasim smirked and said, "I believe he wants to linger behind to have a word with me."

"Fine," I whispered and started to walk off.

"Would you rather I walk you back?" Draki asked.

I stumbled over my footwork and my thoughts. "I …
don't think I'll need your help. I should be able to find my
way back on my own."

"That isn't what I asked. Do you *want* me to walk
you back?"

My heart did a flip, my stomach knotted, and I felt a
smile wanting to claim my lips. "I know that you only leave
me when you have something important to tend to, or you
are remaining unseen for my protection. I'll be fine."

"Sia …"

"Yes?"

"Do you want to be alone right now?"

The way he looked at me wasn't the usual way I had
grown accustomed to. I wasn't sure if I was being pitied, or if
he was upholding his end of the bargain, or if he was
genuinely concerned about me, but the longer he looked at
me, the more I realized that I didn't want to be alone. I had so
few people that I could trust in my life, I was in a new place,
and I wanted—more than anything in the world—to just
have someone hold me and tell me everything was going to
be all right. I just wanted to hear it, even if it was a lie,
because I had enough of struggling and battles and pain. For
a moment, I wanted to be free of everything tormenting me,
and I wanted to feel free of worry. I looked away before I
started to cry. It was easier to mask everything when I wasn't
staring at someone that could pick apart everything that
made me who I was by simply looking into my eyes.

"I'll be fi—"

"Admit that you want me," he commanded.

I was taken aback by his statement and swallowed
whatever I was going to say. My heartbeat fumbled, and I felt
my chest tighten as a rush of heat traveled from my head to

my toes, burning my skin as I nervously reached up to play
with my braids. "I-I-I don't …"

He waltzed over to me like he was on a mission.
When he was practically toe-to-toe with me, he spoke in the
softest voice I had ever heard him produce. "Tell me that you
don't want to be alone, Sia, and I'll walk with you back to the
inn in silence."

My mouth said it before I could stop myself. "Please
walk with me," I whispered.

He held out the crook of his arm and looked back to
Kasim. "We'll meet up again. I've my duties to attend to. You
understand?"

Kasim bowed. "Of course. You and I will meet up
again soon enough."

"Oh, we shall."

By the time we made it back to the inn, I had worked
up an appetite and headed straight for the kitchen to fetch a
snack before I would start working. While we waited around,
I told Elijah about the shops that I had looked at and told him
that when we got enough money, we should both get
ourselves a few outfits and split the cost of any supplies we
thought we would need. I didn't tell him about how I wasn't
sure if we could call this home or not. I even left out that I
had run into another devil. I didn't exactly have a chance to
speak too freely with him due to the fact that I knew we were
being watched. The last thing I wanted to do was tell anyone
that the place we had all deemed as the safest place on Earth
was actually not as safe as we thought. I most certainly didn't

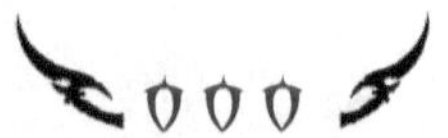

want to express these truths while being secretly watched by everyone, not knowing how they'd take the news. For all we knew, these people could be hiding a special kind of crazy and kill us to keep the truth from getting out to the rest of the people in the city. For now, it was best to be careful and only talk to Elijah about those things when we were absolutely sure that no one was listening. In the middle of the kitchen, a couple of hours before the dinner rush was not that time.

About an hour after the diner had closed up, Dara, Elijah, and I finished up talking about our hourly pay and the daily duties that would be expected of us. With our evening shift over and negotiations handled, he and I walked to our rooms.

Once in the halls, I whispered as quietly as I could, "I found out a few things. We need to talk."

"Maybe we can find some time to ourselves and talk about it tomorrow? I think I found out a few things too," he whispered back.

I nodded faintly and said, "Sleep well, Elijah," as we parted ways in the hall.

"I'll see you tomorrow, Sia. Goodnight."

As I shut the door, I noticed a package on the bed. It was hard to tell with the lamps not lit. There wasn't any point in lighting them now, right before bed. So, I plucked it off of the quilt and took it over to the window. After drawing back the curtains to let in the moonlight and illumination from the street lamps, I turned the package over in my hands curiously. The paper crinkled in my grasp as I started to undo the twine that was wrapped and knotted around it. Slowly, I opened it to reveal a set of jeans, a creamy-white blouse with a pattern of small, red poppies, and a coral-colored dress with a brown, braided, leather belt.

I looked around the room like I would find the culprit for dropping off the package. But there was no one. There was only the faint scent of spice and ash coming from the pile of new outfits.

Chapter 28:

What is Expected of You

Over breakfast the next morning, Dara told us that we would be going to the cathedral. She informed us that we would meet with Grand Master Arland, take care of the initial paperwork, and be set up with a private tutor to teach us the ways of the city and how everything worked. Honestly, it was a lot to take in, and I wasn't sure if I wanted to go and get it taken care of as soon as possible or hide in my bathroom until they gave up looking for me.

"Your eyes look as big as that plate, Sia. You're worrying over nothing. Don't fret over it so much. Once we go there, you'll see that it's nothing more than getting acquainted with the appropriate people so you two can know more about the place you've chosen to call home." Soon after that, Dara went to fetch us an extra helping of food while I pondered over everything we had been told.

Elijah nudged me. "She's right, ya know."

I nodded. But the more that I thought about it, the more that I realized that after she called Saint Augustine home, I didn't feel like that was the right word to describe the place. I frowned as that thought engulfed my mind. "I know.

I—I just don't like that whenever I try to think of this as home …" I looked at him with a sad expression. "I can't."

His lips thinned out into a straight line, and he rubbed me on the back. "Home for me is wherever you are, Sia."

I smiled. "Even if that means that you'll have to fight off demons or devils every night for the rest of your life?"

There was a short pause, but it felt like an eternity. Finally, he said, "If I'm by your side, then, yes."

"Elijah, I couldn't do that to you."

He kissed my forehead. The action was too quick to dodge, and I found myself closing my eyes as I memorized the press of his lips against my skin. "You aren't doing anything to me, Sia. That's the beauty of choice. I choose to go where you go. May that be here, across a thousand deserts, or into a land of eternal night, my home is still with you."

Dara came out of the kitchen with two piping hot plates, and she placed them in front of us, saying, "Dig in. We don't want to keep the Grand Master waiting."

The cathedral felt like it was a living, breathing entity. Any moment now, I was sure it would take in a lungful of air, howl into the afternoon sky, and devour the quiet city below. The closer that we got, the more nervous I became.

Dara wanted to make a few stops along the way to get us better acquainted with the area and to familiarize ourselves with the local shops and the people that ran them.

When the bells began to toll with their thick, hollow song, we were a few blocks away. It was the perfect spot to feel the ringing tremble through my entire being as we made our way up the long, daunting flight of steps.

Overhead, a block of jet-black ravens cawed and fluttered away from the bell tower. The whole scene felt ominous. The only addition that could have made it more poetic than creepy would have been a collection of black-dressed people with matching umbrellas standing out in the rain in front of it.

When we reached the main doors, the shadow that embraced us from the enormous building made the early afternoon air feel chilled. I hoped that inside the building, there would be a reprieve from the strange cold that overtook me.

The massive, wooden doors creaked eerily as they slowly swung open, and men wearing deep brown robes came rushing out in two perfect rows. Their quiet humming kept in tune with the song of the bells.

A single male wearing a creamy-white robe and swinging a silver, ornately designed incense burner bowed to us and several others that were collected around the top of the steps. Without a word, he motioned for us all to follow, turned, and headed back through the main doors. We all quietly trailed behind him.

Inside, wordless singing echoed through the massive building, and I could feel it all over my body. My heart began to race. Between the ringing of the bells and the singing, I felt like I was taking in too much. Worried that I might offend the wrong person, I refrained from making it too painfully obvious that my senses were overloaded. Thankfully, the tolls of the bells stopped not too long after we had entered. We had barely made it halfway across the red carpet lining

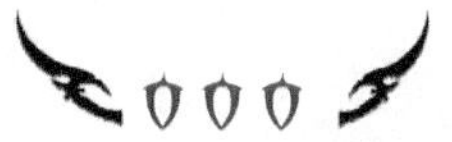

the cathedral's floor when we came to a stop. Someone was blocking our path, though, from the way he held himself, he wasn't just anyone. The male leading us bowed to the man standing in front of him and then shuffled off to the side.

The one that was now before us wore robes of red and white that had thick, bold, gold trimmings. In one hand, he had a bright yellow staff with odd symbols and markings swirling along the length of it. In the other, he held a black leather book with gold letters on the binding. He had soft, hazel eyes and deep brown hair that was cut short and combed back. As I looked at him, I couldn't find a line or crease on his face that would depict an age above his mid-twenties. I was so focused on studying him that Elijah nudging me with his elbow gave my heart a new rhythm to beat to.

Whispering, he said, "I feel a bit anxious and out of place here."

"You and I both," I replied under my breath as I attempted to ignore the zing of energy that raced through my entire being.

He could still hear me, though, and he chuckled lightly. "Good to know I'm not alone."

I silently agreed. This is not how I wanted to spend my day. I wanted to get whatever paperwork I needed to do out of the way and go back to the inn. The longer that I stayed in this city, the more uneasy I became. The more that I explored, the more darkness I discovered. There was a secret buried deep within these walls, and I wasn't sure this was something I could easily escape. Of all the places I had been to, I knew what lay in wait around the corner with all of them. It was devils and packs. Here, though? This wasn't the same. I could feel that this was the calm before the storm. Did

I really want to be here when that storm hit, or should I cut and run before it was too late?

"Greetings, Grand Master Arland," the surrounding group of people stated in robotic unison, their lifeless voices setting me on edge.

"Please separate to your appropriate groups. Newcomers, please, follow me," the Grand Master explained with a smile pointed in our direction.

Guess they know who the newcomers are.

The crowd thinned out, leaving only Elijah, myself, and an older man that stood nearby. The older gentleman had gray hair and sun-worn skin that looked like old leather. His eyes were tired, and he wore a red cardigan over a wrinkled and stained white shirt. I eyed over his dirt-splotched jeans and assumed that he had arrived that day from the Wastes.

After a short moment, we were led deeper into the cathedral. The light tap of the staff gave off a muffled *pang* against the red carpet that made the attached bells jingle with each step. My eyes walked up and down either side of the building, noting the pews with people seated, heads bowed, hands married, and eyes closed. It reminded me of the cave drawings. Had I not seen the rise and fall of their chest, I would have thought them all to be strange statues.

The light pouring in through the stained-glass windows splashed every surface with a vivid glow of color. The inside of the cathedral had turned into a kaleidoscope, and every piece of furniture and person was redesigned in a beautiful rainbow of fractured light.

We stopped at the base of a small stack of stairs that led up to an altar. The Grand Master turned and spoke to us with an excited glint in his eyes. "What a grand day this is to have three newcomers. We are blessed, truly." He bowed his

head and whispered something before lifting back and motioning for us all to come closer. "Normally, we receive one or two newcomers every couple of weeks. This week, though, we have three newcomers all at once. What a gift. What a gift." He chuckled happily. "Tell me, what are your names?"

"Dean," the older gentleman expressed in a soft voice.

"Elijah."

"Sia."

The Grand Master's vision rested respectfully upon each individual as we gave our names. He nodded and drew in a deep breath. "Welcome to our city, Sia, Elijah, and Dean. I hope that you have found rest and comfort within our walls, but—most importantly—I hope that you have found a home." He turned and motioned to the entire cathedral. "Today, you will be gifted with a tutor from us to teach you both our ways and that of the Lord. This is to prepare you for the Hours of Whispered Prayers."

"The Hours of Whispered Prayers?" I asked.

He looked at me with a flash of silent judgment before he explained further. "Yes. It is a ritual that we perform together to keep the city safe each night. It is a burden we share so that our city remains untouched by the darkness that lurks beyond our walls."

"How do you all do that?" Elijah asked.

"In due time, lad. In due time. First, let us set you up with private tutors to ensure that you learn our valuable teachings that will aid in your devoted service later on."

"When are we to serve, Grand Master?" Dean inquired.

Arland grinned and said, "Your first calling will be one week from today."

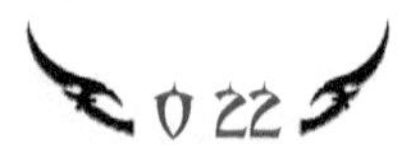

Many thoughts passed through my mind at that moment. What were we learning? How did we do this ritual? Why did we need to be tutored? Should I be concerned? My internal questioning was disrupted by the Grand Master saying my name.

"Sia, I shall pair you with one of my most favorite tutors. She is a faith healer, a wonderful teacher, and a delightful soul." He called over his shoulder, "Ivy, my dear, come greet your new student."

From a hidden room behind him, there came a woman that made every anxiety in me melt away upon seeing her. The girl's golden, curly hair shined like it had been spun from sunshine, and her soft, pink skin looked as though it rarely saw the world outside the cathedral walls. Long lashes hugged her milky-green eyes, and her steps were swift and sure despite the fact that I could tell that she was blind. Her form was covered up in a long, sage-green dress.

Behind her trailed a young man with deeply tanned skin. His deep brown eyes were almost black, and as the young lady stepped forward, he walked behind like a faithful shadow. "Miss Ivy, the steps are ahead," he said in an accent that was as thick as his jet-black hair.

"Thank you, James," Ivy whispered. The faint smile on her pretty pink lips made me mirror the expression as she came to the Grand Master's side. Her short stature made Arland look strangely tall as he faced her.

"Greetings, Grand Master," Ivy proclaimed with a bow.

"Ivy," Arland started and took the girl's hand and then my own. I wanted to pull away but allowed him to bring me to the young lady. "This is Sia. She is to be your new student for the next week. We'll need her ready for the

next round of chosen ones for the Hours of Whispered Prayers."

Her tiny hand found mine and squeezed, and I felt like she could see me as she faced me. Softly, she spoke to Arland, "I understand, Grand Master. Consider her well taken care of. I shall have her fully prepared for next week."

"Good girl," Arland stated with a joyful grin. Then he motioned for Elijah to come forward. "James, how about you take this lad to meet David for me? That'll be a good pairing, I think." As they spoke, their voices were drowned out by Ivy's as she gently tugged me further into the building and toward the doors that led into a deep, dark, and dreary hallway.

I suddenly longed for the massive, open main room with many windows and basking in warm sunshine. The halls we were now in were on the side that was devoid of light during these hours, which made our walk feel cold and eerie. Suddenly, Ivy turned in one direction and then another and stopped. Letting go of my hand, she spun on heel and faced me with a crease deeply set in her brow.

"I'm sorry, Sia, but I will have to ask you to tell your friend to stay behind. Only one student is permitted per tutor."

I looked from her to my side and then behind me. There was no one there. At least, no one that she could see. "I–"

Draki's voice inside my mind caused me to take a pause. *"Seems I can't tag along like usual. I'll meet up with you outside the cathedral when your little learning session is over."*

Attempting to change the subject and not appear nervous while the devil parted ways, I asked Ivy, "Why are people paired up in such small groups? Wouldn't it be easier to teach a class?"

"Every person is different. While more people can be taught, we find that one-on-one sessions are more personal and bring about a healthier learning atmosphere for each student."

They needed all the help they could get in that department. The walk up here, paired with the haunting halls, made the whole experience feel like I was being dragged off to be tortured for a crime I didn't commit. "Oh. Where are we heading?"

She held out her hand to me. "May I?"

Awkwardly, I nodded, smacked my face, and then put my hand in hers, saying, "Yes."

She laughed like she knew what I had done. "Don't beat yourself up. It takes time to get used to being around people that aren't like you. Give it time. You weren't born able to walk. You had to learn."

I smiled. The words were comforting. Unlike Arland, when Ivy smiled, it felt real and made me feel like I could trust her. "Thank you."

We headed deeper into the hall. I honestly started to wonder how big the building was. There was nothing but a never-ending stretch of gray, stone walls. When I thought we would have kept going, Ivy stopped and opened a door. As we entered the room, I took note of the small table and rickety chair in the center. There was a desk tucked into a corner near a chalkboard on wheels, and a small chest near the entrance was nestled next to a tall bookcase with very few books. It looked uninviting, but I said nothing as I waited for Ivy.

"Please, take a seat," she stated, motioning toward the two seating options in the room.

Not wanting to sit at a desk, I opted for the chair at the table and winced as I heard the poor wood whine under

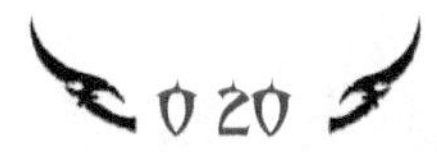

my weight. I drummed my fingers over the surprisingly smooth surface of the old table and gave the room another once-over before asking, "Sooo … what am I going to be learning about?"

"A great deal of things. I will do my best to be thorough and informative, but please ask me anything if you feel lost or confused. This will help you have a better understanding and, therefore, a stronger sense of faith for the Hours of Whispered Prayers."

"Faith in what?" I asked softly in a curious tone.

"It's when you believe in—"

My head immediately started to hurt as she talked. The finer details of the room became hazy and distorted as my vision blurred. Panic swelled within my chest as my eyesight faded for a moment. My blood felt like it was on fire, and it blazed its way through my veins without remorse. My stomach churned, and I felt the urge to expel anything that I had consumed that day. Gripping the table, I sat with my mouth unhinged in soundless agony as each fresh wave of pain mingled with the surge of heat that flowed through my body. As the ringing in my ears faded, I heard Ivy's voice again.

"Does that make sense?"

No, because I didn't hear a single thing you said, I thought. Shifting uncomfortably in my seat, I timidly asked, "I'm sorry. Would you mind repeating that, please?"

There was a short pause before she smiled softly and slightly shook her head. "I don't mind at all. Basically, what I was saying is, when you start to have faith in—"

Again, her voice was drowned out by pain, and my body felt like I was consumed by fire. My head felt like it was being crushed, beads of sweat built on my brow, and I pushed my hand over my heart, where I felt like I had been

stabbed by a hot iron poker. Screwing my eyes shut, I did everything in my power to regain focus on Ivy's voice once again, but the one that I heard was far from the sweet girl before me.

"I would suggest you find a way to end your session early today. Clearly, you aren't strong enough for what they are trying to teach you," Draki hissed, his voice sounding slightly distant.

I said nothing in reply. I didn't have time to before Ivy spoke again. This time, all of her attention was on me, and the expression on her face was disapproving.

Did she know?

I gulped as I watched her and looked at the door to the room. Would it be rude to just get up and walk out without saying anything? Even if I could, that wasn't something I really wanted to do. For one, trying to escape a room with a blind person was beyond rude. She couldn't see, true, but that didn't mean she was stupid. However, I had considered it only because the way she looked at me told me I had done something unforgivable. Was that my conscience eating away at me, or was her unhappy glare in my direction giving me a silent warning that I was about to be met with a horrible fate for being tied to a devil and bravely entering a faith city?

"I can't believe that you would have done this," Ivy started. Blind or not, those eyes pierced through me like she saw the world in a way I never would understand. I felt like she saw things beyond the clothing and skin. It unnerved me. I felt like my flaws were on display. She drew in a long breath and exhaled it slowly before she continued. "And you said nothing to the Grand Master. Do you know what you could have done? The damage that could have ensued would have been irreparable. Do you care so little about yourself that you would have taken such drastic measures?"

"I was only doing what I thought I needed to in order to survive," I half-whined.

"I won't stand for this. Not for another moment," she stated in a stern voice.

"Please, let me explain."

"There's nothing to explain. I will inform the Grand Master of this at once. You shouldn't be here."

"Wait!"

"I will not! You are in pain. I might be blind, Sia, but I'm able to pick up on things."

"I—"

Her countenance twisted in emotional distress, concern swirled in her milky-green gaze. "You have gone through so much out there. I have heard how long you have traveled out in the Wastes. I didn't want to think about it. I didn't want to think about all the pain and struggles that you had to endure, but I can't be unfair to you and pretend that it didn't happen. You had to travel for such a long time … I can't even begin to imagine what you had to face beyond the safety of our walls. Because of that, I will request that the Grand Master give you some extra time to rest. I can tell that you are tired and still in pain from your travels."

She thought that I was tired and still weary from my journey? Talk about a load off my shoulders! I had thought she knew about my pact with a devil. This was a far easier mess to clean up. After quickly collecting myself and rubbing my sweaty palms onto my pant legs, I called out to Ivy before she got to the door. "You don't need to do that. Maybe … maybe there is another way for me to learn?"

"*Don't,*" Draki warned.

I ignored his warning. I saw no threat in anything around me, and I didn't understand why he was acting like it was such a bad thing. I felt unnerved but not in danger.

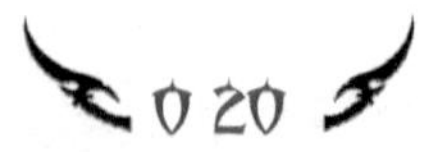

Besides, she didn't know about our deal, and I was sure that she wasn't going to find out about it any time soon.

Ivy turned toward me and stared off into the far end of the room as she contemplated something. "Are you sure you don't need more rest?"

"Yes," I stated. "I just need to learn at my own pace."

"I suppose that is a good suggestion. Hmmm, I wonder …" She walked over to the bookshelf and felt along the bindings of the books as she searched. "It's harder for me to find some things without my special writing to aid me. Can you come tell me what book I'm pointing to?"

I got up and went to her. Once there, I craned my head and read the gold lettering on the black, leather-bound book aloud, "The Holy Bible."

She faced me with a grand smile. "You read, Sia?"

"I can. My mom, dad, and meemaw taught me. We had a pretty good school at the place where I grew up, too."

Ivy nodded approvingly. "Good. Many villages out in the Wastes aren't as lucky." She drew the book from its place on the shelf. "This," she started as she felt around for my hand. After finding it, she raised it palm up, put the book in my grasp, and then gently brushed her fingers over the front cover. "This is the best place for us to start. If you have any questions, I am here to answer them."

For the next several hours, I read the Holy Bible. The more I did, the more fascinated I became. Angels were explained, demons, spirits, creation, prophets, God, and His son, Jesus. For days, this cycle continued. I saw less and less

of Draki, and I saw more and more of Ivy. Oftentimes, the two of us would go on and on about different stories and passages. We would even meet up with Elijah and talk more over dinner together. There was so much to take in. I read the scriptures daily. Ivy even let me take the book back to the inn with me. Faith had become a newfound fire within me, and it burned with the desire to learn.

I was told that in a week, I would be baptized after I confirmed my faith and announced my love and acceptance for God and the One called Jesus. Through it all, though, there were endless revelations and life lessons that I understood now more than I ever had. I got lost in a sea of knowledge, and I started to feel accepted. Only, there was the occasional dark whisper that haunted me from Draki.

"You're not good enough."

"You're not strong enough to handle the Hours of Whispered Prayers."

"God won't love you, not after what you've done."

"You've shed too much blood."

"You've told too many lies."

"You're too far gone to be forgiven."

"Don't forget that you belong to ME!"

"Sia?"

I blinked out of my trance and looked across the table to the two very concerned friends staring back at me. It had been a long week, and we were all out for a celebratory dinner together. Ivy had become such a close friend, and she felt more like family to us, to me.

"Are you all right?" Ivy asked.

Elijah caught my attention, and I knew he was thinking of asking the same thing.

I nodded to him and replied to Ivy with, "Yeah. I just get lost in thought sometimes. It's a lot to take in, but everything makes a lot more sense to me now. I just …"

"You just what?" Ivy urged me to finish.

"I just wish I would have known all of this sooner," I admitted.

"You found out now. There is no need to dwell on the past," she said with a soft smile.

Elijah found my hand and gave it a light squeeze. I smiled, but those words that Draki had spoken shook me more than I cared to admit. He was right … I didn't deserve God's love. Not with what I had done, and not with what I still had left to do. If I faltered in delivering on my end of the bargain, Draki would make sure everyone I knew and loved would suffer. There was no escaping that fate of mine. I at least wanted to ignore it for a little while longer.

"You'll be baptized tomorrow before you will head off to the inner wall to conduct your prayer session," Ivy reminded me.

I pushed the crumbs left over from my meal around on my plate while feeling my stomach turn in knots. "I can't wait," I lied.

I had wanted that day to feel special. I wanted it to feel like I was finally free from everything that weighed me down. I wanted it to break the chains that were tied to me and Draki, but I felt like I was going to suffer a lot more before I would ever know what it was like to be free.

"Come on, Sia. You have a big day tomorrow," Elijah said.

I half-smiled. "So do you, Elijah. You are getting baptized before the Hours of Whispered Prayers tomorrow, too."

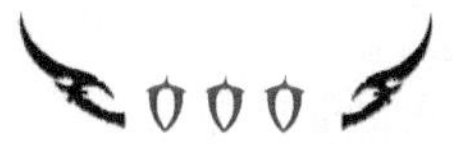

"Good to know that we can do that together," he replied with a grin.

Ivy giggled. "It seems that you two need to head off for the night. I need to head out as well. I don't like to stay out too late recently."

"Oh, why is that?" I asked.

She shook her head with her brows knit in deep thought. "I can't quite explain it. When I feel alone, and it's late at night, anxiety rises up in me, and I feel like I'm being watched or followed. I feel a weight on my feet and like I'm being spiritually dragged down. Sometimes I even hear whispers."

"That sounds terrifying," Elijah mumbled.

Ivy waved the thought away. "It's nothing compared to what you two had to deal with out in the Wastes, I'm sure."

"Do you want me to walk you home?" I asked.

"Don't worry about me. I'm not a faith healer because I lack belief in Him. A few choice words and a prayer full of authority and power and whatever dark energy is lurking around me will always dissipate."

"What about James? Can he come get you?" Elijah asked.

Usually, James would have joined us during our outings or assisted Ivy. Today, he had stayed behind to help prepare for tomorrow's event. If he could drop by and get Ivy, though, I would worry a little less about her. Also, I had to wonder if that dark energy was Draki. He had visited me once or twice, asking if this was where I wanted to make my home. I felt undecided still, and he would sneer, nod, and mumble something under his breath. More often than not, he made his disliking of Ivy known in the foulest of ways, and

since I asked him to stop bringing it up, I saw him even less. The probability that it was him taunting Ivy was pretty high.

"Are you sure?" Elijah pressed.

She nodded. "I'm sure. Now, you two run along and get some rest. Tomorrow is going to be a big day, and I want you guys to get a good night's sleep before I see you at the cathedral."

There was no fighting her on it. She had made up her mind. We hugged and parted ways. But the walk back to the inn and my room seemed longer tonight. From the restaurant to my bed, I was tormented by my own thoughts. My insecurities had their way with me while I went over a million different scenarios that all played out in my head, right down to my fear that I would burn alive after I was dunked underwater. Would Draki show up? Would an army of angels come swarming out of the sky to strike me down for everything I had done up until now? Would I taint the faith city because I brought a devil with me? I shivered from the thoughts and tried to quiet my mind so I could get some sleep.

I should have known better.

"Did you have a fun time?" Draki asked from his lazy perch on the windowsill.

I turned to look at him. He was bathed in moonlight, and he gazed out into the night-washed city. Full of contentment and lounging leisurely against the old, wooden framing, he appeared like there was more to him than the devil I saw. For a moment, he appeared as though he could be redeemed. I wanted to reach out and touch him, but I remained in bed and curled up under my blankets. "Would it bother you if I said yes?"

He slowly faced me and narrowed his eyes. "Would you be disturbed if I told you I would be?"

I gave him a look and sighed. "Yes. I was having fun …" At least, until he was mentally targeting me with things that I didn't want to think about or showing up in my room to pick on me.

He gave a short, clipped burst of laughter and looked away from me. "I wonder what your little black book says about liars," he practically hissed under his breath.

I had had enough of his sass and tormenting. As I swiftly sat up, I snapped at him in a hoarse tone, "Probably the same thing that it would say about you!"

Now that got his attention.

There was a hot rush of air rolling through the room that was unnatural. It was the kind of heat that could have peeled the paint off the walls and melted skin if he didn't control it. And I would be lying if I didn't admit I was drowning in the fear that was claiming me when his gaze held me in place. Slowly, he rose from his seat and waltzed toward me.

"What do you think it says about me?" he asked, but that even tone he questioned me in was betrayed by the heat in his eyes.

Words dried up, and I tried to look anywhere else but at him. However, the threat that he posed was very real, and I couldn't dare avert my attention. I fumbled for some half-baked attempt at speaking. "I don't know. I just thought—"

"Please, Sia," he purred darkly, and my skin rippled with goosebumps. His weight on the bed caused me to involuntarily lean toward him as he finished with, "Tell me everything that you've *thought*."

My vision drank in every bit of his dark perfection. I looked to his lips, down his throat, and to the muscle peeking out from beneath the white robes he wore. I daydreamed for

a moment and thought about throwing myself at him and had to sober up from that thought as our eyes collided once more.

"I didn't read about you specifically. I just thought that it wouldn't speak too kindly of devils."

He was threading a stray braid behind my ear as I spoke, and he went still. "You didn't read anything about me?"

I couldn't be sure, but his voice sounded pained for a moment, like he had wanted to be important enough to be written within the Bible. He sounded like he wanted to be important enough to be remembered. He sounded … disappointed.

Confused, I asked, "Are you written in that book?"

He froze, then. For a long moment, we just looked into each other's eyes and said nothing. Withdrawing his hand, he looked away with a quiet sigh. "Yes."

I rose to my knees and looked at him with slight excitement. I couldn't explain it. I had been learning so much, and there was still a lot I didn't understand. Yet, here was someone right in front of me that had seen countless events that I had been gradually reading and learning about. I opened my mouth to ask probably a million questions, but I could only think to ask, "Who are you?"

Nothing in my life had ever been so clear as the truth that hit me then. Draki looked back to me, and I saw it all. I saw the moonlight glowing off of him. I saw the anger and the pride, and when every moment along our journey came crashing to the front of my mind, it slammed into me like a tidal wave. I *knew*. Instantly, I held my hand over my mouth, and I sat down so fast I started to fall back toward my pillows. He caught me before I went too far and pulled me closer to him than I had been before.

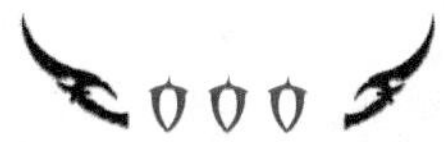

A slight smirk flickered over the corner of his mouth before it disappeared into a thin, unamused line. "And here I was starting to doubt the intelligence that I had come to know you for."

It was too scary to know what I had done. I hadn't made a deal with just *any* devil. I had made one with *the* devil. And now, could I ever be forgiven? I had killed, I had lied, I had made a deal with Draki, and soon I would have to pay up. The price of my sins was too high. I had always tried to be a good person before coming to the faith city and learning everything that I had. But in such a short amount of time, I had done so many things that I didn't think could be washed away. My reasoning was so small in comparison.

I didn't want him touching me. Not with everything that I felt when he did. "Let me go," I whispered.

"And what if I say no?" he whispered back, getting dangerously close to me. "Will you call out to your newfound God? Will you cry out to Him to save you?" He paused, and I didn't have the strength to speak without possibly breaking down into tears, so I angrily stared at him. "Should I call out to Him for you?" He chuckled softly. "Do you honestly think He answers to the likes of you or me? We are two lost souls left to decay in a world that is wasting away with countless others who've all been forgotten. You could scream at the top of your lungs, and you'll find yourself in the same place you are now … helpless and still with me." He yanked my arm, and when I crashed into him, he held me there in his blazing embrace as he whispered with his cheek pressed against mine, "So save your breath."

A tear full of all my regrets and anger welled and spilled from my eye as I thought, *God, forgive me. I'll pay the price for my sins and carry this cross if you'll keep Elijah safe. Just please don't leave my side until the very end.*

Draki pulled back and wiped the wetness from my face as he shook his head at me. "Shhh. You still have me. Until the end, I'll be here." He smiled then, but it held promises of torture. There was no mercy in it, nor was there any in him. He was hell-bent on destroying everything that held me together before he'd let me go. And that truth struck me deep.

Chapter 29:

Within these Walls

Draki warned me that I had until the end of the following day to make up my mind if the faith city was to be called my home or not. I wasn't sure if I would be welcomed by everyone by the time sundown rolled around. After agreeing that I would give a clear answer, I went to bed with a heavy heart.

The next morning, I was awoken by Dara's chipper voice from the other side of my bedroom door. "Today's the day! Rise and shine, Sia. We need to get you to the cathedral for your baptism before the Hours of Whispered Prayers tonight!"

My body felt heavy and sore, and my thoughts were instantly full of gloom. I wasn't sure I'd be able to eat breakfast at this rate, but I wanted to try to keep my strength up for what the day would hold for me.

There was a light knock on the door. "Sia, are you decent?" Elijah's voice sounded worried as he called out to me.

I double-checked my attire to make sure the girls weren't hanging out after a night of tossing and turning and

fussed with my braids as I replied, "You can come in, Elijah, I'm dressed."

After stepping in, he looked out in the hall to make sure the hallway was free of other people. He quickly closed the door and faced me. "So … are we running before everything goes down or going in on a wing and a prayer that your deal with you-know-who doesn't burn the cathedral to the ground during your baptism?"

Even though I was laughing so hard that my side ached, I mentally latched onto one beautiful word that he had spoken when he walked into the room. *We.* He didn't ask what I was going to do or what my choice was going to be. He asked what *we* were going to do. There was such a profound comfort in that. If I wanted to run, he'd run with me. If I wanted to stay, he would as well. Wherever I went, he would be, and it wasn't because he was forced to. It was because he wanted to.

My laughter ebbed, and I shook my head. "I don't think we need to make dust trails just yet. I … I really want to try."

"Getting baptized or calling this place home?"

I looked at him as I let the words sink in. "Both?"

He nodded. "Then I'll make sure our stuff is packed and ready if things go south."

Grinning, I asked, "And if they don't, we decide to stay, and Dara or Micah notice our things neatly packed?"

He shrugged. "I'll tell them we expected to be rehoused soon."

"Logical."

Walking over to me, Elijah took my hands and guided me to my feet. "No matter what, we are going to be okay."

I didn't need him to say anything else. I believed him. "You're right," I said and gave him a big, long hug.

Elijah was going to be baptized first. However, that was planned only after I had insisted that he go ahead of me. If things were going to go bad once it was my turn, I wanted Elijah to be saved. I wanted him to be forgiven and have a fresh start. I wasn't going to take that away from him. Not with everything he had lost … and was going to lose.

I had gone to eat breakfast after packing up my things. Elijah was still getting his things together. As previously discussed, if things made a turn for the worst, we were going to make a run for it, grab our things, and leave the city before anyone could stop us. After everything that we had been through, I didn't put these people above trying to kill us if they discovered that I had a deal with a devil — with *the* devil. When that thought slithered through my brain, I bit my lip so hard I was sure it would bleed.

About halfway through my meal, Elijah showed up and gave me a slight nod to let me know his things were in order. We ate and headed out for the cathedral after making sure that the inn was in good hands. We had to grab an extra set of clothes because we were going to change after the event.

Hours later, we were right outside the cathedral's front doors. It looked as intimidating as ever. I managed to keep my sweaty palms a secret as we headed inside. We said our hellos to the others that were there for their baptism and went up front to stand in line. Each of us were to be baptized

by our tutors. Elijah's teacher was David, who was a tall, thin man with deep brown hair and bright blue eyes.

"Step forward, Elijah," David instructed.

"You've got this," I whispered.

He smiled and squeezed my hand before he let go and walked onto the stage.

I stood behind, wondering if everything that he was experiencing would be something I would get a chance to know. It didn't matter, though. Elijah would. I could feel good about that, at least.

After he came up out of the water, Elijah was all smiles and full of laughter. There was clapping and a roar of excitement from the pews of spectators below. But all of that was drowned out by the voice of the last being that I wanted to hear from that day.

"Getting ready for your new life in the faith city?"

I mentally snapped back with, *"I told you I would give you an answer by the end of the day."*

"I'm looking forward to it. You still have promises made to me, Sia. Forget them and I'll go after everything you hold dear."

"I wasn't planning on it."

"Just remember that if you change your mind and want to build a place to call home … you'll always have me to depend on … Hahahaha."

The chills I felt at that moment made me feel like I had been threatened, and nothing he said was as comforting as he attempted to make it out to be. It was almost as if he knew an outcome to this whole situation, and I was dragged along for the ride. If words held the essence of the intent behind them, I could feel his desire for me to give up on calling this place home. I could feel his hand ushering me toward the path he had laid out for me. Was I really going to do that? This place was so peaceful and clean and free of

worry. Why would I want to give up on making a life here? He was just trying to rattle me and make me doubt this place. He only wanted more from me. He was a devil, after all.

But why did I still feel like there was a darkness lurking?

"Sia," Ivy said. The tone in her voice told me that it wasn't the first time she had called out to me.

Blinking, I awkwardly looked to the sea of patient faces and blushed, embarrassed. I shook my hands at my sides, wiped my sweaty palms on my hips, took a deep breath, and stepped up onto the stage. It was hard to make out any other sound in that moment because my heartbeat was drowning out everything around me. This was the moment of truth.

But a small part of me wondered if any of this would matter at all. If I went through the motions and said all the words right and meant them with all that I was … could I really be saved? Was I really going to be born into a new life? Or were the shackles of my sins too heavy? Were the ties to the devil too great that I couldn't find redemption in this life?

"You're going to be fine," Ivy whispered.

Taking her hand as I stepped into the water made some of my anxiety dissipate. She became an anchor for me. I turned around after I was comfortably in the pool, and she whispered to me again.

"Give it to God. Trust in Him."

"You can't give anything to Him when you are deceiving everyone around you."

I closed my eyes and fought past the sound of Draki hissing his taunt at me and repeated only the words that Ivy spoke. I crossed my arms over my chest and hoped that nothing would go wrong. Ivy pushed me down into the water.

Just like when I had gone under the river current, I was scared as the cool liquid swiftly covered my face. I held my breath, but I still felt the air bubbles as they left my nostrils. This water was kinder than the raging currents from before. These were still waters that consumed all the sound. A gentle hand held me in place as my hair floated beside my face. My eyes opened, and I could see Ivy hovering over me. For a moment, I wondered if she would just leave me there to drown. As if it was a fate I had escaped and was destined to fulfill. Closing my eyes, I took a moment to soak it all in. The silence was a living, breathing entity that hugged me like the surrounding liquid that pressed my clothes against my body. It enveloped me in a stillness that was almost peaceful. I let go of so many things from my past as I remained underwater.

God … if You can … forgive me? Guide me to where I'm meant to be, please. I feel … I feel so lost.

There was no whisper from Draki. There was only the welcomed silence and the cold embrace of the water around me. A second later, Ivy's hand aided me up toward the surface. The moment I felt my forehead break through the top of the water, there was a tingling sensation on my skin. All around the cathedral, everyone was alive with shouts of glee, and the next person was called forward as I stepped out of the pool. I looked back to the water sloshing about behind me. Were my sins left back there? Did I feel lighter? Had I been forgiven?

Did I forgive myself?

Ivy guided me to the backroom to change into dry clothes. After I was dressed, she rushed in and embraced me while wearing a bright smile.

"I'm so happy for you!"

"Thanks," I stated softly.

"Here," she said, handing me a book.

"A Bible?"

"It's yours. We all need guidance in this life, Sia. There are going to be times that you feel so alone in this world that you'll fall into despair and feel like there is no hope left." She pointed to the book. "Let your faith be your guiding star on your darkest night."

I hugged her because I didn't feel like anything that I would say in that moment would have been the right thing. She felt like home when we touched. My worries and doubts were silenced when I was around her. I wanted to stay like this forever. Comforted and accepted.

"I get the feeling that you're going to leave sometimes," Ivy said in a hardly audible tone. "Silly, right?" But she didn't sound like she believed that it was an absurd thought.

"Yeah. Silly," I muttered back.

Elijah met up with us within the hour, and we had a short Bible study session before we were taken to get our ceremonial robes. Afterward, we all waited for the knights to escort the clergy fathers and us to our destination. We made a very long and very quiet walk to the city wall.

The sky overhead was painted in a brilliant-blue hue with big, fluffy clouds that were scattered across every visible inch and washed in deep plums, radiant yellows, and soft peach colors. As we walked, the beautiful scenery swiftly turned dark, and not even the dusting of starlight could make the silent marching less unnerving. I couldn't understand

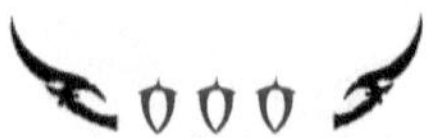

why this feeling of dread kept making an appearance within these walls. Was I that cynical? Had Draki messed with my head?

When we got to the large, metal door that separated the wall from the city, I didn't know what to expect. One of the knights broke formation, stepped up to the barrier, and knocked loudly on it. A moment later, a small, metal hatch was pulled back, revealing a set of distrusting eyes. A seal was presented, and the visor was slammed shut. Soon after, the doors were opened.

Pitch stared back from the mouth of the opening. There were countless whispers, but nothing clear could be made out. The many mutterings were eerily pouring out from the black abyss, making me not want to pass the threshold. However, I didn't have much of a choice. My reluctant feet moved as I was carried away by the crowd, and one by one we all headed inside.

Once inside, we could see down the left stretch of the corridor that there were many slumped-over shapes that went unnoticed within the sea of black. By the entrance, there were several knights standing guard, and a few red-robed people huddled near the mouth of the door. There were also two women, each holding a large, golden flask, while the men held parchment paper and wide-mouthed, ceramic cups. There were more shadows than there was light, and it made seeing what was in the flask or cups near-impossible.

"Please step forward one at a time, brothers and sisters. Let us partake in the ritual wine, and then you'll be seated for the Hours of Whispered Prayers," one of the red-robed men announced.

A female holding a flask stepped forward, poured the fragrant liquid into one of the cups, and the first in line

was given a sip before they were quickly escorted to a vacant spot further down the hall.

"Well, this is going to be a long and delightful evening," Draki grumbled behind me.

I went stiff and didn't move for a split second.

"The next may come forward."

A blazing hand was placed on my shoulder, and the devil's breath played over my ear as he spoke to me in a low tone, "Don't drink the wine. If you want to live, don't drink the wine."

From the lack of astonished looks from those around me, it was safe to say they didn't see or hear the devil on my shoulder whispering his commands. The question was: would I follow his orders, or would I ignore them? So far, everything he told me not to do didn't seem so harmful to me. However, none of them had the warnings of death tied to them either.

The cup was presented to me, and there was only a split second to decide. I took a large sip. Instantly, I was taken off to the side and led deeper into the shadowy void. All the while, I held the bitter drink in my mouth and tried to mask the fact that I had yet to swallow what I had taken. I thought, briefly, about spitting it out while we were walking. It was so dark that I doubted the one escorting me would even notice.

No sooner had the thought crossed my mind, Draki was suddenly walking at my side and speaking hurriedly. "We don't have time. Don't spit it out. They'll notice, and you would have committed a grave sin to them. If you would have just listened to me, we wouldn't be in this situation." He sighed then. "They are going to ask you something when you are seated. I'll have a brief moment to work before it's too late." His eyes flashed to the corner and held me as we

matched our pace. "Don't fight me or regret this. It's the path you chose."

Within minutes, the robed figure stopped and pointed to the floor. "This will be your spot. Do not move from this area until we gather you. You may deny us telling you to leave, but you cannot go before your time is up. Sit down and say: I come to pray for the defense of this faith city in your holy name."

I nodded and looked down to the floor. A clawed finger tilted my head just enough for me to look straight forward. A kiss that could swiftly burn a forest to ash stole the wine, my breath, and all of my senses. My limbs tingled, and I felt like I was melting into his touch. A kiss wasn't enough. I wanted *more*. However, as Draki pulled away and I slumped to the floor, I remembered to speak—even if it only came out in a half-dazed mumble.

"I come to pray for the defense of this faith city in your holy name."

"Good. Now recite the Lord's Prayer and let the Holy Spirit guide you as you guard the city with His words."

I nodded and started to mutter my chant, and the man quickly went back the way we had come. I bowed my head and closed my eyes as I tried to focus on praying. I had barely finished the first one as instructed before Draki was rudely invading my personal space by standing not even an inch away from my kneeling form.

"Are you honestly going to ignore what just transpired?"

Did he mean the kiss? I was struggling enough with everything else. Did he honestly want me to focus on that? Breathing slowly, I cleared my head and focused on anything but how his lips felt against mine. "I was waiting for you to

tell me exactly what happened." *Oh, please be talking about the wine.*

His sigh was loud, and he made sure to hit me in the face with his robes as he turned in a huff and gave me some much-needed distance. I slapped the fabric away from me and glowered in the devil's direction.

"The wine was drugged," he stated blandly.

"Drugged?" I exclaimed loudly and instantly covered my mouth with my hand. After a quick sweep of the surrounding area, I noticed that there wasn't a soul present that had taken notice of my outburst. They all just continued to quietly chant to themselves. "Why would they do that?"

He gave an amused chuckle. "Did you honestly think that they have unwavering faith? Do you see what lurks beyond these walls? Do you hear the terrors that scratch at these stones? Do you see the devils that roam the streets? Ha! The Grand Master and his followers all know the dangers that skulk about. They fake their obedience while they send you all off to fight on the front lines, but the reality beyond this wall is too real for most people—so they drug the wine and have everyone sit in a blissful trance."

"They are trying to comfort those that are praying?"

"Are they, though? Or are they trying to make sure people don't remember how horrifying it is to pray for the safety of the city after the sun goes down?"

"I … I just need to get through tonight."

Draki held up his hand and narrowed his eyes down the narrow path. "Someone's coming. Do what you will, but be convincing about it. Nothing good will come to you if they find out you didn't drink the wine and that you aren't praying," he warned.

I didn't need a second notice. Quickly, I bowed my head and whispered a meaningful prayer. I threw in a quick

word for God to guide me through this night. As I did, I stole a look at those that were passing by. It was another robed figure, and he was escorting Elijah. He was seated a few yards away from me and instructed just as I had been earlier. Soon after, the robed individual departed. I frowned as I stared at my friend. He looked awful. He was slumped in on himself and occasionally swayed about in place as he tried to maintain his balance. His usual bright eyes were bloodshot and glazed with a film of fog.

"Is that from the drugs?" I asked.

Draki nodded. "Yes."

"It's not right," I whispered. "They shouldn't be drugging us."

"I don't know why you are so surprised. After all the different places you've been to and after all that you've seen, why on earth did you think that this place would be any different?"

"I thought that because devils weren't ruling over them … they would be better."

He chuckled darkly. "Are devils really the issue here, or is it people, my dear?"

I didn't reply because I really didn't like the answer that came to mind. I had convinced myself that if I made it to Saint Augustine, everything would be better. I could finally settle down, call this place home, and free myself of worry. Instead, I've felt watched, paranoid, and judged at every turn. This didn't feel right. This didn't feel like the faith city that I had been told about since I was a child. But there had to be some thread of truth to the stories.

There just had to be.

"Hmmm … Seems that I won't need to convince you any further of how this place is. It looks like we are about to

get the most eye-opening show in a moment or two," Draki
informed with a smirk.

Nothing about what he said made me think that
something good was to follow that dreadful statement, and—
much to my disliking—I was right. Off to my left, one of the
hunched-over figures plopped over on their side. As the
hood of their robes was removed from their spastic
convulsing, I could make out that it was an older male, and
his face looked sunken in and his skin looked yellowed. His
mouth was agape in silent horror as his rattling breath
hitched. For a moment, I stood in pure terror. I wasn't sure
what to do.

As soon as I came back to my senses, I rushed over to
the man's side. Spit covered his gray beard, and his hands
grasped at me like it would end his suffering. "H-H-Help …"
And with that final word uttered, he died right in front of me.
I doubted—for a moment—that any of this was happening.
Perhaps some of the drugged wine I held in my mouth had
been accidentally swallowed, and the small amount was
enough to make me hallucinate.

But his grasp on my garments felt real. His ghastly
expression burned itself into my memory. No matter how
much I tried to deny it, the event had taken place. Swiftly,
there came marching knights that came over, checked for the
man's pulse, and then jerked his clutched fist free from my
clothing.

"Another one," one of them said.

"That's the fourth one tonight."

"Ah, drat." The first shook his head and sighed.
"Let's hoist him up over the wall, then."

I looked at them and tried to mask my bulging eyes
and my visage that was twisted in shock. I was appalled by
what I was hearing. This wasn't real. It couldn't be.

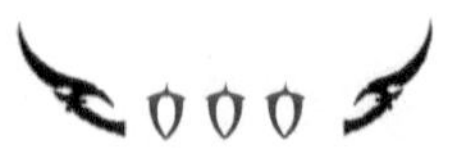

"Hey, you!" The second barked with an angry expression, and he kicked me with his booted foot. "Get back to your spot and pray!"

"Hold up, is she … is she awake?" The first asked with a worried tone.

Draki was next to my ear, and his voice was full of mirth. "They toss the bodies over the wall so they don't have to bury them and let the demons on the other side feast on them. Sometimes, they aren't dead yet. They are holding on to a thread of life but unable to pray, so they have no purpose to the city."

I was aghast and disgusted. My heart couldn't take it. I didn't know who I wanted to hit first, the soldiers for being heartless, Draki for telling me, or the Grand Master for ordering all of this to be done. Or did he even know? If he didn't, maybe he could stop all of this madness.

"I'm not doing this," I whispered and got up from the floor and rushed over to Elijah.

"Hey! Hey! Get back here!"

"You can't do that. Get back to your assigned place!"

From further down the hall, I heard more commotion as I hit my knees in front of Elijah. "Wake up. Come on, Elijah. I need you to come to your senses."

"Good luck with that," Draki said under his breath.

"We've got one that's awake!" one of the knights bellowed.

The sudden sound of more marching feet thrumming over the stone floor made my heart beat to a frantic melody. "Elijah!" I snapped hoarsely and shook him hard. "Wake up! Wake up! We need to leave!"

"Leave?" he asked, confused.

I felt my heart leap with joy at the sound of his voice. "Yes. Yes, we need to leave. Come on."

"Wherever you go, I'll go, Sia," he slurred.

"Best news I've heard all night," I grunted, pulling him to his feet. He weighed like lead, and he had next to no grace.

"Do you see them?"

"See what?"

"All of the people made of light?" he replied in a dreamy tone. Elijah tried to trail with his eyes whatever he was claiming that he could see and spun in place as I struggled to keep both of us from falling over.

"No, I ... don't see anything that you're talking about. I do see some very ... upset people coming our way, though."

He didn't seem concerned. He only giggled and reached out to something with a grand smile, saying, "They're flying, Sia, with great, big wings."

"Tell them to help fly us to safety," I grumbled as I tried to get him to follow my lead. It felt like I was trying to get the drunkest person home at the end of a grand party.

"Stop right there!" a knight with a crimson cape ordered.

"I'm not doing this. I want to see the Grand Master."

Swords were drawn. "By the light, we cannot let you leave your post."

"You're ... You're going to kill me?"

"The protection of the city comes at any cost. We can't permit the faithful to neglect their duty. You cannot leave your post."

"So, people can fall over dead or from exhaustion, but I can't leave because I'm still breathing? Get bent and get out of my way."

"Why do they have swords?" Elijah asked with a loopy expression.

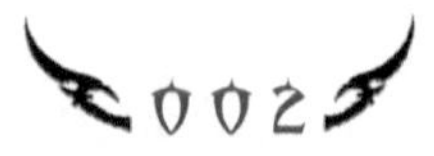

A blade was pointed in my direction. "Return to your post, both of you, and we will overlook this act of disobedience."

I looked around for Draki, but I didn't see him. Was he leaving this up to me to handle? "I'm sorry, but I really need to go see the Grand Master right now."

"This is your last warning. Return to your post or suffer the consequences."

"If you would just listen to me—"

"Take them down," the knight ordered.

"Aww … the light people left," Elijah whined.

"Wait!" I screamed.

But it was too late.

A handful of armored soldiers were rushing at us with swords drawn. They had every intention to end our lives for not obeying their orders. They didn't want to listen to reason. They didn't want to let us go. It was obedience or death. This isn't what I thought the faith city was going to be like. This almost felt as bad as the devil-ran villages and towns. Your peace came at a price.

I held up my arm, put my back to the approaching knights, and tried to shield Elijah from the first foe. They never reached us, though. A great wind blew through the halls and sent every one of them flying. All except for Elijah, Draki, and I were untouched by the blow.

"Run, Sia. I'll buy you some time."

"Thank you," I whispered.

I could hear Draki's displeasure to my thanking him, but I didn't have time to nitpick him over such trivial matters. I needed to focus on getting Elijah and myself to the main exit. Holding up the young man as best I could, we half-ran as we teetered from side to side for the entrance down the corridor.

In no time at all, we were there, and the only ones standing by the opening were the robed people holding the wine and cups. The rest had clearly fled out of fear, while others had gone to get more reinforcements.

"They're bringing more knights. You won't live to see the daybreak," a female snarled at me as we hobbled past. She held the golden flask in her hands like it was a weapon as her heated stare stayed fixed on me.

"I just need to make it to the Grand Master," I mumbled under my breath.

Once we were outside the wall, we heard a commotion by the main gate, and then there was silence. Using every ounce of strength in me, I lugged Elijah along as we headed for the cathedral.

"Looks like you could use a hand."

The red feathers and dark skin were dead giveaways that it was Kasim. I didn't know how to feel about seeing him. Was he really going to be helpful, or was he another hurdle we had to jump? I wasn't fond of the fact that some of my greatest allies presently were devils.

"Don't look so cross, sweetheart. I'm just here doing Draki a favor. Besides, you were entertaining, and this is giving me a little more fun than usual, so I'm here to help you out."

"You didn't hurt anyone, did you?"

His grin disappeared, and his tone got a touch darker. "Let's get you to the cathedral, right?"

I nodded, and he took Elijah from me and pointed with his chin for me to lead the way. Instantly, I headed back up the path we'd taken down to the wall. I didn't walk for the building that loomed over the city. I ran toward it.

"I can take you as far as the front doors. After that, you're on your own," Kasim informed.

"That's all I need," I replied.

Chapter 30:

Confession

It had started to rain along the way. At first, it was only a faint drizzle that made the roads and sidewalks slick. It only took a few moments for the sky to open up and the torrential downpour to soak us to the bone. In the distance, the lights from the cathedral were like beacons in the dead of night. Their yellow glow cast out over the city with the promise of warmth and safety inside. I really hoped that it wouldn't deceive me.

As promised, once we reached the top of the steps, Kasim handed over the drugged Elijah to me, saying, "I'd hurry if I was you. Those knights mean business, and I doubt that it won't be too long before they scale these steps and try to take you down."

"I'll keep that in mind."

"If you ever want to make a deal, though …"

"I've got enough debt. Thanks."

He chuckled, placed two fingers by the side of his head, and gave me a lazy salute before he shoved his hands in his pockets and walked back down to the awaiting city below. I could hear him whistle an eerie song as he departed.

I sighed, resituated Elijah's weight on my shoulders, and headed through the front doors.

Inside, it was warm, and the little chill that was brought on by my drenched clothes was slowly lifting from me. Still, some of the water that had collected on our skin and hair dripped from us and landed with a soft *pitter-patter* on the red carpet that stretched from the doorway all the way to the altar.

Rushing from the other end of the massive room, the Grand Master came darting in our direction with Ivy and a few of the tutors in tow. The fast-paced *tick, tick, tick,* and the accompanying chiming bells of his staff as it tapped against the floors, filled the empty space around us. Arland's quickened steps had him before us in seconds.

"What is the meaning of this? Sia, why are you not attending the Hours of Whispered Prayers? Why is Elijah with you? Has something happened at the wall?" the Grand Master asked with worry creasing his brow.

I shook my head and tried to think of how to start, but it all came out like a frantic child telling a parent about a horrible nightmare that they'd just woken up from. "I saw a man die. He just died right in front of me!" I shook my head as I tried to gain my thoughts. Behind the Grand Master, I could see Ivy and James. Their concern was evident as they listened to my panic-stricken voice explain everything that had transpired. "The guards were talking about dumping him over the wall for the demons to feast on … like he didn't even matter. They pulled their swords on us. I-I-I didn't know where else to go, so I came here. I knew it would be safe here, and I could get some answers. I'm so confused, Grand Master."

He went from looking like he was ready to ring the cathedral bells and sound the alarms to sighing with a sad

expression. "I see. I can understand how traumatic this all must be for you. After all, this is new to you."

"New?"

"Yes."

"Death is nothing new to me, Grand Master. I've seen it more often than you have, I'm sure. What I just saw now was not death, but a lack of compassion for the dead, and I doubt that those on the brink of death get treated any better."

"My dear, the resources we'd have to use to save them or bury them is too great. We live in troubling times."

"Troubling times is when we should show more compassion, not less."

Arland hummed with a knowing expression. "Did you drink the wine?"

How could he be asking me a question like that? He knew the answer. If he wanted me to lie, it wasn't going to happen, and if he wanted me to convict myself, I'd tell the truth and then leave the city before they could ask me to … or worse.

"No, I didn't."

"If you would have but followed our laws and rules here, this wouldn't be an issue right now, my child. The wine wasn't to deceive you. It was to ease you into a state of peace that would be pleasing for the Hours of Whispered Prayers. None of these things would be concerns for you because you would be focused on your faith and not these Earthly matters."

"We're all Earthlings," Elijah whispered in a lazy slur. I wasn't sure how invested he was in our conversation, but I chose to focus on replying to Arland.

"How can you be so cold?"

"My dear, you mistake my understanding of how everything is as having a hardened heart."

"No. I'm not taking you as someone with a hardened heart. I'm seeing you for what you really are. You are manipulating these people by using their faith, our faith, to fuel the safety of this city, and yet you care nothing for those that sacrifice themselves."

He shook his head with a deep sigh. "You speak of those that didn't make it through their prayer session or didn't leave when their time was up. I feel for them, but the fact remains that they failed in their duty."

"Failed? You drugged them! You have no idea of what the lifetime effects of those drugs are, or if mixing them with the wine might have a different effect on different people. How can you act like any of this is their fault when you are the one holding the poisoned vial?"

"Careful, Sia. You are treading on thin ice."

"No, you are just upset that I'm calling you out on your BS."

"If their faith and willpower were stronger, they wouldn't have perished so easily."

"Their faith was stronger than yours! While they are down there, putting themselves at risk on the frontlines, you sit up here in comfort as you call the shots."

"It is written in the sacred book what we should do."

"You are cherry-picking to benefit yourself."

"We are to pray without ceasing!" He bellowed to me.

My face twisted in anger, and I mentally asked for guidance. After taking in a deep breath, I snapped back, "Stay sober and be vigilant!"

He laughed at me and straightened to his full height as he looked down at me like I was a stain in the middle of

the cathedral. With a heated glare, he yelled back, "Without faith, it is impossible to please God!"

My skin prickled with goosebumps, I felt something stir within my chest, and I took in a slow, calming breath. I didn't yell or scream. I met his gaze and let every bit of anger in me die. Sweetly, almost too sweetly for what I was telling the Grand Master, I said, "There are six things the Lord hates, seven that are detestable to Him: haughty eyes, a lying tongue, hands that shed innocent blood, a heart that devises wicked schemes, feet that are quick to rush into evil, a false witness who pours out lies, and a person who stirs up conflict in the community."

He took a single step back as if my words had caused him to lose his balance. Pointing the staff at me, he roared, "You're a witch! You come in here sputtering lies and shaking the foundations of our city and tempting those around you with a seducing tongue to crumble our great walls from the inside out! You are the one stirring up conflict!"

"Grand Master," Ivy whispered, trying to calm him down. She laid a gentle hand upon his upper arm, and he ripped away from her with a cross look.

"Are you defending her? Have you been bewitched by her words?"

"N-N-No. I just feel as though we can handle this situation better if we all calm down," she suggested.

"He can't calm down. I've shown him that he is no better than Satan himself, and I am showing everyone listening in to our conversation right now that he has no intention of changing or repenting."

"Silence your filthy lies! I see you for what you really are now. You had me fooled when you first came here, but

now I see. Oh, yes … I see so clearly now. You come to seek and destroy. You're a child of the devil himself!"

Just then, the soldiers flooded through the main entrance and, one by one, pointed their weapons at me and Elijah.

The half-out-of-it young man whistled and mumbled to me, "Uh-oh."

My sentiments exactly. Nothing good was going to come of this. It was clear in the heated glower from the Grand Master and his flushed cheeks. It was solidified further by his followers, all looking at me like I was a demon myself … or worse. Only Ivy and James had expressions that came across as though they wanted all of this to stop. They wanted to help us, but their hands were tied. I didn't want them to risk everything they had here just to help Elijah and myself.

I made sure to not look at them to ensure that Arland wouldn't find fault with them somehow. Ivy had been my tutor, and I didn't want any blame for my outburst to become her problem. Instead, I made sure that he pointed every bit of that seething rage at me.

"Oh, I see your backup has arrived. Plan on silencing me?" I asked low enough for him to hear and not the cautious knights circling us.

"We are sending you far away from here. You and that young man are to be banished out into the Wastes."

That wasn't so bad. Not like I hadn't been there before. My lack of concern for his decree must have been written all over my face because he added with a hiss, "Tonight."

His final addition to my already terrifying sentence was only concerning because after we left the wall, we hadn't seen Draki. Not a whisper in my mind, not a tormenting

cackle, and not even the faintest scent of spice and smoke. It was like he wasn't even there anymore.

Arland turned to the soldiers. "Have the buckets of entrails and blood the butchers have collected over the past few days spilled over the sides of the walls by the front gates," he ordered.

"Yes, Grand Master," one of the men barked before he bowed, turned on heel, and dashed out of the cathedral.

"You're going to call every demon within miles."

"Yes," he said with a dark smile. "I won't let you live in this city or out there. You're too dangerous."

"Anyone that knows the truth is dangerous to you. Eventually, you'll run out of people to kill, and your city will be empty. Who will pray for your protection then?"

He sneered at me and waved a hand dismissively in my direction. "Bind them and take them to the front gates. We need to make preparations before we offer these two up to the darkness that lurks within the Wastes."

"You'll need those prayers to keep you safe!" I snapped. "Because He knows everything you've done. You cannot hide any of your misdeeds from His eyes. You might feel untouchable now, but your demise is on the horizon! Stop all of this now, it isn't too late!"

"Take them away!" he commanded with an air of righteousness.

I opened my mouth to protest, but the only sound that escaped me was a short cry of pain as the pommel of a sword cracked down below my jaw, and the world was doused in inky black.

The ropes were old, fraying, and scratched aggressively against my skin. My nonstop attempts to wriggle out of the bindings had rubbed my wrists raw, and I was sure that there were minor cuts surfacing as I continued—without avail—to free myself. Despite their age, the ropes weren't brittle and easily broken. A quick glance around the dimly lit storage house proved to me that we hadn't yet been tossed out as a sacrifice. We were still very much within the city. Though from the sound of approaching people and the chatter that I could make out, that wouldn't be true for too much longer.

They were smart enough to set Elijah and me far apart so that we couldn't help one another. It didn't matter much, though. He was passed out and slumped over by one of the poles we had been tied to.

There was a single window on the far side of the room, but around it were stacks of crates, barrels, and boxes that blocked some of the view. From what I could tell, we were at the city entrance, and that it was still night, and the rain had slowed down. There weren't any hints of dawn approaching from what I could see of the sky.

I didn't have a lot of hope that I would be successful, but I wanted to attempt to wake up Elijah. At the very least, I would have someone to talk to. Maybe we could come up with a half-baked plan. Yet, in truth, I knew that it was all ways to avoid a choice that I didn't want to make.

"Elijah!" I hoarsely yelled to him and looked around, listening to the sounds outside to see if anyone was coming. "Elijah!" I called again.

"Mmmm," he groaned.

"Wake up!"

He torpidly shook his head with his brow knitted in annoyance. "Five more minutes," he slurred with a yawn.

With that, his head dropped back down, and I could hear faint snoring. Sighing, I leaned back against the pole and rested my head against the wood. Looking up to the roof, I figured this quiet moment was as good as any to have a conversation with my maker.

"Thank you," I whispered. "I'm not going to blame you for this. My choices led me here. I know that everything, both good and bad, are to shape me into the person you want me to be ..." My eyes burned as I admitted a truth that haunted me. "But I've been so lost for so long, Lord. I still don't know who I am. I don't know what I'm supposed to do. I don't know what my purpose is, and I don't know where to start. Maybe this is the end of my road, and I accept that too, but—if it is your will—Lord, deliver Elijah and me from this place. Put me on the path that you have designed for me."

Thwack!

The door was slammed open, and there were two knights standing on the other side. Both of them stared right at me. One of their gazes was full of disdain and came from a male with black hair and bright brown eyes. The other looked conflicted, and she tried to mask it, but Francis didn't come across as the type that could wipe all emotion out of her expression.

"Time to go," she said with a frown.

"Don't talk to them, they aren't worthy of being spoken to," the male snarled.

"Don't tell me what to do, Chris. I am taking no delight in any of this."

Chris snorted with a smug look and then directed his glare at me. "Oh, but I do," he growled lowly.

She pushed past him to untie me from the pole while Chris went to untie Elijah. As she worked, she whispered faintly to me. "I didn't trust him to come in here alone. I'll escort you to the gates with him. This is all that I can do for you."

Turning to face her, I winced as I felt a dull, aching throb assault my jaw. I waited for her eyes to lock with mine before I smiled and said, "Thank you." And I let every bit of my gratitude flow into those two words.

She stared at the swollen spot on my face where I had been hit by the pommel. Again, Francis looked conflicted, and she quickly averted my gaze. "You're welcome," she mumbled.

Still smiling, I faced back toward the front and was instantly met with Chris's attention directed at me. He made no attempt to hide his hatred as his face twisted in disgust. "What are you smiling about?" he snipped.

"Just counting my blessings," I said.

He spat at the ground near me with a sneer. "Must be a short list," he said with a dark cackle.

"Oh, no … it's quite long when you know how to look at your life and the world around you. Perspective is everything."

His laughter died. Glaring eyes scanned me like he was making a list of my imperfections that he would happily make me aware of. Staring down his nose at me, he let his voice go frigid as he said, "I'll be watching demons tear you limb from limb while you cry for help that will never come. Guess you're right. Perspective *is* everything."

I had expected that kind of reply. He came across as someone that reveled in the pain of others. The curl of my lips didn't waver. "If found innocent, He will send an angel

to close the mouth of the demons just like he shut the mouths of the lions for Daniel."

"You bi—"

"Enough, Chris! We are to escort them, not taunt them."

"Pfft. Whatever," he grumbled and jerked Elijah to his feet. "Let's get this the hell over with."

They led us out of the storage shelter and toward the front gates. The gas lamps were lit, and there were a few fires burning in great, big, iron bowls near the massive doors. An enormous crowd was gathered near the city exit. It seemed that the soon-to-be spectacle had driven some of the city's inhabitants from their beds. All of their faces were shaded and shadowed in ways that made them appear as if they were manifesting into something completely inhuman. They all had turned from a mass of accepting and loving people to these beings that were twisted with judgment and hate.

We were shoved toward the closed doors until we were practically kissing the wood. I spun on heel to look each individual over with a hard frown. Any words I would have spoken failed me. I was beyond disappointed in them, in the city. From further in, the sea of people parted to let the Grand Master and a few of his followers come through.

"Let us cast out this evil before they bring us harm and destruction."

"You are your own destruction. Turn away from your wicked ways," I spat back.

"Still with your lies? Even when you face death, you don't give up the act." Arland shook his head. "You poor girl. You had the chance to be saved."

"I already have been."

His upper lip twitched like a snarling dog, and he shook it off with a forced smile. "Open the gates."

Heavy creaking sounded through the night, but it was followed by the many whoops and hollers from nearby grunts and the screeching calls of other demons. It sounded dangerously close. The throng of creatures was as close to the protected walls of the faith city as they dared to be. The buckets of blood and animal remains the knights had earlier poured over the walls had really done their job. As the vast spread of the Wastes was made visible, we saw it aglow with countless eyes and darting figures moving within the darkness.

"May God have mercy on your souls," The Grand Master announced loudly, and all of those who were watching repeated the phrase. It brought a chill to my bones.

Chris shoved me in the back, and Elijah was thrown next to me. We both grunted in pain as we hit the ground just outside the city. I could see the fog starting to lift from Elijah's eyes, but he was still sluggish and confused.

"Sia," he said my name like he needed me to confirm that I was real.

"Yes?"

The hissing laughter of demons was closer than before.

"This … this is pretty bad, huh?"

I nodded and started to sit up and help him to his feet. I didn't lie. I told him the truth. "Yes."

He slowly looked from me to the encroaching army of demons, and then back to the city entrance, where many were watching us. Taking my hand in his, he turned his back to the faith city and headed further into the Wastes. "Wherever you go, Sia, I'll be with you."

Tears welled in my eyes, and I held his hand a little tighter. Mentally, I wanted to beg them to take us back

because I didn't want to die, but something in me let go of all my fear and accepted my fate. "Protect us, Go—"

"Wrong name," Draki announced as plumes of red, glittering smoke appeared several feet away. Behind him, all of the demons had halted and were waiting for a single word from their master to lunge and devour us. He didn't hide what he was or the power he wielded. For a long moment, we all stared at each other.

Whispers started behind us.

"What's going on?"

"Why aren't the demons killing them?"

"Is God covering them from the demons?"

"Maybe we were wrong."

All of the hushed questions were not received well by the Grand Master. When I turned around, I saw Kasim standing behind Arland. His hands were on the leader's shoulders. The devil's dark features were lit up by his grand smile. I should have known. If a devil gets denied in one way, they don't give up … they just try a different tactic.

Arland's face was flush, and his eyes wild. "Look! She shows her true colors. This isn't divine protection! She is a *witch*. She is full of *wicked* power!"

Suddenly, the knights were rushing about and grabbing for weapons. Bows were snatched up, and deadly arrows pointed in our direction. Meanwhile, Draki stood unmoving within a sea of demons as he awaited a reply from me.

"Build a home with me, Sia."

Turning away from the dangers behind me, I faced the devil, speechless.

His hand was held out, and he grinned madly. "Do we have a deal?"

If I said no, we perished. If I said yes, I tacked on another sin to a long list. I despised myself so much as I let go of Elijah, walked to Draki, took his hand, and said, "Deal."

It all happened at once. A volley of arrows filled the midnight sky. Ivy ran through the streets while being guided by James as she screamed, "Don't! Please!" Draki jerked me forward and then threw me behind him with his arms outstretched, ready to receive the blows to protect me.

I screamed to Elijah, "Come to me! Hurry!" But he hardly made it a few steps before it happened.

The arrows never even had a chance of reaching us. Locusts darted through the air, their numbers beyond anything I could dare to dream. Like they were nothing, the projectiles were consumed, and bits of steel rained down from the collected swarm. But that wasn't the scary part. Abaddon had large, gray wings outstretched, and they beat at a slow pace, bringing him closer to the ground. He hovered several feet from the earth below as he spoke to everyone present at the city entrance.

"Your purpose has been fulfilled. The walls will crumble, and the city will fall by His decree."

My jaw unhinged, Elijah shielded his face from the dust the angel's wings kicked up, and Draki snarled, "Showoff."

"He's … an angel?" I whispered in awe.

Elijah stumbled over to my side and watched it all in horrified wonder. "He's going to destroy the city. I don't think we should stay."

Draki had a strange look in his eyes as he said, "Hmmm, yes. I think we should go."

My heart hurt for so many different reasons. I felt dirty. I felt wronged. I wanted to save them. It didn't seem fair that so many would perish because of one corrupt man's

choices. Silently, I begged God to deliver the innocent people from the city. As I thought it, there was a mammoth-sized wave of locusts rising up. Quickly, it descended upon Saint Augustine like a tidal wave of insects.

Right when it crashed down over the gate, I saw Ivy rush forward, throw up her arms, and scream, *"No!"*

Green light erupted from her, and the locusts hit a barrier and went on deeper into the city.

"God, help me!" Ivy shouted with all her might.

From overhead, green, wispy lights fell from the sky and zipped through the streets. As Draki pulled me away, I had a feeling that those lights were saving those that dwelled within from the destruction that was consuming everything around them. Perhaps that was just my panicked mind trying to soften the blow of the nightmares that were unfolding right in front of me, or—maybe—I was seeing what unwavering faith was capable of.

The sound of the wall's stones toppling over themselves echoed through the night. An army of demons roared with satisfaction, and they quickly flooded the city like a rush of black waters with endless, evil, glowing eyes. Tearing my vision from the hundreds of demons scrambling to enter the city, I watched them avoid Ivy and her barrier at all costs and climb over the rubble of the once great barrier.

I looked to the girl that had been not just a tutor to me but a friend. My feet tried to move in her direction, but Draki grabbed me and jerked me back to his side. "That isn't part of our agreement. I'll get you and Elijah to safety … but those people?" He paused and looked over his shoulder to them. "They are on their own."

Frowning as my heart broke, I turned back to face Ivy as Draki started to pull me away. Again, I felt something stir in my chest, and I called out, "Ivy! Find me in the Wastes!

Stay alive! Be safe and find me!" I didn't know if she heard me or if she even wanted to listen to someone like me, but I hoped that she would find a way to be safe without the protection of the city. "Find! Me!" I screamed.

"She has God. Don't worry. I think she is going to be fine," Elijah reminded.

I felt foolish then. I had put so much trust in the city for so long that I forgot what I had learned. It wasn't the city that protected us all from the demons and darkness. It was faith. It was God. After realizing that, I knew that Ivy would be okay.

Then there was me. Wishing for Heaven but bound for Hell. My eyes were full of pain, sadness, and anger as I looked to Draki, my fated shackle. I could break the chains that bound us together and risk all that I loved and cared for, or I could suffer with him.

He noticed my expression and chuckled darkly as he looked away from me. "Oh, dear, don't look at me like that. Your best interests are always on my mind."

"I find myself doubting that."

Turning suddenly, his hand struck out like a snake, and he held my chin in his blazing grasp. "Careful of the words that you let slip out of this beautiful little mouth, Sia. For—even though it can curse me—it can also sing my praises. Push me enough, and I'll teach you the song."

My breathing hitched, and I licked my lips. "Don't tempt me," I whispered.

His eyes widened, and he froze. As he stared at me, I saw something flash in his eyes. His face dipped dangerously close to mine. I fought every desire in me and stayed as still as possible. When his mouth was almost upon my own, he spoke, and I could feel his lips brush over mine as he did. "But it's my greatest pleasure to do just that."

My heart fluttered, and my stomach flipped. A scream from the city broke the mood, and I felt the spell of lust lift from me. "Take me somewhere safe. Take me to a place I can call home," I reminded him as I fumbled without looking to grab Elijah's hand. He took hold of me and squeezed, silently letting me know that I didn't have to be afraid. He was there. "Please, Draki," I pressed.

"As you wish," the devil purred and pulled me closer to his body so I could feel every muscle hidden away by his robes. Red smoke surrounded us and, soon after, my vision swam in shadows.

Chapter 31:

The Land of Milk and Honey

All I wanted from the start of all this was a place to call home and to live out my life in peace. I had become profoundly aware of my true destiny as time slipped by. After understanding many things that I had tried to avoid and ignore, I finally reserved myself to my fate. It was then that I realized I didn't have any more fear left in me, and all that had once been clouded and hazy was clearer than ever. That realization made me regret making yet another deal with Draki. Was my faith so fragile? Was I really that foolish? Or had I planned this all and was prepared to deny the truth until the bitter end?

No matter the answer, the only thing to do now was to make sure that I had everything in order before I was to pay the price for all of my stupid choices. I wasn't going to let anyone else suffer for them, and there was only one way to ensure that. I had to uphold my end of the bargain. However, Draki had to uphold his first. There was still the matter of his slip-up from early on in our journey that gave me the chance to save my village and family, too. Lots of loose ends and not a lot of time to tie them all up, that's what I had. I needed to act fast and make sure that Draki didn't know what I was up

to, or he would try to hinder me in every way. However—
first things first—I needed a place to put down roots.

As the red clouds of smoke dissipated, I shielded my
eyes from the light of the moon. The magic Draki had used to
get us miles away from the city made me feel like all the
sound in the world had been swallowed up, and things
darker than black had slipped over my vision. When
everything came too, I felt shaky on my feet and sick to my
stomach.

It came as no surprise that the devil had the three of
us standing outside the remains of what looked like a large,
abandoned village. The wind blew up dust clouds, and an
old windmill moved slightly with whining creaks. The place
needed some TLC. When that thought crossed my mind, one
of the doors on the many homes slowly swung open with the
aid of the wind and then fell off its hinges.

Okay … it needed a lot of love.

"Charming," I muttered with a forced smile.

"Please, you have no vision, Sia," Draki said softly
with a light chuckle.

"Or my vision works just fine," I replied under my
breath.

"Wh-Where are we?" Elijah asked while holding his
head.

I came closer to him and helped him stand a bit
straighter. "Far away from the faith city," I whispered.

"Where, exactly?"

Looking over my shoulder, I drew in a slow breath.
"Home," I admitted.

"Home?" He searched the sad buildings and crinkled
his nose. "Better than nothing."

"Yeah."

Draki stepped further away from us and outstretched his hands. "It'll be grander than you could ever imagine."

Hellish sounds rumbled all around us. Shadows ripped through the sky, dipping and diving in the nocturnal abyss as they blipped in and out of sight. I drew in closer to Elijah as he held onto me, and we both watched everything unfold.

Creatures that looked like giant bats with scorpion tails soared through the sky on shadowed wings. Screeching howls pierced my ears as countless things crept, flew, and slithered toward the city. As each being hit a surface, flames rose up and burned at a slow, steady pace. Instead of ash, ember, and coal being left behind, there was spotless steel, stacked stones, and polished wood. All around the buildings, green grass sprouted. Gnarled, dead trees shook and shivered as the branches and trunks became less twisted. Swiftly, bright emerald leaves emerged, and flowers bloomed under the veil of starlight and smoke. Draki was burning a city into existence, and I didn't know if I should be amazed or terrified.

Gradually, the howls and cries ebbed until there was only the unnatural stillness of the night. Pleased with the work that had been done, Draki turned around with a wide grin. "Welcome home."

If I didn't know the price I would have to pay for what he called *home*, I would have been happy. I would have been on the brink of tears and ecstatically dashing off to pick a house, and I would yell throughout the city with laughter until daybreak. But I knew. I knew, and that stole whatever joy I dared to have in that moment.

The devil fixed his sights on me, and I gave a simple nod of thanks to him. "I haven't forgotten our deal."

"And you plan to pay … when?" Greed laced every word he spoke.

Watching Elijah depart from me and turn around to call for me to hurry up, I looked back to Draki and said, "After you uphold the deal we made when I got harmed."

He rolled his shoulders back and stared down his nose at me. "Very well, Sia. We shall discuss this in the morning. Tonight, you have been through enough."

I raised my brows in astonishment. "Oh? You're being so kind. Why?"

The corner of his lips plucked up in a sinister smirk. "Because I'm getting what I want."

Truer words have never been spoken. "I see."

His vision flicked to the Wastes beyond me, but when I followed his gaze, I saw nothing out in the stretch of desert. "Correction: I'll speak with you later on tomorrow evening. In the morning, you'll have guests."

My eyes strained to try to see what hints were out in the blackened void and found nothing. There was only the distant call of a coyote and the close hoot of an owl. That didn't mean that Draki was wrong. It meant that I needed to go get some rest before these guests—whoever they were—arrived.

That night, Elijah and I fell asleep after choosing a home near the village's center. It was fully furnished like all the other buildings, and it had four sizable rooms. When Elijah asked why we needed something that big, I simply told him that it was just a feeling that I had, which wasn't a lie.

When I looked at the house, it felt like I had seen it before, even though I had never been to this place or seen anything close to it. It felt like I should pick it. Meemaw always told me to trust my gut instinct, after all.

We slept soundly through the night and didn't wake up until midafternoon the following day. I was buried under the blankets and feeling really in tune with the thought of just sleeping the day away when Elijah poked my side through the thick comforter.

"Rise and shine, Sleeping Beauty."

"I don't want to."

"Is that the depression talking and you need to be alone, or are you starting to feel awake enough to eat?"

The covers were removed just enough that I could peek out at him. "You cooked?"

"And made coffee," he said with a sweet smile.

I emerged from my warm nest of blankets and stretched. "I suppose I could partake in a few morning pleasures."

"I'll go grab everything. You just focus on waking up."

I nodded while yawning and watched him leave the room. It felt good to just have a lazy day, be served breakfast in bed, and not have to worry about who was going to try to kill me that day. It felt almost too good to be true, mainly because it was. This would all have to come to an end. A reality I wasn't ready to accept, but I would have to because Draki wouldn't give me a way out.

"Get dressed, Sia. They are late, but they'll be here within the hour," Draki warned.

I searched the room and found him nowhere. "Should I be concerned?"

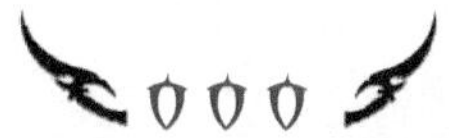

"No. You have nothing to fear. In fact, you're to be their refuge."

"I am?"

"Get ready, and—remember—I'll be speaking with you tonight about our deal."

With that, his voice in my head went quiet.

Moments later, Elijah returned with a tray of food and a cup of steaming, hot coffee. I melted at the sight. Reaching out with grabby hands, I pouted and said, "I need that coffee."

"I'm coming, I'm coming. Don't rush me, or I'll spill it all. My head is still a little foggy from last night."

"Oh, I'm sorry! Are you—"

"I'm fine, Sia. I wouldn't be catering to you if I wasn't. Just don't rush me," he assured with a chuckle.

I suppressed my urge to go help him and let him come to me. The tray was placed on a nearby table, and the coffee mug was carefully handed to me. As he looked at me, he read me like an open book.

"Oh no … something happened. What did Draki do now?"

"More like something he said," I admitted before taking a sip of the hot brew.

He sighed. "Which was?"

I could tell he was preparing for the bad news. After drinking more of the coffee, I said, "We will have guests arriving in less than an hour."

"Guests? As in multiple people?"

"I hope they are people, and yes."

He scratched the back of his neck. "That's a good point. There's no telling what we'd have waltzing up to our doorstep."

"Draki assured me that we are not in any danger."

"Is that because they aren't a threat or because he won't let them hurt you?"

My lips twitched from side to side. "You know, I'm not sure, and that bothers me."

He looked around the room. "Considering that they'll be arriving during daylight hours and Draki isn't roaming about, I'm going to assume that they aren't the threatening sort."

"Let's hope your assumption is right."

After breakfast, Elijah and I went to the front entrance of the village. We drew pictures in the dirt as we played a game to pass the time, and—as promised—within the hour we could see faint outlines of people in the distance.

It was a far larger group than I had anticipated. For a moment, I had worried that those from the faith city were marching toward our newfound home to level it and leave us lifeless in the rubble, but I remembered that Draki had said that they weren't dangerous. Not that I had a hundred percent unwavering faith in the devil, however, I didn't think that he would let a threat of that magnitude waltz up to our front door. Not with the fact that he was so close to collecting his payment and getting ready to set up negotiations for another deal that would be tied to the protection of this city. No, he would want all of my trust … and the debt paid first.

As we watched the group get closer and closer, I squinted my eyes, trying to make out the finer details of those approaching. I saw familiar curly, blonde hair glistening in

the sunlight, and my heart leaped. Before I knew it, my feet were starting to move.

As I headed toward them, I whispered a single name. "Ivy." My pace quickened. Soon, I was running. I stumbled, caught myself, resumed running, and screamed her name. "Ivy!"

I could see her leaning against the arm of James. She stopped in her tracks and reached out into the open air wildly before she let go of him and trotted toward my voice. "Sia?"

I laughed. Uncontrollable tears spilled down my cheeks in warm, unrelenting streams. "Ivy!" was all I could say.

She half-laughed and half-cried as she quickly shuffled her feet in my direction. "SIA! You're alive. Oh, thank God you are alive."

We collided, and I whimpered softly. Frantically, I pulled back enough to see that she had a few cuts and bruises and was a little dirty, but she was alive. She was here, and she was alive. "I thought I'd never see you again."

Her trembling hands patted up my arms until she softly cradled my face. "Are you all right?"

The weight of the world was in that question. For the first time—as I stared into her eyes that couldn't see my streaming tears or my heart breaking—I answered her honestly. "No." I sniffled, and my chest racked with a silent cry. "I can't remember the last time I felt all right, Ivy." Admitting it made me fall apart.

She nodded and drew me in for another hug. "I'm here. I'll help you fight this. You're not alone, Sia. You never have been." Her arms protectively and lovingly embraced me.

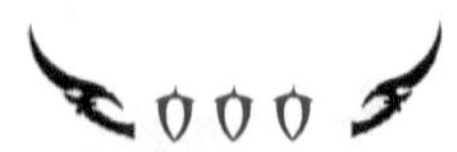

I cried. I let go of things that I thought I had released when I cried back in the cave with Elijah. I let my soul weep for everything I had been through, for all that I was going through, and for the things I knew I was about to endure. I mourned for all those people that had died because of me. It all happened because I had struggled and strived to make it to the faith city.

It's all my fault.

"I'm so sorry. I never meant for any of that to happen!" I wailed into her shoulder.

Her hand rubbed my back, soothing me. "I know. You don't have to be sorry." She squeezed me after a short pause to catch her breath. Her voice trembled with her next reply. "I don't need to be able to see in order to tell that there was something terribly wrong with that place. I was so wrong for ignoring it and denying it for as long as I had. I'm the one that is sorry."

"I feel like it's all my fault."

"Hush now. You couldn't control what happened any more than you could have controlled how people will act. They made their choices long before you showed up. What happened to them wasn't your fault."

Though it was nice to hear her say those words, I couldn't eliminate the feeling that if I had never come to Saint Augustine, those people would still be alive, and the city wouldn't have fallen into ruin.

Elijah was nearby, patient and quiet, waiting for the two of us to finish having our moment. When there was a long stretch of silence, he slowly stepped forward, saying, "Got any room in there for one more?"

Ivy outstretched her arm to one side, and I mirrored her. There wasn't any hesitation in his steps. He rushed in and embraced us without a drop of shame.

"Good to see you again, Ivy," he said softly.

"Oh, it is my greatest blessing to be with you two again," she whispered and nuzzled into our chests.

After gathering ourselves and finding a few things to lift the heaviness that the past couple of days had laid upon us, we headed into the village. Along the way, Ivy told us about how they managed to make it to us without being attacked by the locusts, Abaddon, or the countless wandering demons. She said that a voice had directed her on which way they should travel, and James had dreams of landmarks. All the while, they prayed, sang psalms, and kept each other in good spirits. They had applied the practice of the Hours of Whispered Prayers along their journey, and it had kept them safe. Which confirmed a thought that I had while I resided in the city, and now it gave me an idea.

After we showed everyone around and let them get settled in a large building near the city center, we told them we would get them something to eat. My eyes scanned the crowd, and I went still when I saw Micah, Dara, and Francis heading my way. Part of me wanted to pretend that I didn't see them, rush off, and ignore them, but I found the courage to face them.

Micah was rubbing his arm with the ball of his other arm. "H-Hey, Sia," he said sheepishly.

"We're glad to see you well," Dara added as she gently laid a hand on the young man's shoulder.

Francis looked around. Her eyes were glued to the floor as she cleared her throat. "I'm … I'm really sorry—"

"Don't," I said.

They all three looked at me with wide eyes. I shook my head. "Don't be sorry. I'm glad that you escorted me. Lord knows what would have happened to me if you didn't come, Francis." I smiled then. "I'm glad to see you guys alive and well. I want you to know that this can be home for all of us. What happened in the past, I don't blame you for. Let's start a new chapter, okay?"

"I'd like that," Francis admitted with a weak smile.

"We all would," Dara said.

Micah nodded.

"Here," I said, handing them a small pile of blankets. "Hand a few of these out, and I will get something made for everyone to eat. You all had a long journey."

A few around me asked, "What are we going to do now?" Soft murmurs rose as everyone voiced their thoughts and concerns.

"I am going to help you all figure it out."

"We trust you," Micah announced confidently.

I looked stunned and said, "I'll understand if you all don't trust me. After everything that happened, I even would understand you blaming me for everything."

Dara shook her head. "Sia, honey, we don't blame you."

"But—"

"No buts," Francis interjected. "Ivy believes in you, so we all believe in you."

A little baffled, I left, reminding them that we would make them all something to eat, and Ivy, Elijah, and I all went to our place to talk business while we cooked. Spread out in the kitchen, we all sighed for what felt like the hundredth time.

Enough silence had gone on.

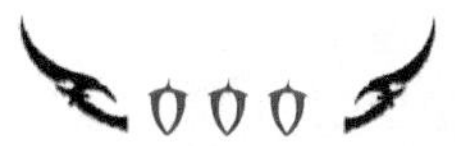

"I think we should try to rebuild the faith city," I blurted out.

"Wow, cut to the chase, why don't you?" Elijah joked.

Ivy sat at the table and took a sip of water before she replied. "I'm with you. But I don't want it to be like it was in Saint Augustine."

Elijah looked baffled. "Are you really suggesting this? Didn't you two learn the first time?'

"Beware of false prophets which come to you in sheep's clothing, but inwardly they are ravening wolves." Ivy sighed and shook her head. "It wasn't the faith city that was the problem. It was the people that were professing things in the name of God, yet knowing nothing of Him. They had no love and, therefore, could not be a true follower."

"Exactly," I said. "The problem wasn't faith, the church, or anything dealing with God. It was people. It was people that went uncorrected, and they slowly corrupted what was good. For starters, the leader of the church should never have been the leader of the city."

"A separation of them?" Elijah asked.

"A council, even. Ways to ensure that the corruption is caught sooner. The church needs to focus on the things like the protection of the city, teaching, and helping others."

Elijah gasped. "What if we applied the prayer practice to moving wagons and we gathered stragglers and wanderers from out in the Wastes?"

"You read my mind, Elijah," I said with a grin.

"Yes!" Ivy cried out happily. She clapped her hands excitedly and smiled as she asked, "Where do we start?"

Several hours went by. Plans were made between cooking, serving food, and trying to get everyone settled in comfortably. Well into the night, we all jotted down ideas, rules, and mapped out a smooth system for the city to run on. We designed it in a way that would ensure the village lasted long after the three of us were gone. I waited until the right time to tell them that I wanted Ivy and Elijah to be the leaders of each respective role. Ivy was to be the head of the church, while Elijah was to be the head of the village. They asked me why I wouldn't be a leader as well, and I told them that I would be on the council with a few other trusted members of our group. They were happy with that and didn't bring it up again. I was glad they didn't. I had other things to worry about aside from building our city.

Excusing myself for the night, I yawned, stretched, and expressed how tired I was. Elijah and Ivy stated that they would continue with a few more points and stepped outside after bidding me goodnight.

As soon as I closed my bedroom door, I knew that *he* was there. "I haven't forgotten about you, Draki," I muttered with a hint of annoyance.

"Hmmm ... I was starting to wonder."

"Let's get this over with."

"Someone's moody."

"I'm tired," I expressed with a look that matched my groggy tone.

"Very well." He motioned for a chair in the corner of the room next to a small table under the window. I didn't

fight him. I didn't have the energy to. I simply went over and sat down. "When can I expect you to pay up?"

"As soon as you free my family from the devil of my old village."

He sat up straight and smiled. "Then I shall be on my w—"

"Wait!"

His eyes narrowed at me. "Don't try to test the waters with me. I've given you ample time to fulfill your end of the bargain. If you are attempting to deceive me, you'll be disappointed, and I'll make sure I do more than make you cry. I'll break you in ways you didn't know you could be broken."

"The first warning that you ever gave me was more than enough," I said with my hand raised to try and stop his anger from rising. "I don't plan to trick you … it's more the other way around."

To that, his lips twitched and curled. "Oh?"

I nodded my head. "Yes. I want to make sure that I can get them all here safely. You said that you would break the hold that the devil has over the village. You didn't say anything about keeping them safe."

He laughed. "Hmmm. You're not wrong." Sighing, he stood and asked, "So, what do you have planned?"

"Give me a few days to build caravans. Ivy said that she and a few others will go out in them and retrieve everyone from my village."

"Why Ivy? Why not you?"

"I didn't think you'd let me go or put myself in harm's way. She offered to help while I stayed here to handle other affairs. I figured it was a win-win."

For a long moment, he stared at me as if he were picking me apart. I didn't like being under the weight of his

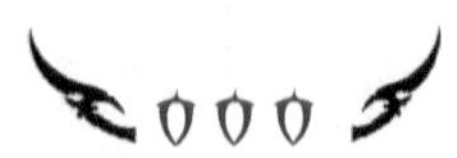

gaze while he stood looming—unmoving—over me. If it
wasn't for the rise and fall of his chest and the slow sweep of
his vision inching all over my body, I would have thought he
was an angry statue in the middle of the room.

"Very well. You may have your few days."

"Took you long enough. I was starting to think that
you had trust issues."

"Hahaha. You would, wouldn't you?" He paused
and then spoke again. "When will the construction of the
caravans begin?"

"If everything goes according to plan, tomorrow."

"Are you missing anything?"

"Not that I'm aware of. I didn't think you'd be so
thorough with the creation of this place. We have livestock,
farms, food, and everything from the basic needs to medical
supplies. It was more than I asked for."

"Trust me, I'll ask for something that will be equal in
price," he warned in a tone that made my blood run cold. A
threat was woven in that promise.

"Yes. We can talk about that later."

"No."

"What?"

"What will you give me in exchange?"

"Can't we deal with one debt being paid at a time?"

He drew in a slow, calming breath. "I suppose I can
wait. I'll even do you one even better. Since my request will
be quite hefty, I'll even give you time to grieve after I've
collected my first payment."

I gave a mock grin. "How kind."

He was in front of me before I could blink and
leaning in too close. "Oh, Sia, you've seen nothing. I can be
kind …" he flashed me a pearly white smile, "… for a price,"

he finished and then laughed in a way that sent shivers
racing down my spine.

Chapter 32:

Soul Collector

I wanted a place that everyone could find refuge in. I knew all too well the dangers that lurked out in the Wastes. I knew how unforgiving and cruel they could be. I didn't want anyone to feel like hope had been taken from them because the faith city had been met with ruin. I wanted to be more than a marker on the map. I wanted to help people find their way. We were all willing to take the risks to bring people to a place—a home—where they could feel at peace and like they could build a life. Everywhere I had been had a price that you needed to pay, and the cost was often higher than any positive emotion that was offered in return. I didn't want people to feel like they had to compromise for a life free of constant fear.

The next morning, Elijah, Ivy, and I went to tell the others what we were planning to do. After a few days of discussions, I went to work on writing out the rules and handled the mapping out of everything onto paper. Even if I wasn't going to be here anymore, I wanted them to be able to continue on without me. That was all that I could do. I could prepare them for a world that I wouldn't be a part of

anymore, but (hopefully) the message that I left behind would live on.

We had four caravans constructed within three days. I was in the library with the others, marking out the path that I had taken to get to the faith city. With the help of Draki the night before, I had the new city's location pinpointed on the map. Using it, I was able to show everyone how to get to my old village. Ivy and the others departed in the morning before the sun rose, and I had never been so scared to see someone off.

As the days crept by, I felt my nerves start to fray and unravel. It was one thing to reserve yourself to a specific fate, and it was another thing to prepare your heart, body, and mind to follow through with the act. It was a lot of convincing, a lot of breaking down, and a lot of putting on a mask to try and fool everyone around me. And maybe—if I was lucky—I could convince myself while I was at it.

There wasn't much to talk about. The caravans left, and I knew it would be almost four days before I'd see them again. I thought about how I could wrap my arms around my dad, taste Momma's cooking, and feel Meemaw's fingers running through my curls as she braided my hair. Elijah had tried to help me maintain them, God bless him, but he couldn't compare with the skill those old hands possessed.

For two days, sleep eluded me, and not even Elijah trying to keep me company could stop me from pacing randomly or staring out the window for long hours while I was lost in thought. It was the evening of the second day since the caravans left, and I had a blanket around my shoulders as I stood out on the porch looking up at the sky.

"Sia," Elijah called softly to me, and I could tell by the sound of his voice that it wasn't the first time that he had said my name.

Blinking, I turned away from the vision of the rising moon and twinkling stars in the distance and hugged myself. "Hmmm?"

"Are you really that worried about your family coming here? You know that the prayers work. You know that the caravans, your family, and Ivy will all arrive safely. Let go of that worry. Fear is not your portion … remember?"

I smiled at his words, but my heart broke. He had no idea of what was about to happen, and I didn't have it in me to tell him. "Yeah. Yeah, you're right," I said softly.

He took a step toward me, and I took a step back without thinking. "Really? Back to this song and dance?" he asked with pain swimming in his hazel eyes.

I frowned and opened my mouth to speak, but nothing came out. Looking away, I sighed. "I'm sorry. I've just been inside my own head lately," I admitted.

"You aren't mad at me, are you?"

Snapping my vision back to him, I looked baffled. "Why would you even ask that?"

"I mean, you've been pretty distant lately, Sia. Why wouldn't I ask that?"

"It's not you, Elijah. I care for you, I do … I just feel like something is coming our way that we won't be able to escape, and I don't want to hurt you more than I'm going to."

"You plan on hurting me?"

"I'm tied to a devil, Elijah. I'm bound to hurt everyone around me one day."

"Is that what's been on your mind? You think your family is going to find out?"

Honestly, the thought never crossed my mind. Now I had a new thing to tack onto my list. *Great*. "Yeah," I said. At least it wasn't a complete lie.

Before I could notice or stop him, Elijah had his arms around me, and he was drawing me in for a hug. "Stop carrying all of this on your own. You have me. You have Ivy. If you won't talk to us, you know that you can always take it to God."

I doubted that God would want me anymore. In the end, I could at least make up for all my mistakes by what I was going to do in the days to come. At least I had a few more days with Elijah in blissful silence and could live a life that felt normal despite the impending doom that loomed on the horizon. At least I could see my family one more time.

"I'll be okay. I already feel better," I whispered and wrapped my arms around him and squeezed. The tighter that I held him, the more I found myself unwilling to let go. I feared that if I didn't say everything that was left in me, I wouldn't have the chance to later on.

I said the words that I had been afraid to speak for so long. "I love you, Elijah."

Suddenly, I felt him hold his breath and go very still. Panic rose in me, and I went to look him in the face, but he stopped me and rested his head on my shoulder.

"I love you, Sia. God, I love you. I'll do everything I can to make you happy."

The sting of hot tears burned my eyes. "You already have," I squeaked out.

We pulled back enough to kiss, and I let it be both deep and meaningful but also short and sweet. He took my hint and didn't fight for more. He let me pull away. A soft laugh escaped him. "It's getting pretty late," he said breathily.

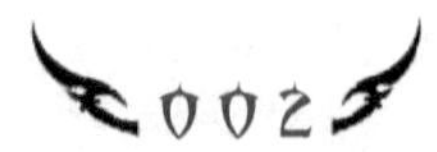

I nodded, my forehead resting on his. "Yeah, I'm pretty tired."

He kissed my head and said, "Go rest, Sia. Tomorrow is a new day."

"Thank you." I made sure to look him in the eyes when I said it. "Goodnight," I whispered.

"Goodnight."

Slipping into my room, I closed the door gently and rolled until my back rested on it. Looking to the ceiling, I said, "God, please help me."

"Trust me, He isn't listening," Draki stated. His back was to me, and he was looking out the window.

Fear gripped me. "What are you doing here?"

He looked over his shoulder and then back out the window. "I finished my task. Your old village is no longer bound by its devil, and you won't have to worry about it ever coming to seek revenge."

I didn't want to know what he had done in order to achieve that. Whatever it was, I was sure it wasn't good. The more I realized that Draki had done something terrible to uphold his end of the bargain, the more that I felt the lighthearted mood shift into something darker. I pulled the blanket around my shoulders and frowned a little bit. Something didn't feel right. Everything felt ominous, somehow.

"Are you ready?"

"For?"

He turned around with a smile as bright as the moon and as dark as the midnight sky. "For you to pay up."

I almost choked on the air I was breathing. "Now? I thought I had until my parents and everyone else got here."

Laughing, he started to gradually close the distance between us, but the bed acted as a barrier, halting him in his approach. "Why would I do that? You got what you asked for and more. I've done more than my fair share. I think it's time you show me a little kindness and pay up. Of course, as agreed, I'll let you have your time for mourning before we talk about the next payment."

"You never planned to let them get here before I would have to pay, did you?"

He looked unbothered by the question. "Did you think that your happiness was what I was after? I revel in your despair. I build you up to watch you plummet to the unforgiving ground. My greatest joy is seeing you get close to God and then watching you fall away from Him. My thrill comes from seeing you feel like there isn't a thing in this world that can break you, and then I come along and leave you shattered at my feet. My joy is your *pain*, Sia. How did you ever think that there was more to you and me than that?"

It shouldn't have hurt to hear him say it, but it did, and I knew exactly why. "I guess when you're friends with the biggest monster in the room, you tend to forget that it's always hungry."

His grin widened. "I'm so very hungry, Sia. And it's time for me to collect what is rightfully mine."

There was no escaping it now. There was no turning back. I had to pay him what I promised at the start of all this. A choice that I thought that I would be able to endure, but it's funny how you think that you can do anything in order to stay alive …

My voice sounded like it was made of sandpaper as I yelled, "I want to … make … a deal."

"What kind of deal?" he purred darkly.

My mind raced, and the sensation of his nails scraping over my tender skin didn't make me feel like I had a lot of time to decide. One thing was for certain, I wanted to survive and find somewhere to call home. I didn't want to tie myself down to a place I had never seen with my own two eyes and then find out it wasn't what I expected it to be, so I made the best choice for myself at that moment.

"Protect me until I find a place to call home and do whatever is in my best interest for me."

His grin was too wide and twisted. "Hahahaha … look at you being so clever. And what do I get out of the deal?"

"When I die, you can have my soul."

His smile melted away. He gave me a smug look with a quick, nasally laugh. "It's no fun for me if it's that obvious. Your soul wouldn't make this deal enjoyable for me. No, no, my dear. I'll need something a little better than that."

My heartbeat swallowed every nerve in me, and my eyes widened. Was I being denied? Was I going to die? "Then what do you want?" The worry was evident on my face as I searched his golden gaze. He had all the power in that moment, and he knew it.

For a long moment, he turned his head from side to side, inspecting me like he was a predator and I was prey he had caught right after a meal. Was he still hungry? Did he devour me or let me go? After a long moment, he said, "I want the soul of your first love."

"I've never been in love."

Dark chuckling erupted from him, and it crashed into my chest like a punch. His free hand reached out and moved a braid from my blood-spattered cheek as he let the laughter fade. With his face inches from mine, he let his nails retract, and he whispered happily, "And that, my dear, is how this arrangement just became all the more interesting." The hand that once held me captive reached out in my direction. "Do we have a deal?"

I didn't love anyone, so there couldn't be any harm in accepting. Besides, how hard could it be to not fall in love with someone? I would live, no one would die … I failed to see the problem. Without batting an eyelash, I took his hand and felt heat dance over my palm.

"Deal," I grunted out between aching breaths.

I stared at Draki with stunned surprise. "I—"

"You what?" He had a bored expression that was laced with a hidden anger. "You just needed more time? You just wanted to stall? You just wanted to escape the responsibility of staying true to your word?"

With every word spoken, I felt my heartbeat quicken, and it drummed to a painful rhythm. The truth to everything he asked was *yes*, but I wasn't about to say that out loud to him, though.

"I just expected my family to be here first."

The look in his eyes told me everything that his words never would. There was refined rage brewing under that blank expression. There was a sadistic joy tucked away beneath his perfect mask.

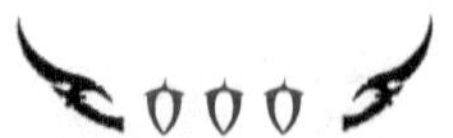

"I've given you more than enough. I want a taste of what belongs to me. No more running, Sia." That last part hit home a little more than I wanted it to. My lip quivered, and he smiled. "It's time to pay up," he whispered gently, but there was no kindness to his words.

It went without saying that I wasn't ready, and I never would be. There was no fighting him or avoiding it any more than I had. Up until this point, I did everything that I could and took all the possible steps to try to extend an inevitable fate. The blanket couldn't fight back the chill that assaulted me. Nothing would take away the harsh reality that froze me from the inside out. It was more than realizing I had made a horrible choice from the start. It was the fact that I had to pay one way or another. I had decided that I wasn't going to let anyone be the victim. Not if I could help it.

Draki still stood by the window. It was just like him to want people to go to him instead of the other way around. Now that I let go of everything and had nothing to lose, I saw all the things that I had blinded myself to for so long. In such a short amount of time, he had become a stranger to me. Did I ever really know him, or had I made it all up so that I could forget the monster that he was?

Gradually—his actions full of triumph—the devil lifted his hand, stretched it out palm up, and said, "Give me what is mine."

With a shaky exhale, I gave up and gave in. My eyes locked with his. My watery, blue hues didn't flinch as his molten-golden orbs glowed victoriously at me.

"Okay," I said, but I never moved from my spot. I stood my ground as I held him in my sights.

For the first time, I saw Draki's brow bend ever so slightly as he tried to understand why I wasn't walking out of the room defeated. "What game are you playing, Sia?"

"I'm not playing, Draki."

His chest rose and fell slowly. "You're trying my patience."

"I promise you, I'm not tricking you, Draki. I'm giving you the soul of my first love."

The creases on his forehead deepened. The damage was already done. I could see the sparks of it in the middle of the darkened room. His eyes flicked over to a slight glow that had softly illuminated the shadows. The skin of his hand looked like paper slowly burning. The edges of his fingers were alight with orange before they turned to soft, gray ash that floated away at the slightest movement of air.

He snapped his heated gaze to me and snarled, "Me?"

I didn't reply. I only stared at him quietly. The silence stretched, and the sound of an unseen fire burning broke through the stillness of the room.

The storm clouds in his eyes rolled in. Thunder rumbled in his throat. Rage twisted his features until I felt the need to take a step back from him out of fear that he would rush at me and snap my neck. I knew that there was no escape from his wrath. Death awaited me tonight with him. I had reserved myself to that fact when I stood out on the porch earlier that evening. I just didn't think that it would be so soon, that it would be right now. But there was a time, even before that, when I had made the choice to love him. It wasn't as hard as I thought it would be, and that made me disgusted with myself. It made me feel so disappointed in every inch of my soul. How could I love someone like him so easily? I had hushed that voice within me with the fact that I wouldn't be the one to take away someone's life. I wouldn't fall in love if it meant I would sacrifice that person in the end. That didn't sound like the love I thought of when I looked at

Momma and Daddy. They raised me better than that, and I wasn't that selfish.

Draki brought his hand closer to his face. The light made dark shadows play across his face and illuminated his pale skin with a soft, ginger hue. "Are you serious?"

"I love you, Draki."

"You heartless wench!" he growled. "You stupid girl!" he roared and threw the bed that was between us out of the way like it was nothing. It splintered on the opposing wall, and I flinched from the sound. "Why me? Of all the people you could have chosen, why me? I'm a devil. I'm. A. Devil!"

"I know," I said simply, in a voice that was far too sweet and calm for what was happening.

He snarled, "I'm *the* Devil!"

I saw the line of orange that was burning over his skin reach the midpoint of his fingers, and the tip fell off and instantly floated away like gray snowflakes in the blackened void of my room.

"I know," I repeated softly.

A moment ticked by where we held each other's gaze in tension-filled silence.

"I would have never loved you, Sia. I never will."

I sighed again. "I know, Draki. I know that there isn't a single reason I should have fallen for you, but I did. I found reasons to love you until it became horribly unnatural to do so. I'd make excuses for your venomous words, I would ignore your hurtful actions, I made so many things my fault, and I picked apart everything you said and did until it made sense, even when it didn't. I did it until there was nothing but positives that had manifested from my own lies. I should have never loved you … but I did. In the end, we used each other. I used you for protection, and you used me for

amusement, and now?" I laughed with a devilish smile. I wasn't going to be weak in my final moments. "Now we are done, and I'm making sure that you won't hurt anyone *ever* again."

"You're foolish if you think that I can't tear everything down before I die."

"It would go against our unfinished deal."

"I hate you!" he bellowed.

"Love and hate are two sides of the same coin."

"You bitch!" He screamed and moved faster than I could follow.

So, I closed my eyes.

I waited in those seconds that stretched out like hours for him to reach me and make me suffer. But I had already won. I just wish it didn't have to end like this. I wanted to see Meemaw, Daddy, and Momma again. I wanted to hug Elijah and tell him I love him one more time. I wanted to laugh with Ivy. I wanted to watch the village grow and prosper. I wanted so many things that I couldn't be a part of anymore.

Outside of my room, I could hear Elijah banging on my door. Fresh panic prickled across my skin. I prayed.

God forgive me for all my sins. I repent and hand all my troubles, worries, and problems over to You. May You guide and guard me through this storm. Keep him safe. Keep them all safe and watch over them. Please! Please help me!

I heard a voice that was unfamiliar, just as a light erupted in the room like I had a bonfire started right in front of me. Any moment, I would feel the stinging pain of my burning skin.

"YOU WILL NOT TOUCH HER, FALLEN ONE!"

I opened my eyes just in time to see Draki fly backward and slam into the wall. The impact was so great that the window broke. Glass rained down on the hardwood floors, and I could hear it tinkle against the ground outside. The devil fell in a heap below the busted opening with a grunt of pain. Tangled, white strands of hair half-hid his face as he struggled to stand. A clawed finger pointed in my direction, but he was pointing at something behind me. Something I was too afraid to look at. Yet, from the corner of my vision, I could see golden wings curling around me.

"You can't be here. She is mine! Step aside!!"

"I don't follow your commands. I follow the will of the Father. She is no longer yours. Her body and spirit now belong to Him."

"That wasn't part of the agreement!"

"Flee from this place before His judgment finds you."

A fraction of a second went by as I watched the flustered devil wrestle his emotions. Suddenly, plumes of red smoke billowed, and the devil that had kept me helpless for so long was gone. Around me were golden, fiery wings that felt warm but didn't burn. There was a sword covered in wildly dancing flames, and there was a light so bright that I was sure that the sun had risen in the middle of my room. I turned slowly to face the being. I tried to see some finer details, but I could never see them past the blinding light coming off of him. The outline of a person was there, but it hurt to look at him.

"Sia?!" Elijah yelled, and the door bowed as he threw his weight upon it.

"I'm okay! Don't come in!" I wasn't sure that it was a hundred percent safe to. "Are you … going to kill me?" I asked in a hushed voice that was only for the winged being of light and fire to hear.

His sword was lowered. "The pact with the devil is now over. You have no more ties to the fallen one. You are now a child of the light. Your covenant is with the Father. He protects this place, and you will be watched over by me, as I am your angel."

"My a-angel …?"

He nodded. "Everyone has at least one," he explained.

"Do I need to do anything?"

"Only to love with all your heart, believe in the Father and the Son, and love them with all that you are."

"Nothing more?" I seemed disappointed as I questioned him.

I couldn't really see it, but—somehow—I knew that he was smiling. "If you love with all your heart, you cannot kill, steal, cheat, corrupt, or sin. If you love, you forgive. There is nothing above this. Love is the greatest commandment." Turning slowly, he motioned for the exit. "Your friend is waiting for you."

I found myself following the sweep of his hand and stopped before I could reach the door. Breaking out of my trance, I called back to him, "Wait. I just have one more question. What's your name?"

He smiled and said, "Michael," as the feathers on his wings rustled like they were shivering with excitement. The sword with dancing fires was sheathed, and he pointed to the door again. "Know that I am watching, and the Father is always listening."

"You mean … you mean God heard me?"

"He always has, Sia. There was never a moment your voice or thoughts were hidden from Him," Michael replied, and then he faded from sight.

My eyes welled with tears, and I sniffled. It was the

pounding of Elijah's fists on the door that made me turn, and in a haze of wonderment, I rushed to open the door. Tears were freely streaming down my face, and I hit my knees as soon as I saw Elijah. My hand covered my mouth, and I let the other grab at my chest and twist the fabric in my hand.

"He's gone," I croaked out. "Draki's gone," I stated between sobs.

"What?" Elijah gasped.

At that moment, I felt every part of me understand what it meant to love Draki. I accepted it. I knew it. I hated it—and yet—I found myself missing him already. Despite all the torture and pain he put me through … I loved him. I could never accept him like I once had. I knew that everything I thought Draki was … was all an illusion. I had fallen victim to him. Even though there was nothing about him that was good or healthy, I embraced him without batting an eyelash. But, at the end of the day, I knew that there was never a future for him and me. Not one that I could be happy in. Knowing all of this didn't stop it from hurting. It didn't stop me from feeling like a villain for loving the wrong man when all I wanted was to give Elijah my heart from the start. For so long, I felt horrible for caring about Elijah while loving Draki. A necessary evil doesn't mend a broken heart; it defines one. Yet, it had become a blemish on my soul that made me unhappy every time I caved to my desire to be with Elijah. I tormented myself because I loved two men at the same time for entirely different reasons. But, in reality, my heart knew that the love that I felt for Draki was forced. I latched onto his strength and told myself that he cared about me, too. The truth was—at some point—I didn't have to force myself to love him anymore. It just happened naturally … and that tore me up. In the end, Draki was gone, but my heart was still broken no matter how much I tried to make sense of

it all.

I tried to find an even breath between sniffles. "He's gone," I repeated, my voice no more than a strained whisper.

"What happened? Are you okay?"

I knew that he was refraining from asking how we would keep a city this large safe from the demons that lay in waiting out in the Wastes. Controlling the tears proved to be more difficult than I would have ever thought. I struggled to inhale and not have it immediately turn into more weeping. I sputtered every time I tried to speak. My mouth opened, and sorrow flowed out. No matter what I thought about myself, after everything that had happened, I had been forgiven. I was saved.

I was alive.

Slowly, I found my voice and laughed as I said, "He heard us. God heard us. We don't need devils. We have Him. He sent us an angel. Our village is protected by an angel sent by God, Elijah!"

He stared at me in awe and then laughed happily before he crashed into me with a hug that made me cry even harder. His mouth found mine, and he stole my breath with his kiss. After breaking away from me, he said, "You did it, Sia. We are free. We are free!"

"I didn't do anything. God did it." And I realized then that every step that I took wasn't cursed from the start. Every bit of hell I went through was taken and made to fit a plan that I didn't understand until the end. We were to rebuild the faith city. I had been blessed, we all had been, and we could finally live without being dictated by devils. We could be free of them without fear that demons would overrun our homes.

I knew that this was just the start of something bigger than me. I could feel it in places beyond blood and bone. We

weren't going to stop here with this place. We were going to break the bonds of all the devils and free the people of this land.

"I shall show you the way," a voice whispered sweetly to me.

At that moment, I felt a love that was beyond words and a blessing greater than the breath in my lungs wash over me. After everything I had been through and suffered, I was not only alive, but I had been given gifts that I never would have imagined that I would be worthy of receiving. Despite all my failures and all of my mistakes, I was still loved. I was still forgiven. The devil was wrong about how God would never accept me. I had been a threat to Draki from the start … I just didn't know that until now. No matter what, I knew what the first steps of my journey were—what they were for all of us.

In a world of endless night:
Be the love.
Be the light.

Epilogue:

He is the Hope

A burnt hand with a few missing fingers reached out and slammed against the night-washed ground of the Wastes. Small puffs of dry earth rose into the air when a second slapped over the rocky dirt, and extended claws dug deep as Draki dragged his body over the desert floor. His white robes were now soiled, his long hair was a tangled mess, his brow was beaded with sweat, and his face was twisted with anger as he struggled to reach a destination that even he was unsure of.

After dragging himself a little further, he tiredly hit the ground with a grunt. Not a moment later, a scorpion skittered out from behind a small collection of stones and repeatedly stabbed the devil's hand with its tail. Draki seemed to register no discomfort. He only snatched it up in his grasp and snarled as it squirmed and struck at him with its poisoned tip. Suddenly, red threads of mist came rolling out of the creature. Strange, high-pitched screeches of agony poured out from the scorpion as its essence was drained. Opening his hand, the devil inspected the husk that remained therein. With a sneer, the carcass was tossed away into the shadows of the dying night.

With newfound vigor, Draki resumed his crawling travels. However—a few feet later—he miscalculated the shadowy depths and rolled down a rocky hill. Landing at the bottom with a howl of pain, the devil screamed out into the night in frustration. Rolling over, he reached out again to pull himself forward, only his hand didn't touch dirt or stone.

It landed on something soft.

A quick glance revealed to him a human, sandaled foot. Draki's lips twitched and slowly curled into a devious smile. Grabbing hold of the foot, the devil made sure his prey wouldn't be able to run away from his burning touch.

"Oh, You're about to have a bad day," he announced with a dark chuckle. Slowly, he looked up, and then all of his confidence drained from his face.

"No, I am not. However, you are …" the stranger informed.

The Man that spoke had short, woolly hair that was whiter than snow. His eyes were a bright hazel color that held hints of orange, like they had been kissed by a flame. His skin was like burnished bronze, and His robes were a deep and vibrant red, like they had been soaked in blood. His crown atop His head glittered in the moonlight, but the rest of His face was so bright it was hard to make out any other features.

"No!" Draki shrieked and flopped over in his sad attempt to flee.

But he never made it far. His body ignited into flames as a pillar of blazing fire rained down from the sky. One second, the devil and the pillar of fire were there, the next … they were gone. A hole in the ground surrounded with singed dirt was all that was left behind. Smoke rose up from the opening, and cries from within it faded into the night as the pit gradually closed shut, forever sealed.

The crowned Man then faced the direction of a newly built faith city, and He drew in a mighty breath. With a grand smile, He headed toward it just as the dawn broke over the horizon.